FOOTPRINTS ON MY DOORSTEP

Elaine Hankin

Published in 2017 by FeedARead.com Publishing

Copyright © Elaine Hankin

The author asserts her moral right under the Copyright, Designs and Patents Act, 1988, to be identified as the author of this work.

All Rights reserved. No part of this publication may be reproduced, copied, stored in a retrieval system, or transmitted, in any form or by any means, without the prior written consent of the copyright holder, nor be otherwise circulated in any form of binding or cover other than that in which it is published and without a similar condition being imposed on the subsequent purchaser.

A CIP catalogue record for this title is available from the British Library.

With grateful thanks to all my writing friends for their encouragement and help during the writing of this book.

THE EARLY YEARS

I was built in the year the old queen died. Black drapes hung from windows, many people went into mourning as if she were a member of their own family. However, my very first occupants had much to be happy about for they were embarking on a new life in a new house and with the expectation of a new baby. No one suspected that in a few short years war would throw Europe into chaos.

Since getting married a year earlier, Jack and Daisy Webster had been living in one room in Jack's parents' house in Wandsworth when the vacancy for a railway porter cropped up and, in the blink of an eye, as Daisy put it, they were whisked away to live on the South Coast. So even if the rest of the country was in the doldrums, their luck had changed.

'Opportunities like that don't crop up every day, my boy,' said Jack's father, sucking at his pipe, *'a job on the railway is a job for life.'*

And so in mid February they moved in. They were only renting of course because I went with the job. I had been built by the Railway Company to house employees. At that time, this was a small town with a population of around 25,000; nestled at the foot of the South Downs it had a rural feel and, indeed, when Daisy looked out of the top back bedroom window, she could see gently sloping hills and, closer to hand, an abundance of fruit trees.

I am Number Seven, which is in the middle of a block of terraces that were built on land purchased from a market gardener. This was a godsend for Jack and Daisy because, instead of finding themselves confronted with a stretch of uncultivated back garden, there were mature apple, plum and pear trees and leftover raspberry and gooseberry bushes to provide them with free puddings to help feed their growing family.

The lavatory was built into the side of the house near the back door so that the occupants didn't have to traipse to the end of the garden, as was the case for residents of houses built before the turn of the century. There was a covered walkway behind the houses to give all occupants easy access to the communal laundry facilities. When they saw what was being offered to them, Jack and Daisy were over the moon.

And so begins their story...

ONE

'Let me look you over just once more,' Daisy Webster insisted, brushing invisible specks from Jack's lapels for the tenth time. 'You look so smart in your uniform. Are you sure you've got everything you need?'

'Stop fussing, sweetheart, I've checked everything.' When she stood on tiptoes to kiss him, he laughed and added, 'If you get much fatter, you won't be able to reach me.'

'Go on with you,' she giggled. Giving his shoulder a gentle push, she stood on the doorstep to watch him stride off to his first day in the new job, losing sight of him as he rounded the bend in the road after stopping briefly to wave at her.

She went back indoors, leaning against the doorframe, partly to ease her aching back and partly to sigh with pleasure at the start of this exciting episode in their lives. Who would have thought, a year ago, that they would be living in their own three bed roomed house snugly cradled between the sea and the countryside?

She shuffled along the floorboards - they couldn't afford a runner yet although she had her eye on an attractive one called Kashmir Red she'd seen on a visit to a department store in Clapham Junction prior to their move south. She hadn't told Jack about it because, like his father, he was inclined to be a bit tight-fisted and she knew he would say it was way out of their league. A twinge of pain caught her and she was obliged to sit down on one of the two dining room chairs her parents had given them. The twinge didn't last long and she was sure it wasn't the real thing, not yet. The baby wasn't due for another two weeks. She hoped it was a boy. Jack would like that. But she also hoped that one day they would have a girl as well. An only child, she had always longed for siblings, envying Jack his large family.

After a few minutes she put her hand on the table and pushed herself to her feet. There were chores to be done; so much more to do in a whole house rather than the twelve by twelve-foot room they'd come from. Not that she minded. She would have twirled around with delight if she hadn't felt so clumsy. The house was perfect, Jack was perfect and they were distanced from her interfering mother-in-law. It wasn't that she didn't like Gladys but her non-stop advice and endless suggestions had begun to grate after the first few months of her pregnancy. It was lovely to be away from all that even if she did feel a bit lonely sometimes.

Despite the assurance he demonstrated to his wife, Jack felt nervous at starting his new job. And as he rounded the corner, his jaunty walk took on a slower gait as if something were holding him back. He loved his Daisy so much but the responsibility of the expected child was beginning to weigh heavily on him. He was frightened too because Daisy's mother had nearly died giving birth to her and was subsequently unable to have more children. Suppose this weakness ran in families! He wanted a lot of children. He was used to the chaos of eight people squashed around the kitchen table, of squabbling brothers, of teasing sisters. And now they had this wonderful house there was room for a large family.

He mounted the steps to the station entrance and approached the ticket office.

'Hello mate!' The ruddy-faced cashier greeted him cheerily, indicating with a nod for him to go round to the side door. 'Jack, isn't it, welcome aboard? I'm Bert Stanwick.'

Jack began to relax; he joined the man in the tiny office, watching while he sold tickets to a couple of passengers.

'You might have to double for me sometimes, Jack. You know, holidays and week-end shifts.'

'They didn't say anything about that.'

'Didn't they...must have forgotten to mention it. Don't worry it won't happen for a while.' He looked over his shoulder. 'Here's Steve, he's going to tell you your duties. There are seventy trains a day, weekdays that is, Sundays the number is half that. 'Course, you'll be working shifts, you know that, don't you?'

The eight-hour day passed swiftly. Jack soon found there wasn't all that much to learn but Steve turned out to be meticulous and insisted on showing him the ropes over and over again.

At six o'clock, a man called Chas took over and Jack made his way home.

Daisy's face lit up as he let himself in. She hurried to meet him, reaching up to kiss him on the lips. 'How did it go today, darling?'

'Fine, piece of cake.'

'So you think you'll settle in? I mean, after your last job this must seem very different.'

'Do you think I can't handle it?'

She bit her lip. Her husband could be touchy sometimes and, in a bid to calm the waters, she said cheerfully, 'Go and get washed, I'll have the dinner on the table in next to no time.'

When he returned from the wash-house, they sat down to mutton stew, eked out with plenty of vegetables. It was going to take Daisy a long time to persuade her husband that they could afford something better now that he had regular work.

'Is this new?' asked Jack slapping his large hand down on the colourful oilcloth table covering.

Daisy jumped guiltily. 'I bought it the other day in a little shop I found in town. It's such a pretty pattern, don't you think? And it will protect the surface of the table.'

'Hmm...' Jack shook his head. 'You mustn't go spending money recklessly, sweetheart, just because there's a bit more coming in each week. We must put some by for a rainy day.'

She lowered her gaze, allowing her auburn curls to fall forward to hide her face. Was it always going to be like this? Was he always going to quibble about every penny she spent?

He realised he'd upset her and reached out to touch her, saying, 'It's very nice, Daisy.'

She looked down at his hand on her arm. How big and strong it was! His arms were brawny with a layer of black hair. She remembered that he'd once won a pint of beer in The Rose and Crown for arm wrestling. It was when they were still living in Wandsworth. He had come home, slightly the worse for wear, proudly proclaiming that the lads thought he ought to be a wrestler. *I'm glad he's not*, she thought, *wrestlers are always ugly with twisted noses and cauliflower ears*.

'Well,' he said mopping up the last of the gravy with a chunk of bread, 'it's an early night for me, got to get up at the crack of dawn tomorrow.'

She struggled to her feet and collected up the empty plates. 'You go off to bed while I wash up the dishes. Then I'll join you. I'll try not to wake you if you're already asleep.'

Jack got up and tenderly kissed the top of her head, saying, 'Don't worry, I'll be dead to the world by the time you come up.'

Daisy gave a little shudder at his turn of phrase.

Left on her own, Daisy boiled up a kettle of water and set about washing the plates and cooking utensils, scraping off the residue of ground-in fat with a wire scourer. As she dried her hands she couldn't help wishing they were as white and smooth as they had been before she became a married lady. And now that her time was nearly due she was finding the housework tiring. In Wandsworth there had only been one room to keep clean since her mother-in-law had taken care of the shared staircase, sometimes doing it herself, sometimes ordering one of her daughters to do it.

Slipping off her apron, Daisy switched off the gas lamp and lit a candle before making her way to the hall. The flight of stairs ahead of her was daunting. The stairs were narrow and steep and it took all her strength to drag herself up.

As predicted, Jack was already asleep so placing the candle on the chest of drawers, she started to get undressed. It was such a relief to discard some of the layers: the shawl knotted around her shoulders, the woollen blouse that by the end of the day made her skin itch, the heavy serge skirt and, last of all, the starched petticoat. Gingerly lowering herself into the rocking chair her mother had insisted they bought for nursing purposes, she kicked off her boots without undoing the laces and slid down her lisle stockings.

Going to the bed, she carefully removed Jack's arm which lay across her pillow and drew out her winceyette nightdress from under it. She slipped it over her head, untangling it when it wrinkled over her protruding stomach. Utterly exhausted, she blew out the candle and sank between the sheets.

TWO

Daisy's two-week wait extended into three and by the end of the third week she was desperate to get the whole business of giving birth over and done with. To make matters worse, her mother-in-law paid them a visit and regaled them with disturbing accounts of her own first confinement. Even Jack could see how upsetting this was for his young wife and attempted to change the subject but Gladys enjoyed giving voice to her own experiences.

'Ma, you're upsetting Daisy,' he butted in after she had given a lurid account of how, after giving birth to Leonard, her eldest, the bedroom had looked like a slaughterhouse.

'Sorry, love,' she leant over and patted Daisy's hand as it rested on her protruding stomach, 'it's not always like that so I'm sure you'll be all right.'

Fortunately, Gladys was called home when her youngest went down with measles, putting paid to her intention to stay over until after the birth.

The day after her departure, Jack was reluctant to go to work. 'Are you sure you'll be all right, sweetheart?'

Daisy nodded her head. She wasn't at all sure but knew that Jack needed to get to work, particularly on this day because he had been enrolled on a training course, the first step towards promotion.

She saw him off in her dressing gown, returning to lie down on the bed for a further half hour before fixing herself some breakfast. The doctor had said she must keep her strength up by eating regular meals but she didn't feel hungry.

'Don't forget, my girl,' her mother-in-law had repeatedly reminded her, 'you're eating for two.'

She fell asleep, waking an hour later with a terrible backache and when she tried to prise herself off the bed, the contractions began. She waited, seated on the edge of the bed for the first ones to pass then levered herself up and slipping her feet into her carpet slippers, she struggled downstairs, clinging to the handrail for support.

By the time she reached the hallway, the contractions were coming thick and fast. Tearfully she thought about Gladys, sorry now that she had departed. Her waters broke just as she reached the front door. Doubled over in pain, she shouted to her neighbour, a kindly soul who had befriended Daisy shortly after she and Jack had moved in.

She appeared at the door, wiping her hands on her brightly coloured apron. 'I've just been doing some baking,' she said then frowned. 'So your time's come, Mrs Webster. Don't worry, dear, I'll send young Jimmy to fetch the midwife.'

She shouted for her nine-year-old grandson, who appeared almost immediately. 'Go and get Mrs Sparks, my lad and be quick about it otherwise Mrs Webster will drop the baby on the doorstep.'

She ushered Daisy back into the house. 'You'll never get up those stairs,' she said, 'it will have to be the settee.'

Daisy was too distressed to explain to Mrs Durrant that they hadn't yet been able to afford a settee. But the lady was not put off. Helping Daisy to an upright chair, she hurried upstairs, returning with several pillows and an eiderdown.

'These will do just fine,' she said.

The midwife arrived in time. Daisy had only met her on one occasion and she wished she could have had her original midwife, Mrs Phelps from Wandsworth, a woman she had got to know quite well.

Mrs Durrant was helpful. She sent Jimmy to the station to ask Bert to get a message to Jack but as he had gone to Brighton for his training it was unlikely he would get back before nightfall.

The contractions continued and, afterwards, Daisy could remember little of what went on. All she could think of was the terrible time her mother had had when giving birth to her.

'It could be a difficult one,' muttered the midwife to Mrs Durrant, not intending Daisy to hear her. 'She should be in hospital.'

'Shall I send Jimmy to call for an ambulance?' whispered back Mrs Durrant.

'No, maybe it will be all right.'

Daisy felt remote from the two women. Despite the awful circumstances of her own mother's confinement, Mary Manning had never gone into details about it. Her daughter had only learned how terrible it had been when, as a little girl, she had asked her father why she was an only child when all her school friends had brothers and sisters. How she wished her mother was by her side now!

'It's time to push, dear.' She heard the midwife's instructions through a haze. 'Come on now, push hard and it will all be over.'

Summoning up all her remaining strength, Daisy obeyed and to her relief, she heard a small cry.

'Well, my dear,' said Mrs Sparks as the baby's cries grew in strength, 'you've done it. You've got a lovely little boy and he's got a healthy pair of lungs.'

The relief was so great that Daisy wanted to shout for joy but all she could muster was a feeble whimper. Closing her eyes, she let the two women do what was necessary, holding the baby to her breast after they had cleaned him up.

While she nursed him, she could hear the two of them whispering anxiously.

'She'll be confined to bed for a week at least,' said the midwife. 'Has she got anybody to look after her?'

'Well, there's her mother-in-law,' said Mrs Durrant. 'She was here only yesterday but she's gone home.'

'What about her own mother?'

'I don't know anything about her.'

Daisy tried to raise herself from the pillows. 'She's not well, she can't walk; Mum's crippled with arthritis.'

Mrs Durrant came over and looked down at her. 'I didn't know that.' Her eyes were full of sympathy as she added, 'Not to worry, I'll look in on you every day, two or three times if necessary.'

'You can't do that, Mrs Durrant, you've got too much to do looking after your grandchildren and your invalid husband.'

'We'll work something out.'

'We'd better get the new mother upstairs to bed,' said the midwife briskly.

It took the women ten minutes to help Daisy up the steep flight of stairs. She sank into a deep sleep only to be woken with instructions that it was time to feed her offspring.

Once the news reached him, Jack was allowed to go home. Nonetheless, it was evening before he arrived. He raced up the stairs, two at a time, to find Daisy nursing his son.

'A boy!' Pride made his voice screech. 'Was it bad?'

Daisy smiled through the tears she couldn't hold back. 'Not too bad. I've survived, haven't I? But I am supposed to have some bed rest.'

Jack looked worried then his brow cleared. 'Ma will sort something out. Maybe she'll come back or maybe she'll send Ruthie to help out.'

'But Ruthie's only fourteen,' protested Daisy.

'She's very sensible.'

There was little choice since Gladys firmly refused to leave her youngest when he was suffering so badly with measles and the next day, Ruthie arrived carrying a battered cardboard suitcase secured with string.

She was a skinny girl with mousey hair tied into plaits and a complexion marked by adolescent spots, the latter made worse by constant scratching. She greeted her brother with a wide smile but managed only a nod at Daisy. Jack showed her where everything was and explained the quickest route to the shops.

During their first year of marriage, Daisy hadn't had much to do with Ruthie but she had felt sorry for her. Gladys had insisted that she should leave school at thirteen to help look after her younger siblings instead of taking advantage of the extra year of education currently allowed by the Government. There was an ongoing row between mother and daughter about this state of affairs and Daisy could well understand Ruth's resentment. She vowed to make things as easy as possible for her during her stay.

Mrs Durrant continued to call in from time to time. 'I just like to check up on things, ' she said and, turning to Ruthie, added, 'I'm sure you're very capable, my dear but it doesn't hurt to have me to fall back on if needs be. Where did you say you live, Ruth?'

'Wandsworth,' was the grunted reply.

'Ah...' Mrs Durrant clasped her hands across her apron clad stomach and sighed. 'I went up to London once. It was very busy.'

'Your mean it's alive, not half asleep like...'

Daisy caught her sister-in-law's eye in a bid to stop her saying anything else and Ruth shuffled her feet and shook her head so that her twisted little plaits bobbed on her shoulders.

Fortunately, Mrs Durrant didn't take offence easily and a possible confrontation was averted. However, it didn't make Daisy's 'lying-in' any easier because she was always on tenterhooks.

Something happened towards the end of the week that revealed a different side to Ruthie. Daisy woke up feeling much stronger and gingerly made the descent down the narrow staircase to the living room. Much to her surprise, she found Ruthie engrossed in a book. As far as Daisy knew, the Websters were not book lovers. During her stay in Wandsworth she hadn't seen a single book lying around. She had noticed this because in her own home there were several bookshelves housing an assortment of novels and biographies. Daisy herself had read all the Jane Austin and the Bronte classics, encouraged by both her mother and father, who were avid readers. Jack had frequently teased her about always having her nose in a book, and when she had recommended a title to him he had laughed her off.

Ruthie looked up guiltily when she entered the room. Flustered, she put the book down and stammered, 'I was doing no harm; I just wanted to see what it was about.'

Daisy was swift to reassure her. 'Go ahead, Ruthie, take a look through the bookshelf. You can borrow any of the books.'

Ruthie eyes lit up. 'Can I?'

This proved to be the 'open sesame' to their friendship. From that moment on, Ruth treated Daisy with respect and by the time she was due to leave for home they had formed a warm relationship. In fact, the evening before her departure, the young girl opened up to her. They were seated at the dining-room table, Jack having scoffed his meal and gone up to bed, which was often the case after a hard day's work.

'You can take a book with you, Ruthie,' said Daisy, 'more than one if you want to.'

'I'll take great care of them,' mumbled Ruth, picking up the one she was currently reading and hugging it to her chest. 'I won't let Davey or Gerald grab 'em.'

'Is Davey still as difficult these days?' asked Daisy, recalling the troublesome eleven-year-old who would never do what he was told and was prone to angry outbursts.

'He's worse,' said Ruth, 'Pa says he oughta be sent away but Ma won't hear of it. She finds it hard looking after him and Gerald. Gerald thinks he's funny, you see and goes and copies him. The doctor says Davey's got something wrong with him and he oughta be institu…'

'Institutionalised,' finished Daisy.

'Yes, he should be in the loony bin but Ma says no 'cos I'm good at handling him.'

'Is that why you haven't found yourself a job since leaving school?'

Ruth nodded and to Daisy's amazement she burst into tears. It all came out then: the rows with her parents when the fourteen-year-old wanted to spread her wings and find herself a job enabling her to meet other young people instead of being stuck at home with the disagreeable Davey, who had been expelled from three different schools.

For a split second, Daisy was tempted to suggest that Ruth stay down by the seaside living with them. After all, the house was big enough with three first floor bedrooms and a box room in the attic. Just in time she thought of Jack's reaction to this suggestion. He would not welcome his young sister becoming a permanent fixture in their lives. Like his father, he was not the most tolerant of men.

The next day, Jack escorted his sister to the station. He carried her battered suitcase and she clutched three books under her arm, held together with an old leather strap, protecting them as if they were gold nuggets.

Three months later when Daisy had regained her health, Gladys, Ruthie, Davey and Gerald came down for the Christening. Alf Webster decided not to come, stating that he didn't believe in all that rigmarole. Jack's other brother,

Leonard brought his wife and his other sister, Lizzie took time of work to come too.

Daisy had planned the event for weeks beforehand. The baby would wear the Christening gown she had worn twenty-one years earlier and her mother had worn before that. It was so beautiful, creamy white with a lacy hem and cuffs! She searched her wardrobe for a suitable outfit to wear for the occasion. At the back of the cupboard she found her wedding dress covered by a sheet, and drawing it out, she spread it out on the bed. The white dress with its frilled neck-line and nipped in waist brought back memories of her wedding day. They had got married in Highgate and she remembered how happy she had been because her mother was able to attend, albeit in a wheelchair. She heaved a sigh: she couldn't wear the white wedding dress for Teddy's Christening. Maybe she could dye it. The idea was quickly dismissed because she had a dream that one day she would have a daughter who would wear it for *her* wedding.

In the end, she plucked up courage and on his next pay day, she asked Jack if she could buy a new dress. He frowned at first, then relented and delved into his pocket, handing her a bundle of notes. She flung her arms around his neck, kissing his face all over. He laughed and hugged her back, adding, 'Don't get too excited I won't be this generous very often but, after all, it is for our son's Christening.'

It was a beautiful summer's day and the family formed a crocodile as they made their way to the church. Mrs Durrant came too, bringing with her the grandson who had played his part on the day of Daisy's confinement. The general idea was that since he and Gerald were close in age, they would be company for one another. This proved to be a catastrophic mistake since, once they reached the churchyard they took great delight in playing 'catch' around the gravestones even before the family had entered the church. Once inside, they were kept apart by Mrs Durrant and Gladys.

Over the preceding weeks, Daisy and Jack had discussed the baby's name at length, settling at last on Edward.

'It's only right,' said Daisy, 'because our little boy is one of the first Edwardians.'

'Isn't it a bit la-di-da naming our son after the King? We'll probably end up calling him Ted anyway.'

In fact, almost from the start, the child was called Teddy.

The Christening ceremony went off without a hitch although Mrs Durrant and Gladys looked grim faced as they left the church, having had great difficulty keeping their young charges under control. The company filed home to squeeze into Number Seven where Daisy aided by the two older women bustled around serving sandwiches and cups of tea.

By the late afternoon, Leonard and Lizzie had departed but the others had decided to stay on for a couple of days to take advantage of the sea air. Ruth, Davey and Gerald even ventured into the water but none of them was happy about the pebbly beach and, when he stubbed his toe, Davey lost his temper and ended up throwing stones at all and sundry.

Ruthie managed to calm him down, giving Daisy yet another insight into her sister-in-law's caring nature although she hated the way Gladys left everything to her daughter. By bedtime everybody was ready for an early night, the sea air having played its part in wearing out the younger boys. After feeding Teddy, Daisy went to join Jack who was already asleep. She felt content: the Christening had gone well and a day by the sea seemed to have kept everybody happy.

She was woken up in the small hours by a terrible kafuffle on the landing, followed by a scream and a loud thump. Jumping out of bed she rushed to the door and, in the half light, saw to her horror that Gladys was lying at the foot of the stairs in a crumpled heap. Davey stood at the head of the stairs swinging his arms and kicking one leg back and forth as if it were a pendulum.

Ruth and Jack arrived seconds later. Shoving Davey aside, Jack raced downstairs to his mother.

'Take Davey back to bed, Ruthie,' said Daisy before going downstairs to join Jack.

But the girl didn't move. She just stood staring down, traumatized, while her brother continued to swing his leg back and forth, wailing at the top of his voice.

'Is she conscious?' asked Daisy as Jack gently turned Gladys' head towards him. She clapped a hand to her mouth when she saw that her mother-in-law's eyes were wide open, staring.

Jack shook his head. 'She must have knocked her head on the handrail as she fell.' He looked wildly at Daisy. 'How did this happen? Why was she going downstairs?'

Daisy looked up and saw that, thankfully, Ruth was no longer transfixed. Somehow, she had pacified her young brother and was now leading him back to the bedroom. But Davey's wail had been replaced by Teddy's cry. It was time for the early morning feed and Daisy knew that if she didn't put him to her breast, his cry would turn into an ear-splitting scream.

What happened after that would always be a blur to Daisy. Jack pulled himself together and dashed along to the station in order to use their phone to call for an ambulance. Disturbed by all the noise, Mrs Durrant came in and took charge while Daisy breast-fed Teddy. The good lady helped Ruth get Davey back to bed; his younger brother, Gerald, had slept through the entire incident.

They all knew, before the arrival of the ambulance that there was no hope for Gladys. Ruthie seemed panic-stricken rather than saddened by her mother's fate, and

Daisy wondered whether she had already realised the onus that would now fall on her frail shoulders with two little brothers to be taken care of.

THREE

After a few fraught months, life returned to normal and Jack and Daisy were able to look forward to their first Christmas in their own home. Once he had completed his six-month trial Jack was given a substantial rise so that Daisy was at last able to buy the hall runner she liked so much and to choose a settee to complete the furnishing of their front room.

That first Christmas was one of the happiest in Daisy's life. The trains weren't running on Christmas Day so she was able to celebrate with the two people she loved the most without being tied to a routine. It was true that Jack had to report for duty the next day but the train timetable had been changed and he was able to stay in bed for a little longer on Boxing Day.

'That was a wonderful meal, love,' said Jack, leaning back in his chair. He patted his stomach. 'I wish I had room for a bit more of that Christmas pudding.'

'You'd burst,' laughed Daisy. She got up from the table. 'Go and relax on our new settee while I see to the dishes. Turn the wireless on; there might be some music for you to listen to.'

'Send me to sleep, more like,' said Jack. And he was right because no more than five minutes later, Daisy peeped into the room and saw that he was fast asleep, his mouth hanging open and a gentle snore making his chest reverberate.

She finished the washing-up and then attended to Teddy, who was beginning to whimper for his feed. She loved breast feeding him. In her arms he felt so soft and small and vulnerable. Sometimes she wished he would stay like that forever. Other times she imagined him as a young man: tall and strong and handsome. All the girls would be after him, of course, but she would be picky. Her boy's future wife would have to be just right. She would suddenly come to her senses and laugh. Why think so far ahead? Besides, her Teddy would not countenance an interfering mother. He would be perfectly capable of choosing his own wife.

She always day-dreamed during feeding time; sometimes this made her happy, sometimes sad. As she swayed in the rocking-chair her thoughts went back to the day of Gladys' accident. For days afterwards she had scrubbed at the blood-stains on the floorboards at the foot of the stairs, but she was never able to completely remove them. Now of course they were hidden by the new Kashmir Red runner. She kept in touch with Ruthie, writing to her regularly every week and offering to lend her more books to read. Ruthie replied but Daisy could tell that she was very discontented with her lot. Even though Davey had been sent to a special home for disturbed young people, Ruthie still had the responsibility of looking after her father and her little brother. Gerald was now ten and had turned out to be a bright pupil at school, but he was a handful at home.

The clock struck six and Daisy heard Jack's footsteps on the stairs.

'Still up here, sweetheart,' he said, poking his head round the bedroom door. 'I could do with a cuppa.'

Daisy sighed and moved the baby from her breast. 'I'm just coming. Put the kettle, there's a love.'

They went to bed at nine o'clock and despite his afternoon nap, Jack still fell asleep the minute his head hit the pillow.

The next eighteen months flew past and the couple were delighted when Daisy found she was pregnant again. This time the confinement went well and Margaret, or Madge as she came to be called, was born on a sunny April morning.

'We really must take the children to see their grandparents,' said Daisy. 'After all, my ma and pa have only seen Teddy twice and I know Ma will be excited to see her new granddaughter. On the way we could call in to your folk in Wandsworth. I know Ruthie will want to see her niece.'

'Well, I've got some holiday due so why don't we go in June. By then, our little Madge will have settled into a routine.'

And so it was that Teddy and Madge were taken to meet the family. The Highgate visit where Daisy's parents lived was a little awkward. Jack had never seemed able to come to terms with Daisy's background. In fact, it was only when they visited her home that she noticed how gauche his manners could be. Her mother had a daily maid, something that his mother could have done with when her six children were little.

The stop off in Wandsworth delighted Jack but it upset Daisy to see how downtrodden his sister Ruth had become. She had brought a couple of romantic novels for her but when she handed them to Ruth, the girl sighed and said, 'Thank you, Daisy, but when am I going to have time to read them?'

Things were going well. Jack had been given another rise and they were able to spend money on a few extras, even buying a second-hand Columbia phonograph. They were only able to afford three records to play on it and there was a long discussion in the shop before the choice was made.

'I love *In the Good Old Summertime* and *The Entertainer*, maybe we should buy both,' said Daisy.

Jack disagreed. 'We've got to buy *When You Were Sweet Sixteen*.' He gave his wife's waist a squeeze.

Daisy jumped away, feigning indignation, although secretly she liked it when her husband displayed affection. 'What do you think you're doing, Jack Webster, here in a shop full of customers?'

In the end they settled for Daisy's choice of *In the Good Old Summertime*, Jack's *When You Were Sweet Sixteen* and a stirring Sousa march.

These records were played over and over again until Daisy began to think they would drive her mad. Teddy loved them, especially the Sousa march, which surprisingly helped to lull his little sister to sleep. And in the evening, after the children were in bed, Jack would play the records again, always finishing with his favourite whereupon he would pull Daisy to her feet and waltz her around the room.

Everything seemed wonderful to Daisy and she seemed to be floating through the days with a smile on her face. During the summer following Madge's birth she would prepare a picnic and take the children down to the beach getting to know other young mothers who were doing the same thing. In later years, she would reflect that June, July and August of 1903 were halcyon days.

Jack too was content. He was still a porter but hoped that eventually he would be promoted to ticket collector or even guard. He got on well with his colleagues but didn't spend very much time in the pub after work, as most of them did. He was friendly with the regulars, those who travelled daily to London or Portsmouth. And occasionally, he would take advantage of the concession fares granted him to take the family on a day trip to Brighton or Eastbourne.

While they were in Eastbourne, Daisy pointed to a tower at the end of the pier. 'What's that?' she asked.

'It's a camera obscura, love.'

'A camera obs....what did you say?'

'You go up in the tower and they close all the windows so it's pitch black then through a pinhole they show you all the surrounding area just as if you're actually out there.'

'What's the point of that?' said Daisy, wrinkling her nose.

'Tell you what...' said Jack, delving in his pocket for some coins, 'we'll go up there and you can see for yourself.'

'I don't know about that,' said Daisy, holding back, 'I mean, won't Teddy be frightened?'

'Not if I hold his hand. Look...' He pointed to his daughter. 'And Madge is fast asleep anyway.'

And so, much to Daisy's delight, they paid a visit to the camera obscura. She was awestruck and wouldn't stop talking about it all the way home. She loved those outings and usually came back with a memento, a paste statuette of the Brighton Pavilion or a postcard featuring Eastbourne pier. On that occasion she bought a postcard of the camera obscura tower.

She persuaded Jack, who liked to do a bit of carpentry, to build a little cubbyhole in the dining-room wall for her souvenir knick-knacks. He even constructed a little door with a lock.

'There you are, Daisy,' he said, proudly handing her the key, 'now you've got somewhere to keep all your little secrets.'

'What secrets have I got?' scoffed Daisy, delighted with her husband's handy-work.

On a visit to Brighton, Jack was amused by the shock on his wife's face when a group of young women came out of a bathing machine wearing the most up-to-date swimsuits.

'How can they show their arms and legs like that,' she whispered in his ear.

'But sweetheart, they're not showing very much in those long-sleeved dresses and frilly bloomers,' he replied. 'You will have to get used to modern ways; it won't be long before lady's skirts will be well above the ankle.'

He was on duty one foggy October day. Most trains had been cancelled due to the weather and to get out of the penetrating cold, Jack joined his mate Reg in the signal box for a cup of tea. All at once, a message came through that a train was approaching. Reg quickly closed the level crossing gates but there were already several people walking across the track. Jack raced down the signal box steps yelling at the top of his voice. A couple of people heard him and hurried off the track but an elderly woman seemed deaf to his warning and continued to meander on, head down, looking neither to left nor right. Without hesitation, Jack leapt over the barrier and rushed towards her, pushing his hands into the small of her back so that she landed face-down on the opposite side.

The next minutes were a blur. As he catapulted himself forward he knew that he had been hit, but it was to be days before he would learn the truth.

Daisy opened the door with Madge in her arms and Teddy pulling at her skirt. A policeman confronted her. His manner seemed overly respectful and she instinctively knew he was the bearer of bad news.

'Mrs Webster?' he enquired.

Daisy nodded. Her mouth had gone dry and she knew that if she tried to speak only a squeak would come out.

'I'm afraid your husband has been involved in an accident.'

Daisy found her voice. 'He's not ....?'

'No, Mrs Webster, but I'm afraid he's in a bad way. They've taken him to the hospital.'

'Can I go to him?'

'Yes of course but is there someone who could look after your children?'

'My neighbour will help out.'

At this point, Mrs Durrant opened her front door and joined the group on Daisy's doorstep. 'What's happened?' she gasped.

Forcing herself to appear calm, Daisy said, 'Can you take care of the children, Mrs Durrant, only I've got to go to the hospital as my husband's been in an accident?'

'Not serious, I hope. And of course I can take care of the children.'

'I can give you a lift,' said the policeman addressing Daisy.

Still traumatised, Daisy went indoors to collect the necessary baby paraphernalia to hand to her neighbour then grabbed her purse and her shawl and followed the policeman to his waiting vehicle. She had never been in a car before but the experience which would normally have been exciting was far from that. On the way, the policeman explained what had happened.

'Your husband was very brave,' he said, 'he saved a lady's life.'

'What actually happened?'

'He jumped over the barrier just as a train was approaching because the lady in question didn't hear his shout of warning. He didn't give a thought to the danger...' he swallowed before continuing, 'it was one of the bravest things I've ever heard of.'

'Is he badly injured?'

'I can't say, you'll have to ask the Doctor about that.'

At the hospital, the Sister in Charge led her to a private ward. Jack's face normally quite ruddy due to the sea air, was as white as the sheets on which he lay. His eyes were closed, his hands on the counterpane, scratched. But her gaze was drawn to his left leg, which was suspended in a sling. Briefly, she experienced relief. So he'd broken his leg, surely that would mend?

The Sister whispered although it was clear that Jack was unconscious to the world. 'It's his foot, I'm afraid.'

'It looks as if his leg is broken.'

The Sister shook her head. 'No, his leg is cut and bruised but unfortunately, it was his foot that took the full force of the hit. It was trapped between the rails.

'Oh God!' Daisy felt her head begin to spin as the impact of what the Sister was about to tell her sank in. She felt behind her for the arm of a chair, glad of its proximity.

'We don't know for sure yet, but it's possible they'll have to amputate. I'll get the Doctor to talk to you. Would you like a cup of tea?'

The Sister took Daisy's arm and led her out of the room, settling her in a waiting area while she ordered one of the nurses to pour some tea. 'Make it sweet,' she said.

'I don't like sweet tea,' protested Daisy.

Nonetheless, when it arrived she was grateful for the sugar boost.

Daisy got a horse-drawn cab home. Mrs Durrant was looking out for her and opened the door immediately.

'Come and sit down, dear, you look as if you've had a terrible shock. Tell me about it.'

Daisy's hands were shaking as she accepted another cup of tea, this time without sugar. Mumbling through her tears, she gave Mrs Durrant a garbled account of what had happened.

The woman put her arm around her, gently stroking her bowed head. 'You poor, poor, dear...'

Over the next few days, while Jack lay in a coma, Daisy tried to carry on as normal. With two young children, there was always so much to do and, in a way, this helped to deaden her emotions. You couldn't spend your day crying when there were two hungry infants to attend to. When Jack regained consciousness, she visited as often as she could but cab fares weren't cheap and money problems began to worry her.

On several occasions she spoke to the Doctor only to be told that they were hoping to save Jack's foot, although a decision about amputation may eventually have to be made. Jack himself was in reasonably good spirits. His cuts and bruises had cleared up and the question of whether or not his foot could be saved seemed to have gone over his head.

When Daisy mentioned this to the Sister, she said, 'This often happens with possible amputees. It's too traumatic for them to be able to face up to it.'

Persuaded by Jack's refusal to accept that this could happen to him, Daisy took the view that as bad as things were they were bound to get better.

FOUR

After a couple of weeks, Jack was allowed to get up as long as he didn't try to walk on his damaged leg. This entailed being pushed around in a cane wheelchair, which seemed a bit of a lark at first but soon became annoying. The Railway Company paid Jack's wages for a month, after which they wrote him a letter saying that his salary would be cut to half pending his return to work. This threw Jack into a frenzy of impatience resulting in him demanding to see the doctor. Daisy tried to calm him down with assurances that they could manage. 'I'll cut back on meat,' she said, 'after all Teddy will thrive on vegetables and fruit and I'm still breast-feeding Madge.'

She hoped she had reassured Jack but, in fact, worry and lack of protein were causing her milk to dry up and she wasn't sure how much longer she would be able to breast feed her baby. She was troubled too because Jack complained that she didn't visit him enough and when she explained that the cab fare was biting into their savings, he slipped into sullen silence so that she was only too pleased when the visiting hour was over and she was able to make her escape.

Six weeks after his accident, the doctor called in a colleague for a second opinion and when Daisy paid her usual visit, the Sister waylaid her. 'The Doctor would like to see you, Mrs Webster,' she said and Daisy could tell by her tone that this wasn't good news.

Numbly, she followed the Sister to a private room. As they entered, the Doctor put down the pen he was using and rose to greet her. 'Ah, Mrs Webster, thank you for coming. Please take a seat.'

After studying the report on his desk, the Doctor looked up. 'I'm afraid the news isn't good. After consideration, we have decided to amputate your husband's left foot.' When Daisy gave a gasp, he went on, 'we have done all we can to save the foot but the infection is affecting your husband's general health. He will be much better once the amputation has been performed.'

Daisy closed her eyes and clenched her fists. In her mind's eye, she saw Jack stumbling about with crutches. How would he manage the stairs? How could he return to work? In that moment, their whole beautiful future exploded into a thousand pieces. The good times they were going to have; the improvements they were going to make to their home; the education they were going to give their children. Neither of them wanted Teddy and Madge to leave school at thirteen as Jack had been obliged to do. Then the worst thought of all blasted her mind: if Jack couldn't work for the Railway Company, they would have to move out of Number Seven.

'Are you all right, Mrs Webster, can I get the nurse to bring you some water?'

Daisy blinked her eyes open. 'Have you told my husband yet?'

'No, we thought you should know first.'

'When are you planning to tell him?'

'This afternoon... Would you like to be present?'

She nodded. 'But there's something I want to ask you.'

'Yes?'

'Will my husband be able to walk, I mean, can he be fitted with an artificial foot?'

'Yes, of course he can. Great advances have been made recently in the manufacture of artificial limbs, all down to the genius of a certain Mr Gillingham.'

Daisy clasped her hands to her face. She couldn't believe it. Now there really was hope for a better future.

The Doctor smiled. 'Yes, Mrs Webster, and I think you'll find that in view of the accident occurring on railway premises and the partial loss of a limb, your husband is entitled to compensation.'

'Oh.'

It had never occurred to Daisy that her husband's accident could be the fault of the Railway Company, but of course it was. If the train had been running in accordance with the signals, the level crossing gates would have been lowered several minutes before it shot through. This realisation lifted such a weight from her shoulders that Daisy felt almost light-hearted.

The Doctor spoke again. 'Of course, the hospital will back up any claim your husband makes.'

The next few months were difficult with Jack learning to cope with his artificial foot. He made a big effort to manage the steep staircase but it was a clumsy business. However, once the wheels for claim of compensation had been set in motion, the Railway Company seemed eager to have Jack back as an employee. It transpired that if they re-employed him, the compensation package would be lower so, eventually, he returned to work in the ticket-office where there was a chair to sit down on should he need to rest. And by the end of the year, the Railway Company decided to take advantage of the publicity by nominating Jack for a George Cross.

Daisy was so proud of Jack. Until now, the horror of his injury had eradicated his bravery. Now her husband was on the mend, they were no longer living on the bread line and Jack had been proclaimed a hero. In 1904 they were invited to a ceremony at Buckingham Palace and this time there was no question about Daisy having a new outfit.

One of the young mothers she had met on the beach went with her to choose it. She opted for a deep blue ankle-length skirt with a cream blouse, trimmed with lace; there was a navy veiled hat, matching gloves and fashionable ankle boots to go with it. The boots even had a two inch heel which pleased Daisy because, at just over five foot, she had always longed to be taller.

'You look wonderful, sweetheart,' said Jack when she tried the outfit on to show him.

Daisy beamed at him. Since their life had improved, she had regained some of the weight she had lost and the dimples in her cheeks had returned.

'Give us a twirl, there's a dear.'

She did as he asked, feeling like royalty as she caught a glance of herself in the long mirror on the wardrobe door. Even Teddy looked in awe of her but she had to get Jack to hold him back in case he grabbed her skirt with his sticky little fingers.

Jack too had to be fitted out with a new suit. 'Why can't I wear the one I wore for our wedding?' he said. 'There's nothing wrong with it and it's only taking up room in the wardrobe covered in mothballs.'

'Don't be silly, darling, for an honour like this you need a new suit. I won't hear of you turning up to meet the King in an out-of-date suit.'

Jack begrudgingly agreed and he was secretly pleased when he inspected himself in the mirror, especially when Daisy oohed and aahed over his appearance.

Both of them floated through the ceremony as if in a dream. Daisy would recall one aspect which Jack had completely missed, and vice versa, he would pick some facet of the regalia that had completely passed her by. When they got home, Mrs Durrant, who had once again taken care of the children, was agog to hear every detail.

'And did the King actually speak to you?' she asked Jack.

Jack nodded.

'And what did he say?'

This floored him. For the life of him, he couldn't remember. They all laughed and Mrs Durrant said, 'One day, you will be able to tell your children all about it.'

Despite the pain he sometimes experienced with his artificial foot, life improved for Jack. He found that working in the ticket office afforded him the opportunity to talk to people. He enjoyed the contact and made friends with some of his regular customers. Daisy was happy with her lot. She loved motherhood although they mutually decided that two was enough, especially as they now had a pigeon pair.

They often took the children for walks on the Downs with Jack just about managing to carry his young daughter on his back when she got tired. The town was expanding: an infant school opened up along the road, just in time for Teddy. In 1908 a Museum and Art Gallery was built and in 1911, the Kursaal Entertainment Complex was opened, affording the Websters the opportunity to have the occasional evening out while the kindly Mrs Durrant sat in with Teddy and Madge.

The children did well at school with Madge being good at English and even learning to type, while Teddy found that mental arithmetic came easily to him. Their parents were proud of them and felt confidant that they would be assured of a job when they left school.

Little did they know that everything would change so suddenly. One June evening in 1914, Jack hurried home from work with dramatic news.

'Have you had the wireless on?' he asked as he burst through the door.

Daisy stopped stirring the stew to which she had just added a pinch of salt. 'Why, what's happened?'

'There's been an assassination.'

Daisy's eyes widened. 'Here, in England?'

'No, in Sarajevo, an important archduke has been murdered.'

'Thank goodness it's not in this country. Where is Sara...that place you mentioned?'

'It's in a country called Bosnia, near Austria.'

She put the lid back on the saucepan and turned to her husband. 'I've never heard of it. They're always having fights in that part of the world. What has it got to do with us?'

But she was taken by surprise because Jack looked serious. 'There's talk of war,' he said, 'the Germans are up in arms about the assassination.'

'Huh,' scoffed his wife, 'it will never come to that, not in our country anyway.'

But Daisy was wrong and by August, war had broken out. In the first flush of patriotism, men flocked to volunteer but by 1916 conscription had begun. For once Daisy counted Jack's accident as a blessing. He would not be able to go to war and neither would her son because at fifteen he was too young. She realised they would face shortages but as they lived in an area abundant with market gardens they would not starve.

As the conflict progressed she would lie awake at night feeling guilty for her own good fortune when her friends received news of missing husbands or sons. Then one day Mrs Durrant received the dreaded telegram informing her that her grandson, Jimmy, had been killed in action. The roles were reversed and now it was Daisy's turn to do the comforting.

By this time, Teddy was working as a delivery boy for a local butcher. Jack was delighted that his son had found this position and encouraged him to work hard and learn the trade. But with the progress of the War meat became scarce and Teddy was laid off. He moped about the house, getting under Daisy's feet and with the difficulty of making sure the family had enough to eat, she was on a short fuse. Mother and son often exchanged harsh words and sometimes, Teddy would stomp out of the house, staying away for hours at a time until Daisy would fear he would never come home.

On one such occasion, he returned looking jubilant.

'Have you found another job?' she cried on seeing his smiling face.

'Not exactly...'

'What d'you mean?'

Jack looked up from his newspaper. 'Answer your mother properly, son.'

For a moment, Teddy was silent then he burst out, 'I've enlisted.'

'What!' both his parents shouted in unison.

'I've joined the army.'

'But you can't, you're only fifteen.'

'Nearly sixteen...' Teddy cheekily corrected his mother.

'Hold your tongue!' Jack threw the newspaper onto the floor and leapt up from his chair. 'I should box your ears you impudent young whippersnapper.'

Teddy stood his ground. He had felt the hand of his father many times during his childhood but he wasn't going to back down now. Praying that Jack wouldn't notice the trembling in his legs, he thrust out his chin and said defiantly, 'It's too late; you can't do anything about it. I pick up my uniform tomorrow.'

'No!' Daisy's high-pitched shriek brought Madge running down the stairs from her bedroom.

'What's happened?' she demanded.

Teddy turned to his sister, seeking support. 'I've joined up. I want to do my bit for the country.'

Madge's eyes widened with shock. 'But Teddy, they don't accept fifteen-year-olds.'

Edging towards the door, he insisted again, 'Nearly sixteen, I said I was eighteen and they believed me.'

Daisy turned to her husband. 'Jack, do something.'

Slowed by his artificial foot, Jack took a step towards his son but the boy was too quick for him and before he was halfway across the room, Teddy had rushed out slamming the door behind him. The next day, Jack tried to countermand his son's recruitment but it turned out that the enlistment couldn't be undone and Teddy was sent off for training the following week.

For the next month, Daisy went about her chores with tears in her eyes. She couldn't understand why Jack hadn't been able to stop Teddy and no amount of protest on his part would convince her that he had really tried to rectify the situation. She had always been proud of her son who was tall for his age. She was sorry now that people had always taken him for two or three years older than his actual age.

After the third month, he wrote saying that he was being posted abroad although he had no idea where he was going. *Don't worry,* he wrote, *I know how to take care of myself. Besides it will all be over by Christmas.*

He meant the War but sadly it turned out to be his life.

FIVE

Daisy opened the door. The telegraph boy handed her the telegram and ran off down the road. She knew him. He was Seth Hunter's boy who had joined the Post Office after leaving school.

She stood in the hallway for several minutes unable to bring herself to open the envelope. *It could mean he's been wounded and that they've taken him to a field hospital* she told herself. She slit the envelope open with her nail and read the dreaded words: *Killed in Action.*

Stumbling into the living room, she slumped onto an upright chair, placing the flat of her hand on the table for support, just as she had done sixteen years earlier, in the days before Teddy was born. Her mind conjured up a horrendous image of her little boy lying in a muddy trench, his mangled body covered with blood. She felt nausea rising and rushed to the sink, wiping her mouth with her apron afterwards and returning to take up her place by the table.

Madge found her like this on her return from work. 'What's the matter, Ma?' she cried on seeing her mother's motionless figure. Then she saw the telegram still clutched in Daisy's hand. Snatching it up she read the brief message. 'Ma, when did this come?'

When Daisy remained silent, Madge turned on her heel and left the house running all the way to the station where her father was on duty. Out of breath, she picked up her skirt and climbed the steps to the station entrance. This was a quiet time of day; the homeward-bound rush had not yet started. Tearfully, she pushed the telegram under the glass partition, just as Bert came into the kiosk to join Jack.

'No!' Jack's gulp of anguish echoed around the tiny room.

'What is it?' Bert took the telegram from him. 'Take your daughter home, Jack; I'll cover the rest of your shift.'

Numbly, Jack snatched his coat off the hook behind the door and left the ticket-office, passing in front of his daughter without greeting her. He strode as fast as his artificial foot would allow him with Madge running along behind him, just as she used to when she was a little girl.

Daisy heard the front door open and, jolted out of her catatonic trance she rushed to greet her husband, throwing herself into his arms. But he thrust her away and marched through to the garden, drawing his packet of Craven As out of his pocket as he went. His wife and daughter stared after him until, all at once, Daisy crumpled to the floor and burst into tears. Madge crouched down next to her then gently helped her to her feet. She guided her mother upstairs and led her to the bed.

'You rest, Ma,' she said. 'I'll make you a cup of tea.'

From the kitchen Madge could hear Daisy's heaving sobs. They seemed to reverberate throughout the house. This must be what it's like when an earthquake strikes, thought Madge as she struck a match and lit the gas under the kettle. She busied herself opening the cupboard and getting out three cups and saucers, placing them neatly in a line with a teaspoon on each saucer. She poured the required amount of milk into the cups: lots for Pa, a mere drain for Ma and something in the middle for her. She got out the sugar basin, replenishing the contents and even reached for the biscuit tin. These small tasks kept her from breaking down. If she let go too, where would they be?

She took her father's tea out to him. There was a biscuit - one of his favourite's - balanced on the saucer but his hand shook so much as he took it from her that the biscuit landed on the ground. He didn't say a word. Madge went back indoors and using a tray, she climbed the stairs taking care not to slop any of the tea into the saucers.

Daisy was propped up on the bed, dabbing her eyes with a handkerchief. Heaving sobs still rent from her throat but she managed to give her daughter a grateful smile.

'Thank you, darling,' she muttered. 'I need to know what happened; do you think they will tell us?'

Madge didn't know what to say. Questions were spinning around her mind too but she didn't know what the procedure was. Would the War Office issue details of fallen men?

The weeks that followed were a nightmare for Madge. At so young an age she was ill-equipped to cope with such devastating grief. In the insurance office where she worked, she had seen people torn apart by news from the Front and, being blessed with a sympathetic nature, she was one of the first to offer a shoulder to cry on. But getting a direct hit with news like this was a different matter. She knew her mother was putting on a brave face; going about her daily chores with her usual vigour, greeting acquaintances with her usual smile, accepting awkward condolences from neighbours with her usual grace.

She was more worried about her father. He had withdrawn from both his wife and daughter. He barely spoke and started coming home from work later than usual. Daisy and Madge knew he was spending more time in the pub although he never appeared to be drunk.

A few months later, one spring day, he failed to return at all. By ten in the evening, Daisy was at her wits end. She told Madge to hold the fort while she scoured the local public houses. Entering such establishments was alien to Daisy but, plucking up courage, she made her way to the George and Dragon where she knew her husband sometimes went. Ignoring the drinkers' stares she went to the bar and asked if anybody had seen Jack.

One of the men grunted, 'Not today, missus, try the Hare and Hounds.'

She left the George and Dragon and, hitching up her skirt, ran through the dark streets to the Hare and Hounds. On reaching the pub she paused, panting for breath on the doorstep. Her courage almost failed her for this was a lively alehouse frequented by rough and ready fishermen whose language, she felt sure, was not fit for a lady's ears.

I have to do this for Jack's sake, she told herself and, taking a deep breath, she pushed open the door, entering into a low-ceilinged, beamed saloon. A haze of cigarette smoke hung over the occupants. There was a hush as she entered and all heads turned in her direction. Doing her best to look composed, Daisy approached the bar.

'Erm, excuse me, barman,' she said in a low voice, 'but have you seen my husband lately?'

Before she could even give his name, there was a guffaw of laughter from a group of men seated at a nearby table. 'Why, missus, have you mislaid him?'

Daisy fought to control her welling tears. 'His name's Jack and he some...sometimes come...comes here,' she stuttered.

'There are a lot of Jacks around here, which one in particular?' This banter from the barman raised another chorus of laughter and a clink of tankards.

Daisy clenched her fists. 'He's tall and good-looking, his hair's dark and he walks with...'

'Oh,' said the barman, 'you mean Peg Leg Jack.'

Daisy gasped. So this is how they saw her wonderful husband! She felt the blood rush to her head and was forced to thrust out a hand to the bar counter to steady herself. This silenced the men and one of them stepped forward and guided her to a bench, telling her to lower her head to allow the dizziness to recede. Some of the others crowded round.

'Get the lady some water, Al,' shouted a beefy fisherman, while another man placed a cushion behind her back.

The barman produced a flagon of ice cold water, which was passed from one gnarled hand to the next until it reached Daisy. The laughter that had greeted her had now turned to concern.

'What's going on?' A blowsy-looking woman appeared in a doorway behind the bar.

'The lady's had a funny turn, Trixie.'

With a swish of her serge skirt, the woman lifted the counter flap and came out from behind the bar. 'Stand back! Give her some space,' she ordered and the men surrounding Daisy moved away to allow her room to pass.

The big man provided information, saying 'She says she's looking for her missing husband, Trix.'

Trixie sat down on the bench next to Daisy, revealing as she did so a bulging cleavage. She put her arm around her shoulders and said, 'Here, love, what's the matter?'

This unexpected kindness was too much for Daisy. Looking into the woman's concerned brown eyes, she spilt out the whole story.

Trixie listened, nodding sympathetically. Then she took charge. 'Look to it, lads, organise a search party.' She gesticulated to the onlookers. 'You three take the west side of town and the rest of you go and search the east side.' She pointed at a man snoozing in the corner. 'Mick, you lazy good-for-nothing, wake up and escort the lady home.'

At Trixie's command, the drinkers, gulped down their ale and sprang to life while Mick, blinking wearily, dragged himself to his feet and shuffled over.

'Where d'you live, love?' asked Trixie and when Daisy told her she glowered at Mick and said, 'Make sure the lady gets home safe and sound.' When he started to protest, she added, 'Move yourself, you bleeding bastard.'

Normally, Daisy would have been shocked at hearing such language from a member of her own sex but all she could do now was smile gratefully. Getting to her feet, she took Mick's proffered arm and let him lead her out of the pub into the street, ignoring the lingering smell of fish that seemed to ooze from his every pore.

After Mick had left her in Madge's care, Daisy did her best to calm down convincing herself that the voluntary search party would track Jack down and bring him home. The hours dragged and when there was still no news by the early hours she sent Madge off to bed and went to lie down herself. But neither of them managed to sleep and Daisy was pleased when her daughter crept into bed beside her.

'Pa will turn up tomorrow, Ma, he'd never miss work,' said Madge in a bid to comfort her, but in the morning Bert sent word that Jack hadn't reported for work.

'This isn't like Jack,' he said, 'he's usually so reliable. Maybe you should contact the Police.'

Two days later, the Police discovered Jack's rucksack behind a beach hut. His body turned up further along the coast, discovered by a group of schoolboys who came across it when they were foraging for crabs on Shoreham Beach. Hidden by a mound of seaweed, it had remained unnoticed for several days.

SIX

Mother and daughter were devastated. Things like this happened to other people, not to their family. The pair talked for hours trying to make sense of it.

'I should have seen the signs,' lamented Daisy.

'How could you, Ma? Pa didn't behave differently the day he left.'

Daisy wrung her hands. 'But he'd been acting strange for ages.' The tears spilled out and ran down her cheeks. 'He was never the same after Teddy died.'

'You mustn't blame yourself. Teddy was your child too and you didn't fall apart.'

Her mother wiped her eyes with a corner of her apron. 'But your pa adored that boy. When Teddy was born he was so happy to have a son.' She looked up realising how hurtful this would seem to Madge. 'He loved you both so much,' she added, touching her daughter's hand.

Practicalities took over. There was a funeral to arrange and Daisy's niggling worry was that after Jack's funeral the Railway Company would want her to move out. But thanks to the backing of Jack's faithful work mates the Company agreed that Daisy could stay there for the time being. This left Daisy feeling insecure, always afraid that a letter would arrive telling her to leave, but when a year went by and then another and this didn't happen she began to believe that she would see out her time in Number Seven.

The years rolled on and Madge started dating a recently demobbed army officer called Charlie Bilston who had joined the insurance company where she worked. Daisy was a little wary of Charlie. She felt that his family must be a cut above their working class roots. She voiced her misgivings. 'Madge dear, Charlie's parents must be quite well-to-do if he used to be an officer.'

Her daughter hastened to reassure her. 'Some men rose from the ranks very quickly during the War,' she said, a reminder to Daisy that many of the young soldiers died very soon after being sent to the Front.

Gradually, Charlie charmed Daisy by doing odd jobs around the house, proving to be handy with a hammer and screwdriver and she was genuinely pleased when the pair became engaged.

One spring day, Madge came home from work bursting with excitement. 'Ma, you'd better go and buy yourself a new dress because me and Charlie are getting married in June.'

Daisy gasped. 'That's wonderful news, darling but it's a bit sudden, isn't it? And where will you live? Of course, you could move in here. There's plenty of room.'

'I've got some more news for you, Ma,' Madge's eyes twinkled, 'Charlie's put the deposit down on a house.'

Daisy looked startled. 'A deposit on a house, can he afford that?'

'Yes, isn't it exciting?'

'Why didn't you tell me before?'

'We wanted it to be a surprise.'

'Well, it certainly is. Where is this house?'

Madge hesitated before replying. 'It's on the east side of town but don't worry Ma...'

Daisy's heart was pounding for despite the joyful news she couldn't help panicking that her daughter would not be living close by. Madge must have read her thoughts. 'We won't be very far away, Ma, only a stone's throw. You'll be able to come and visit us, stay for the weekend.'

But Daisy couldn't assimilate the news. 'Is there a bus that goes that way?' she asked.

'Well, you'll have to change buses down in town, but don't worry I'll check the timetables for you.'

'Oh dear, I shall miss you so much,' sniffed Daisy.

She turned her head away to hide her tears but Madge noticed and, despite her excitement, she felt the prick of tears too. Daisy recovered first. 'Dearie me,' she said. 'June! Then we don't have much time to plan the wedding. It will have to be St John's. We must arrange for the bans to be read at once…'

'Ma!'

'Yes.'

'Everything has been taken care of. We're getting married at St Paul's in Brighton and…' Madge's eyes shone with excitement. '…Charlie's father has booked the reception in a Brighton hotel.'

'No…no!'

'What's the matter?'

'A Brighton hotel, I can't afford that! Why don't we have it in the tea rooms at the end of the pier? They do lovely sandwiches and cakes.'

'Sorry, Ma but it's all arranged,' muttered Madge tightly, 'and it won't cost you a penny because Charlie's father is footing the bill.'

Daisy's lower lip quivered, then she brightened. 'I'll look out my wedding dress for you to wear. Do you remember? I showed it to you once.'

Madge look embarrassed. 'Please don't bother to get it out, you see Charlie's mother's taking me up to the West End to choose a dress.'

'What?'

Madge reached for Daisy's hand. 'Why don't you come too? That way you can meet Mrs Bilston and…'

Daisy drew away from her daughter, dismissing the suggestion with a flick of her wrist. 'No, dear, you go ahead and choose your wedding dress with Mrs...Mrs Bilston.'

'Ma, I know you're disappointed but fashions have changed, you know; I don't want a floor-length dress, I want an up-to-the-minute frock with a short skirt. We've seen a lovely one with a handkerchief style hemline and a low back.'

'We?'

Madge lowered her gaze realising that things weren't going well. 'Mrs Bilston is very keen on the latest fashion; she buys *Vogue* every month,' she said in an attempt to justify her actions.

Clearly this didn't impress Daisy, who nodded and moved swiftly towards the kitchen, calling back, 'I must get supper ready.'

After that, conversation between mother and daughter was awkward. Both women were feeling hurt but as the big day drew closer, they knew they would have to put aside their differences.

'I've never even stepped inside a hotel,' complained Daisy for the umpteenth time. 'I won't know what to do, how to behave. I shall feel uncomfortable.'

Madge tried to reassure her. 'It's only going to be family and friends.'

Daisy stifled a sob. '*His* family, *your* friends, you mean, but what about me? I'll be all alone.'

Exasperated, Madge said, 'Ma, Charlie and I wanted you to meet Mr and Mrs Bilston but you said you'd rather wait until the wedding.' Her mother's doleful expression prompted her to add, 'But don't worry you'll feel at home in next to no time.'

But it did worry Daisy. Charlie's parents were from North London, his father was a solicitor, his mother was a school teacher and most of their friends worked in offices. Daisy who knew nothing about office work had been terribly proud when Madge had passed her shorthand-typing exams and found a job as a stenographer with an insurance company. Looking back over the past few months, she realised that Madge had been spending a lot of time with Charlie's parents. She couldn't help noticing that her daughter's attitude and manner of speech had changed. She had started using expressions unfamiliar to Daisy, expressions which she associated with toffs in matinées she had seen at the Picturedrome.

And Daisy *did* feel uncomfortable at the wedding ceremony, especially at the reception. Madge did her best to keep an eye on her but there was so much going on and so many people to greet that Daisy got overlooked. Charlie's mother made an effort to introduce her to various relatives but Daisy had never learnt the art of small talk and found herself tongue-tied. Anyone who approached her soon gave up trying to make conversation and drifted away. She felt like a fly on the wall. Everybody was laughing and joking, talking about things she knew nothing about. She wanted to go home but knew that was impossible. Eventually, she was rescued by Charlie's grandfather who came to sit down beside her.

'Oh dear, a lady all alone,' he said, offering her a cigarette.

'No thank you, I don't smoke,' she replied.

'Can I get you a drink?'

'Lemonade please...'

'My goodness, dear lady, I think a glass of Champagne is more in order.'

Before Daisy could protest, he headed in the direction of the bar returning with two glasses of bubbly.

'Let me introduce myself,' he said, 'my name's Charles, my grandson was named after me. Tell me Mrs Webster...'

'Daisy, please...' she replied after taking a sip of her drink and rather enjoying it.

'Tell me Daisy, you sound like a Londoner? Which part of the great metropolis do you hail from?

For a moment, Daisy was flummoxed. What did he mean: the great metropolis? 'Oh,' she gasped, 'I was born in Highgate but we moved to the South Coast when my husband was offered a job down here. I've been here ever since.'

'You're a war widow?'

Daisy shook her head and wished she hadn't. Until now, the only alcohol she had ever tasted was the occasional glass of port and lemon.

'My husband died as a result of an accident,' she explained, hoping he would leave it at that but he seemed intent on drawing her out.

'Dear me, how did that happen?'

'He drowned, and...and I'd rather not talk about it if you don't mind.'

'I'm so sorry, dear lady I didn't mean to distress you. I can't apologise enough.'

The three-piece band started to play and couples moved onto the dance floor.

'Would you care to dance, Daisy?'

He took her hand and led her onto the dance floor. She had always loved dancing but once Jack had lost his foot, he had become rather clumsy so dancing had been out of the question. Five minutes later when the band paused and the best man announced that it was time to cut the wedding cake, Daisy found herself standing beside the newly married couple with another glass of champagne in her hand. She felt more relaxed now and glowed with pride as everybody clustered around her daughter. Madge looked lovely in her fashionable calf-length dress in cream lace. An Alice band of flowers adorned her cropped auburn hair. Daisy had been heart-broken when her daughter had decided to have her long hair cut. Nothing would have induced *her* to chop off her own long hair, which still retained a hint of auburn although there was plenty of grey showing through. What a beautiful daughter she had and, one day, there might be a grandchild or two to brighten her life.

SEVEN

Daisy was lonely without Madge. How she wished she had brothers or sisters. Since Jack's death, she had rarely been in contact with his side of the family and her own parents had died several years earlier. There were a few distant cousins of her mother's somewhere in the London area but she had long ago lost touch with them.

During the summer months she found solace in the garden. The area nearest the house benefited from full sun from June to September and Daisy took advantage of this by digging up part of the lawn and planting an assortment of flowers. She would often sit out there in a deckchair with an afternoon cup of tea watching the butterflies and bees flitting from plant to plant.

The winters were the worst. When it got dark by four o'clock, she felt there was nothing to live for. She would look back to the days when Jack had arrived home from work and related the goings on of his day at the station. To fill the gap, she considered taking in a lodger but thought the Railway Company might not like that and, although she listened to the wireless and played her records - she now had quite a collection - the days dragged. She washed curtains that had no need of a wash, she cleaned windows that she'd cleaned only days earlier and she constantly rearranged ornaments.

One day when dusting, she got out Jack's favourite record and placed it on the turntable. The words of *When You Were Sweet Sixteen* took her back to when she had teased him about playing it so often. She picked up a cushion, hugging it to herself and started waltzing around the room, swirling her skirt against the furniture. But the words were too nostalgic and she sank down onto the settee and burst into tears.

The record ended, leaving the turntable whirring. It reminded her of when she and Jack had met. As a special treat, her father had taken her to the Easter Fair at Hampstead Heath. It was so exciting. They had tried out all the rides, laughed until they cried in the Hall of Mirrors, and she had screamed at the top of her voice during a ride through the House of Horrors. It was when they were having a go at the Coconut Shy that a young man came to stand beside her. Daisy desperately wanted to win a prize but after three failed goes, she turned away disappointed.

'Can I have a go?' said the handsome young man at her shoulder.

Jack made several attempts without success but it didn't matter because when she looked up into his blue eyes, she knew this was the man she wanted to marry. Under her father's watchful eye, they had exchanged addresses and Jack had courted her for three months before her parents agreed that they could get married. Jack had promised to take her back to Hampstead Fair one Easter, but the birth of two children had put paid to that idea.

Then change came in a way that Daisy least expected. A letter arrived one day informing the tenants of the entire terrace that the Railway Company had decided to put the properties on the market.

'As the current resident, you are being afforded the opportunity to make an offer of purchase in advance of the house being advertised on the open market. Your offer will be considered most favourably,' the letter read. It went on to say that they had three months to find other accommodation.

Daisy was thrown into panic. Leave Number Seven! When the Railway Company had failed to turn her out after Jack's death, she had hoped she would end her days there. All her memories were locked up in this house; her children had been born there, her husband's funeral had been conducted from there. How could she settle in any other place? Madge found her in tears on her next visit.

'Ma, maybe it's a good thing,' she said, 'after all, this house is much too big for you now. You spend your life cleaning rooms that are never used. Charlie and I will help you find a nice little flat somewhere nearer the centre of town within walking distance of the beach.'

'But I don't want to move,' wailed Daisy, 'I'll be lonely...'

Madge placed an arm around her mother's shoulders. 'No lonelier than you are living here all by yourself. Why, only the other week, you told me the neighbours you used to chat to had moved away.'

Daisy shook her head and sniffed into her handkerchief. 'Living somewhere else wouldn't be the same, I'm used to this house and it has such fond memories for me.'

Her mother's words almost brought Madge to tears too but she knew that inevitably Daisy would have to move out. Selfishly, her thoughts turned to her own situation; she and Charlie had decided they didn't want children although of course she hadn't mentioned this to her mother. They were a reclusive couple who enjoyed one another's company almost to the exclusion of everybody else. She was excessively possessive of her good-looking husband and didn't want to share him. In an attempt to justify her feelings, she reasoned that despite Charlie's efforts to please Daisy they had never quite hit it off. Hardening her heart, she tried to press her mother into moving to a flat, but it was no good.

'You can come and live with us, Ma,' she whispered finally.

Daisy straightened up. 'Won't Charlie have something to say about that?'

'I'll talk him round,'

'What about my furniture, all my knick-knacks?' asked Daisy, thinking of the mementos she had collected over the years.

Madge took a deep breath. 'Of course you can bring your souvenirs and we might have room for one or two larger items.'

'I wouldn't want to part with my settee.'

Madge felt a mixture of sympathy and irritation. She knew how hard it was going to be for her mother to move out of Number Seven. 'Well, maybe you could have one of the larger bedrooms so that it will fit in,' she said.

After a cup of tea and a piece of fruit cake, much to Madge's relief, Daisy cheered up but as she left the house, she couldn't help wondering what Charlie was going to say when she told him.

A couple of weeks later, a second-hand dealer came to collect most of the furniture. Reminded of the day she and Jack had moved in, Daisy stood on the doorstep with Madge watching the van drive away. When she and Jack had moved in there had been very little to manoeuvre through the narrow hallway; just a bed, a table and a couple of chairs. This time there was an endless stream of furniture being carried out. She couldn't help wondering where it was going to end up.

She was still smarting over a disagreement she and Madge had had earlier in the day. Before the dealer arrived, Madge had brought up the subject of the box-room.

'Ma, what about all that stuff in the attic?' she said.

'I'm keeping it,' replied Daisy.

'But Ma what's the point of keeping all those old things from our childhood?' protested Madge.

'They've got wonderful memories for me; I don't want to part with them.'

Madge threw up her hands in exasperation. 'Cots, prams, baby clothes! You don't need those any more, and what about the toys and story books? Why don't you give them to the family along the road; they've got a couple of kiddies. I'm sure they'd like them.'

'What about you and Charlie? They might come in handy for you one of these days.'

Madge tried to be tactful. 'Ma, we probably won't have any children,' she said quietly.

Daisy misunderstood. 'You never know, stranger things have happened. Just as you give up hope, a baby comes along. You may be twenty-seven but that's not too late.'

Madge heaved a sigh. The same conversation had been repeated on several occasions and she knew that her mother would not give up the idea of one day cradling a grandchild in her arms. She had never explained that she and Charlie didn't intend to start a family; it was easier to prevaricate so that her mother still had hope. The trouble was the contents of the box-room would no doubt end up in their loft and she knew Charlie wouldn't like that.

She ushered her mother back indoors, saying cheerily, 'Well, Ma, there's a lot more space now; how on earth did you and Pa collect so much rubbish?'

'It's not rubbish to me,' retorted Daisy.

Realising her mistake, Madge hastened to rectify the situation. 'Oh dear, I didn't mean rubbish I meant possessions.'

'You meant rubbish,' snapped her mother.

It was arranged that Madge and Charlie would pick Daisy up the next day but she couldn't bear to spend the hours ahead in idle reminiscence so donning her apron she set about cleaning the entire house from top to bottom even though she had already done it the day before. She washed the downstairs windows and scrubbed the doorstep, giving it a polish with red gumption and swept the path. Even the wrought-iron gate was given a vigorous dusting.

At eight o'clock she went to bed to spend a restless night until the first signs of dawn filtered through the net curtains. By the time her daughter and son-in-law came to collect her, she was waiting in the hall with her packed carpet bag on the floor beside her. She had dressed with care: a tailored white blouse with a sombre black skirt and coat, topped by a matching veiled hat, an outfit which seemed fitting for the occasion.

Madge and Charlie arrived with a small van to transport her last remaining possessions. Dry-eyed, she stood, arms folded across her chest, watching the procedure of loading her bed, the settee and the gramophone onto the van, together with a box containing her collection of china ornaments and another crammed with toys and baby clothes.

'Come on, Ma,' urged Madge taking her arm, 'the taxi's waiting.'

Daisy didn't move.

'Hurry up you two,' called Charlie as he gave the go-ahead for the van to leave so that they could follow in the taxi.

Daisy stood transfixed until Madge firmly closed the front door behind them and guided her mother out to the waiting cab.

*****

BETWEEN THE WARS

During the second decade of the century Europe witnessed upheaval when the Bolshevics executed the Romanov family; Emmeline Pankhurst and her followers provoked unrest by staging protests and hunger strikes until the People Act brought in votes for women over the age of thirty and in America prohibition incited bootlegging, gambling and prostitution. In 1933 Adolf Hitler became Chancellor of Germany and new laws were introduced proclaiming Jews as second-class citizens. Ethnic Cleansing had begun.

At home, the town's population increased to nearly 38,000 with parish boundaries expanding to include outlying villages. In 1933 the Town Hall was rebuilt and the Plaza and Odeon cinemas opened to bring the number of picture houses to four.

My status changed too and I became a privately owned dwelling. However, it took time for the estate agents to find the right occupants. The 1920s brought a brighter more open décor into favour with the consequence that most viewers were put off by the heavy woodwork inside the property. This was because Daisy had never up-graded to the more fashionable art deco style of the early twenties. She had insisted on redecorating my rooms with the exact same colour and pattern of wallpaper every time. The cornices, dado rails and skirting boards were always dark brown.

'That's the way I like it,' she would tell Madge whenever she suggested a change. The only thing she agreed to was the installation of a telephone.

Walter and Hetty Parker came to view me one late autumn day. On entering the hall, Walter shook his head. 'This place is too dark, Hetty.'

His wife wasn't so sure. 'Walter sweetie, I have a good feeling about this house. It's welcoming. Let's at least have a look round.' Taking his hand she persuaded her husband to follow her from room to room. Her excitement grew. 'Just look, Walter, there's a dear little cubbyhole hidden in the wall. I wonder what secrets it holds.' She gripped his hand tighter. 'We can transform this house, darling, I know we can.'

Her husband was still doubtful. 'It will cost a lot to bring it up to scratch.'

'Nonsense, it only needs a coat or two of paint. You're so clever, darling, you'll have this place looking just the way we want it in next to no time.'

'It needs an inside bathroom, and electricity.'

'We can have both installed before we move in. Oh, Walter, I can just see us living here. The garden's lovely with all those fruit trees and flowerbeds.'

Their twin daughters, Patsy and Paula were as enthusiastic as their mother and so the Parker family moved in after an extension bathroom had been added. It only encroached on the back garden by a foot or two, leaving Daisy's carefully tended flowerbeds intact.

EIGHT

'It's just that she's high-spirited. I'm sure she didn't mean any harm and if there's any damage to your gate we'll pay for it,' said Hetty, switching on her sweetest smile.

The woman from Number Five sniffed and said, 'There's no need for that but I wish you'd keep your children under control, Mrs Parker.'

To satisfy their neighbour, Hetty gave her errant daughter a gentle cuff round the ear and ordered her up to her room but once indoors with the front door closed, the culprit burst into giggles and it wasn't long before Hetty started laughing too.

'What's going on?' demanded Walter, lowering his newspaper and peering at them over the top of his spectacles.

'Nothing to worry about, darling...' said his wife, 'just a little misunderstanding.'

Walter frowned. 'Come on, out with it, what has Patsy done now?'

His daughter tried to suppress her giggles as she mumbled, 'Mrs Daly caught me swinging on her gate. Honestly Daddy, I don't know why she made such a fuss about it.'

'You've no right to annoy people, young lady, tomorrow you must go and apologise to Mrs Daly.'

'All right, Daddy,' agreed his daughter looking suitably contrite but she had to bite her lip to keep a straight face.

He retired behind his newspaper again knowing that in a house full of women he could never win. From time to time, he tried to impose discipline but Hetty wouldn't back him up. She saw every situation through rose-tinted glasses and although he adored her he sometimes wished she would take life a little more seriously. He was twenty years older than her and had to admit that he had been flattered when the attractive nineteen-year-old had agreed to be his wife. Hetty was the ideal partner for a successful company director. She enjoyed entertaining and was an expert at putting her guests at ease. He would be the first to admit that she had brought custom to his export business. But she liked expensive clothes and couldn't pass a shop without buying that must-have hat or pair of shoes. She indulged the girls too and had persuaded him to put their daughters into the best private school in the area.

He heaved a sigh. Who could have predicted Black Tuesday, that October day barely a year ago when Wall Street had crashed, bringing down his business and all his hopes for the future? The American Market had been his best customer and without it there was no way he could carry on. Their life changed overnight but to give Hetty her due, she had coped marvellously, not uttering one word of complaint when they had been forced to down-size in a hurry. Thanks to a timely inheritance from one of Hetty's distant relations they had still had enough money in the bank to buy Number Seven, a very modest residence compared to their home in Putney, but Walter had been obliged to sell his luxury Ford with the family relying on Hetty's small Austin Seven.

The Parkers filled the house with noise. They were either laughing or squabbling. Raised voices could be heard by neighbours along the road but nobody minded too much because they were as generous of spirit as they were quarrelsome. Hetty it turned out was always willing to help a neighbour out by lending a cup of sugar or providing a bucket of coal.

Like the Websters before them, it was work that brought the Parkers to the town. Following the collapse of his company Walter managed to find a post in Brighton. It was a far cry from being his own boss but Walter counted himself lucky to have found a post which would enable him to provide for his family.

While her husband was at work and the children at school, Hetty would busy herself around the house, singing along with the wireless at the top of her voice. Once or twice the next-door-neighbour complained about the volume. Hetty obligingly turned the volume down, only to increase it again after a few minutes.

Hetty adored her daughters but she was far from the motherly type and indulged them outrageously. She just couldn't bring herself to be the strict parent that Walter wanted her to be. He was always accusing her of being unable to say the word 'no' and she had to admit that when they wanted something they only had to look up at her with pleading eyes and she invariably gave in.

On one occasion, Walter was furious when he came home and found that his daughters had adopted a black and white kitten.

'Where did this come from?' he demanded when he nearly trod on it.

'Oh daddy isn't she sweet?' cried the twins in unison.

'Hetty, haven't I said no animals, especially cats?'

Hetty joined the girls. 'I know, but we love it.'

'Where did it come from?

'Mrs Baldwin's cat had a litter and said we could have this one. It's the littlest,' said Patsy.

'And the prettiest,' piped up Paula.

Walter looked from one to the other of them. 'Hetty,' he said, 'you know cat's fur makes me sneeze, why did you let them bring it home?'

'Sorry, darling. If it proves to be a problem I'll get the girls to take it back.'

Hetty suppressed a smile knowing this was unlikely since Patsy and Paula had set their hearts on keeping the kitten.

'Well,' agreed Walter, still unwilling to concede. 'Keep it out of my way and don't forget, girls...' He thumped the table with his fist, '...it's your responsibility to look after it.'

'Attention, ma chérie, ne t'énerve pas.'

Hetty knew that it irritated Walter when she spoke French, a throwback to her childhood days in Brittany. She softened the reprimand by putting her arms around his neck and kissing his cheek.

And so the kitten, named Mimi took up residence in Number Seven.

But it wasn't long before Hetty grew bored with her role of housewife. In Putney they had employed a girl straight from school to look after the chores. Ivy had fitted in well with the family. The girls loved her and Hetty knew that she could safely leave them in her care while she went off to play tennis or bowls. A leading figure in a local group assisting 'fallen women', Hetty had proved to be an inspiration with her cheerful attitude and positive thinking. She held evening soirées and organised cultural outings. But here in this small seaside town she knew no one of her own social standing and although she didn't consider herself a snob, she didn't enjoy gossiping with the neighbours.

Patsy and Paula attended the local school, which satisfied the former, who favoured her mother's easy-going personality, but left the other twin feeling like a misfit. Although alike in looks, their personalities often clashed, with the more serious twin coming off worse.

Although the town had grown over the years with a couple of picture houses and a rugby club it was still a backwater in Hetty's eyes. However, during the summer months, the beach provided a diversion.

'It's a beautiful day, let's go down to the beach, darling,' she said to Walter one Sunday in August.

He looked up from the crossword he was ruminating over and said, 'You go sweetness, I'll sit in the garden and enjoy the sunshine out there.'

Hetty and the twins gathered up their towels and costumes and headed for the beach. Patsy and Paula were in their element, running in and out of the water and making sand castles. Hetty wore a swimsuit she had purchased in Knightsbridge during their time in Putney, a fashionable blue and white striped one with a flattering neckline. She knew it suited her curvaceous figure.

The three of them splashed about in the water until Patsy spotted an ice cream vendor cycling along the promenade.

'Mummy, can we have an ice cream?' she cried, already tearing half way up the beach, her sister at her heels.

'Wait a minute,' called Hetty, 'I don't think I've brought my purse with me.'

'Oh Mummy!' moaned the twins.

A tall fair-haired man stopped in his tracks. 'Did I hear you say you wanted an ice cream?' he said addressing the girls.

'Yes please.'

'I'm afraid they're out of luck today,' said Hetty catching up with them.

The stranger pulled a face, making the twins laugh. 'We can't have that, can we?' he said.

Delving into the pocket of his slacks, he brought out some coins. 'Here you are, ladies, my treat.'

His reference to 'ladies' sent the twins into a fit of giggles but Hetty was horrified. 'I can't let you do that,' she cried, 'sorry, girls you will just have to go without ice cream today.'

'Oh Mummy...!' Patsy stamped her bare foot and Paula's brows met in a frown.

'You can't disappoint them,' said the man, 'please let me help.' Holding out his hand to shake, he said, 'My name's Freddie Egan and I can assure you that it would give me great pleasure to buy us all an ice cream.'

After a slight hesitation, Hetty took his hand. 'I'm Hetty Parker and these are my daughters, Patsy and Paula.'

'Now we're no longer strangers, you *are* going to let me buy those ice creams, aren't you?'

The twins started hopping up and down in their eagerness making it difficult for Hetty to refuse. 'Very well,' she agreed, 'but you must let me pay you back some time.'

'Look!' Freddie Egan pointed along the beach. 'Do you see that beach hut, the one painted yellow? That's mine so why don't you all go along there and make yourselves comfortable and I'll be back with our ice creams in next to no time?'

Without waiting for her agreement, Freddie turned on his heel and made his way to the ice cream seller. Feeling slightly bewildered, Hetty gathered up their towels and buckets and spades and the three of them trudged along the beach to the yellow beach hut where two deckchairs were ready on the patio.

After a few minutes, Freddie returned with four large ice cream cornets. 'What do you say, girls?' said Hetty as her daughters each took one.

'Thank you, Mr...'

'Please call me Freddie.'

'*Uncle* Freddie,' corrected Hetty.

After they'd finished their ice creams Patsy and Paula amused themselves once again by building sand castles, leaving the grown-ups to themselves.

'Are you here on holiday or do you live here?' asked Freddie.

'We moved to the town quite recently because of my husband's job.' She thought she had better let Freddie know she had a husband. 'What about you?'

'I live and work in London,' he replied, 'but I come down nearly every weekend.'

'We used to live in London, Putney to be precise,' said Hetty with a sigh.

Freddie picked up on it. 'Do you miss it? I mean the energy, the crowds; it must seem awfully quiet down here.'

Not wanting to appear discontented with her lot, Hetty replied carefully. 'Sometimes, but the children love it.'

'What about your husband?'

'He likes a quiet life.' She laughed. 'At this moment he's sitting in the garden doing his crossword.'

'More fool him,' grinned Freddie. 'If I were him I'd much rather be sunning myself beside a beautiful lady on the beach.' When Hetty wrinkled her brow, he added quickly. 'Oh dear, that was out of order. I'm sorry.'

He seemed genuinely contrite and to ease his embarrassment, Hetty went on to explain about Walter's business venture going down as a result of the Wall Street Crash.

'How terrible for you,' sympathised Freddie. 'Your husband must feel sad after all the hard work he put in. Gone in a flash! I don't think I could bear that.'

'Walter's very philosophical,' said Hetty, wishing that her husband would show his anger instead of accepting his fate so dispassionately.

As the air began to cool, Hetty ordered the children to collect up their things ready to go home.

'Do we have to, Mummy?' pouted Patsy, 'only it's been such fun today.'

Hetty smiled. She felt the same. It was wonderful to talk to a man who came from the big metropolis she loved so much. Walter seemed to have lost all interest in London. He even complained about the crowds in Brighton.

'Are you on the telephone?' asked Freddie. 'Only I may be down here during the coming week. Perhaps I could invite you - and your husband of course - to a cup of tea at the café in Marine Gardens.'

Hetty thought quickly. Should she accept his invitation? She knew he was only extending the invitation to include Walter out of politeness. But there was the question of paying him back for the ice creams, so surely there was no harm in giving him her telephone number? Impulsively, she reeled it off.

By the time she got home, Hetty had decided it had been a mistake to give Freddie her telephone number. Of course, there was no way she could keep the encounter secret because the twins would be bound to spill the beans about the ice creams. She was right about that because Paula related the incident to her father the minute they got in. He seemed unperturbed, merely grunting, 'So you met someone on the beach, Hetty?'

'Yes, a gentleman bought us all an ice cream. Wasn't that kind of him?'

Paula started to go into detail. 'Uncle Freddie's ever so nice.'

'Uncle Freddie?'

Hetty hastened to reassure him. 'I told the girls to call him Uncle Freddie when he introduced himself. He wanted them to call him Freddie and I thought that was inappropriate.'

'Oh, I see.'

Making light of it did the trick although Hetty couldn't help thinking that had the situation been reversed with Walter meeting a young lady on the beach, she would have bombarded him with questions. His complacency irked her.

That night in bed she couldn't get the incident out of her mind. She saw again the tall handsome figure with broad shoulders and slender hips. His eyes were deep blue, matching the polo shirt he was wearing. She remembered how they crinkled at the corners when he smiled. His voice too was attractive, soothing yet commanding. Turning away from Walter, she tried to push the image from her mind.

NINE

Hetty listened for the ring of the telephone for the entire week. She chided herself that she was being foolish, that it would be better if Freddie didn't contact her. Then she changed tack and persuaded herself that it was only right she should repay him for the ice creams.

By the following weekend she had decided she must forget about him. But she couldn't let go of the possibility that perhaps she had given him the wrong number or that he had written it down incorrectly. After all, her decision to give him the number had been made rather hurriedly.

It was a fortnight before the call came.

'I do apologise for not getting in touch earlier, Hetty, but I had to travel up North on business.' When she didn't reply immediately, he went on, 'Hetty, are you there?'

It took Hetty a moment to gather her wits together. 'Hello Freddie. Yes I'm here but the line's rather bad.' In fact, the line was perfectly clear but she needed an excuse for her hesitancy.

'I wondered if you would care to have tea with me this afternoon. We could meet by the pier, perhaps take a stroll along the prom and then stop for tea in the Marine Gardens café.'

'And I can repay you for the ice creams,' said Hetty with a light laugh.

And so a meeting was set up with Hetty making sure she had her purse with her this time. Whatever happened, she was going to insist that she repaid him.

The sun was shining and there was a gentle breeze as she made her way to the pier. She felt happy though slightly guilty and found herself looking around in case one of her neighbours should be on the seafront and see her meeting a strange man.

She spotted Freddie from a distance. His tall figure was unmistakable. He was wearing light-coloured slacks and a blue and maroon striped blazer. His fair hair was brushed back from his forehead in a quiff. She was pleased she'd taken care with her own appearance, brushing her short black hair until it shone and applying her favourite shade of lipstick. She considered using the false eyelashes she had recently begun to experiment with but decided that would be a step too far. The low-waist flowered voile dress she had chosen to wear suited her figure to perfection. She was carrying her white floppy straw hat instead of wearing it, fearing that the breeze might blow it away.

He saw her, waved and strode forward with his arms outstretched. Taking her hands, he looked into her eyes and smiled that charming smile she had been unable to resist on the occasion of the ice creams.

'I'm so glad you decided to come,' he said, 'only I was afraid you might have forgotten all about me, or worse still, decided you didn't want to see me again.'

'Oh, but I did want to see you again.' The words burst from her lips before she could stop them.

He offered his arm and they started to stroll along the promenade when, almost immediately, they were accosted by a street artist.

'Lovely lady, let me draw your picture,' he said, pleadingly.

Hetty threw up her hands in horror. 'Oh no!'

'Yes please,' said Freddie and, before she could stop him, he had drawn a couple of notes out of his pocket.

'I'll do two for that amount, one of each of you,' said the artist, setting to work immediately.

It took him less than ten minutes to produce a good likeness of both Hetty and Freddie. They were delighted with the result. As they continued on their way, Freddie again glanced at Hetty's charcoal portrait and said softly, 'No wonder, he insisted on sketching you, Hetty, you're beautiful.'

Hetty felt the colour rise to her cheeks. In the course of her role as managing director's wife, she had received her share of compliments. She had always accepted them graciously while Walter had looked on beaming with pride. This was different. She wasn't being buttered up for the sake of her husband's business; Freddie's words rang true.

'How are your daughters?' asked Freddie.

'They are fine.'

'Have they settled down well here?'

'Patsy made herself at home at once but Paula took longer. She's all right now that she's made lots of friends.'

'And your husband...hmm does he mind you meeting me?'

'I...I haven't had time to tell him,' stuttered Hetty.

Freddie turned to look her in the eye. 'Does he need to know?'

And in that moment, a clandestine pact was sealed. They met on a Wednesday and one windy autumn day they were caught on the promenade in a heavy shower.

'There's nowhere to shelter,' cried Hetty, holding her bag above her head to shield her from the downpour.

'Oh but there is,' said Freddie.

Pulling her by the hand he led her onto the beach, stopping outside the yellow beach hut to withdraw a key from his pocket. They stepped inside and shook themselves like a pair of puppy dogs.

'I'd forgotten about your beach hut,' said Hetty. She looked around. 'It's really quite comfortable, isn't it?'

'Yes, I installed the couch last summer. Please sit down and make yourself at home, Hetty. I'll find you a towel for your hair.'

'I'm soaked to the skin,' cried Hetty, 'I'll spoil your new couch.'

'Hmm, if you're not too modest, I would suggest that you take your damp dress off and hang it up to dry.' He pointed to a line running from front to back of the hut.

'Oh!' For a moment Hetty was alarmed then she realised that it was a sensible suggestion. 'Well...all right.'

Turning away from him, she slid out of her dress, revealing her cream silk petticoat. Freddie reached for the dress without looking at her, quickly hanging it over the line. Then he turned to face her and for perhaps ten seconds, his blue eyes met her hazel ones and, as their gaze locked, she knew they would be lovers before the afternoon was over.

He broke the moment, by handing her a towel. 'Here, dry your hair.'

She took the towel and started rubbing her hair vigorously and when she caught a glance of herself in a mirror on the back wall, she let out a hoot of laughter. 'Just look at me, fit for nothing with my hair sticking up all over the place.'

'I love you like that,' said Freddie.

He took her hand and they sank down onto the couch. It seemed the most natural thing in the world when he leant over and pressed his lips to hers. She wound her arm around his shoulders and let her fingers tease the hair curling into the nape of his neck. An inner voice told her to stop before it was too late but another, more persuasive voice, told her that it was already too late.

As his caresses became more urgent, she felt her slip ride up over her thighs revealing her stockings secured by a minute suspender belt. Freddie released the suspenders and rolled down the silk stockings. She lay back on the couch delighting in his touch and, reaching out her hand to stroke his cheek she detected the beginnings of a five o'clock shadow. His aftershave was deliciously sweet and lingering, not stringent like Walter's.

He seemed instinctively to know how to please her, his exploring tongue finding orifices that Walter had never explored. Hetty couldn't hold back. This was the missing piece to the jigsaw of her life. Until now she had been incomplete. Walter provided security and affection but he could never give her the physical excitement for which she yearned. Freddie could fill the gap. Could she be selfish enough to embrace both?

The thundering downpour drowned out Hetty's moans of ecstasy and it wasn't until they lay inert and satiated that she realised how cold the room was. Freddie noticed her give a shiver and got up to fetch a blanket from a cupboard.

'I know what will warm you up,' he said, going to another cupboard and taking out a bottle of Johnnie Walker and two glasses.

'I shouldn't, not at this time in the afternoon,' protested Hetty.

'Why not?' laughed Freddie.

'Walter might notice alcohol on my breath.'

'It will have worn off by the time he gets home.'

As she sipped her whisky Hetty's mind was racing. She had to get home in time to wash away the tell-tale signs of their lovemaking; the girls and Walter must never find out. Seized with contrition, she said sharply, 'Freddie, this mustn't happen again.'

Freddie raised an eyebrow and smiled. 'So you didn't enjoy it?'

'Yes...no.' She looked at her watch. 'Just look at the time, I must go.'

'But it's still pouring with rain.'

She threw off the blanket and hurriedly put her damp dress back on before going to peer out of the beach hut window. 'The rain's easing off a bit. I'll be fine.'

'Don't go, Hetty, not yet.'

His pleading smile disarmed her. 'Five more minutes...'

The five minutes somehow extended to ten, after which she rushed home, arriving just before the twins got in from school.

From then on their Wednesday trysts took place in a hotel room and sometimes Freddie would pick her up in his Alvis Silver Eagle and drive her into the country.

Hetty's moods alternated between delirious happiness and abject shame and in a bid to clarify her emotions, she began keeping a diary, locking it away in Daisy's little cubbyhole. With Walter at work all day she had plenty of time to agonise over her dilemma. On one occasion, Paula caught her scribbling but she managed to brush her aside with, 'I'm only jotting down a few notes.'

'Why, mummy?' asked Paula, always the inquisitive one.

'So I don't forget things.'

'What things?'

Patsy overheard the conversation and giggled, 'Perhaps mummy's writing a novel.'

On another occasion, her daughters crept up on her in the back garden. She had plucked a shoot of blossom from the apple tree and was holding it to her cheek while swaying and softly singing the lyrics of a romantic ballad.

'Mummy's gone all starry-eyed,' giggled Patsy, prompting Hetty to abandon her moment of bliss and slot back into her role of wife and mother.

The mid thirties saw the rise of Hitler and Mussolini with unrest growing throughout Europe. Cocooned in a bubble of happiness, Hetty paid no attention to the gloomy tidings being broadcast on the wireless. Like most British people she felt unconnected from countries on the other side of the Channel. Hadn't those Europeans always fought amongst themselves? Their squabbles had nothing to do with the Brits.

Meeting Freddie had turned her world upside down; her everyday life with Walter contrasted sharply with her secret life with Freddie. In her role of wife and mother she performed her tasks of housework, shopping and cooking with cheerful resignation, but when she met up with Freddie she threw off that dutiful persona and emerged once again as the carefree young girl she used to be. She no longer suffered pangs of conscience because, in different ways, she loved both men. What harm could there be in her adultery if Walter was unaware of it? She was, after all, still his caring wife, occasionally even sharing his bed. As for her daughters she was sure they had no idea that she still met up with 'Uncle Freddie'.

These afternoon liaisons continued through the years. They exchanged confidences with Hetty explaining that in the early days, she had been flattered by Walter's attention. 'I was only nineteen and marrying him made me feel grown-up and important,' she said, 'then when the twins were born, Walter was delighted. You see, they were a surprise; he believed he was too old for fatherhood.'

'I've only seen your daughters once and that was a while ago.'

'They're fourteen now, too old for sandcastles and ice creams.'

'But they brought us together, didn't they? Sadly, my beach hut rarely gets used these days?'

'How did you come to have a beach hut down here?' asked Hetty, wrinkling her nose.

'My aunt lived in Sussex; she was a keen swimmer. I used to stay with her during my school holidays and when she died I hadn't the heart to sell it.'

Freddie went on to confide that when he was in his early twenties he had come close to getting married but the girl's family had persuaded her not to go through with it.

'Why ever not?' asked Hetty.

'Her father's a snob. He didn't approve of his daughter marrying a journalist and she wouldn't stand up to him.'

'More fool her but lucky for me,' said Hetty, giving Freddie a kiss on the cheek.

Freddie told her about his work as a reporter but never aired his views on the political situation. She had no idea as to whether he favoured Neville Chamberlain's Conservative Government or was of a Socialist turn of mind. In any case, Hetty wasn't interested in politics. She was always eager to hear about Freddie's encounters with famous people, especially movie stars and theatre celebrities.

From time to time, he would travel up North but she never learned what he was doing there. When it fleetingly occurred to her that he might have another woman, she resolutely thrust it from her mind. She loved him, she trusted him.

It was a newspaper report that opened her eyes. Walter came home from work, outraged by the news of the Cable Street riots.

'Just look at this, Hetty,' he said, spreading the paper out on the dining room table. 'I would never have believed things could come to this in our country.'

Hetty was shocked by the images plastered all over the front page.

'That Mosley fellow must be stopped. He's the cause of all this.'

Hetty had never seen Walter so angry. Even the twins were drawn to question him. 'What's happened, daddy?'

'You don't need to know, girls. Go and do your homework.'

For once, Patsy and Paula obeyed their father.

After supper when Walter had perused the story from start to finish, Hetty read it too. Her thoughts flew to Freddie. Would he have been reporting on the event?

Hetty had always found politics boring and although she valued her right to vote - after all, those suffragettes had fought hard for that right - she resented it when Walter shushed her if she started to chatter while he was listening to political reports on the wireless. But, all of a sudden, it was important for her to know what Freddie's political views were. The stories being broadcast together with the placards denouncing Hitler and the situation of the Jews in Germany had been seeping into her sub-consciousness without her being aware of it. She shared her husband's outrage and she needed to know how her lover felt.

The next time, after booking in under their assumed name, they hurried to the lift. Hetty had long ago lost her embarrassment about the signing in procedure and giggled as they rushed, hand-in-hand, along the plush carpeted corridor to their room. Once inside, Freddie took her in his arms and kicked the door shut with the heel of his shoe. Smothering her with kisses, he shunted her across the room until she fell back onto the bed.

Coming up for air, she laughed and said, 'Darling, you seem to be in a terrible hurry this afternoon.'

'I'm always in a hurry to make love to you my angel.'

With his usual tenderness, he undressed her, encouraging her to do the same for him. His lovemaking was even more passionate than usual, his ardour almost sweeping away her determination to question him but, afterwards, as they started to get dressed, her niggling doubts returned. She needed to question him. If he loved her, he wouldn't hold back.

'Freddie...'

'Yes, my love,'

'Were you involved in reporting those dreadful riots in the East End the other day?'

He stopped buttoning up his shirt and asked, 'Why bring that up?'

'I'm worried about you, that's all.'

He continued with his shirt buttoning. 'There's no need to worry.'

She tried to sound casual. 'What's your opinion of the BUF?'

He frowned and catching hold of her elbow, twisted her round to face him. 'What are you talking about?'

'The British Union of Fascists...'

'They're a political party.'

'I know they are, so what d'you think of them?'

He drew her close. 'Let's not talk politics.'

She persisted. 'What about that awful Mosley man?'

Freddie's grip on her elbow tightened. 'What makes you think he's awful?'

Despite feeling slightly intimidated, Hetty pressed on. 'He's pro-German, pro-Nazi, he's...'

'The Germans are putting their country in order. Hitler is proving to be a great leader.'

'You're hurting me,' said Hetty, looking pointedly at his hand on her arm.

Freddie smiled and moved away. 'Sorry, darling, let's forget about this nonsense and enjoy the rest of our afternoon together.'

Hetty knew she should let it go but somehow she couldn't. 'I've heard the Nazis persecute Jews and imprison innocent people. They're calling it ethnic cleansing.'

Freddie picked up his trousers and pulled them on. 'Darling, don't worry your pretty little head about such things. It can't affect us in this country.'

'I hope it can't,' she said.

He drew her to him and gently stroked her cheek, smothering her anxiety. They separated with a lingering kiss. Happiness overwhelmed her. If her lover didn't want to discuss politics then she wouldn't bring the subject up again. After all, she had no reason to believe that he was one of Mosley's followers. He couldn't be.

But that evening when Walter pointed out more references to the BUF in his paper, she couldn't help feeling uneasy and almost against her will, she started recording in her diary the seemingly insignificant remarks that Freddie made.

1936 proved to be an eventful year. Besides the Cable Street Riots and the outbreak of the Spanish Civil War, the scandal of the King's association with Wallis Simpson hit the headlines leading to his abdication in December of that year. Never had there been so much dramatic news in such a short space of time!

Hetty started taking an interest in world news and grabbed Walter's newspaper the minute he had finished with it. He noticed. 'Why the sudden interest in politics, darling?' he asked.

She tried to make light of it. 'I think I ought to make myself more aware of what's going on in the world.'

'Hmm, we may soon find ourselves more aware than we want to be,' he observed.

'What d'you mean?'

'War in Europe is looming.'

'Don't say that.'

Hetty was old enough to remember the other world war. She had lost an uncle on the Somme and she recalled her aunt's tear-stained letter informing her mother of her loss. What about the twins? They were coming up for seventeen. She couldn't bear to think of them spending their adolescence in a deprived country with rationing and other shortages. There could be bombing too.

Walter put an arm around her shoulders, 'Don't worry, darling, it might not come to war, after all Chamberlain is known to be a peacemaker.'

TEN

Hetty started to buy the newspapers every day. When Walter had gone to work and the twins had departed for their secretarial course at a college in Brighton, she would spread the broadsheets out on the dining room table and read about current affairs both at home and abroad.

She continued to meet up with Freddie but was careful to keep off the subject of politics. Their time together was brief - most of it taken up with lovemaking - which meant their conversations mostly centred on the personal. However, he surprised her one day when he revealed that he would not be able to see her for a couple of weeks because he was going away.

'Are you taking a holiday, darling?' she asked him, not for the first time wishing she had the courage to leave Walter and offer herself full time to Freddie.

'You could say that.'

'Where are you going?' She felt suspicious. Had he got another woman?

'Berlin.'

Surely he wouldn't choose Berlin for a romantic dalliance? Trying to keep her voice level, she said, 'What a strange choice darling! Isn't there a lot of unrest in Germany at the moment? 'I've heard those Nazis are rounding up people and sending them off to internment camps.'

He stopped in the middle of tying his tie. 'Where did you hear that?'

'I read it in the newspaper.'

He continued adjusting his tie but his expression hardened. 'You shouldn't believe everything the press write.'

Hetty was puzzled. Why would he say that, after all he was a member of the press. His attitude put her back up and propelled by an obstinate streak in her nature she persisted in questioning him. 'Have you got friends in Berlin?'

'Why?'

'I'm interested.'

'Just acquaintances…'

Turning away, he fastened his cufflinks and when he turned back he had once again become the charismatic lover she adored.

'Come here, my beautiful, gorgeous Hetty, let's go down to the bar and have a cocktail. I'll order Blinkers, your favourite.'

'Isn't it a bit early for cocktails?' said Hetty looking at her watch. 'It's not half past five yet.'

He threw back his head and laughed. 'It's never too early for a cocktail, darling.' But to Hetty his humour seemed contrived.

She got home just before Patsy and Paula. They burst into the house and it immediately resounded with their chatter and laughter. Two cocktails had brought out the sentimental in Hetty. She listened to her daughters, reflecting on how lucky she was and admitting to herself that they, rather than Walter, had been the reason why she had not considered leaving the marital home. But they were almost grown-up and it wouldn't be long before they left the nest either to get married or to pursue a career. Would that be the right time to break away from Walter? When she recalled that Freddie had never once suggested she should leave her husband, she swiftly brushed the thought aside. Freddie was too much of a gentleman to expect that of her.

No, when the time was right, it would be up to her to broach the subject of divorce and marriage.

Walter arrived home shortly after the girls. When she asked him how his day had been, he replied, 'Nothing special, just the usual.' He noticed that she seemed to be in a happy mood and asked, 'Have *you* been doing anything special today, my dear?'

She blinked at him and said quickly, 'No, like you, nothing special.'

He switched on the wireless to listen to the news while Hetty set about preparing supper. He sat sucking at his pipe, surreptitiously watching her as she moved back and forth from room to room. He loved her passionately. For him there could be no other woman. He had met her at a friend's party and had been unable to take his gaze off this lovely, young, light-hearted girl who drew everyone she met to her. Her hazel eyes had sparkled as she had self-consciously flicked ash from the long cigarette holder she was holding. Clearly, she wasn't used to smoking and since their marriage she had not continued with the habit. At the party, she had flitted from group to group and he had been convinced that one of the younger men would have taken the opportunity to escort her home. In fact, no one did and the enviable task fell to him. He could hardly believe that after only a few months courtship she would agree to be his wife.

However, in the last few years he had noticed a change in her and at first had put it down to maturity but when her moods began to fluctuate, he guessed that the inevitable had happened: she had found herself a lover. He decided not to confront her. Wasn't it better to hold on to part of the woman you loved rather than risk losing her altogether? He hoped she would tire of her new love and come back to him but years had passed and this hadn't happened. At times, fury boiled inside him like a raging furnace and on one occasion he had bitten so hard into the stem of his favourite cherrywood pipe that it had snapped and he'd had to buy a new one. As retirement approached, he wondered how things would pan out when he no longer went off to work everyday. How would Hetty manage to keep her secret trysts then?

The two weeks without Freddie seemed endless. Hetty spent time weeding the flowerbeds, bottling plums from the tree in the garden and taking long walks along the beach. She still read the newspapers every day and what she read disturbed her. Why on earth would Freddie choose to visit Berlin? If he needed a break from work, why not go to the South of France or the Italian Riviera? By the end of the second week she was feeling very unsettled. Could a woman be luring him over there?

He contacted her, as promised and they arranged to meet the following afternoon. Once again, she met him at the entrance to the pier and once again, her heart leapt the minute she caught sight of his familiar figure. She practically threw herself into his arms all fears of being seen by one of the nosy neighbours dismissed. They went onto the pier and made their way along the wooden boards towards the tea rooms facing out to sea. As they walked she linked her arm through his, leaning her head on his shoulder, aware of his chin resting on the top of her head. He patted her hand. 'So you've missed me, my darling?'

'How could I not miss you? Have you missed me?'

'Of course...why wouldn't I?'

'I was afraid...'

'Afraid of what, my dearest...?'

'It's nothing.'

'Tell me what you were afraid of.'

'I was afraid you wouldn't come back.' The words rushed out of their own volition.

He stopped in his tracks and took her in his arms, ignoring the inquisitive glances of passers-by. 'I would never leave you, Hetty.'

'Promise...'

'I promise.'

Reassured, Hetty allowed him to lead her to the end of the pier. There was a stiff breeze causing white horses to dance on the sea. She leant her elbows on the barrier content to feel Freddie's protective arm around her shoulders. By mutual consent they hurriedly retraced their steps.

'I've booked a different hotel this time,' he whispered as they crossed the road. 'It's not far from here.'

He collected the key from Reception and they went to wait impatiently for the lift to come. Once inside the room, Freddie slipped her coat off her shoulders and started to undo the buttons of her blouse.

'Why do you wear such awkward clothes?' he teased.

'Let me.' She undid the fiddly buttons and unzipped her skirt, allowing it to fall to the floor.

He pulled her to him and stripped off her underwear, kicking her shoes across the room. They made love on top of the candlewick bedspread, lying in one another's arms afterwards, exhausted yet content.

'Happy, darling...?' he asked.

'Deliriously...'

'I love you, Hetty.'

She turned her head to look at him. He had never uttered those words before. 'I love you too, shall we...?' The phrase in her head never reached her lips because there was a knock on the door.

Freddie frowned. 'Who can that be?'

'Room service, sir...'

'Oh yes, I forgot.' Freddie got up from the bed and snatched a towel to fasten around his waist. 'I ordered tea for four-thirty.'

Hetty's opportunity to suggest that she break free from Walter was gone. She had lost courage but she told herself she could always bring the subject up next time they met. They sipped tea and dunked biscuits sitting on the edge of the bed, half dressed, neither of them wanting the afternoon to end.

'Will I see you next week?' asked Hetty.

'I'm sorry, sweetheart next week's difficult; I have to go up North.'

'What for...?'

'Oswald Mosley's holding another rally. I need to cover it.'

'Don't get caught up in any rioting,' she said.

'Don't worry about me, my darling, Mosley and I know one another well.'

'Mosley? He's a friend of yours?'

'We're acquaintances,' corrected Freddie.

'He's an awful man, darling promise me you won't get involved with him.'

'No chance of that,' said Freddie a little too hastily.

Later, at home, she reflected on their conversation. Acquaintances! Freddie liked that word. He used it a lot. Hetty frowned thoughtfully; the word 'acquaintances' could cover a multitude of sins. What was he up to? The need to rationalise her thoughts drove her to seek refuge once again in her diary. She unlocked the door to the little cubbyhole and took out her purple-covered notebook, spending the next hour scribbling in it. She wrote swiftly in an untidy scrawl with frequent crossings-out and corrections. She never re-read what she had written, afraid to face her doubting self.

The twins tumbling in through the front door prompted her to quickly return the notebook to the cubbyhole, locking the door and slipping the key into her pocket.

Turning away from the little cupboard, she saw Patsy wagging a finger at her. 'Have you been writing down more of your little secrets, mummy?'

Paula joined her sister, adding her taunt to their mother's confusion.

Hetty tried to make light of it. 'Away with you, girls, I haven't got any secrets.'

'We all have secrets,' retorted Paula.

'Who says?' countered Patsy.

Paula pointed at her twin. 'You have, for one.'

'No I haven't. Don't tell lies.' Patsy swung her bag hitting Paula on the head, whereupon the latter retaliated until the giggling pair disappeared upstairs to their bedrooms.

Hetty smiled, grateful that the attention had been switched from her but she wondered what secret Patsy was keeping from her.

Freddie didn't telephone Hetty until three weeks later by which time she had put aside her suspicions about his political activities, replacing them with the conviction that he had another woman. She needed to find out and became obsessed with ways in which she could do this, playing out imaginary conversations with him, scenes in which she was nothing less than a dominating goddess, he the contrite lover begging for forgiveness. She promised herself to be cool when he contacted her but her resolve melted away at the sound of his voice.

'Darling I'm so sorry I haven't been in touch. I got delayed in Manchester. It was impossible to get to a phone and...Hetty I've missed you so much.'

'Me too,' she murmured. 'When can we meet?'

'I'm coming down to Brighton tomorrow, are you free?'

'Yes,' she replied. The arranged afternoon cup of tea with a friendly neighbour could be postponed.

'Can you meet me by the Royal Pavilion at two?'

'Yes,' she said, 'I'll be there.'

They had never met in Brighton before and for a fleeting moment Hetty had a mental image of bumping into one of her daughters in North Street where their secretarial college was situated. She shook the idea away. Impossible, her girls would be busy drumming away at their typewriters all the afternoon. Nonetheless, she was relieved when they checked into a hotel.

Freddie was as attentive as ever, sweeping away Hetty's lingering doubts about his faithfulness. He often brought her small gifts and on this occasion she was bowled over when he produced a necklace set with diamonds.

'It's too beautiful,' she whispered, lacing it between her fingers. 'I can't wear anything as extravagant as this.'

He fastened it around her neck. 'You look wonderful in it, Hetty, diamonds suit you.'

She gazed at herself in the mirror, smiling as the sun caught one of the diamonds so that reflected in the looking-glass it winked at her. She shook her head and unfastened the necklace, placing it on the side table. 'No darling I can't accept it. When would I be able to wear it?'

Freddie took her in his arms. 'If you can think of a suitable excuse to give your husband, I could take you away for a romantic weekend in a five-star hotel, then you could wear it.'

She fondled the back of his head where his fair hair curled into the nape of his neck. 'Do you really mean that?'

'Of course I do.'

He kissed her fiercely, sliding his hands beneath her blouse to caress her breasts. That unmistakable frisson of pleasure erased misgivings from her mind. She *would* think up an excuse to give Walter so that she and Freddie could spend a whole wonderful weekend together.

Their lovemaking that afternoon was more passionate than she could ever remember. Reluctantly they left the bed and got dressed. Then the phone rang. Freddie answered it.

'Yes, please put him through...' He put his hand over the receiver and turned to Hetty, whispering, 'I'm sorry but I must take this call, darling.'

She smiled her understanding and while he waited for the caller to be put through, she picked up the necklace and held it up to the light. It really was a beautiful piece of jewellery and she wondered how he could afford it on a journalist's salary. She put it down on the dressing table.

While he was talking to the unseen caller, Hetty finished getting dressed. Sitting on the edge of the bed she started to put on her shoes but something in Freddie's tone caught her attention. Clearly, he was annoyed and even though he was muttering quietly into the receiver she heard the name *Mosley*.

He raised his voice. 'They can't do that the BUF is a legitimate party.'

He listened while the caller responded then said angrily, 'There were rumours about its dissolution before but nothing ever came of it.' He paused to listen then said, 'If war breaks out, it will bring more followers to the BUF.'

Hetty's shoe slipped from her hand. The BUF! She remembered Freddie's evasive reply when she had questioned him about it and she remembered Walter's disdain of it.

When the call ended Freddie continued getting dressed and noticing the necklace laying on the dressing table, he asked, 'I hope you're pleased with my present, darling.'

Hetty stood up and looked directly into his eyes. 'Are you a member of the BUF, Freddie?' she asked.

He stared back at her. 'What if I am?'

'Are you?' He smiled winningly and reached out to her but she backed away. 'Are you, Freddie?'

He took a step towards her, placing the flat of his hands on the wardrobe door, trapping her. Leaning forward to kiss her, he whispered, 'Why are you worrying your pretty little head about something you know nothing about?'

She twisted away feeling his warm breath on her cheek and where once his closeness would have thrilled her, this time it felt menacing. She pushed him back. 'Why don't you give me a straight answer, Freddie?'

His eyes narrowed as he said, 'Spoiling for an argument, are you?'

'I just want a *yes* or *no*.' Hetty felt a cold chill run down her spine even though the late afternoon sun warmed the room. He seemed like a stranger, a man she didn't want to know.

As Freddie turned away to pick up his tie, she saw his shoulders stiffen and knew she had riled him. Tie in hand, he turned to face her. 'Yes I am a member. People must understand it's the only way to maintain the country's moral and social well-being.'

She gave a gasp. 'What on earth do you mean?'

'Foreigners infiltrating the country - immigrants from God knows where bringing in their medieval culture. The Government must put a stop to it. You've seen what happened in Germany...'

'Ethnic cleansing, you mean?' snapped Hetty.

'Call it what you like, it's necessary.'

'No it isn't.'

Hetty's trepidation changed to anger. What about the Jewish family who lived along the road? She often stopped to chat to Mrs Cohen and, when they were younger, her own daughters used to play with the Cohen children. And what about that nice Polish man with the unpronounceable name? He sometimes came to give her a hand with the heavy work in the garden. She picked up her coat and bag and went to the door.

When he realised she was about to leave, Freddie's attitude changed. 'Don't let's fight, darling. What difference does it make, we are both still the same people.'

'No.' Hetty shook her head. 'You're not the same, not to me anyway.'

He touched her arm but she brushed his hand away.

'Darling, don't leave like this, please.'

'I don't want to talk about it.'

He glanced at the dressing table, said, 'You've forgotten your present.'

'I don't want it. Keep your nasty Fascist necklace.'

'Don't be like that, Hetty.' Freddie's brows met in a pleading frown. 'Let's make up. What about the lovely weekend we're planning to spend together?'

Hetty jutted her chin. 'I'm not going away with you, Freddie. And I don't want your present.' She pushed past him and snatching up the necklace, flung it at him, narrowly missing his ear.

'Hey!' he shouted, as it landed on the floor behind him.

'What's more, I don't want to see you ever again.'

'How are you going to get home?'

'I'll take a taxi.'

Hetty left the room and, with her head held high, she walked along the corridor to the lift. She half expected him to follow her but he didn't. Going down in the mirrored lift she stared at her own reflection seeing for the first time a naive middle-aged woman who had been strung along by a misguided extremist.

ELEVEN

Over the next few days it became clear to Walter that something had upset Hetty. She no longer hummed a happy tune while going about her chores; she didn't even bother switching on the wireless. She listened listlessly to Patsy when she confided in her parents that she had a boyfriend. She lost interest in her appearance and sometimes didn't even bother to apply powder and lipstick.

He wanted to ask her what was wrong but instinctively knew she wouldn't tell him. Besides, if she knew he had noticed her change of mood it might make matters worse. Then one day, she asked him again about the BUF Party.

'What do they do exactly?'

'Huh, they're a group of louts,' replied Walter, 'the Party won't come to anything. That Mosley fellow will probably end up in jail.'

'What about his followers?'

'They'll get out quick or get what's coming to them I expect.'

'Oh.'

'Why the interest, Hetty?'

'No reason.'

She seemed to have lost interest in the conversation so Walter went back to his crossword. But her questions had made him suspicious and he had a feeling that something drastic had changed in Hetty's life. A glimmer of hope rose: maybe, just maybe, she would come back to him.

But in the September of 1939 the outbreak of war changed many people's lives. For the very first time the twins were separated. They each joined up but to different services: Patsy joined the WRENS to follow her boyfriend into the Navy while Paula joined the ATS. Walter was too old for call-up and besides, after a lifetime of heavy smoking, his health was beginning to fail.

Hetty often thought about Freddie and wondered whether he had forsaken the BUF Party and joined up. Would he be in favour of fighting the regime he had blatantly admired? She wanted to know his fate yet something told her that it would be better to remain in ignorance.

The town seemed to change overnight. Street shelters appeared, barbed wire was strung along the promenade preventing people from going onto the beach. Propaganda notices urging citizens to *Dig for Victory* or *Grow your own vegetables* were on display. There were also admonishing placards saying *Loose talk can cost lives*.

Bombing raids began in earnest in 1940 and Walter erected a corrugated iron shelter in the back garden. He also took on the role of air raid warden leaving Hetty in the house on her own in the evenings. Unused to spending time alone at night she found this unsettling.

They both worried about Patsy and Paula. So far the latter had remained in England but Patsy had been sent overseas and they only heard from her occasionally. The town was in a direct line to London and that coupled with its proximity to Ford Aerodrome made it vulnerable to attack and there were often dog fights between the RAF and the Luftwaffe.

'I saw a barrage balloon being shot at today,' said Hetty as the couple ate their supper before Walter went off to do his warden shift. 'It looked frighteningly close.'

'I know.'

Hetty tried not to talk about their daughters because bringing up that subject seemed tantamount to tempting fate. She only mentioned them when a letter dropped through the letter box and she knew that up until the moment the letter had been posted they had been safe. This was a strange philosophy but it comforted her.

She was now in her late thirties, too old to sign up. She helped out locally with food kitchens, jam making and knitting afternoons but she wanted to be more directly involved in the war effort.

Then in May 1940 news came through that the Germans had driven the allies back to the sea. A call went out for seaworthy boats, large or small, to aid in the evacuation of 300,000 men stranded on the beaches of Dunkirk. There was a call also for ambulance drivers to convey the wounded from their arrival point at Dover to hospital.

Walter and Hetty listened to the announcement with growing alarm until, all at once, Hetty's eyes lit up.

'I could drive an ambulance,' she gasped.

Walter frowned. 'Don't be ridiculous.'

'It's not ridiculous; I've been driving since I was eighteen.'

'Driving an ambulance is different to driving a small car,' Walter pointed out.

Hetty jutted her chin. 'I'm going to volunteer,' she said, 'and let them decide whether I am capable or not.'

After that things happened rapidly. A few days later, Hetty departed for Dover, where she was given basic training and then conscripted to convey wounded soldiers to hospitals in London. What she saw shocked her: young soldiers with terrible wounds, in pain and traumatised. There was very little time to rest; a catnap on a camp bed in a tent. Whenever the tension eased, between the docking of one lot of boats and the next, she thought about Freddie. Had he had a change of heart and joined up to fight for his country? Was he amongst those stranded on a beach in Northern France? She found herself scanning the faces of the exhausted young men crowded onto the trains after their terrifying journey across the English Channel, and studying the wounded in case he was amongst them. Perhaps Freddie would turn out to be a hero. He had been a hero in her eyes; that is until she learnt the awful truth about his political beliefs. In darker moments, she told herself bitterly that he was probably languishing in prison with other members of Mosley's followers.

Back at home, Walter spent sleepless nights worrying about her. He told himself that the opportunity for her to help in the war effort could be a good thing. It would focus her, help her to get over her thwarted love affair and maybe soften her feelings towards him. Once the emergency was over, she would come home to him a more hopeful, positive person.

But this didn't happen because ambulance drivers were in short supply and Hetty volunteered to stay on. She was sent for more training and instead of returning home on her first leave, she chose to spend it with a nurse she had befriended at the training camp.

Walter was devastated. This brush-off was even harder to take than the years he had spent knowing that she had lain in the arms of someone else. He withdrew into himself, pining over a life wasted in the pursuit of an impossible dream. If all those years ago she had refused his proposal of marriage, he would have taken it on the chin but to lose her like this was too much to bear. He tried telephoning her but their conversations were awkward.

'Are you coming home to collect some of your things, Hetty?' he ventured.

'What things?'

'You've left a lot of clothes in the wardrobe and there are other things belonging to you, books etc.'

'Oh *those*! Throw them out, or on second thoughts, give my clothes to the Salvation Army. I'm sure they could use them.'

'What about that fur stole you love so much.'

'That old thing! It's probably full of moth holes by now.'

'It would be nice to see you, Hetty. Couldn't you come home for a weekend?'

There was a pause before she answered. 'I'll see but I can't promise anything. I never know what my schedule's going to be. I might be sent abroad.'

Walter was shocked. 'Abroad? You mean you might be sent to the Front?'

'I could be.'

Walter's voice betrayed his concern. 'I hope not. Couldn't you refuse after all you joined up for home duties.'

Hetty's tone hardened as she replied. 'Why should I? If they ask me to go overseas I shall go.'

The call finished abruptly and although he wasn't a habitual drinker, Walter poured himself a stiff whisky before leaving for his shift as air raid warden.

On putting down the phone, Hetty experienced a stab of remorse. Why had she been so curt with Walter? She almost rang back to say she would come home for a visit after all but she knew that facing her devoted husband would heighten her own sense of betrayal. Since her split with Freddie, Walter's presence had jabbed at her conscience like a knife to her heart, reminding her of what she might have had and what she had lost. In the end, she justified her refusal to visit by rationalising that if she saw Walter again she would have to admit that she had actually volunteered for overseas duties, thus upsetting him further.

Her work as an ambulance driver had given her a purpose. She would never be able to shake off Freddie's memory but now her days were occupied it was easier to behave normally. The call for her departure came sooner than she had expected. The destination: France.

Meanwhile, Walter continued with his usual routine: going to work, coming home, reading the newspaper and doing the crossword before performing his air raid warden duties. When he got home he went straight to bed. Of course, he had to cook his own dinner but he was a man of simple tastes and due to the rationing, cooking didn't take much effort. Occasionally, one of his daughters would spend a few days leave with him but, for most of the time, he was on his own.

The war years rolled by and peace came. By then, Patsy had married her young man and Paula was going out with an officer in the Royal Engineers. Walter was relieved that both his daughters and their young men had come through the fighting unscathed.

Hetty never returned to Number Seven. In the summer of 1944 Walter received news that she had been killed on active service. Sadly he never learnt the full details of her death. He grieved for her in his own quiet way. Not unnaturally, his daughters were upset, but many years of separation from their mother lessened their loss, especially now that they had both started out on a new life with husbands and children.

Walter stayed on in Number Seven for a few more years by which time he was due for retirement. His health was poor, a lifetime of heavy smoking having left him with emphysema. He knew his days were numbered and next time Paula visited him he told her he had decided to sell the house and move into a rented flat in the centre of town.

'Why rent, Daddy, you could easily buy a nice flat closer to me or Patsy.'

But Walter was adamant. 'Paula, darling, I haven't got much time left so what's the point of moving away from here?'

'I still don't understand,' argued his daughter, 'why rent when you could buy?'

Walter smiled. 'If I sell now, the proceeds can go to you and Patsy straightaway; in that way you won't have to wait until I kick the bucket.'

Paula was upset. 'Please don't talk like that, Daddy, you've got years of life ahead of you. If you move closer to me or Patsy, you could enjoy your retirement and see more of your grandchildren.'

Walter was touched by Paula's concern but he kept to his plan and the next day he contacted a local estate agent and set the wheels in motion.

*****

THE COLD WAR

After the bleak years of the War, the 1951 Festival of Britain lifted the country's' spirits. The following year saw the sudden death of King George VI and brought a young queen to the throne. Winston Churchill's prediction of an Iron Curtain dividing Europe proved true but perhaps the greatest shock to the nation was the soviet spy scandal of the mid-fifties.

During this period the town saw an influx of royal visitors. In May 1951 the then Princess Elizabeth paid a visit, in 1956 the Duchess of Kent attended the opening of a new technical high school and in 1959, Princess Margaret came to visit a special school in the area.

Housing estates were built and the population increased to over 77,000. Due to the demand for new style housing, it was months before a buyer was found for Number Seven, which fell into disrepair. Weeds sprang up and apples and plums were left to rot where they fell. This was a sad time. I missed the aroma of Daisy's baking, Hetty's tuneful singing, Walter's sweet-smelling pipe tobacco for despite the tragedy of Teddy's death, Jack's suicide and Walter's heartache, both the Websters and the Parkers had brought joy to Number Seven.

Finally, mother and daughter, Cora and Thelma Stokes moved in. Their relationship was contentious; they were always quarrelling. If Cora liked something, Thelma disliked it and I wondered what was in store for me.

Cora was in her late seventies, Thelma in her mid-fifties. Cora's husband had deserted her after her daughter's birth and, from then on, she had played the martyr. Self-pity and bad-temper had etched lines into her features giving her a permanently disgruntled expression. In addition, she had unfortunately broken her left leg while running for a bus during the Blitz, resulting in a stiff knee which meant she had to use a walking-stick.

From the age of sixteen, Thelma had worked in a West End department store. Never having married, it had not occurred to her to leave her mother. She was ungainly with mousey hair, poor eyesight obliging her to wear thick lens spectacles which often slipped down her nose. Had fate decreed to remove her from Cora's influence, her life might have been happier.

They had lived in rented rooms since being bombed out of their London home, and now that Cora was 'getting on a bit' she had decided they should move to the coast. They were a far cry from my previous occupants and my walls were to echo with their discontent.

TWELVE

Cora and Thelma were at each other's throats from the moment they moved in. They squabbled about how to arrange the furniture, they fought about who should have the front bedroom, they argued about how much they should tip the removal men. If there was nothing to argue about they would invent something.

'I really like this house, Mother,' said Thelma after the removal men had departed. 'Just think, this will be our first real home since we were bombed out.'

'It's too big,' sniffed Cora.

'No it isn't.'

'It is. I said as much when the estate agent showed us round.'

'I don't remember you saying that.'

'You've got a short memory when it suits you.'

Determined to be positive, Thelma persisted, 'The garden's lovely, you'll be able to sit out there in the summer.'

'It's too big.'

'No it isn't. Don't forget now I've left work I'll have plenty of time to look after it.'

'The downstairs badly needs decorating.'

'I can do that too.'

'You don't know one end of a paint brush from the other,' scoffed Cora.

Thelma weaved her way between the piles of boxes cluttering the floor. 'I'll start decorating this room next week,' she declared. Looking around, she pushed her glasses further up her nose and added, 'Yes, I'm looking forward to getting started.'

'Hadn't you better get unpacked first,' snapped her mother, waving her walking-stick in the air and narrowly missing the centre lamp.

'Mind the light, Mother,' warned Thelma.

Cora looked up and pulled a face. 'That awful thing must go for a start.'

It was a Tiffany lampshade chosen by Hetty in her first flush of enthusiasm on moving in to Number Seven.

'I like it.'

'It's hideous it makes the place look like a bordello.'

Thelma gave a laugh. 'Really, Mother, you do exaggerate.'

Cora pointed at the boxes piled up in the kitchen. 'Start in there. Do you know which box the kettle is in?'

'How would I know? You were the one who packed the kitchen utensils,' retorted her daughter.

After a five-minute search she found the kettle and returned with teapot and cups balanced on a small tray. 'Mother, make a space for the tray please.'

Using her walking stick, Cora swept aside a pile of papers from the table and for a little while a cup of tea and a chocolate biscuit restored peace.

Thelma was true to her word and the following week she started stripping off the wallpaper ready to redecorate.

'I think the funky yellow and red pattern or the terracotta lion design would be nice in here, don't you?' she said, flicking through a wallpaper pattern catalogue.

Cora disagreed. 'I want flowered wallpaper, Magnolias.'

'Flowers are old-fashioned, Mother.'

'Well what's wrong with old-fashioned?' argued Cora. 'And what are you going to do about that silly little cupboard over there?'

Thelma stood back to study it. 'It's rather sweet,' she said, 'but it's locked and there doesn't seem to be a key. We'll have to get a man in to chip it out of the wall.'

'Get a man in! I'm not paying someone to do that job you'll just have to paper over it.'

'It'll leave a bulge in the wall.'

'We can hang a picture over it.'

'All right, I'll do my best to disguise it,' said Thelma. 'I'm looking forward to trying my hand at decorating, you know.'

'Huh!' Cora was scathing. 'You'll mess it up. Don't expect me to pay for someone to come and clear up after you.'

'Oh ye of little faith,' declared her daughter, for once choosing not to take offence.

In the end the pattern they agreed upon featured little green birds which would be easy to match up. Thelma bought a book of instructions on home decorating and she turned out to be quite a dab hand at wallpapering. Even the bulge made by the little cupboard wasn't too unsightly.

Winter was approaching and Cora was impatient to get the rest of the house decorated.

'Are you going to do my bedroom next?' she asked.

'It's cold upstairs Mother, can't the rest wait until the spring?'

'You should have thought of that and done upstairs first.'

'You said you wanted the front room done before the winter,' protested Thelma.

'I don't remember saying that,' grunted Cora, 'and by the way, isn't the coalman supposed to be delivering today?'

'Yes, this afternoon.'

'Well, just make sure you count the number of bags he carries round the back. Last time we were a bag short.'

'That was ages ago, Mother, when we were still living in London.'

Cora gave a dismissive shrug. 'They're all the same so keep an eye on him.'

When she'd left work the company had presented Thelma with a wooden mantel clock and a card signed by all the staff. Mr Bateman, the Managing Director, gave a speech commending her on forty years service, forcing Thelma to stand through it all, red-faced with embarrassment. Shuffling from one foot to the other, she longed for the ground to open up and swallow her. As Mr Bateman finished speaking everybody clapped and wished Thelma well, with one or two declaring that she must stay in touch.

'Keep us up to date with all your news, Thelma,' said Nora, the woman who was taking her place, 'and don't forget to give me your address.' She thrust a piece of paper into Thelma's hand. 'Here's mine.'

Some of the girls from *Cosmetics* invited her to join them in the pub for a drink after work but she knew they didn't really want her. They were in the habit of going to the Black Horse on a Friday evening to meet up with some of the boys from *SportsandLeisure* and they had never included her before. But she was touched when young Ellie from the canteen came up to her just as she was leaving the building and handed her a pack of embroidered handkerchiefs tied up with a pink ribbon. 'You've always been kind to me, Miss Stokes,' she said, looking tearful, 'I shall miss you.'

On the train going home, Thelma couldn't help thinking about the genuine sadness in Ellie's eyes as she had handed her the gift. Ellie had always greeted her with a cheerful smile and often added an extra scoop of ice cream when dishing out the apple crumble. As the train passed through a tunnel, she stared at her own reflection in the window wondering dolefully why, after forty years, she had made so little impression on her workmates. She was sure that by Monday Ellie would be the only one to give her a passing thought.

Cora grumbled incessantly: the house was too cold; the newspapers never arrived on time; there was too much passing traffic.

'I can't open the windows because of the noise,' she declared. 'It keeps me awake at night.'

'It's your own fault, Mother,' replied Thelma, resolutely adjusting her spectacles to sit on the bridge of her nose, 'you shouldn't have insisted on taking the front bedroom.'

'Hmm, and those kids from next door are always throwing their ball over the wall. You must go round there and complain to their mother, Thelma.'

'I'll do no such thing,' retorted her daughter although, privately, she was finding it rather tiresome having a grubby-faced eight-year-old constantly knocking at the door with, 'Can we have our ball back, missus?'

While she had been working, Thelma had put up with her mother's whining with stoicism but now they were together all day long, she was becoming more and more irritated. She began taking long walks along the beach, hands thrust in pockets, toeing pebbles as she allowed her imagination to run riot. Thelma had a vivid imagination and she enjoyed conjuring up ways of silencing Cora's moaning: stealing into her bedroom at dead of night and smothering her with a pillow; lacing her bed-time drink with arsenic so that she'd never wake up; pushing her down the stairs. She brightened up. Yes, that was the best way. She could say her mother had tripped over that damned stick she always carried. Of course, she knew she would never put any of these plots into practise but it was comforting to imagine them.

Cora's discontent stemmed from a broken heart. Alfred, the husband she adored, left her for a Tiller girl.

Betty, her best friend at the time, had commiserated with her. 'Don't worry Cora dear he'll tire of her in next to no time, you mark my words.'

'She's so glamorous,' lamented Cora, 'how can I compete? Why, she's got legs up to her armpits!'

Betty smothered a giggle. 'She's common. Your Alf will come to no good playing around with the likes of her.'

'But if he divorces me...'

'He can't do that, you're the injured party, he's the one in the wrong,' protested Betty. 'Anyway, look on the bright side, you're still young and if he doesn't come back to you, there are plenty more fish in the sea.'

This was no comfort to Cora who had set her heart on hanging onto her man and when Alfred did not tire of his long-legged Tiller girl, shamed by his desertion, she refused to file for divorce. Instead, she sneaked away and found digs on the other side of London, bringing up Thelma all by herself. A skilled seamstress she managed to keep body and soul together with the help of the small amount of money which, during the early years, Alfred provided. He never enquired about his daughter so Thelma grew up without knowing her father. It was hard-going but somehow mother and daughter won through and once Thelma left school and started working at the department store, things improved. By then, Alfred had disappeared.

'Your father's gone forever and "good riddance" I say,' proclaimed Cora when, on one occasion, Thelma became curious and plucked up the courage to ask about her father.

Betty kept in touch with Cora for a while but eventually gave up trying to pull her friend out of her *poor me* frame of mind. Working from home meant that Cora had very little contact with the outside world. Over the years, Thelma did all the shopping and most of the cleaning despite working a forty-hour week at the department store. No one ever visited them and since Cora was always dissatisfied with their rented accommodation, they had frequently moved house.

When, at the age of fifteen, Thelma started work, she would obediently hand over her pay packet to her mother. Every Friday evening Cora would count out the pennies to go into the appropriately labelled jam jars she kept on the kitchen shelf. There was one for coal, one for electricity, another for the gas meter and, of course, one for a 'rainy day'. Having performed this weekly ritual, she would hand back a modest amount of pocket money to her daughter. Cora appeared not to care that their lives were so predictably monotonous but Thelma never ceased to dream of something better.

On one occasion, while they were living in a rather seedy area of North London, she had challenged Cora. 'What's the point of saving for a 'rainy day', Mother we both need a holiday, why don't we go to the seaside for a weekend: Folkestone or Eastbourne?'

Cora's lips tightened. 'What nonsense, my girl, we might need that money for something important.'

'Like what?'

'How will you manage if I fall ill?'

'The NHS will take care of you.'

'Tch, the NHS is nothing more than charity.'

'No it's not, mother,' cried Thelma indignantly, 'it's there for everybody.'

Then their luck changed. The authorities got in touch with Cora to tell her that Alfred had died of a heart attack. Apparently his liaison with the Tiller girl had ended when he lost most of his money on the horses, prompting her to make off with a bookmaker from the betting shop. Over the years he had become a habitual gambler, his fortune vacillating from race to race. As luck would have it, his heart attack occurred when he was riding high, thus his winnings passed to Cora as his next of kin, making it possible for her to purchase Number Seven. Thelma never dared ask her mother how much money was involved and despite being better off, Cora continued to moan about their living expenses.

'I always said this house was too big for us,' she grumbled, 'we would have been better off finding a two bed-roomed flat.'

'We could rent out a room,' said Thelma, half joking.

To her surprise, Cora nodded her head. 'For once, you've come up with a good idea, my girl.'

They placed a card in the local newsagent's window and received a number of applicants. Cora insisted on showing them round despite her difficulty in getting about.

'Why don't you let me show people the room?' suggested Thelma, 'it would save you having to struggle upstairs.'

'I go upstairs to bed, don't I,' snorted Cora, 'so who says I can't manage? Besides, I don't want some stranger poking his nose into the other rooms up there.'

'I wouldn't let anybody do that, Mother.'

But Cora couldn't bear to relinquish authority to her daughter.

Then Leslie Dempster answered the advertisement and arrived on their doorstep looking dapper in a dark grey pin-striped suit and a trilby hat. He sported a narrow moustache over thin lips and wore tortoiseshell-rimmed spectacles. When Cora answered the door, he took off his hat to reveal sleek black hair smoothed across his head as if to hide his receding hairline.

'Good morning, Mrs Stokes, I believe you have a room to let,' he said politely.

One glance at him convinced Cora that the fifty-something man standing in front of her was respectable. This impression was further confirmed when he explained that he was employed by the Tax Office. Anyone working for the local council must be trustworthy.

She went ahead of him up the stairs; her visitor followed at a discreet distance in order to avoid a brush with her rather large rear which tended to swing out as, encumbered by her stiff left knee, she made her shambling progress upwards.

Leslie Dempster liked the room. 'Well, Mrs Stokes,' he said with a little bow, 'this will suit me admirably. How much will you charge for it?'

Cora quoted a figure half expecting her prospective lodger to shake his head and barter but he agreed immediately. They made their slow progress downstairs to where Thelma was waiting expectantly.

'This is our new lodger, Mr Dempster,' said Cora triumphantly. Leaning her hand on the table for support, she beamed at her daughter and waved her stick saying, 'Thelma dear, show Mr Dempster the kitchen and bathroom.' She turned to him. 'By the way, did I mention that I cannot allow any form of alcohol on the premises?'

'Of course not,' replied Leslie. 'I myself was brought up in a strictly teetotal environment.'

Thelma smothered a smirk knowing that her mother was in the habit of drinking a pint of Guinness each evening before retiring to bed. Forcing herself to keep a straight face, she escorted their prospective lodger through the kitchen to the bathroom.

After glancing around he made Thelma blush by saying, 'Thank you, young lady, this seems eminently suitable for my needs.'

They returned to the dining room where Cora was waiting. She cleared her throat. 'Mr Dempster, in order to reserve the room for you I shall need a deposit.' To justify this request, she burbled on, 'We've got several other people interested in the room, you know.'

'No problem,' he replied, taking out his wallet and extracting the required number of notes. 'I shall arrive on

Monday afternoon at around five o'clock if that's convenient.'

'That is most convenient, Mr Dempster. By the way, if I am to be cooking your meals, I shall need your Ration Book.'

'There's no need for that, Mrs Stokes, I prefer to cater for myself.'

'Of course, of course,' said Cora.

Thelma wasn't very happy about this arrangement. It was she not Cora who cooked most evenings and as the kitchen wasn't very big two people using it at the same time could cause a problem.

However, Cora seemed pleased. Waddling ahead of Leslie Dempster to the front door, she said, 'It will be so nice having a man in the house again.'

After he'd left, Cora's eyes glinted with satisfaction. 'Isn't it lucky I thought about taking in a lodger?' she said.

'Mother, it was *my* idea,' protested Thelma.

Ignoring her, Cora continued to enthuse about their lodger. 'Such a well-educated gentleman,' she said, 'and he's got a really important job on the Council.'

'Mother, he's a clerk in the Tax Office,' Thelma pointed out.

Her mother wasn't listening. 'Thelma dear, we've got the weekend to get the house spick and span. You must start spring-cleaning first thing tomorrow morning.'

Thelma could hardly stop herself from hitting Cora. Why did all the chores fall to her? Resorting to sarcasm, she said tartly, 'You can't *spring*-clean in the *autumn*. Besides he's only paying for the use of *one* room not the whole house.'

THIRTEEN

Leslie Dempster moved in on a damp October morning. He didn't have much luggage, just a suitcase with his clothes and several boxes. For the first few days, Cora was in her element. 'It's so nice having a man in the house again,' she gushed, giving the impression that her husband's demise had been only recent. Thelma found it difficult to hide her giggles but her mother's glowering frown warned her not to spoil the cover-image she was so carefully creating.

During the ensuing days she watched her mother's antics with amusement. Cora fussed over her lodger as if he were a member of the gentry. On the first Saturday after his arrival she invited him down for tea and cake and although Leslie was extremely polite, Thelma detected a hint of hesitancy before he accepted the invitation.

At the appointed time, Cora directed him to an armchair by the window, and on the pretext of giving him a place for his cup and saucer she cleverly arranged an occasional table in front of him. This made it difficult for him to stretch out his legs thus preventing a quick get-away once the tea had been drunk and the cake eaten.

'Dear Mr Dempster,' she began after pouring out the tea, 'have you been employed by the Council for very long?'

'I've been in local government all my life, Mrs Stokes,' explained Leslie, taking a sip of tea and dabbing his lips with Cora's floral napkin. 'But as I told your daughter, I lived in Salisbury until I was transferred down here.'

All smiles, Cora leant forward. 'A great career if I might say so and tell me, how do you find this part of the world?'

'Very agreeable, I love the sea. Have you and your daughter been living here long?'

Cora conjured up an air of sadness. 'Alas we were bombed out in the Blitz but fate smiled on us and found us this charming house by the sea.'

Thelma, who had taken a back seat so far, couldn't help saying, 'But Mother, I thought you didn't like it here. You're always moan...'

Cora flicked a hand at her. 'Nonsense dear, what put that idea in your head?' She went on. 'Tell me, Mr Dempster...'

'Please call me Leslie.'

Cora beamed at him. 'I'm Cora and my daughter's Thelma.'

'You were saying?'

'Oh yes, do you come from a large family, Leslie?'

'No, I'm an only child. Sadly, my parents died some ten years ago so now I'm all alone.'

Cora raised her eyebrows. 'No aunts, uncles, cousins?'

'Unfortunately, not.'

Thelma listened to their conversation without contributing much. She was embarrassed both by her mother's fawning tone of voice and by her probing questions. She wanted to put an end to them but didn't know how to change the subject.

An hour and a half later and after several more cups of tea, Leslie made his escape. On his way out of the room, he passed Thelma who caught a fleeting expression of sympathy in his eyes. She stood still for a moment, thinking about him and came to the conclusion that there was more to Leslie Dempster than met the eye.

Over the winter, Cora and Thelma had little contact with their new lodger. He never again accepted Cora's invitation to tea, cleverly finding an excuse each time she asked him. Returning from work he would cook a hasty supper before shutting himself away in his room. Sometimes, Thelma could hear him playing classical music on the gramophone he had brought with him but, for the most part, he seemed to be engrossed in his books. He never had visitors except for the man from Littlewoods Football Pools. Thelma couldn't help sniggering because, despite Cora's fortunes being changed by Alfred's race winnings, her mother despised gambling and would give a huff of disapproval whenever the collector came to call. In Cora's eyes, this was the only black mark against Leslie until one day he approached her asking if she could arrange for some shelves to be put up in his room.

'I would be most grateful,' he said in his quiet, polite manner, 'I have rather a lot of books and they are in the way on the floor and they may get damaged.'

'Well…' Cora pursed her lips, 'calling in a joiner will cost money; you know how expensive carpenters are these days.'

'Oh dear lady, I didn't mean that you should pay for it. I'll foot the bill if you would kindly arrange it.'

Cora's expression softened; smiling she said, 'Of course, Leslie, I will see to it at once. Run down to the corner shop, Thelma and make enquiries; that Mr Royston knows all the local handymen.'

As Thelma went to collect her coat from the peg in the hall, Leslie tried to stop her. 'There's no rush, tomorrow will do.'

'Thelma doesn't mind, do you dear?' insisted Cora.

When Thelma looked undecided, Leslie said, 'In that case, my dear, we'll go together. Please wait while I get my coat.'

As Leslie mounted the stairs, Thelma caught her mother's glance and knew that Cora wasn't happy. 'Mother, we can't let him pay for the carpentry,' she said.

'Of course we can, after all he knew there were no bookshelves when he took the room? I'll have to put his rent up if he keeps asking for extras.'

Thelma looked aghast. 'You can't do that, Mother!'

Their argument was interrupted when Leslie appeared wearing his hat and coat.

'We won't be long,' called out Thelma as they left the house.

While they walked along, Leslie said, 'Do you like to read, Thelma?'

'Yes I do.'

'What sort of books do you like?'

Thelma coloured as she replied, 'I love a romance but I don't suppose you would be interested in those.'

'Do you read Daphne du Maurier?'

'Yes, and Barbara Cartland and Catherine Cookson,' replied Thelma, spouting the names of famous romantic novelists she had heard of. She didn't want to admit that she only ever read Mills and Boon.

When March drew to a close and spring sunshine brought out primroses and daffodils, Thelma resumed her walks on the beach. Since leaving work she was obliged to spend a great deal of time with her mother and walking on the beach was a means of escape. One Sunday afternoon she was surprised to come face to face with Leslie on the promenade.

'Well I never,' he said, 'I didn't know you were a keen walker too.'

To her chagrin, Thelma found herself blushing. 'I've always loved walking by the sea,' she said.

'In that case, do you mind if I join you?'

After half an hour they ended up in a seafront café. 'It's getting a bit nippy now,' said Leslie, hugging a beaker of tea. 'But perhaps we can do this again.'

'I'd like that.'

'Tell me about yourself, how long is it since you left your job?'

'Eighteen months. I used to work in a big London department store.'

'That must have been interesting.'

'It was sometimes,' fibbed Thelma, unwilling to tell Leslie how much she had hated the job.

'Your mother is a very stalwart lady.'

'Stalwart?'

'She tells me she was inconsolable when your father died and you must miss him too. Was his demise recent?'

Thelma almost burst out laughing. So that was the story her mother had fed their lodger! 'I never knew my father, he died several years ago.' Taking pleasure in disproving her mother's version of events, she added, 'He left us when I was a baby.'

'But I was under the impression...'

'I know, mother makes everything into a sob-story.' Thelma lowered her gaze feeling a twinge of guilt at her unkind words. She tried to rectify the situation. 'I mean, she tends to be melodramatic.'

'I see.'

They fell silent and Thelma's gaze fastened on the salt-sprayed café window. The sky had clouded over and the wind had picked up so that white crested waves splashed against the breakwaters lining the beach. Seagulls screeched overhead and both she and Leslie drew back as one soared close to the window.

'I thought it was coming in for a cup of tea,' joked Leslie.

The incident broke through their awkwardness and, after paying the bill - Leslie insisted that he did it - they left the café and walked towards home. As they passed the newsagents, Leslie slapped his pockets. 'I need some cigarettes,' he said, 'you go on ahead.'

Thelma was grateful for his discretion. It wouldn't do for her mother to think that she had been having a tête-a-tête with their lodger.

The Sunday afternoon walks became regular and by tacit agreement they met at the entrance to the pier. Thelma felt comfortable in Leslie's company and found herself opening up to him. They exchanged confidences, describing their lonely childhood. Like Thelma, Leslie had only ever had one employer: the Council. He explained how he had been exempted from call-up during WWII due to a heart condition brought on by an attack of rheumatic fever when he was eleven.

'I wanted to do my bit,' he said, 'but they wouldn't have me. In any case, my job in the Council was granted exemption.'

'If I had been younger, I would have joined up,' said Thelma, 'although it would have been difficult leaving mother.'

'Have you ever thought of moving, striking out on your own?'

Thelma recoiled with shock. 'Oh, I don't think I could.'

As time passed she learnt that Leslie was fifty-one and that he was dissatisfied with his job.

'Have you got any hobbies?' she asked him.

'I collect stamps,' he replied, 'I'll show them to you one day.'

'Sometimes I can hear you playing music,' she said.

'Oh dear, I hope it doesn't disturb you.'

'Not at all, I like it.'

'What about your mother. Does she mind?'

Thelma laughed. 'Mother's a bit hard of hearing so you don't need to worry about her.'

In fact, most evenings Cora retired to her room early armed with her bottle of Guinness. She always got Thelma to discreetly dispose of the empties while Leslie was at work.

'Do you like classical music?' asked Leslie.

'I don't know anything about it,' she confided.

Leslie smiled at her. 'In that case, I shall invite you to a concert one of these days.'

FOURTEEN

As the summer progressed, Thelma and Leslie grew closer. They even took to walking arm-in-arm which, for Thelma, was a strange experience. She had never been close to another person. On thinking back, she couldn't remember a single moment when anybody had hugged her. She supposed that as a baby her mother must have nursed her but during her toddler to teenage years she could not recall Cora ever comforting her when she fell over or sympathising when something went wrong at school. In fact, Cora had never attended any of Thelma's school plays or sports days.

Thus displays of affection were alien to Thelma, and when one day while they were sitting in one of the promenade shelters Leslie drew her into an embrace and gently kissed her cheek, she froze.

'I'm sorry, I shouldn't have done that,' he muttered, sliding sideways along the narrow bench so that there was a gap between them.

The incident spoilt their afternoon and they returned home with Leslie carefully keeping his distance. As they walked close to a shop window, Thelma caught a glimpse of their reflection: a stout soberly attired woman and a spruce middle-aged slightly-built man. She was a head taller than Leslie and probably weighed twice as much as him. All at once, she felt ridiculous and resolutely vowed to curtail their walks. It would be easy to do that without giving offence because autumn was approaching and the weather was not conducive to walking.

'Will you be going for a walk today, Thelma?' asked Leslie when he met her on the landing the following Sunday morning.

She shook her head. 'No, there's a lot to do in the garden at this time of the year; you know, cutting back and clearing up leaves.'

'I'll give you a hand.'

Thelma was stunned by the offer. 'That's very kind of you but I can manage,' she said.

'I'd like to help you.'

'No really, I can manage.'

'Manage what, dear?' Cora appeared at the foot of the stairs.

'Oh, I was just saying that I can manage the garden, Mother.'

Leslie started walking downstairs, a smile on his face. 'And I was offering to help.'

'Why, Leslie, that's very kind of you. After all gardening can be strenuous work and I'm sure Thelma could do with some assistance.'

Thus Thelma and Leslie set to work pruning, cutting back and sweeping up leaves. She tried not to appear too friendly but Leslie's eagerness to help and his cheerful manner soon melted her resolve and she felt comforted to have someone working alongside her.

Leslie stopped to remove his pullover and roll up his shirt sleeves. 'It's hot work,' he said as he took a packet of Capstan Navy Cut out of his pocket. 'Do you mind, Thelma?'

'Not at all,' she replied. It pleased her to see that he was a smoker, simply because she knew her mother disapproved of smoking.

Leaning on his spade, he removed his glasses and wiped the sweat from his brow. When he replaced his spectacles and started digging again, his bare arm brushed Thelma's hand and she experienced a frisson of excitement. She could smell him too: besides the cigarette, he carried the aroma of a working man, something that would have disgusted her had she come across it on the underground or in a bus. Something strange stirred inside her, something she had never quite been able to conjure up from all those Mills and Boon novels she had read.

Anxious to dispel these embarrassing feelings, she said, 'It's hard work and I'm grateful for your help, Leslie.' Just using his name made her blush but she knew he wouldn't notice because they were both quite red in the face from their exertions.

He grinned and replied, 'Actually, it makes a change from sitting at an office desk all day.' Then he sprang a surprise on her. 'Hmm, Thelma, would you like to come to a concert with me next Friday evening? It's a programme of light classics and I think you'd enjoy it.'

Taken aback, Thelma pushed her glasses to the bridge of her nose, mumbled her acceptance and went back to raking the lawn with added vigour.

The following Friday Thelma broke the news to her mother that she wouldn't be in for supper.

'Where are you going?' asked Cora. It was after all unknown for Thelma to go out in the evening.

Crossing her fingers behind her back in a bid to fend off the anticipated barrage of questions, Thelma replied, 'I'm going to the pictures, there's a film I want to see.'

'What's wrong with a matinée performance? We could go together tomorrow afternoon.'

'I'm sorry, Mother but I've decided to go this evening.'
'Which film is it?'
'It's one you wouldn't like.'

'How do you know? What's it called?'

'*Rebel without a Cause*,' mumbled Thelma, knowing that it was currently showing at the Odeon. 'It's not your sort of film.'

Cora gave a sniff of disapproval but, much to her daughter's relief, she didn't persist with the argument. Thelma took a long time deliberating on what to wear. The decision shouldn't have been difficult since her wardrobe was limited. Even when working at the department store, she had seldom spent money on new clothes and never bothered to follow the latest fashions like the other women employed there. In the end she chose a calf-length navy blue pleated skirt topped by a pale blue lambs-wool twin-set and once ready to leave, she crept downstairs and through the front door, calling out a hurried *goodbye* to her mother.

Leslie came straight from work and she found him waiting for her at the station entrance. He greeted her with a smile and her heart leapt when he kissed her cheek. This time she didn't draw away. After a quick meal of fish and chips in a seafront restaurant, they took their seats just as the concert was about to begin.

'I know you're going to enjoy this,' whispered Leslie, taking her hand in his.

Thelma felt as if she were in a dream. For the first time in her life, she was out on a date with a man. During the interval, Leslie bought her a drink at the bar. Thelma wasn't used to alcohol and despite Cora's liking for a glass of Guinness, she had never felt the urge to imbibe.

'I've brought you a Dry Martini,' he said, returning with two glasses, 'I hope that's all right.'

Thelma hadn't the least idea what a Dry Martini was. She had heard the girls from *Cosmetics* talking about the drinks they had tried in the pub but no one had ever explained what the ingredients were.

'It's very nice, thank you.' And she really meant it.

As they made their way back to their seats, she began to feel slightly light-headed and was grateful for Leslie's steadying hand on her arm.

The concert ended before ten so they had another drink in an adjacent pub before catching the train home. The alcohol soothed away any inhibitions Thelma still harboured. She felt deliriously happy and didn't mind when Leslie placed his arm around her waist while they were walking to the train station.

This time they went into the house together because Thelma knew that Cora would be in bed. Nonetheless, Thelma took off her shoes and carried them as they crept upstairs. Leslie followed suit.

'It's been a lovely evening, Thelma,' he whispered when they reached the landing. 'Would you care to come in for a nightcap?'

'Oh, I don't think I should.'

'I would really like you to; it would round off the evening.'

Thelma giggled. 'Another Martini?'

'I'm afraid not. I haven't got any gin or vermouth but I have got some sweet sherry.'

He put a finger to his lips and opened the door, ushering her into his room. It seemed strange to Thelma to be in a gentleman's bedroom but she reminded herself that this was her mother's house and Leslie was only the lodger. She sank down into the armchair to wait for him to pour their drinks.

'Here you are, my dear,' he said handing her one of her mother's tumblers. 'I haven't got any sherry glasses either so these will have to do.'

Drinking from Cora's tumbler made the illicit drink taste even more daring. How shocked her mother would be if she could see her now!

Leslie sat on the edge of the bed and raised his glass - another of Cora's tumblers. Fleetingly, Thelma wondered how they came to be in Leslie's room. Usually, her mother noticed if anything went missing from the kitchen.

'Come and sit next to me, it's more comfortable.'

Thelma obediently joined him to sit on the edge of the bed, experiencing a warm glow when he slipped his arm around her. She continued to sip her drink, vaguely wondering which was nicer: the Dry Martini or the sherry. Sliding closer, Leslie took her empty tumbler and put it on the side table.

'Did you enjoy the concert, my dear?' he asked and, responding to the warmth of his presence, she leant her head on his shoulder and whispered, 'Oh yes, thank you for a lovely evening, Leslie.'

Thelma would never understand what made her do it but, all at once, her need for affection overwhelmed her. Impulsively, she turned her head and kissed Leslie on the lips. For a fraction of a second, he was taken by surprise and in that tiny moment, Thelma lost her nerve. Drawing away, she stammered, 'I...I don't know what came over me... I must go.'

She went to stand up but lost her balance, collapsing down onto the bed and in an endeavour to cover her embarrassment, giggled, 'Goodness, just look what the drink has done to me!'

Leslie took her hand. 'There's no hurry, Thelma, stay a little longer.'

She hesitated. 'Erm, all right...'

'Can we repeat the kiss, Thelma?'

She gave a nervous nod and let him remove her glasses. This time the kiss took longer, allowing a myriad of sensations to swamp her: the prickly sweep of his moustache, the faint aroma of Capstans on his breath, the moisture on his lips. She felt mesmerised and encouraged by her compliance, Leslie's kiss became less tentative. No one had ever tried to kiss her before. She was sure Leslie must be able to hear her heart beating against her ribcage.

The heat rushed to her cheeks and unnerved, she shrank back. Without her glasses she couldn't read his expression as he murmured, 'Why are you trembling, my love?'

'Oh Leslie…' With a sob she pressed herself close to him, seeking his mouth again.

What remained of the evening would forever be a haze to Thelma but at six o'clock the next morning she woke up to find herself lying on Leslie's bed while he was slouched in the armchair covered by a blanket.

Thrown into panic, she sat up and stared at the wall opposite as if pleading for support. Her head throbbed and she couldn't focus properly. What had happened? Had Leslie made love to her? She looked down at herself and saw that her skirt was caught up revealing her navy blue knickers. Surely that meant nothing could possibly have happened! Nonetheless, overwhelmed with embarrassment, she tugged down her skirt, cringing at the thought that Leslie had seen her old-fashioned underwear.

Had she passed out? Seized by shame, she got to her feet and picked up her glasses. An inspection in the mirror showed an ageing face with heavy bags below the eyes. She raked her fingers through her hair in an attempt to tidy it but the result wasn't encouraging. Reaching for her bag, she tried to make her escape before Leslie or her mother woke up and then she remembered her shoes. Where were they? She couldn't see them so she dropped to the floor and on hands and knees began to grope around for them.

'What are you doing down there?' Leslie yawned and sat up.

'Where are my shoes?' she gasped hysterically. 'I must get out of here.'

'Why? Am I such a tyrant?'

Leslie's jocular tone calmed her and struggling up from the floor, she sat down on the bed. 'I'll just have to leave without my shoes.'

Leslie took her hand. 'Nothing happened, you know. You fell asleep. I would never take advantage of you, my dear.' He looked at her earnestly. 'You do believe me, don't you?'

Suddenly, it all seemed too much. Lowering her head into her hands, Thelma burst into tears. Leslie went to sit beside her. 'Don't be upset,' he said. 'Go and get some sleep. I'll find your shoes and return them to you.'

Thelma crept along to her own room and quickly undressed. Her emotions were in turmoil. She had spent the night in Leslie's bed. He had assured her that nothing untoward had happened but how could she be sure? And her shoes were still there, kicked into a corner or under the bed. Could she trust Leslie to be discreet about returning them?

Tiredness overcame her and she fell into a deep sleep to be woken at eight o'clock by her mother's angry shout from the bottom of the stairs.

'Thelma, where are you?'

'Coming Mother,' she called.

'Are you going to stay in bed all day? Hurry up!'

She stumbled out of bed pulling her dressing-gown around her. Reaching the top of the stairs, she saw Cora standing below looking irate and brandishing her walking-stick. She hurried downstairs and followed her mother into the kitchen.

'I'm making breakfast, do you want eggs and bacon?' grunted Cora.

'No thank you, toast will do.'

'Are you ill?'

'I'm not ill, Mother, just tired.'

'You look like something the tide washed up.'

Thelma's heckles rose. That was exactly what she didn't want to hear but she felt too exhausted to retaliate.

'Was it a good film?'

'What?'

'The film you went to see, was it good?'

Thelma blinked then hastily adjusting her thoughts, said, 'Oh yes, quite good.'

'What was it about?'

'Good morning, ladies.' Leslie stood in the doorway. Thankfully he was not holding her shoes. 'Eggs and bacon, that smells nice.'

'Good morning, Leslie, would you care to join us for breakfast?'

'Thank you, Cora, that's very kind of you.'

'Take a seat in the dining room and I'll bring it in.'

Leslie's timely appearance saved Thelma from further interrogation. She sat at the table between them nibbling at a piece of toast and feeling ill at ease in her pink quilted dressing-gown when the other two were fully dressed. Both Cora and Leslie enjoyed a full English breakfast and while Leslie tucked in to his eggs and bacon he somehow managed to keep Cora off the subject of the film Thelma was supposed to have seen.

On returning to her room, Thelma found her shoes placed neatly beside the chest of drawers. It troubled her that Leslie had taken the liberty of entering her room without asking permission but she decided that discretion had prompted him to do so. Throughout the rest of the day, she analysed her motive for not wanting to tell her mother about their growing relationship and she always came back to the same conclusion: if Cora found out and disapproved she might terminate Leslie's tenancy. At all costs, that mustn't happen.

FIFTEEN

A week passed. Leslie returned from work each evening, greeted his landlady and her daughter in his habitually polite manner and after preparing his meal, he retired to his room to play his music.

Thelma had never been troubled by insomnia. She would retire to bed with one of her Mills and Boon novels and after a couple of chapters, the book would slip from her fingers and she would drift to sleep dreaming of love and passion. Thelma was a romantic and in rare moments of self analysis, she knew this characteristic was the only thing that had kept her sane throughout the years of co-habiting with Cora. But after the concert outing, her sleep pattern changed and she would toss and turn all night fearing that Leslie was deliberately avoiding her. She tortured herself by re-visiting the events of that Friday night. Had she made a complete fool of herself? Had she said things she shouldn't have said? That must be why Leslie wanted nothing more to do with her.

After only a few hours sleep, she would wake at six o'clock to the rattle of the milkman's float as he trundled along the road delivering milk. She would drag herself out of bed, feeling tired and ill-tempered. This would lead to squabbles with Cora and to avoid this constant bickering, she endeavoured to get out of the house as much as possible. But autumn had turned to winter and the weather was too cold for lonely seaside walks.

One evening, a week later, after Cora had gone to bed, she bumped into Leslie on the stairs. She was on her way up, he was coming down.

'I was just going to make a cup of tea, Thelma,' he said, 'would you care to join me?'

She nodded and turning round went ahead of him into the kitchen where he took the initiative, striking a match to light the gas under the kettle and taking cups and saucers off the dresser shelf. When he opened the larder door and took out her mother's biscuit barrel, it crossed Thelma's mind that to a fly on the wall observer Leslie would seem to be the landlord, she the lodger.

While they were waiting for the kettle to boil, Leslie asked, 'Are you and your mother getting along all right?'

'Why?'

Leslie warmed the teapot and went on casually, 'No reason really except that you seem a bit upset lately.'

Thelma forced a laugh. 'We've always quarrelled. I'm sorry if it disturbs you.'

'It doesn't matter to me but I think it must be upsetting for you. Hmm, I get the impression that Cora isn't easy to live with.'

Thelma hesitated before replying. Would it be disloyal to discuss her mother with Leslie? 'She's not the most easy-going person in the world,' she confessed.

'I thought not.' Thelma wondered where the conversation was heading but, thankfully, Leslie changed the subject. 'Look, I'm sorry I haven't seen much of you this week but I've been very busy at work because a colleague's been off sick.'

'I understand,' she replied.

'Would you like to come with me to the pictures next week?'

'Well, er, I don't know what's on.'

He smiled as he poured out the tea. 'I'll find out and let you know. Shall we take our tea upstairs?'

Thelma found a tray and Leslie arranged the tea and biscuits on it. 'Right, after you,' he said with a slight bow.

So once again, Thelma found herself in Leslie's bedroom. This time, she made a point of staking her claim of the armchair, leaving him to perch on the edge of the bed.

'Is that a photo album?' she asked, pointing to a glossy-covered scrap book on the table.

'No, it's my stamp collection; would you like to have a look at it?'

'Yes please. Are you a philate...?'

'Philatelist...yes I suppose I am.' He proceeded to flick through the album pointing out various stamps, murmuring wistfully. 'One day, I might hit on the big one.'

'The big one...?' Thelma pushed up her glasses to settle more securely on the bridge of her nose.

'Yes, one day I'll come across a really valuable stamp and then I'll make my fortune...' His eyes glazed over for a moment as he said with vehemence, 'then I'll be able to thumb my nose at the boss and say goodbye to that stuffy office.'

Taken aback by his outburst, Thelma asked. 'Could that really happen? I mean could you make a lot of money with the right stamp?'

'Yes, indeed,' replied Leslie quietly, clearly realising that he'd let his excitement run away with him.

'What would you do if that ever happened?'

'I'd buy a boat and sail the seven seas. Thelma, just imagine being able to go where you liked, stop off where you liked...' Leslie drew in his breath and exhaled slowly, 'ah...the joy of freedom!'

'That sounds lovely,' said Thelma, quite captivated by Leslie's yearning tone. 'It's good to have a dream. Everybody should have a dream.'

Undoubtedly feeling coy after his show of enthusiasm, he brushed a hand over his receding hair and laughed. 'Of course, it's only a pipe dream but I play my records and amuse myself for hours just studying the stamps and sometimes I come across a new one. I often browse the stamp shops; there are a lot of interesting ones in Brighton. I'll show you one day.'

Thelma felt flattered that she had been privy to Leslie's secret dream. She had read many romantic novels and shared the protagonists' innermost desires but she had never before met a real life person who, like her, let their imagination steer their life. She had been fascinated too by his knowledge of stamps as he explained their origin and their geographical importance. *No wonder he spends so much time looking through them,* she thought.

From then on, Thelma spent many happy evenings in Leslie's company. She felt safe in the knowledge that, due to her nightly intake of Guinness, her mother was a sound sleeper, although occasionally a creak in the woodwork on the stairs or the landing would make her stiffen with alarm.

'It's only a ghost, Thelma,' teased Leslie.

'...a ghost?'

'Come here, my love.' He wrapped his arms around her and gently kissed her lips.

'It might be mother checking up on me,' she protested.

Leslie laughed and Thelma was seized with embarrassment. She was behaving like an adolescent. 'I'm sorry,' she whispered, resolving to rid herself of Cora's shadow.

That night, she slept with Leslie, waking in the early hours wrapped in his arms. Her emotions were in turmoil. At the age of fifty-six she had at last lost her virginity. She felt young again and wanted to shout to the world that somebody loved her. Recalling the latest Mills and Boon novel which lay open on her bedside table, she reflected that real life was quite different to the paradigm portrayed in the story. In fiction, Chapter Five ended with the bedroom door firmly closing on the lovers, leaving the reader to imagine the rest. It didn't describe the fumbling under the bedclothes, the shock of that initial penetration and then the ecstasy of release.

She studied Leslie's sleeping form. He was no Adonis, rather weedy actually, but he had a certain charm and the more she got to know him the more she liked him. Could this be love? Thelma, the middle-aged spinster - reader of romantic novels - turned her face into the pillow to hide her tears of happiness.

Cora began to notice the change in Thelma. Her daughter no longer reacted when she made scathing remarks. In fact, it was getting more and more difficult to ruffle her feathers.

'Thelma, are you listening to me?' she snapped on one occasion when she had been blowing off steam about the lights being left on and had received no response from her daughter.

'Yes, Mother.'

'Really Thelma, you must speak to Leslie about leaving the light on in the hall.'

'All right, Mother.'

Cora felt irritated. Ever since her daughter was old enough to talk she had faced up to her. Battles had raged and Cora had always won but until now she had not realised how much she enjoyed Thelma's opposition. She missed her daughter's cutting retaliation to her own spiteful remarks. Nowadays Thelma seemed to live in a bubble. She spent most of her time in her room, only coming downstairs at meal times when she would gobble up whatever was on her plate, dutifully do the washing-up and hurry back upstairs.

'What do you do up there all day, Thelma?' Cora demanded one afternoon.

'Read.'

Cora snorted. 'Have you still got your nose stuck in those silly romantic Mills and Boons novels?'

'No, Mother as a matter of fact, Leslie has leant me some classics...'

'Classics - like what?'

'Jane Austen, the Bröntes...' Thelma reeled off the titles.

'Oh I see all that high-brow stuff.' Cora's heart was racing and she knew that she ought to calm down but when Thelma didn't rise to the bait she felt propelled to provoke her. 'What nonsense that man is feeding you!'

'It's not nonsense,' replied Thelma patiently.

Cora clenched her fists, aware that a vein was throbbing at her forehead. 'Maybe it's time he moved on. What do you think about that, Thelma dear?'

This *did* provoke a reaction. 'You can't do that,' replied Thelma hotly, 'not while he pays his rent on time and keeps his room tidy...'

'How do you know he keeps his room tidy?'

A flush spread over Thelma's cheeks. '*You've* never had cause to complain about it,' she retorted.

Cora's eyes glinted wickedly. 'And how do *you* know?'

'I...I don't but I'm sure he keeps it clean. If you don't mind I want to get back to my book now.' Thelma turned and left the room.

After she'd gone, Cora sank down onto a chair. Pressing a hand to her chest, she tried to catch her breath. This breathlessness was happening more and more often although she hadn't mentioned it to Thelma. Maybe it was time to play the invalid?

Thelma stomped upstairs in a fury. Over the past few weeks she had been patience personified, ignoring Cora's moaning, refusing to react to her sarcasm. But criticism of Leslie was a step too far. And what if she actually *did* ask him to leave?

She threw herself onto the bed, thumping the counterpane and shedding tears of frustration. It was only when she heard the front door open and Leslie's footsteps on the stairs that she pulled herself together. There was a gentle knock on her door and, quickly drying her eyes, she went to open it. Leslie stood on the threshold looking animated and before she could say anything, he took her arm and pulled her into his room.

'What's happened?' she cried.

'My love, you'll never guess.' His voice was hoarse with emotion.

'Don't tell me you've come across a valuable stamp in your collection?'

'No even better than that.'

Thelma had never seen him so excited. 'Don't keep me in suspense, what's happened?' Selfishly, she hoped it wasn't something that would entice him to move out of Number Seven.

'Thelma, I've won the pools.' Thelma's mouth dropped open. 'What do you think of that?'

'That's wonderful, Leslie. Is it a large amount?' She remembered one of the assistants in *Furnishings* winning a hundred pounds. He had invited everybody to the pub for a drink after work.

Leslie laughed and squeezed her hands. 'Yes rather.' His grip tightened and for a moment, Thelma thought he was going to take her in his arms and waltz her round the room. Enunciating every word, he said, 'One hundred and seventy thousand pounds.'

Thelma was speechless. She just couldn't imagine that amount of money. Leslie let go of her hands and took off his glasses, cleaning them with a handkerchief. As he looked at her with wide eyes, she noticed what a strange colour they were: a mixture of brown and green.

'That's an awful lot of money, Leslie.'

He placed his hands on her shoulders. 'My dear, do you see what this means?'

She shook her head, still unable to comprehend what he was saying to her.

'We can go away together, Thelma...'

'Me and you?'

Doubt cast a shadow over his enthusiasm. 'Don't you want to, am I being too hasty?'

'It's...it's a bit sudden.'

'Don't you want to escape?'

'Escape from what; you mean from Mother?'

'Yes, my love, she treats you like a skivvy...'

Thelma felt a twang of conscience. 'Mother's not *that* bad; she's ailing and she needs me.'

Leslie looked at her in astonishment. 'Thelma, you've been under her thumb all your life, this will give you the chance to break away. I'll give in my notice and buy a boat and we can go and live on it, sail away to far off lands. I can already smell the salty sea, feel the spray of the waves as they lap the hull; Thelma, you'll love it.'

'Wait a minute!'

'What's the matter?'

Backing away, Thelma stuttered, 'It's too sudden, Leslie, I need time to think.'

Opening the door, she rushed back to her own room.

SIXTEEN

Over the next few days Leslie seemed preoccupied and Thelma saw little of him. She couldn't believe he had actually asked her to go away with him. Had he really won that amount of money on the pools? If he had, why weren't there hoards of reporters banging at the front door? On the other hand, maybe he had put a cross in the privacy box.

Concern for her mother took her mind off it. On several occasions, after a bout of coughing she had seen Cora gasp for breath and lean against the wall for support.

'Perhaps you'd better go and see the doctor, Mother,' she suggested.

'There's no need,' snapped Cora.

'You don't seem very well.'

'What do you care? I'd be all right if you'd stop going around with that love-sick look on your face.'

Thelma gasped. 'What do you mean?'

Cora gave a sly grin. 'I know you're hankering after Leslie.'

'I am not!' her daughter hotly denied.

'So why do you go all gooey-eyed when he looks your way?'

'Don't talk rubbish, Mother,' retorted Thelma, striding out of the room.

But the exchange sobered her and, by the end of the week she had persuaded herself that Leslie had been teasing her, that the big pools win was a joke. Next time she saw him he'd tell her he was only kidding. Whenever she caught glimpses of him he looked rather down in the mouth. Either he had been joking or he had made a mistake when checking the coupon. Perhaps he was feeling depressed. She decided to seek him out and, the next day, an opportunity presented itself. On her way to post a letter she came face-to-face with him in the street. They both stopped in their tracks.

'Thelma, you seem to be avoiding me. Why?'

'I thought it was the other way round,' she said.

'I've been busy arranging things. Have you decided, Thelma?'

'Decided?'

'You know, about coming away with me?'

So he had been serious. 'Well...no,' she mumbled, 'to tell you the truth I didn't think it could be real...winning the pools, I mean.'

He threw back his head and laughed. 'You thought I was joking! It's no joke, Thelma; Littlewoods have been in touch and the money's in the bank.' She stared at him in stunned silence, as he went on, 'Well, my dear, have you decided? Will you come with me?'

Thelma couldn't think straight. The whole adventure seemed like a scene from one of the novels she loved to read. With a jolt she realised that Leslie was giving her a means of escape from the monotonous existence she had hitherto endured. Leaving with him would mean freedom from Cora's domination; Leslie was right, her mother had treated her like a skivvy over the years. She had never tasted freedom and it was tantalising to imagine it.

'Thelma?' Leslie's quiet voice broke into her thoughts.

'Give me time,' she said at last, 'it's a big decision to make.'

'I know that but I would love you to come. It's going to be so exciting. Just imagine, we can visit all those wonderful places in my stamp collection.'

'So you're really going to buy a boat?'

'Yes, did you think I wouldn't?'

'No...but...' She turned away from him.

'Please decide, Thelma.'

'It's the biggest decision I've ever had to make,' Thelma murmured.

Leslie touched her arm but she drew away. For years she had longed for something to change her life but now the opportunity had come along she wasn't sure she was brave enough to take advantage of it.

Leslie waited patiently, than said, 'I shall have to give Cora my notice soon so please think about it Thelma, then we can break the news to her together. Don't you want to get out from under the old witch's feet?'

'She's not an old witch.'

Leslie gave an awkward laugh. 'I'm sorry, I shouldn't have said that.'

'No you shouldn't.'

'I didn't mean it.'

'I don't know how she would manage without me,' muttered Thelma as if she were thinking aloud. Glancing at her watch, she excused herself with, 'I must post this letter; it's nearly time for the collection.'

Spinning round, she hurried off leaving Leslie looking after her.

During the following couple of weeks, Thelma avoided Leslie as much as possible and, out of consideration or indifference - she wasn't sure which - he didn't approach her. In bed at night she lay awake tossing the alternatives over in her mind and she came to realise that for the first time in her life she would have to make a life-changing decision. Until now her life had followed a pattern: school, then the job in the department store arranged for her by the headmistress, resignation from the job brought about by Cora's decision to move to the coast. When had she ever made a decision for herself? On top of this was Cora's failing health. How could she abandon her mother when she needed her most?

She tried burying herself in one of her Mills and Boon romances but these days the stories seemed tedious and unrealistic, featuring good-looking men and attractive women falling in love and living happily ever after; not like real life at all.

After three weeks Leslie told her he was going to tell Cora he was leaving.

'I'm sorry you can't make up your mind, Thelma dear,' he said, 'because I think we could have been happy together.'

'I haven't ruled it out,' she objected, 'it's just that mother...'

'I understand,' he said quietly. 'Your mother must come first.'

'I...I...' It was no good she couldn't bring herself to break away.

The next day, Thelma listened as Leslie broke the news to Cora.

'I'm sorry to hear that,' replied Cora. 'I hope we haven't done anything to upset you. I mean, Thelma can be a bit moody sometimes...'

Thelma's hackles rose. 'What are you talking about, Mother?' she demanded.

Cora ignored her. 'Is your room comfortable, Leslie? If you would prefer the other bedroom I am sure Thelma would be only too willing to do a swap with you.'

Her daughter could hardly believe her ears. Was she nothing more than a pawn on a chess board? She opened her mouth to protest but Leslie spoke first. Shaking his head he said, 'Dear lady, my stay with you and your daughter has been most enjoyable. As a matter of fact, I am going to buy a boat.'

Cora raised a surprised eyebrow. 'A boat! Why?'

'I've always been drawn to the sea and I've decided to take the plunge...' Leslie chuckled at his own pun. Yes...' he continued jovially, 'from now on it's a life on the ocean waves for me. '

'My, my, that does sound exciting,' Cora sucked in her lips and cocked her head to one side. Clearly she didn't believe him. 'You wouldn't be keeping a secret from us, would you Leslie? You're not getting married by any chance?' She chuckled. 'Have you got a lady friend hidden away somewhere?'

Thelma felt the colour rise to her cheeks as Leslie jokingly replied, 'No nothing like that...' He gave a chuckle and winked at Thelma. 'After all, who would have me?'

Cora glanced at her daughter. 'What do you think, Thelma, is Leslie holding out on us?'

Thelma was thrown into panic. Did her mother suspect anything? Were her jibes deliberately directed at her or was she just being facetious?

Cora turned back to her lodger. 'You're an excellent catch, Leslie, a man like you in the prime of life, why... you must have had plenty of opportunities.' She heaved a sigh. 'Of course, it's different for you, a man can marry at any age, but sadly a woman...' She glanced pointedly at Thelma, '...is on the shelf once she passes thirty.'

'Really, Mother...' Thelma fought the urge to stamp her foot.

She wanted to march out of the room but shame rooted her to the spot. She longed for Leslie to announce his feelings for her, for him to say, *Cora, as a matter of fact I've asked your daughter to marry me.* But he didn't and all at once she realised that although he had suggested she move in with him the word *marriage* had never passed his lips. She blushed even more. What a fool she was!

She hardly slept that night. Once, in the early hours she got up and, wrapping her dressing-gown around her, went out onto the landing with the intention of knocking at Leslie's door. But with her hand raised she heard Cora's hacking cough echoing along the landing. How could she abandon her? Wasn't it a daughter's duty to care for her mother? Swivelling around, she scurried back to bed and howled into the pillow.

On the evening before his departure, Leslie came to her bedroom. She ushered him in and quickly closed the door. They stood opposite one another, neither knowing how to reach out to the other.

Then without making a move to touch her, Leslie said, 'Well, Thelma, can I get you to change your mind?'

Thelma's legs felt as if they had turned to jelly. Without uttering a word, she sat down on the bed, tears welling in her eyes.

Leslie sat down next to her. 'I have to go, my dear,' he said, taking her hand in his. 'The offer is still there, if you want to come with me it would make me extremely happy. The reason you haven't seen much of me lately is because I've been taking sailing lessons. You should just see the boat I've bought. You'd love it. It's called, 'The Skylark'. It's moored in Portsmouth Harbour.'

Thelma gave a sniff into her handkerchief. 'It sounds lovely,' she muttered.

'Go and tell your mother now.'

'How can I leave her all alone?'

'It's time you broke free, Thelma,' retorted Leslie, 'I can tell you really want to.'

'Thelma, where are you?' Cora's voice reached them from downstairs, 'I need you to help me up the stairs.'

Thelma snatched her hand away from Leslie's and jumped to her feet. 'Coming, Mother.'

Leslie moved out and Thelma sank into depression. Cora on the other hand seemed to take on a new lease of life. The day after their lodger's departure, she started giving orders.

'Thelma dear hadn't you better clear out the spare room' - she seemed incapable of referring to their former lodger by name - 'ready for our next tenant?'

'There's no rush, Mother.'

'We'll miss the money.'

Thelma gritted her teeth. How could her mother talk about money when her daughter's heart was broken! She recalled the number of times she had empathised with a Mills and Boon heroine never imagining that she would one day find her own emotions in such turmoil.

Forcing herself to regain control, she said, 'We can manage, after all we managed before.'

'Just the same,' sniffed Cora, 'next time you go shopping place an advert in the newsagents and I think we should insist on a lady this time.'

But Thelma was in no hurry to prepare the room or to place an advert in the newsagent's window and she deliberately put off doing both. Their relationship grew progressively more antagonistic as she began to suspect that Cora was not as ill as she had made out.

Their rows became bitter, laced with sarcasm and once again, Thelma began taking long walks along the promenade. She strode out at a brisk pace, head down, shoulders hunched. If a passer-by greeted her she grunted a reply and hurried on. Again, her imagination ran riot and she re-ran her conjured up plots to dispose of her mother. Leslie had been right, Cora was an old witch.

Time passed and mother and daughter settled back into their former life pre-Leslie. Despite the fine weather, Thelma couldn't summon up any interest in the garden. It had been fun digging and trimming with Leslie by her side but now she could see no point in tending flowers he wouldn't see and cutting a lawn that no one would sit out on.

'Why haven't you cleaned the spare room, Thelma?' Cora demanded again, 'someone might answer our ad and the room won't be ready.'

'All in good time, Mother,' snapped Thelma.

'You did place that ad, didn't you?' her mother asked suspiciously.

'Of course I did.' Thelma had no compunction about lying. She couldn't bear the thought of someone else taking up residence in Leslie's room.

Her resentment grew. One night she got up and went to her mother's bedroom. Opening the door quietly she went to stand by her bed. Cora's mouth hung open and a dribble of saliva trickled onto her pillow. She gave a reverberating snore making Thelma jump back in alarm. For several seconds, she froze but once she was certain Cora was still asleep, she again approached the bed. A cushion had fallen off the Lloyd loom basket chair and lay on the floor. Out of habit she picked it up and shook it into shape. Standing there with the cushion in her hands, she recalled her plot to finish off Cora, to do away with her moaning and nagging. How often had she wanted to change the daily routine her mother insisted upon! Would it matter if the washing was done on a Tuesday instead of a Monday, if the sheets were changed on a Wednesday instead of a Saturday? What difference would it make if they ate sausages instead of fish and chips on a Friday and if the Sunday roast was replaced by lamb stew? She gripped the cushion tightly.

She got up the next morning and went downstairs. Cora wasn't in the kitchen. Normally, she rose early and started on the breakfast before Thelma got up. Feeling concerned, she hurried upstairs and knocked on her mother's door.

There was no reply. After a second knock, she went in. Cora looked to be asleep.

'Wake up, Mother,' she said in a loud voice.

Cora didn't stir so Thelma shook her arm. It slipped limply from her hand. She gasped and stepped back then remembering that you were supposed to feel for a pulse, she held her mother's wrist, but she had no idea how to check. She felt her neck and leant close to her slightly parted lips half expecting Cora to snap open her eyes and shout at her. But this didn't happen.

Thrown into panic, she shook her by the shoulders but Cora slumped back lifeless. Bursting into tears, Thelma threw herself over the bed, beating at her mother's body. 'Wake up you old witch, wake up!'

Ten minutes later, when the truth had settled into her consciousness, she went downstairs and phoned for the doctor.

Still numb with shock, Thelma went about the business of arranging the funeral, even going to the expense of buying a smart black suit and cream silk blouse to wear. She chose the Crematorium in favour of having to stand around a hole in the ground while the coffin was lowered into it. To her surprise, several of the neighbours attended the service, even Mrs Wilton, mother of the boy who was always calling to ask for his ball back, put in an appearance. Everyone greeted her sympathetically with assurances that she only had to call if she needed any help.

'I expect you'll miss your mother, my dear,' said Mrs Wilton, 'it will be very quiet without her.'

'Yes,' agreed Thelma although she wasn't quite sure what that meant. She had often wondered whether the neighbours had been able to hear Cora's ranting through the walls.

She was just about to make her departure from the Crematorium when she spotted a man's figure some distance away. She frowned and adjusted her glasses. Was it? Could it be? The man was the right build but, wearing slacks and a sports jacket with an open-neck shirt he was dressed quite differently to the way Leslie habitually dressed.

At that moment, another neighbour touched her arm. 'Perhaps when you are feeling rested and things have settled down, you might care to come and have tea with us. My sister and I would love to see you.' The Misses Turpin were two ageing spinsters who lived at Number Three.

'Thank you very much,' replied Thelma, nervously trying to look back over her shoulder. By the time she was able to get away, Leslie - if it had been Leslie - had gone.

'The car's ready for you, Miss Stokes.'

She turned to find one of the funeral attendants gently prodding her into the limousine and, as they drove her home, she wondered guiltily whether she should have arranged tea and sandwiches for the people who had taken the trouble to attend the funeral. Then she comforted herself with the thought that their attendance had been totally unexpected because the only people she had invited were Cora's erstwhile friend, Betty, Nora, the woman who had taken over her job at the department store and Ellie from the canteen. None of them had come, although Betty had sent flowers.

Over the next few weeks, Thelma discovered how friendly the neighbours were but she also realised that her mother's demise had evoked a great deal of pity. At first she thought their pity was related to her loss but, after a while, it dawned on her that it was, in fact, a form of commiseration for what she had been obliged to endure during Cora's lifetime. It had never occurred to her that anyone would understand her ongoing predicament.

She experienced a mixture of gratitude and shame when they tentatively commiserated about how much she must miss her mother, how quiet the house must seem without her. Even the genteel Misses Turpin looked at her with unguarded sympathy. And it *was* quiet but it was a quietness which, to start with, Thelma welcomed. However, once she had disposed of Cora's clothes, given her blankets and sheets to the Salvation Army and forced herself to clean Leslie's room, time hung heavily on her hands.

At night she suffered pangs of conscience when she remembered the ridiculous plots she had conjured up in order to see Cora off, and she sometimes wondered whether she had actually committed the crime. At these times she longed to talk to Leslie and, yes, to have his scrawny arms encircle her while he uttered words of comfort.

She got up one morning having made a firm decision - probably the only one she had ever made in her entire life: she would sell the house. After all, she told herself, a three bedroom house plus an attic room was too big for one person. It would be much better to move somewhere smaller and have a nice little nest egg to stow away in the Bank.

Several months later, one sunny August day in 1962, Thelma closed the front door of Number Seven for the last time. She stood for a couple of minutes on the doorstep, her suitcase at her feet. Would she regret her decision? She shook her head, picked up her case then went out to the waiting taxi. Her destination: Portsmouth.

*****

THE SWINGING SIXTIES

My next occupants didn't move in until the end of 1963 by which time my garden was completely overgrown. Daisy's beloved flowerbed was covered with weeds, and brambles had sprung up between the raspberry and gooseberry bushes. The Toplin's move had been delayed due to their sale in North London falling through at the last minute.

Mark Toplin worked in London and as there was a direct train service to Victoria, the family decided to settle by the sea. Mark's wife Sandra was a stay-at-home housewife, their son Robert would be starting college in the autumn, daughter Vicky was coming up for her 'O' Levels while four-year-old Amanda was due to begin school in September.

1963 proved to be the worst winter for nearly twenty years, with snow piled up by the kerbs until April. The youth of the country exploded into life with adolescents being renamed teenagers; pop stars and boy bands were venerated with the Beatles topping the charts; June saw the first woman to go into Space and the Profumo scandal hit the headlines. Even more shocking was President Jack Kennedy's assassination in November.

Things changed in the town too with the opening of a new swimming pool and a Ten Pin Bowling Alley. On the downside the Rivoli Cinema was destroyed by fire and seaweed, floating in from further along the coast, covered the beach causing an environmental problem.

Before moving in, Mark and Sandra discussed the renovations needed. Fourteen-year-old Vicky came up with suggestions but sixteen-year-old Robert was too busy sulking because he was going to miss his girlfriend. By common consensus, it was agreed that the Stokes' little green bird wallpaper would have to go and Mark said he would get in a builder to remove the dining-room fireplace. Both bathroom and kitchen would need renovating.

'A yellow bathroom suite, I think,' said Sandra, her brow wrinkled and a pensive look on her face as she imagined the finished result. 'Dark blue tiles are the 'in' thing these days. As for the kitchen, farmhouse style with a breakfast bar. The walls would look nice in cream with bright orange curtains at the window.'

Sandra liked bright colours and this penchant for colour reflected the Toplin family's relationship. They laughed a lot, played cheerful music and even owned a colour television set. By and large, it looked as if I could look forward to a rosy future.

SEVENTEEN

'I'm so happy we found this house,' said Sandra, snuggling her wavy red mane against Mark's shoulder when they went to bed for the first time in their new home.

'I like it too,' replied Mark, 'but I hope the kids settle down in their new schools.'

'Robert is the only question mark but I think he'll soon get over Cindy and find another girlfriend.'

'Let's hope so,' said Mark turning away to switch off the bedside lamp.

Mark had taken two weeks holiday in order to supervise the removal of the dining-room fireplace. He started decorating the attic room at the top of the house, which was going to be his study. Sandra had argued that it was better to start from the bottom and work up but Mark was adamant. Their three-bedroom house in Pinner had not allowed him the luxury of a place of his own in which to hide away and make his model aeroplanes. Trying to fashion such intricate models in the living room had always frustrated him. Come meal-times and Sandra would order him to clear away his mess so that she could lay the table.

Sandra liked to call herself the proverbial earth-mother. 'I love staying at home and looking after the family,' she said when any of her more career-minded friends asked her why she didn't get bored. 'Bored? Not me. I love cooking and there's always my needlework and knitting. Besides,

Mark hasn't got time to look after the garden. That task falls to me.'

She hadn't worked since Robert was born and, in truth, after all this time she wouldn't have felt comfortable catching up with all the latest office equipment: electric typewriters and such like. She had great plans for the garden, spending her evenings sketching out designs for additional flowerbeds and, of course, a patio where they could eat outside during the summer.

Her red hair was frequently tossed over her shoulder and her bright blue eyes were forever flashing with enthusiasm. Mark always said that the old axiom 'the eyes are the windows to the soul' was certainly true in Sandra's case. He was a past master at reading her thoughts.

By contrast, he was easy-going although when roused, his anger could be intimidating. In company, he liked to take a back seat and let his wife take the limelight. Not that Mark was overly reserved or ineffectual. When it came to important issues, he would take charge. He was a tall man with dark hair and eyes. Keen on sport, he was determined to join the local cricket club and become a member of the golf club as soon as work allowed.

By mid-August most of the building work, except for some additional decorating, was finished and the family were able to enjoy the rest of the children's school holiday by spending time on the beach and taking long walks on the Downs. Robert often missed out on these activities, saying that he'd rather go to the swimming baths or try out his new roller skates along the promenade.

'We ought to get a dog,' said Sandra on one such countryside walk. 'It would be lovely to have a cocker spaniel or a Yorkshire terrier.'

'And who would take it for walks? Mark asked.

'I would.'

'I would.'

Both his daughters volunteered but he laughed and shook his head. 'You,' he said, pointing at Amanda, 'are too little to take a dog for a walk on your own, and you...' He swung his pointed finger in Vicky's direction, '...wouldn't have time because you've got to concentrate on your schoolwork.'

'*I* could walk it,' chirped up Sandra.

Mark waved her offer away. 'No, darling, no dog - end of story.'

Of course, it wasn't the end because Sandra chipped away at his refusal until, for the sake of peace, Mark gave in and they went along to the Animal Rescue Shelter and came home with a mixed breed terrier. The children agreed to call him Patch because he was predominantly black with just a small white patch on his nose.

By October, the Toplins had settled into their new home. Mark had got used to his daily commute to London; Robert had forgotten about Cindy since meeting a girl at college; Vicky had made friends at her comprehensive and Amanda had taken to primary school like a duck to water.

This left Sandra with time on her hands since despite her claim that she had plenty to do - and she did - she missed her Pinner friends. Most of those who were following a career only worked part-time so she had frequently met up with them. Here she knew nobody. The neighbours on one side were out at work all day and, on the other side, there was an old widow living alone. Being of a friendly nature, Sandra decided to call on her and introduce herself. It took a long time for the woman to open the door.

'Yes?' Her greeting didn't sound encouraging.

'We've recently moved in next door and I just wanted to say "Hello" but if this is an inconvenient time...'

'I know you moved in.'

Sandra put out her hand to shake. 'I'm Sandra Toplin.'

'Are you?' This didn't seem to be going too well.

'I thought it might be nice if you came in for a cup of tea one afternoon so that we could get to know one another.'

'I don't know about that...' came the grunted reply.

'Oh well, I'd better leave you in peace.' Sandra turned to go.

'Just a minute, could you wait while I put my teeth in?'

Sandra nodded. So that was the reason why the old dear was reluctant to engage in conversation. A few minutes later she came back, having removed her apron and combed her hair as well as putting in her false teeth.

'My apologies,' she said, 'you took me by surprise; no one ever calls on me these days.'

'I'm sorry to hear that,' said Sandra, her blue eyes full of sympathy, 'haven't you got any family?'

'They've all moved away.'

There was no answer to that so Sandra repeated her invitation for tea and this time, it was accepted. The following day, the good lady appeared on her doorstep at three o'clock precisely, smartly dressed in a navy skirt and white blouse with a hand-knitted Fair Isle cardigan over it. The latter gave Sandra the lead into conversation - not that Sandra was ever at a loss for words - as knitting was clearly a mutual pastime.

'I love your cardigan, Mrs Maybridge.' She had learnt her neighbour's name by now. 'What a delightful mix of colours! Did you knit it yourself?'

Mrs Maybridge plucked at the cardigan's sleeve. 'As a matter of fact, I did.'

'I love to knit. Perhaps you could lend me the pattern some time.'

'Of course, dear...'

They talked about many things with Sandra asking her neighbour to let her know if the children or the dog were too noisy. 'I would hate them to disturb you,' she said.

'To tell you the truth, I miss hearing children playing,' Mrs Maybridge replied, 'my last neighbours were very noisy but not in a good way. They were always quarrelling.'

'Oh dear...!' Sandra furrowed her brow in sympathy. A slip of the tongue by the young woman from the Estate Agents when they were being shown around the house had already revealed that the previous owners had, by all accounts, been difficult people.

Mrs Maybridge chatted on about how nice the town was, how convenient it was having the shops just up the road and about the favourable climate.

'It's much warmer down here than where I used to live,' she told Sandra. 'You see, I come from up north and they can have bitter winters. Here, it seldom snows.'

Sandra laughed. 'Don't tell that to my children.'

The removal of the fireplace made the dining-room seem much bigger and now that the plaster had dried, Sandra was impatient to get the room decorated. The old carpet had been pulled up and it was while she was sweeping the wooden floorboards beneath that Vicky found a little key.

'Look, Mum, isn't it dinky?' she cried. 'It's got a fancy edge and a little flower thing in the middle. Can I keep it?'

'You may as well but I don't think it will be much use to you,' replied her mother.

Vicky held it up between finger and thumb. 'It's really sweet,' she said, 'I wonder what it opens.'

'It must be something really small.'

'I shall try every lock in the house until I find one it fits.'

It didn't take long for the matching lock to come to light. The following day her father started stripping off the Stokes' green bird wallpaper, revealing the secret cupboard Jack had fashioned for Daisy.

'Well I never, it actually fits,' said Mark, 'shall we open it?'

'Let me!' cried Vicky, hopping up and down with excitement. Her little sister immediately joined in, crying, 'It isn't fair, I want to do it.'

'Well, Amanda,' said their mother, 'Vicky was the one who found it so I think she should open it.'

They all stood watching while Vicky tried the key. The little door swung open, it's hinges as functional now as they had been in Daisy's day.

'What's inside?' burst out Amanda, pulling at her big sister's sleeve.

'Give me a chance to find out.'

Vicky put her hand into the cupboard and drew out a small notebook.

'Let me see?' Her mother wanted to make sure it didn't contain anything unsuitable for her daughter to read. 'Why, it's some sort of a diary.' She flicked through the pages. 'I don't think you'll find anything very interesting in it, Vicky.'

Nobody noticed the folded sheet of paper that had fallen out of the back of it. Vicky all but snatched the notebook from her mother's hand. Turning tail, she bolted upstairs to her bedroom, leaving Amanda howling that it wasn't fair.

She threw herself onto her bed, stomach down and resting her elbows on the pillow, opened the notebook. The first page bore a name: Hetty Parker and underneath in brackets (née H-Bonneville). Vicky turned to the next page which described the walks the writer had taken along the seafront. It wasn't until she got further in that she realised her mother had missed something. The diary was the account of a love affair and Vicky's teenage eyes widened as she read the passionate language filling the pages.

At one point she rolled onto her back and held the notebook at arms-length, repeating aloud Hetty's loving sentiments. She lowered the notebook musing that Freddie Egan wasn't a very romantic name. *She* wouldn't have settled for anything less than say, Fitzwilliam Darcy or Edward Fairfax Rochester - she was studying Jane Austen and the Brontës at school. Even Rhett Butler would be better - her mother had dragged her to see a showing of *Gone with the Wind* only a week or two ago. She had tried to wriggle out of it but by the time the film ended, she had quite fallen for Clark Gable. She read through almost the entire diary but when she got to the part where Freddie reveals that he favoured the politics of a politician called Mosley, she felt puzzled.

That evening at dinner, she asked her father. 'Dad, who's Oswald Mosley?'

'Why on earth do you want to know that?'

Vicky shrugged. 'Just interested...'

Her father went on to explain that just before the Second World War Mosley had tried to form a fascist party but ended up in prison because favouring fascism was tantamount to being a traitor.

'Were the British fascists friendly with Hitler?' she asked. She knew a little about the War from lessons at school.

'Yes, and of course, we had to put a stop to it.'

Robert poked a forkful of sausage into his mouth and said, 'Why are you interested in all that rubbish?'

'Don't talk with your mouth full, Robert,' reprimanded Sandra.

He swallowed a large chunk and asked the question again.

'I heard someone mention it and I was curious, that's all,' replied his sister.

But Vicky's curiosity had been aroused. She read on, learning that shortly after Freddie's revelation, poor Hetty broke up with him. No wonder she was heartbroken: her lover was a traitor, an enemy of the country. She flicked through the pages again and was surprised when a folded sheet of paper dropped out. It had somehow become stuck to the inside of the back cover of the notebook. She smoothed it out and saw that it was a charcoal sketch of a man. The charcoal had smudged a bit but she could still see that he was young and good-looking. With a deep sigh, she dropped the picture to her lap. So this was the man Hetty was head-over-heels in love with. What a pity, there wasn't a picture of Hetty too! Vicky's eyes glazed over as she conjured up the image of a beautiful heroine struggling between love and patriotism.

That night she couldn't sleep. Thoughts about Hetty whirled round and round her head until, in the early hours, she made a decision: she would do all she could to find out what had happened to Hetty. Was she still alive? Of course, she would be a very old lady by now but perhaps she went on to find a new love. Without telling her parents, she went to the library, spending time in the Reference Department looking up old records. She became such a frequent visitor that the librarians began to acknowledge her and when she summoned up enough courage to ask for help, one of the ladies promised to see what she could find out.

EIGHTEEN

'I'm off to the library, Mum.'

'Again? Make sure you're back in time for tea Vicky, and don't forget you've got to do some studying. You can't get away with it just because it's half-term.'

'Okay, Mum.'

Sandra heard the front door slam and paused in the middle of the letter she was writing. Why was her daughter, who generally loved to spend her spare time out of doors, so interested in going to the library? She had never been a bookworm. Could her fourteen-year-old have a boyfriend? Sandra shrugged off that possibility; so far Vicky had shown no interest in the opposite sex, she was too keen on tennis and netball. And, unlike her brother, Robert, who was nearly always top of his class and had a university place in his sights, Vicky needed to be goaded into studying for her 'O' Levels.

Vicky ran along the road to the library. She ran everywhere; in her eyes walking was akin to loitering. The lady at the check-in greeted her.

'Hello again, have you finished that book already?'

'No,' replied Vicky, 'I'm only half way through it.' In truth, she had only taken out the book to justify her frequent visits to the library. 'Can I go up to the Reference Department?'

'Yes of course.'

She made straight for the woman at the desk who was bent over the task of repairing the cover of a book.

'Hello, Miss Pelling,' she said.

Miss Pelling looked up. 'Shh! You're supposed to talk quietly up here.'

'Sorry,' giggled Vicky.

Beckoning her closer to the desk, the librarian smiled and said kindly, 'I've found out a little about your Hetty.'

Vicky's eyes lit up expectantly.

'It's not very much I'm afraid. The name Hetty Parker threw up nothing but the surname Bonneville is listed in *Who's Who*. Hetty could be short for Henrietta and you'll never guess, I came up with someone called Henrietta Bonneville.'

'Could that be her?' Vicky could hardly contain her excitement.

'I'm not sure. What puzzles me is the reference to H-Bonneville in the notebook.'

'Could that be Henrietta?'

'I suppose it could be, although there is another possibility.'

'Yes?' Now Vicky was agog with excitement.

'I had a flash of inspiration...' smiled Miss Pelling, '...I started looking through the double-barrelled names and low and behold, I found this reference.'

She twisted the book in front of her to face Vicky and pointed to an entry.

'Henrietta Hastings-Bonneville!' squealed Vicky.

Miss Pelling put a finger to her lips and gave her a warning look. 'I thought you'd be pleased. Tomorrow, I'll do some more research now I've got the full name. Come back in a couple of days' time.'

Vicky left the library and ran all the way home. She was on cloud nine and once indoors, she raced straight upstairs to her room to take another look at the contents of the notebook.

'Tea's ready, Vicky.'

Her mother's voice reached her from the bottom of the stairs.

'Coming, Mum.'

Putting the notebook in the top drawer of her desk, she went downstairs. 'Where have you been, Vicky?' demanded Amanda. 'You promised to play doctors and nurses with me this afternoon.'

'Sorry, I forgot, I'll play with you tomorrow.'

'I shall be the nurse and you'll be the patient,' said Amanda firmly.

'Whatever you say...'

Sandra looked at her eldest daughter with surprise. Usually, she wasn't so obliging with Amanda. 'Did you get a book out of the library?' she asked.

'Erm, yes,' came Vicky's non-committal reply.

For Vicky, the next two days seemed to drag although she had plenty of revision to do. She would sit at her desk facing the window and after reading a couple of paragraphs from her history textbook, her gaze would be drawn to the gently swaying trees in the garden and she would think about Hetty Parker. On the second afternoon, Sandra allowed her out to play rounders with her friends on the green near the beach.

The next day, she couldn't wait to get to the library but she was destined for disappointment. It transpired that Miss Pelling was off sick.

'When will she be back?' asked Vicky.

'I'm afraid I don't know. She's got a chest infection and it could take some time to clear up.'

Vicky felt close to tears. She knew Miss Pelling with her grey hair and wrinkled neck was old, at least seventy, although that wouldn't make sense because at that age she wouldn't still be employed by the library. She dawdled home and, once again, went straight upstairs to her room.

Sandra was in the kitchen and she heard the front door open and close. She also heard her daughter stomp upstairs instead of racing up two at a time. Rinsing flour from her hands, she abandoned the pastry she was rolling out and went up to Vicky's room.

Vicky didn't answer when she knocked at her door. She knocked again and said, 'Can I come in?'

'If you want to.'

Sandra went in and found her daughter curled up on the bed. She went to sit down next to her. 'What's the matter, Vicky?'

'Nothing.'

'I know when something's wrong; tell me what it is.'

All at once, Vicky felt the compulsion to confide in her mother. Jumping up from the bed, she fetched the diary.

'You've still got it!' exclaimed Sandra.

'Yes, it's not what you think.'

'What d'you mean?'

She opened the book and pointed out the name at the beginning then flicked through until she came to the very last page. Very deliberately she read out Hetty's words: 'I can't bear to stay here any longer. Walter is better off without me, the twins are independent. I won't be missed...'

Sandra was horrified. 'Is this a suicide note?' she gasped.

'Suicide?' Vicky shook her head. 'Oh no, Hetty wasn't going to commit suicide. Listen to the rest...' She went back to the notebook. 'I'm going to sign up as an ambulance driver for war duties. I'm going to play my part. Freddie is a traitor so I must compensate for his actions.'

'Who's Freddie?' Sandra was intrigued now.

Vicky proceeded to give her mother a garbled account of what the diary had revealed. 'You see, Mum,' she said, 'Freddie was involved with the fascist movement; that's why Hetty stopped seeing him, even though it broke her heart.'

'What a romantic story!' Sandra whispered when she had finished. 'And now I understand why you've been going to the library. What have you found out?'

Vicky explained about Miss Pelling being ill and her worry that perhaps she wouldn't come back to work.

'I expect she will. Listen, darling, next week you'll be back at school but we'll go down to the library on Saturday and try and find out more. No wonder you're interested and now you've got me hooked too.'

She went to leave the room then remembered the sheet of paper that had slipped out of the diary when Vicky had found it. Without paying much attention, she had picked it up and shoved it among some papers stacked on a shelf in the kitchen. Was it still there?

'What is it, Mum?' Vicky followed her downstairs.

'Look!' Sandra triumphantly handed it to her daughter. 'I think it's a portrait of Hetty.'

Miss Pelling was off sick for several weeks and Vicky began to despair that she would ever find out about Hetty. But when she returned she had some news.

Mother and daughter went to see her together. Vicky introduced her mother.

'I'm sorry to have kept you waiting for so long, Vicky,' said Miss Pelling, 'but while I was at home I made some enquiries and you are going to be surprised when you hear what I've found out.'

Vicky could hardly keep still and Sandra was hanging on the librarian's every word.

'Well, it transpires that your Henrietta Hastings-Bonneville was a brave lady.'

'Was?'

'Yes, sadly she's no longer with us; she died in 1944. After Dunkirk, she volunteered as an ambulance driver serving abroad. Apparently, she died in France although the exact circumstances are unclear...' Miss Pelling's words petered out, prompting Sandra to suspect that she was holding something back.

She gave the librarian a searching look but Miss Pelling wasn't forthcoming.

'What a shame,' said Vicky, sniffing into a tissue, 'I was hoping we could get in touch with her.'

Sandra put her arm around her daughter's shoulders and gave her a gentle hug. Then she said, 'I remember reading something about her a long time ago but I didn't take much notice.' She sighed. 'What an interesting story, to think that Henrietta Hastings-Bonneville used to live in our house!'

Vicky smothered a sob, making Sandra realise how much her daughter had become attached to Hetty and her story. 'Mum, show Miss Pelling Hetty's picture,' she whispered.

Miss Pelling adjusted her glasses and studied the faded charcoal drawing. 'Where did you find this?' she asked.

Sandra explained how it had fallen out of the notebook and been put away among some other papers.

Miss Pelling smiled. 'Well,' she said, 'that *is* a find. It's faded but you can see what a beautiful woman Hetty was. If you're interested, I daresay you will be able to get hold of a copy of her Obituary now that you have all the details.' Handing back the diary and the portrait, she added, 'You've got a piece of history there, Vicky my dear, treasure it.'

NINETEEN

Although Hetty's story was no longer a mystery, Sandra wanted to know more. Without telling Vicky, she got in touch with a company who specialised in storing old newspapers. Miss Pelling had provided them with the date of Hetty's death and it wasn't difficult to trace the newspaper in which her obituary had appeared. A copy of the paper dated 30th June 1944 arrived several days later.

Sandra couldn't wait to open the package. And there it was: Henrietta Hastings-Bonneville's Obituary. She read it eagerly.

"IN LOVING MEMORY OF
HENRIETTA PARKER
(NÉE HENRIETTA HASTINGS-BONNEVILLE)

Henrietta Parker, known as Hetty was born in France on 11th August 1902 and died in Brittany on 19th June 1944. Her parents, Brigadier Bernard Bonneville and Ellen Hastings were British. Henrietta was the eldest of three siblings, having a brother Paul and a sister Sybil. Married to Walter Parker in 1921, she was mother to twin daughters, Patricia and Paula.

In 1940 Hetty Parker left her home on the South Coast to volunteer as an army ambulance driver. The following year she was recruited as an agent when it was discovered that she was a fluent French speaker with a working knowledge of German. Because of her familiarity with the Brittany landscape, she was frequently parachuted into that territory by the RAF. During her time as an agent Hetty constantly put her own life in danger while helping British soldiers and airmen escape from the Gestapo and French collaborators. In June 1944, just prior to the Normandy Landing, she was caught by the Germans while escorting escapees through a Brittany forest. She died by firing squad the following day.

Henrietta Parker has been recognised posthumously by the British and French Governments for services to both countries during WWII. She is survived by her two daughters."

There was also a photograph which portrayed an older Hetty, a Hetty who had seen too much bloodshed.

When Vicky arrived home from school that day, Sandra had to suppress the urge to tell her about the find right-away. But the exams were imminent and she decided to wait until they were over. When Mark got home, she told him about it but he didn't seem very interested and she let the subject drop. It was another two weeks before she was able to break the news to Vicky.

'Darling, you remember that information Miss Pelling kindly found out about Hetty Bonneville, well I've delved further into it and look what I've discovered?'

She produced the yellowing newspaper to show her daughter.

'Wow Mum, that was clever of you.'

Vicky spread the broadsheet out on the dining-room table and scrutinised the fading print. 'Crikey, look at this Mum, Hetty was a heroine, a wartime spy and look...' She pointed a finger at the bottom line, '...Hetty's daughters are still alive, why don't we get in touch with them?'

This possibility had not occurred to Sandra and, instinctively, she held up her hands in rejection. 'I don't think we should do that, dear.'

'But Mum, wouldn't it be cool to actually talk to someone who knew Hetty.'

'Let's not be hasty, Vicky, they may not like our interference...' Sandra clenched her hands together. '...and besides, we don't have their address or addresses. They are probably both married so they won't have the same surname.'

Vicky looked disappointed. 'I didn't think of that.'

Despite her wise words to Vicky, Sandra couldn't stop thinking about Hetty's family. By rights, the diary belonged to them as next of kin but if she managed to trace one of the daughters, would Vicky be willing to relinquish her find? She fretted about what to do for several weeks until, one day, finding herself in the library she went up to the Reference Department to look through the telephone directories from various parts of the country. There was no harm in looking and the possibility of locating either Patricia or Paula Parker was so remote as to alleviate her conscience.

She started with local areas first and found there were quite a number of "Parkers". Then she moved on to outer London and there she found a Paula Parker listed. She made a note of the number and went home.

Now she had a further dilemma: should she tell Vicky before or after telephoning the number, or indeed, should she telephone the number at all? In the end, unable to let it go, she took the plunge one afternoon while Vicky was at school.

The phone rang several times and she was on the point of replacing the receiver when a woman answered.

'Hello,' she reeled off the number.

'Hello,' said Sandra, finding to her surprise that her heart was beating rapidly and her throat had gone quite dry. 'Can I speak to Ms Paula Parker please?'

'Speaking...'

'Hmm...' Sandra cleared her throat. 'Forgive me for asking, but did you once live at Number Seven...'

She didn't finish the sentence because the other woman interrupted her. 'Yes...but who are you?'

Sandra went on to explain that she now lived there and had discovered the Parkers had been former residents.

'My father sold the house to a mother and daughter. Let me think, the mother's name was Cora something or other, would that be you?'

'No, my name's Sandra Toplin and I live here with my husband and children.'

'I thought you couldn't be Cora because she was quite elderly and you sound young but...' There was a pause. '...may I ask why you are phoning me?'

It all came out then: Vicky finding the diary, the search through library records and the discovery that Hetty Parker had been a heroine.

'Oh my goodness, to tell the truth after Patsy and I left home we seldom went back. Once Mummy left, we occasionally visited Dad...' Again she paused. '...actually I still feel a little guilty about Daddy.'

Did Sandra detect a sob in Paula's voice? All at once she too felt guilty. If the daughters didn't know about the diary, the likelihood was that they didn't know about their mother's affair with Freddie Egan. By showing them the diary she would be letting the cat out of the bag.

'I hope I haven't upset you,' she said 'I wasn't sure what to do. Look, forget I rang.'

'Don't go!'

Sandra bit her lip, wishing she hadn't made the phone call.

Paula started speaking again. 'What did you say your name was?'

'Sandra Toplin, I live at...' She stopped realising that, of course, Paula knew exactly where she lived.

'Look, I'd like to get in touch with my sister and then perhaps we could come and visit you.'

Things were getting out of control. 'Yes...' Sandra replied hesitantly.

'It would be at your convenience of course.'

The warmth in Paula's voice convinced Sandra. 'Yes, of course you can come. We'd love to meet you. My daughter and I were so impressed by your mother's heroism. You must be proud of her.'

The visit was arranged for the following Saturday. Robert said he would be out with friends and Mark promised to take Amanda and Patch to the park so that Sandra and Vicky could greet their visitors on their own. At three o'clock, they were both on tenterhooks as they waited for the doorbell to ring.

'Suppose they don't come, Mum,' said Vicky anxiously.

'They will.' Sandra was confident although by three fifteen, she too was beginning to wonder whether the Parker sisters had changed their minds.

They turned up at twenty past, explaining that their train had been delayed. Paula introduced herself and her sister, who's married name was Stevenson.

'It was lucky that I was able to trace you through the name Parker,' said Sandra.

'Yes, if I'd kept my married name after my divorce you wouldn't have found me,' agreed Paula. 'You see, I reverted to Parker for business purposes.'

If they hadn't been dressed differently and hadn't worn different hairstyles, Sandra would not have been able to tell them apart. They sounded alike too and broke into one another's sentences, using the same gestures when they explained anything.

Sandra let Vicky make the tea while she broke the ice because she knew that her daughter was feeling shy.

'It was such a surprise to find out about your mother's exploits during the War,' she said, taking a seat opposite them. 'My daughter's search began as a bit of a schoolgirl lark but when I started looking into it with her, we realised that this was a piece of history.'

'I suppose it is,' said Paula.

Patsy leant forward eagerly. 'We can't wait to see the diary. I remember Mummy writing notes in that funny little notebook of hers but I didn't realise she was keeping a diary, did you, Paula?'

Her sister shook her head and Sandra experienced a frisson of apprehension. How would they feel after reading it?

Patsy spoke again. 'If you're worried about some shady goings-on coming to light, we already know about Mummy's affair. Actually, we were there when she met Freddie Egan or Uncle Freddie as we used to call him.'

Sandra's eyebrows shot up. 'So you knew him?'

At this point, Vicky came in carrying a tray of tea and biscuits. 'Knew who?' she asked.

'Paula and Patsy knew about their mother's affair all along.'

'That's cool!'

As the conversation progressed, it became clear to Sandra that Patsy was the more dominant twin. She laughed a lot and something told her that she was the daughter who most resembled her mother. Each sister skimmed through the diary in turn, Patsy with a smile of amusement, Paula looking perturbed. 'I didn't realise Mummy was so much in love with him,' she said.

Patsy frowned. 'Well, you know what Mummy was like: fun-loving and flirty. I'll never understand why she married Daddy.'

'There was nothing wrong with Daddy,' snapped Paula.

'I didn't say there was but you have to admit, he was a bit dull.'

'Just because he was quiet and liked reading doesn't make him dull.'

'Do you think he knew?'

'Of course he knew. And he must have known about Uncle Freddie being a fascist.'

'Why didn't he stop her seeing him then?' retorted Patsy.

Sandra began to feel uncomfortable and, changing the subject, asked, 'From her obituary, it seems your mother received posthumous awards, did you attend the ceremonies?'

'We did in England but neither of us was able to go to France for the French award.'

Sandra suddenly remembered the charcoal sketch of Hetty and went to fetch it. The twins scrutinised it eagerly. 'Fancy Mummy never showing us this portrait,' said Patsy. 'Was it with the diary?'

'Yes.'

Paula sighed, 'Mummy was very beautiful.'

Patsy laughed. 'What a pity she didn't pass her good looks on to us!'

Sandra wanted to contradict her but thought better of it. As regards looks, the twins were well endowed but, by all accounts, their vivacious mother had outshone them. She recalled the sketch of Freddie but instinctively felt that it would be better not to mention it.

Vicky had kept quiet for most of the afternoon and Sandra couldn't help noticing that her daughter's gaze was constantly drawn to the diary as it was passed from twin to twin. *She's realised that she will probably have to part with it,* thought Sandra, dreading the moment when either Patsy or Paula would ask to keep it.

At half past four, Mark and Amanda returned. Patch bounded in and Sandra had to stop him from jumping all over their visitors. Amanda was fascinated by the identical twins and went to sit between them on the sofa.

'I have a daughter called Amanda,' said Patsy.'

Amanda jumped to her feet and waved her arms, bursting out, 'Is she the same age as me? I'm nearly six.'

'My Amanda is grown-up and has a family of her own,' revealed Patsy, giving Sandra to understand that the twins must be a little older than she was.

Mark greeted them politely before excusing himself by saying he had to fix a broken fence panel in the back garden.

'Down, Patch, down!' ordered Sandra when Patch started getting a bit excited again.

'We never had a dog,' said Patsy, 'but we had a cat called Mimi. Do you remember her, Paula?'

Paula chuckled. 'She was so sweet and we had a job persuading Daddy to let us keep her, but I suppose you couldn't blame him; after all he was allergic to cats.'

'I wonder what happened to Mimi after Mummy left.'

'I suppose Daddy gave her away. I'm sure he didn't take her with him when he moved.'

Mention of their father gave Sandra a jolt. 'Is your father still alive?' she asked.

'No, daddy died a long time ago. He was a heavy smoker and suffered from emphysema.'

'I'm sorry.'

Patsy explained, 'We wanted him to come and live near one of us but he refused saying he preferred to live by the sea. He sold the house and rented a flat so that he could give us each enough money for a deposit on a property. It was very generous of him.'

'Indeed it was,' agreed Sandra.

This conversation reminded Sandra that Number Seven had once been home to Patsy and Paula. 'Would you like to have a look round?' she said.

'Yes please. I expect you've made quite a lot of alterations since our time here,' said Paula.

Sandra led them upstairs and showed them the en-suite shower room they had added to the main bedroom. She explained that the attic box room was now Mark's study. It was five o'clock by the time she had shown them the rest of the downstairs and proudly escorted them into the garden, which she had so painstakingly re-landscaped.

'The garden's lovely and I think you've made the house look very nice too,' said Patsy, and Paula agreed.

The conducted tour completed, they all went back indoors and Sandra watched as Patsy picked up the diary from the coffee table. Vicky's gaze was fixed on her and, for a dreadful moment, she was afraid her daughter would try to snatch it back. She needn't have worried.

With Paula nodding in agreement, Patsy said, 'Sandra, we would like to take that sketch of Mummy but we think Vicky should keep the diary because, after all, *we* know our mother's history, but it was your daughter who found this.' She handed the diary to Vicky. 'Please take care of it for us.'

Vicky's eyes lit up. Losing her shyness, she threw her arms around Patsy's neck and then around Paula's. 'Thank you so much,' she cried.

TWENTY

Mark and Sandra had always harboured great hopes for Robert. He was a smart boy, had no trouble with his studies and was more than capable on the sports field. He was also popular with his peers and once he had got over leaving Cindy, Sandra saw a succession of his girlfriends pass through Number Seven.

He had passed his 'O' Levels with flying colours and was now studying for his 'A' Levels but Sandra had begun to notice a change in him. He no longer seemed motivated, rarely communicated with his family and cleverly avoided any questions about his studies. He started staying out later than the agreed curfew time, and at home he locked himself away in his bedroom playing recordings of the Rolling Stones or the Beach Boys loud enough to drown out the television.

One evening Mark lost his temper and stormed upstairs to his son's room. From downstairs, Sandra could hear every word of their altercation, their voices raised above the music. When it was suddenly switched off, the row between father and son was even more audible.

'What's the matter with you, Robert, don't you realise that racket can be heard halfway down the street?'

'It didn't sound all that loud to me.'

'What about your studies?'

'I *was* studying, Dad…'

'You can't study and listen to music at the same time.' Mark pointed at a sheet of paper his son had hastily shoved under his exercise book. 'And what's that?'

'Nothing Dad.'

'Let me see.'

Before Robert could stop him, Mark had snatched the paper from off the desk. 'Another bloody drawing,' he said, tearing it into two pieces.

'Don't Dad.'

'You should be studying not doodling.'

'I'm not doodling, I'm drawing.'

'Well, no more drawing until you've passed your exams, d'you hear me?'

Robert muttered something almost incoherent. His father frowned. 'Mind your tongue!'

Sandra could picture the two of them facing one another in Robert's small bedroom. At eighteen, the boy was already taller than his father and strong too. If it came to fisticuffs she knew who would win.

'Music helps me study,' Robert's voice was petulant.

'Not any more. Keep it switched off for the rest of the evening and get your head down over those books. If you switch it on again, I'll confiscate it.'

Sandra didn't catch Robert's reply as Mark came stomping downstairs, anger clouding his brow.

'What's the matter with that boy,' he ranted, '...doesn't he want to do well? He won't get a place at uni if he doesn't study.'

Sandra tried to placate Mark. 'He's just going through a teenage phase, darling. Keeping on at him will only make things worse.'

'He deserves a good thrashing. My father wouldn't have stood for me answering back like that.'

Sandra could remember Mark's father, a formidable figure trapped in a Victorian mindset. She knew her husband had not had a very happy childhood, unlike her own which had been wonderfully easygoing.

But Mark's tough stand did the trick and by 1966 Robert had passed his 'A' Levels with adequate grades although they didn't show the potential his 'O' Level results had shown. Sandra got ready to drive him to various universities so that he could decide which ones he would apply to. Thus it was a shock for her when, one Saturday afternoon, she came home from a shopping spree in Marks and Spencers to find Mark and Robert sitting in front of the television with glowering expressions on their faces.

'What's up?' she asked, dumping her shopping bag down on the floor, her intention to show Mark her purchases forgotten.

'Ask him,' snapped Mark.

Sandra turned to her son. 'Well, what's happened?'

'Nothing...'

'Don't grunt at your mother like that.'

In response to his father's reprimand, Robert got up and stormed out of the room.

'Come back here!' shouted Mark, also getting to his feet.

But it was too late. Before he could reach the hall, the front door slammed shut.

Feeling deflated after the high she had been on after the shopping spree, Sandra sank down onto the sofa. 'You'd better tell me what's going on,' she said.

Mark's features were taut with anger. 'He's doesn't want to go to university, that's what's going on.'

'Doesn't want to go?' repeated Sandra.

'That's what I said,' snapped Mark.

'But that doesn't make sense...'

'No, it *doesn't* make sense.'

'Mark, for goodness sake, explain...'

'He wants to go travelling.'

Sandra let out a sigh of relief. In her mind's eye she saw a much worse scenario: drugs or crime or Robert getting a girlfriend pregnant.

'What's wrong with that? He can always take up his university place when he gets back, after all they're crying out for engineering students and, besides, lots of young people take a gap year.'

'He doesn't want to be an engineer.'

'Well, I expect his grades are good enough to let him switch courses.'

Mark was so red-faced that Sandra was afraid he'd have a heart attack. 'Calm down,' she said, 'this is only a passing phase; he'll come to his senses.'

'He wants to be an artist.' Mark enunciated each syllable.

'What?' For a moment Sandra was astonished then she remembered the number of times she had seen her son busily sketching and she had to admit that he was rather good.'

'Sandra, he's serious. He says he wants to go to Australia to gain some life experience and build up a portfolio, I ask you!'

'I'll put the kettle on.' Sandra stood up and went into the kitchen.

'Weren't you listening, Sandra?' said Mark following her.

'Yes, I heard every word but he's only young.' She switched on the kettle and went on, 'Did you know what you wanted to do at eighteen?'

'He's nearly nineteen,' Mark corrected her, 'and yes, I *did* know what I wanted to do when I was his age.'

'Leave it to me, I'll talk to him,' said Sandra, planting a kiss on her husband's cheek.

Mark turned away abruptly and went back to sink into an armchair in front of the television to watch the football results.

In actual fact, Sandra wasn't as confident as she appeared. She knew how obstinate Robert could be once he got an idea in his head. She recalled the fights they'd had about getting his hair cut and the occasion when Mark had nearly hit the roof when his son had come home wearing a pair of doc martens, saved up for with his paper round money. She decided to leave it until the following day to approach him.

The next morning as soon as she heard movement coming from his room, she went to knock at the door. 'Robert, can I come in?'

'There's nothing stopping you.'

'I know that but I won't come in if you don't want me to.'

'Come in, Mum.'

She found him sitting at his desk looking through a pile of travel brochures.

'If this is what you've come to talk to me about, you can forget it,' he said, planting his hand firmly on the top of the pile.

'Well...you did give your father and me a bit of a surprise. We thought you were all set to go to uni. What changed your mind?'

He swivelled round and reached for her hand. 'Look, Mum, I like studying and I've worked hard but engineering isn't what I want to do.'

'What *do* you want?'

He looked somewhat sheepish and said, 'I want to be an artist. Please don't laugh.'

'I'm not laughing.'

'Dad laughed; he made me feel like an idiot. What's wrong with being an artist?'

'Nothing, darling but it's an uncertain career whereas engineering could bring in good money.'

He wrinkled his brow. 'I know, but I must give it a try.'

'Why not get your university degree first then...'

Robert shook his head. 'I've made up my mind. I've already booked my flight to Sydney.'

'You've what?'

'I didn't take the decision lightly, Mum,' he said earnestly.

'Where did you get the money?'

'I've been working, you know that and…'

'And what…?' Sandra was beginning to get worried.

'You know those premium bonds you took out for me when I was little? Well, as they were in my name, I've cashed them in. Please don't be angry. I don't want to leave home under a cloud.'

Sandra reached out and hugged her son. 'That won't happen, at least not from me. I would only ask one thing. Please keep your university place open so that if you change your mind, you can take it up next year. It's not much to ask, is it?'

Robert held his mother at arms-length and smiled down at her. 'For you, Mum, I'll do that.'

Robert departed a month later. Waved off by his disgruntled father and his tearful mother, he checked in at the airport, encumbered by an enormous rucksack. His intention was to backpack around Australia, working in bars and restaurants. It was going to be a great adventure and he was up for it.

During the journey his excitement grew and much as he tried to catnap he failed. In consequence, he was bleary eyed and had a thumping headache by the time he landed in Sydney the following afternoon. It was getting late and finding digs was of paramount importance and when a stranger offered to show him a respectable hostel, he readily agreed. It turned out to be in a back street but it looked all right: basic but clean.

Thinking how friendly the Aussies were, he thanked the man, paid for two nights and slumped down on the narrow bed without bothering to unpack. He slept for sixteen hours, waking up when he heard voices in the corridor. Getting up, he stumbled out of the room to look for the bathroom, which he had been told was halfway down the hall.

When he got back, he decided to change into some clean clothes and it was then that he noticed his rucksack was unfastened. He frowned, trying to remember whether he had opened it the night before. Concerned now, he emptied everything out. His clothes and washing accoutrements were all there. He delved into the side pockets. His passport was there and so was his visa but the wallet containing his Australian dollars was missing and so was the expensive camera he had saved up for with his dad providing the shortfall. He sank back onto his haunches: Robert Toplin had been conned on his first day in Oz.

Sandra rushed to greet the postman, who handed her an airmail envelope. She tore it open and started to read Robert's letter. It was cheerful and gave an account of his journey, clearly scribbled during the flight. Then the tone changed. He seemed a bit lost, said Australia was very expensive and money was tight. "*...but don't worry, Mum, I've already found a job.*" Feeling puzzled, Sandra dropped the letter to her lap. Before leaving, he had assured his parents that he had sufficient money to last at least two months before he needed to look for work as he intended to do some sightseeing first.

Sandra's intuition was seldom wrong and the more she thought about the letter - rereading it several times - the more convinced she was that something was not quite right. When she showed the letter to Mark he shrugged off her concerns.

'I expect he's decided to test the waters on the job front before striking out on his travels,' he said. 'That sounds sensible for once.'

For a while she was reassured but a second letter increased her concern when Robert confided that his beloved camera had been stolen. Sandra paced the floor, the letter screwed up in her hand. If only she could speak to him but so far he had not given them an accessible telephone number. The minute Mark came home from work, she spilt it all out.

'The young fool!' Mark was angry. 'How did he let that happen? Hasn't he learnt to look after his belongings yet?'

Sandra jumped to Robert's defence. 'Have a bit of sympathy,' she insisted, 'he's far away in a foreign country…'

'It's not as though they don't speak English over there, Sandra. Being in Oz is home from home for us Brits.'

Sandra lost her temper. 'I think you're being terribly unfair. He's only a lad, just out of school, give him a break.'

'Give him a break! I'd break his neck if he was here. That camera was top of the range, cost a fortune.'

'There's worse,' said Sandra quietly. 'He says he needs money, his earnings from bar work barely cover his food and accommodation.'

'Where's he staying for God's sake,' thundered Mark, 'in a five star hotel?'

Mark stomped upstairs to change from his work suit into jeans and a t-shirt, leaving Sandra close to tears. She gave a sniff, knowing that her husband would eventually calm down. In any case, she decided, she would despatch the necessary funds over to her son the very next day.

And so, with his mother's help, Robert was able to continue his tour of Australia but he had to cut his stay down to nine months instead of a year. Armed with a cheap instamatic, he hitch-hiked whenever he could, sometimes taking the Greyhound bus. But the incident taught him a lesson and he began to realise that, although up until now things had invariably gone his way, there was no guarantee that this would continue and he started to think seriously about taking up his university place.

But fate has a way of showing its face in extraordinary ways. During a ride on the Greyhound bus he met a girl from Wales, who was also on a gap year. They decided to continue travelling together. Her name was Bethan and she was due to start a Textile Design Course at Leeds University the following autumn. When she heard that he wanted to be an artist, she enthusiastically went into details about the course she was about to take.

'Have you done much drawing?' she asked him.

'I'm always sketching something or other.'

'Let me see some of your sketches.'

As the bus sped along the long straight road, Robert raked through his backpack and took out some of his more recent drawings. Heads touching, they poured over them together.

'These are really good, Robert,' she said, looking up at him, 'why don't you apply for a graphic design course?'

'I don't think my dad would take kindly to that idea.'

'Has he seen your drawings?'

Robert shook his head. 'I've shown them to Mum and Vicky but Dad isn't interested.'

Bethan got excited. 'You should apply to Leeds; that's where I'm going. It would be great, Robert, you'd love it.'

Robert couldn't help smiling as, in her eagerness, Bethan's Welsh accent became more and more pronounced.

'When I was looking to take an engineering degree Leeds didn't crop up but I suppose if I changed direction, I could apply.'

'Your grades are good enough; did you take A Level Art?' He nodded so she went on. 'Why don't you take a foundation art course first and if you do well, you can apply to Leeds next year? It would be great us being at the same university.'

Robert thought about this and persuaded by Bethan's enthusiasm, he wrote to his mother asking her to make enquiries. Her response was positive although he wasn't sure whether she had mentioned this to his father. He decided to wait and find out about that when he got home.

Nine months sped by and just before Christmas 1965, Robert kissed Bethan goodbye at the airport. He would be home for Christmas; she was due to fly home in the New Year. His parents were at Heathrow to meet him and he hoped his father would have mellowed during his time away. While they were in the airport concourse nothing was said but once the luggage was stashed in the boot of the car and he was sitting in the front passenger seat, his father brought up the subject of his change of direction.

'So you've definitely decided to switch courses?' said Mark as he manoeuvred the Audi into the correct lane. 'An art course...?'

In an endeavour to justify his decision Robert didn't choose his words very sensibly. 'Honestly, Dad, it'll be a blast,' he said.

His father's response was not encouraging. 'Son,' he said with a deep sigh, 'we didn't keep you at school until you were eighteen for you to have *a blast* but I suppose at the end of the day, you have to do what you want to do.' He cast a brief glance in Robert's direction. 'And thanks to your mother, it looks as if you've gained a place at Leeds provided you enrol for a foundation course first at a local college to prove yourself capable.'

'I will, Dad, I'm so relieved; I thought you'd go ape when I told you.'

'Mum says you met a girl down under and that's why you chose Leeds University. Was that the draw?'

Here we go, thought Robert. 'No, Dad,' he said firmly, 'it's just that Bethan showed me the way I can fulfil my ambition.'

He knew his mother, sitting in the back of the car, was smiling. She had always been on his side. He promised himself that he would make up for all the hassle he had caused her.

TWENTY-ONE

Time waits for no man and it wasn't long before Robert and Vicky had fled the nest. They were both at university: Robert doing his second year at Leeds and Vicky her first year at Durham. Although Amanda often brought friends home, the house seemed quiet without them, prompting Sandra to look for a part-time job.

She found employment in a florist and with her hours filled with flower arranging and dealing with customers, she felt content. Surprisingly it was Mark who became restless.

'How about we move house, darling,' he said one day.

Sandra was taken aback. 'I like it here,' she said, 'besides it wouldn't feel right for Robert and Vicky to come home to a different address.'

'Maybe you're right.'

Much to Sandra's relief, Mark let the matter drop and they remained at Number Seven for a few more years, by which time, Mark was beginning to think about retirement.

Robert's marriage to Bethan in 1973 was quickly followed by Vicky's engagement to a fellow history student.

'We're losing our children,' wailed Sandra.

'Gaining a daughter and son-in-law you mean,' Mark corrected her.

'The family hasn't been together at Christmas for years and now we've got to share our son and daughter with two other families.'

'Would you rather they didn't get married and have families of their own?' Mark huffed.

'Of course not, I want to be a grandmother while I'm still young and fit enough, not an old biddy who can hardly prise herself out of a chair.'

Mark laughed. 'You'll never be like that.'

By 1975 Bethan was pregnant, giving birth to baby John during the autumn and much to Sandra's delight the family congregated at Number Seven for Christmas. Sandra was concerned about their son's future. Robert and his wife had so far managed to make ends meet but now they had a baby to care for it looked as if, for a while at least, they would have to rely solely on Robert's income.

'You can't worry about them forever, darling,' Mark told her, 'Robert made his choice. If he'd gone for engineering like he was supposed to, his future would be assured.'

Sandra gave a guilty shudder. Hadn't she been the one to encourage her son to follow his dream?

Once the festivities were over, Mark sprang a bombshell on her. 'I've decided to take early retirement.'

'Won't you get bored being stuck at home all day long?' She flashed him a quick glance, 'I'm not giving up my job.'

'Are you sure about that?'

'What d'you mean?'

'Well, darling, I've got plans for us.' Leaning forward, he touched her knee. 'Let's do something daring.'

'What do you mean?'

'Let's sell up and go and live in Spain. You know how much you love it there, all that sand, sea and sun…'

'You're not serious?'

'Of course I am. Now that Amanda's at uni, there's nothing to stop us.'

'Don't be silly, Mark…damn, now look what you've made me do, I've dropped a stitch.'

'Fuck the dropped stitch, just listen to me, Sandra.'

'Mark!'

'Sorry, darling, but I am serious about this. Hear me out.'

Sandra put her knitting down on the chair beside her and clasped her hands together, resting them on her knees and looking rather like a school girl waiting to be reprimanded by the head teacher.

He leant closer and said, 'I've thought about this a lot and now that I'm going to retire and the children are off our hands, I don't see why we can't do it.'

Sandra had never seen Mark so animated. Usually he was the most unenthusiastic person in the world. Over the years she had been the one to plan holidays and suggest outings. She saw in her mind's eye the Costa del Sol's coastline, soft sands, surfers and sail boats. Mark's idea was appealing.

'They're not completely off our hands,' she said, 'remember Amanda's only eighteen.'

'Old enough to marry, drive a car and to vote…'

Sandra laughed. 'Old enough but not yet wise enough.'

'And,' went on Mark, 'properties are cheaper there and we'd have a nice little sum in the bank in case of emergencies…'

'Emergencies…?'

He shrugged. 'So we could help Robert and Bethan out if they were in trouble; you know how unpredictable the art world is'.

Sandra burst out laughing. 'Oh, I see…'

'Well?' He caught her hand and squeezed it. 'Does the idea appeal to you?'

Sandra blinked and adjusted her glasses. 'Of course but I'm still doubtful about Amanda?'

'Why?'

'She'd have nowhere to come home to at weekends and half-term.'

'She could fly over to join us or stay with either Vicky or Robert.'

'Yes, I suppose…'

Sandra frowned as she considered the drawbacks but these were fading fast as she thought about the positive aspects. It would be wonderful if they could afford a villa large enough to accommodate the whole family during the holidays. Their little grandson would love playing on the beach and Amanda could spend her entire summer break with them. She sighed. Was she ready to move out of Number Seven?

'I'll have to think about it,' she said, picking up her knitting.

Mark went back to his newspaper, smiling smugly, confident that in a year's time they would be soaking up the sun on an Iberian beach.

*****

THE IRON LADY

In December 1980, the world was shocked by the assassination of John Lennon and 1984 brought news of the murder of Indira Gandhi. In 1981 the wedding of Prince Charles and Diana Spencer was televised live and in 1982 Michael Jackson's 'Thriller' video exploded onto our TV screens. In 1984 Mikhail Gorbachev became leader of the Soviet Union and the decade drew to a close with the Berlin Wall being torn down. By this time, Margaret Thatcher, Britain's first woman prime minister had been in power for ten years.

Closer to home, during the 1984 Conservative Party Conference, the IRA bombed Brighton's Grand Hotel killing several people and injuring many more but, on a happier note, the emergence of language schools in the town brought an influx of foreign students throughout the summer months.

Anthony Sanders and Jasper Cole moved in during a heat-wave. Anthony suffered from the heat but he was a conventional man of some forty-eight years and insisted on never being seen in public without a jacket and tie. This was partly because he was the proprietor of The Sanders

Menswear Shop, which called for a smart appearance. He was a large gentleman, several stone overweight and addicted to cigars. He also liked to indulge in a tot or two of Whisky each evening.

His companion, Jasper Cole was slight in build and sometimes had a nervous twitch over one eye. Where Anthony was even-tempered and slow of speech, Jasper was constantly on the move and words tumbled out of his mouth uncontrolled. Jasper was an aspiring actor-cum-song writer some twenty years younger than Anthony. The older man bought Number Seven so they could set up home together after they had got to know one another on a protest sit-in staged to save the local theatre from closure. Anthony brought home the money, Jasper provided the entertainment although, occasionally, when stage work was really scarce, he would lower his sights and take on a temporary job as a call centre operator.

'We'll have to change everything, Ant,' declared Jasper looking round at Sandra and Mark's decorations. 'That'll have to go.' He pointed at Daisy's cupboard.

'Let's wait until we've settled in,' said Anthony, running a hand over the wall to test the smoothness of the plaster. 'The house has been well looked after.'

'Their choice of décor's terribly unimaginative, darling.' Jasper went to look out of the window. 'The garden will have to be completely re-landscaped.'

I resented that. Sandra had made a good job of my garden and I didn't want her well-tended lawn and carefully planned flowerbeds dug up. But there was nothing I could do about it: Anthony and Jasper were here to stay.

TWENTY-TWO

'You know, Ant, this is my very first *real* home,' said Jasper as they closed the door on the removal men. 'I was brought up in a children's home, did I tell you?'

'Yes, many times,' replied Anthony with an indulgent smile.

This didn't deter Jasper, who went on, 'I don't remember my mother although I'm told she was very beautiful, and she came from a good family. She couldn't look after me you see. She was only sixteen when I was born.' He giggled. 'It isn't true, you know, that old adage isn't true; I mean about girls being sweet sixteen and never been kissed. They've all been kissed by the time they're sixteen.'

'I dare say they have,' agreed Anthony. 'We'd better start unpacking.'

'We'll need to buy more furniture. We could go to Brighton on your next day off and pick up a few things. We'll need a larger table and, of course, a *king*-size bed to replace that old one of yours.'

'Let's see how everything fits in first. There's no rush.'

'Well, I'll start upstairs,' said Jasper, picking up a box and heaving it towards the stairs. You do the lighter stuff; after all I'm younger than you.'

'No need to remind me,' laughed Anthony.

He sometimes wondered how it was going to work out with Jasper. During his forty-eight years he had had several affairs but he had never taken that extra step and asked anyone to move in with him. Much as he loved and trusted his chosen companion, being cautious by nature he had taken the house out in his sole name. Better to be safe than sorry.

His doubts were dispelled during the evening when, surrounded by boxes they sat side by side on the sofa watching television. Jasper never ceased to amuse him by mimicking the actors or comedians they were watching. He really was a talented impersonator. Anthony hoped that one day he would be spotted by an agent; he knew Jasper had his sights set on a serious acting career but he wasn't sure that was right for him.

Jasper was an innovative chef. He could turn simple everyday ingredients into something special. Prior to meeting him, Anthony had lived on takeaways and ready meals, a habit which had contributed to his substantial girth. At times, Jasper fancied becoming a vegetarian or a vegan but this seldom lasted more than a week or two because there would always be a cookery programme on the television which would tempt him back into being a meat eater.

At the end of the first month, during which there were a good few arguments about how to decorate the house, Anthony gave in and left Jasper to make these decisions.

'But don't go overboard with the cost, Jasper,' he warned. 'I draw the line at anything too expensive; I know what you're like.'

'What on earth do you mean, darling?' Jasper let his bottom lip droop and regarded his companion with lidded eyes.

'I mean you're prone to change your mind and might want to alter things.'

'Spoilsport!' Jasper feigned annoyance and flapped his wrist.

The ill-matched pair spent a lot of time going to the theatre and cinema. Jasper loved horror films although Anthony could never understand why since he always covered his eyes at the sight of blood and ghost stories sent him into hysterics.

Anthony liked classical music and opera, which bored his companion so if he was in the mood for something more serious than Top of the Pops, he would retire to the attic box room to listen to Tosca or Wagner on his Bang and Olufsen stereo system.

'Oh duckie you're not going to sneak away to your hidey hole again this evening, are you?' moaned Jasper, his tone wheedling. 'I was hoping we could have a quiet evening in together, share a bottle of wine and have a game of cards.' He winked, 'Strip poker or something...'

Anthony laughed and patted his portly belly. 'Not likely, I'm too old for those games. Anyway, you'll have to watch telly on your own this evening because they're playing some Beethoven on Radio Three and I particularly want to listen to it.'

Jasper frowned and said in a petulant voice, 'Why tune into that stuff? It's fucking boring. Can't you move with the times, Ant?'

'Don't swear, you know I don't like it. And I'm afraid you'll have to spend the evening on your own. I need a dose of culture once in a while.'

'A dose of culture!' Jasper clamped a hand to his forehead in exaggerated dismay. 'You make it sound like you've got some terrible disease, cancer or something...'

'Don't talk nonsense.'

'Take a bloody aspirin instead of filling the house with all that noise. Why don't you get yourself some earphones?' grumbled Jasper.

'Because it doesn't sound the same through earphones,' snapped Anthony beginning to get riled, 'and I don't want to end up deaf like half the youth of today.'

'Suit yourself, but don't throw a wobbly if I play my guitar into the night.'

'Throw a wobbly, me!' Anthony burst out laughing. 'I thought that was your prerogative.'

They went their separate ways for the evening but Anthony knew that his highly-strung partner would have forgotten their disagreement by bedtime. Friction between them was part of their daily routine but it was always short-lived, the argument resolved with a hug and a promise to be more tolerant in the future.

The Sanders Menswear Shop didn't make Anthony a fortune but it had kept him comfortably off for more than ten years. He employed a couple of part-timers, allowing him to take the occasional day off. Like Anthony himself, the products he sold were conservative, intended for the older man. He didn't sell jeans, trainers or anoraks; he went in for the tailored suit complete with matching waistcoat, his tweed jacket and shoe ranges were limited to the Windsor classic and the country brogue.

He was aware that the young men who ran the shop when he was absent made fun of him behind his back, but this didn't worry him. They had proved to be honest and that was all that mattered.

Once in a while he took time off without telling Jasper because much as he loved having him around, his partner's constant chatter could be tiresome. On one such day, he decided to take a trip to Brighton, partly to chase up one of his tailoring suppliers who seemed to be taking too long over an order and partly for a change of scene.

'I won't be in this afternoon, Mike,' he informed the part-timer, 'will you be able to manage without me?'

'Sure thing, Anthony, I don't foresee a rush of customers today.'

It irked Anthony that his employees addressed him by his Christian name but he knew it wouldn't go down well to correct them.

Rather than go home to collect his car, he took the bus to Brighton, enjoying the ride along by the seashore. It was a beautiful day with the sun glistening off the mirror-like water. There were plenty of people about: mothers playing with toddlers on the beach prior to fetching older children from school; old age pensioners taking a stroll; ice cream sellers pitching their wares. The bus ride gave him the opportunity to reflect on his own life. An only child, he had been a loner at school. During the holidays his parents would pack him off to stay with his Aunt Florrie in Eastbourne. She in turn, would pack him and his cousin Jamie off to the Downs for the day, armed with a picnic lunch. Jamie had been a bit of a daredevil and had goaded him into doing things he would never have done on his own. He recalled being coerced into stealing apples from a tree in someone's garden. When the owner had come out ranting and waving his arms in the air, Jamie had taken flight, leaving him to take the blame. And there was that time when he had been persuaded to climb down a chalk pit and slipped, ending up with a sprained ankle. Somehow, with his cousin's help, he had limped all the way home, only to be castigated by his furious aunt when she saw that he had torn a hole in his trousers.

The bus pulled up near Brighton Pier and he got off. This was the summer of 1977 and although not as hot as the year before, it was hot enough to cause Anthony to wipe a handkerchief across his forehead. The height of the season had drawn day trippers to the resort; the promenade was busy. He decided to walk along the pier for a bit of fresh air.

A street photographer waved a camera in front of his face. 'Photo, gov'ner?'

'No thank you.'

He walked on, sometimes peering down between the wooden floorboards at the lapping waves beneath, sometimes looking towards the Seven Sisters cliffs, clearly visible in the distance. From the end of the pier he stared back at the shore to watch people moving in every direction, like ants.

A hurdy-gurdy started playing and next to it, a performer set up a Punch and Judy kiosk in readiness for his eager after-school audience. He bypassed the fruit machines; Jasper liked those and would waste money on one-armed bandits.

Returning to the promenade, he looked up at the big wheel thinking that it was the perfect day for a ride, but resisted the temptation. Volk's Electric Railway chugged by as he made his way into town to choose a place for lunch. After tucking into a plate of plaice and chips and a pint of bitter, he paid the bill and strolled past the Royal Pavilion into Regent Street. The tailor he was planning to visit had premises nearby.

Then he saw him. At first he couldn't believe his eyes: ahead of him Jasper was walking arm-in-arm with a flame-haired youth. They were absorbed in one another. Anthony froze. Should he catch up with them and challenge Jasper or should he wait until they both got home? Should he ignore the incident and assume it meant nothing - maybe the youth was an old friend or a relative? No, Jasper had told him he didn't have any relatives.

Turning on his heel, Anthony almost ran back down the hill to the bus stop. All he wanted was to get away from Brighton. His day out had been ruined.

Unaware that they had been spotted, Jasper and his companion continued on their way. If Anthony had confronted him, Jasper would have been devastated. Toby, as his companion was called, was merely a diversion for apart from Anthony supporting him when he was *resting*, he was genuinely fond of his conformist partner and did not want to hurt him.

The pair arrived at a corner pub and went inside where loud music drowned out conversation. Jasper ordered two beers and they sat down at a small table. He tore open a large packet of crisps for them to share, taking time to study the youth. He was certainly striking with his dyed red hair and a good deal of body piercing. Jasper looked at his fingernails. They were short and clean. Jasper was fastidious about cleanliness and couldn't be enticed by anyone the least bit grubby.

'Have you got someone regular?' Toby asked him.

'Nah.' Jasper's conscience plagued him when he lied but he managed to hide it.

'Nor me.'

'What, a good-looking boy like you! I thought they'd be falling all over you.' Jasper knew how to flatter.

They chatted for half an hour with Jasper impressing the youth by exaggerating his stage roles. Finally, he came to the point. 'Where do you live?' he asked, hoping he wasn't one of those down-and-outs moving from hostel to hostel but judging by his appearance, he guessed the boy had some kind of permanent residence.

'Not far from here.'

Jasper's innocent blue eyes met those of the boy. 'Well, what's keeping us,' he said, reaching across the table to stroke his hand.

'Got any weed?'

Jasper pulled a face. 'Nah, what d'you think I am?' Then he laughed and patted his top pocket. 'Only teasing…'

Unlike on the journey to Brighton, Anthony barely noticed the scene from the bus on the way home. He ignored people getting on and off as the vehicle progressed westwards, gazing fixedly up at the clear blue sky. He made the short walk home from the bus stop in record time and once inside Number Seven, he slumped down onto a chair and lowered his head into his hands.

'How could you do this to me, Jasper?' he wailed aloud, his shoulders rocking as sobs overtook him.

He remained seated there until, an hour and a half later, Jasper came home. The younger man gave a start when he saw his partner's tear-stained face.

'What's up?' he asked, a concerned look in his eyes.

'How can you ask that?'

'What's happened? Has someone died?' Jasper said carelessly.

Anthony's next words shocked him. 'Why are you double-timing me?'

Me! Double-timing you?' Jasper knew he had been tumbled but he instinctively tried to bluff it out. 'Whatever gave you that idea, lover boy? As a matter of fact I went to Horsham to see about a role. The local rep are auditioning.'

'Oh yes...' Anthony's tone was heavy with sarcasm, 'and what play are they doing?'

Jasper thought quickly. 'It's a Pinter play,' he said but he couldn't control the irritating twitch over his left eye.

Anthony stood up. He was half a head taller than Jasper and twice as heavy and, momentarily, Jasper experienced a tremor of trepidation, knowing that if his partner turned nasty, he wouldn't stand a chance against him even though he was years younger.

'You didn't go to Horsham, you went to Brighton,' said Anthony, the certainty in his voice convincing Jasper that he should come clean.

'I told a fib; I *did* go to Brighton and I was going to tell you, honestly I was.'

'When were you going to tell me?'

'When I got home, of course...' Again his eye twitched.

'Then why did you mention Horsham at all?'
'I got confused.'
'Confused eh!'
'How did you know?'
'I know because I saw you with my own eyes.'
'Where?'
'In the street...'

Jasper's hopes began to rise. Maybe it was before he picked up Toby. Maybe this was Anthony being overly possessive. It happened sometimes. 'You can't expect me to give you an account of everywhere I go, Ant,' he said, belligerence creeping into his voice.

Anthony almost snarled as he said, 'Who was your young friend?'

The cat was out of the bag, or was it? Jasper held his breath, praying that Anthony hadn't followed them to the pub. 'He's an old mate I bumped into.'

'It didn't look like an *old* mates' meeting to me. It looked more like a new friendship; have you been...?' Anthony couldn't bring himself to say the word *unfaithful*.

His brown eyes bored into Jasper, who reached for his hand and using all his acting skills, murmured contritely, 'Oh love, I'm *terribly* sorry, believe me it didn't mean anything.'

Anthony shook him off. 'Get out of my sight.'

Jasper's eyes filled with tears. 'But Ant darling, you have to forgive me. I promise I'll never do anything like that again.'

Anthony fought down the urge to take him in his arms. Focusing on a picture of the Taj Mahal hanging on the wall behind Jasper's head, he snapped, 'It'll take more than a hollow promise to convince me.'

Realising that he'd lost the battle Jasper shambled out of the room.

'You can sleep in the spare room tonight,' Anthony shouted after him.

TWENTY-THREE

For the next few days they didn't speak to one another. Anthony walked around the house with a haughty expression on his face while Jasper vacillated from slavish docility to childish impudence.

The impasse was broken when Jasper received the offer of the part of Albin in *La Cage aux Folles* in Eastbourne. Rehearsals were to start almost immediately.

'Yippee!' He replaced the receiver when the call ended and forgetting all about their disagreement, he raced up the road to the Sanders Menswear Shop to find Anthony.

At the entrance, he caught sight of his reflection in the window and stopped to pull up his joggers and zip up his sweatshirt. Anthony was showing a customer some Harris Tweed swatches and didn't look pleased to see him. Jasper waited impatiently while the white-haired client wavered between an Orkney and a Coniston. At last he left the shop having placed an order for one of each.

'They'll be here in a week's time, sir,' said Anthony, shaking hands with the customer. 'Good afternoon to you.'

Thankfully no one else came in.

'What brings you here, Jasper?' he demanded as he carefully returned the swatches to their place in a drawer.

'I've never seen you at work before,' tittered Jasper, tweaking the end of the tape measure which was hanging round Anthony's neck.

'What do you want?'

'Listen, sweetie, I've had the most wonderful news and I just have to share it with you.' He took a step closer to Anthony and assumed a persuasive tone. 'Please let's be friends again. I can't bear it when you're cross with me.'

Anthony did his best to assume a serious expression. 'This isn't the time or the place to discuss our relationship. I suggest you go home.' He turned to go into the storeroom at the back of the shop. Jasper followed him.

'Don't be like that, Ant. Don't you want to hear my news?'

Anthony took a corduroy jacket from a rail and proceeded to give it a brush. 'What news?'

'I've got a job. It's fantastic. I've got a big part in a musical in Eastbourne. It could run for months.'

'That's a long way to travel every day.'

'Oh, I'd have to go into digs for the duration but I'd come home every Sunday and on my days off.'

Anthony frowned. 'I see.'

'Aren't you pleased for me, darling?'

Jasper's enthusiasm won his partner over. 'Of course I am,' he said, giving Jasper a peck on the cheek.

'Don't I deserve a hug?'

When he heard a customer come in, Anthony glanced past Jasper through the beaded curtain dividing the storeroom from the shop. 'Not now. Look, go out the back way and I'll see you at home.'

'Are we friends again?'

'Of course we are.'

And so the episode with Toby blew over and the couple were as loving as ever. But Anthony was not happy about Jasper staying over in Eastbourne and he voiced his misgivings. 'How can I trust you after what happened in Brighton?'

'I'd never deceive you, darling, never again.'

'But you'll be mixing with lots of showbiz people and I know what they're like.'

Jasper gave a shrug. 'They're mostly women.' He was on safe ground because he was pretty sure Anthony knew nothing about the show. Secretly he was pleased when his partner showed signs of jealousy. 'You *will* come and see it, won't you?'

'Wild horses wouldn't keep me away.'

Because he wasn't needed for every rehearsal, Jasper travelled to Eastbourne on a daily basis. He came home complaining that he was dog tired but exhaustion didn't blunt his enthusiasm and he regaled Anthony with all the trivia the day had provided. Anthony tried to calm him down by talking about his own mundane existence, sometimes envying his partner's exciting lifestyle. *Still,* he told himself, *it's just as well one of us has got his feet firmly planted on the ground.*

He went to the opening night and waited for Jasper after the performance so they could have a drink in the bar afterwards.

'You were wonderful as the drag artist,' said Anthony, 'my goodness, I almost didn't recognise you.'

'Make-up had their work cut out making me look older,' said Jasper, casting a sneaky glance at his reflection in the mirror behind the bar.

After a pause, Anthony asked, 'The guy who plays the part of Renato, is he gay?'

Jasper guffawed. 'No worries there, Ant, he's married to one of the chorus girls.'

But Anthony couldn't let go of the idea that Jasper would hook up with somebody else while he was in Eastbourne. He knew from his experience of *sitting in* to save the local theatre how flirtatious some of the actors could be. He had observed both girls and boys switch from one partner to another without batting an eyelid and he knew how easily Jasper could be carried away by flattery.

Indeed, hadn't he tried it out himself when he was courting his partner? Jasper placed great store on looks and Anthony was well aware that it was not *his* good looks that had won him over. He knew that, although most of the time Jasper enjoyed his company, the draw was the stability their partnership afforded him. He knew also that sometimes Jasper found him too conformist.

He shuddered at the memory of the barb in Jasper's tone when he once joked, 'If I didn't know better I'd take you for a straight guy.'

On several occasions during the rehearsal period, Jasper had stayed out all night, claiming on his return that he had missed the last train home and had been obliged to spend the night in a B&B. Once when Anthony was loading the washing machines he found a pair of boxer shorts he knew didn't belong to Jasper. Disgusted, he took them out into the garden and set light to them, watching as they turned to ashes. He wanted to challenge Jasper but fear of losing him was even greater than his jealousy, so he said nothing.

And despite the heartache living with this unpredictable bundle of energy brought him, Anthony knew there was a kind side to Jasper. He had, on one occasion, brought home a waif he came across in a shop doorway. It was a cold evening and he begged Anthony to let her stay with them.

'It's only for one night, Ant, just look at her, she's freezing. There's a gale blowing out there tonight.'

'We're not a hostel for down-and-outs,' protested Anthony.

'At least let her have bath and a meal,' insisted Jasper.

'All right but then she must go.'

The unfortunate girl didn't utter a word during this exchange but she willingly accepted the offer of a bath and a meal and while she was safely in the bathroom, Anthony made further protestations.

'She can't stay here, Jasper.'

'Why not, we've got a spare room and it's only for one night. We can send her off home tomorrow.'

'Send her back on the streets no doubt so that she can beg shelter from some other sucker tomorrow night,' said Anthony bitterly.

Jasper got angry. 'No, I can tell she's from a decent family. Besides, she didn't beg, I offered.'

'You had no right to bring her here,' snapped Anthony. 'If she's a run-away her parents must be worried sick. As soon as she's finished in the bath, we must get her to ring home.'

After giving her a meal, Jasper made up the bed in the spare room for her. It transpired over a bedtime cup of cocoa that she was barely sixteen and had run away after a row with her parents. With gentle understanding, Jasper persuaded her to ring her parents to let them know she was safe and, in the morning, he borrowed money from Anthony so that she could get the train home.

Then there was the time, he brought home a stray dog. It was a small scruffy-looking mongrel but it had a pathetic look about it.

'Where did *that* come from?' demanded Anthony, 'we haven't got room for animals here.'

Jasper untied the piece of string he'd threaded through the dog's collar and let it lick his face. When it turned to Anthony, he leapt away.

'I don't want it licking my face. You don't know where it's been.'

'I'll take it to that dog rescue place in Shoreham tomorrow,' promised Jasper.

'Take it right now.'

'It's too late, they're closed.'

Anthony pointed to the dog's collar. 'Have you looked to see if the owner's telephone number is on it?'

'It isn't but it says the dog's name is Buster.'

Anthony took a deep breath. 'It can sleep in the shed until someone comes to pick it up.'

'It will be lonely.'

'Lonely, my foot! It must have been on its own when you found it.'

'It was wandering around sniffing all the garden gates. If we take it to the rescue place they will probably be able to trace its owners, or they might ring up and ask if it's been handed in.'

'Whatever,' sniffed Anthony, 'it sleeps in the shed.'

Soon after they moved in, Anthony arranged for the local newspaper to be delivered every week. He claimed he had a social conscience and that it was their duty to keep up with local events. He took to writing letters to the editor complaining about cyclists riding along the promenade, people letting their dogs run free on the beach and the outlandish parking charges in the town centre.

Jasper scanned the paper for forthcoming attractions or titbits of scandal. One day he came across a piece of news about a woman who had walked into the local police station to make a confession.

'Here Ant, listen to this,' he said.

Anthony put down the book he was reading and took off his glasses. 'What is it?'

Jasper paraphrased the article. 'An eighty-four year old local woman claims she murdered her mother in her bed some twenty-six years ago…'

'What made her confess after all this time?'

'It seems that there were no unusual circumstances surrounding the mother's death at the time, so no one suspected anything. The Death Certificate said she died from natural causes.'

'Who is this woman, she must be loco?'

'They say there could be some truth in her story.'

'What's her name?'

'Thelma Stokes.'

'That name rings a bell.' All at once, Anthony got up and hurried from the room.

'Where are you going?' called Jasper.

'I won't be a minute.'

A puzzled frown creased Jasper's brow. It was unusual for his partner to move so rapidly; normally Anthony was as measured of movement as he was of speech.

After five minutes, Anthony returned with a bundle of documents under his arm.

'What have you got there?'

'The House Deeds...' He picked up his glasses, exasperating Jasper by taking time to polish the lens before placing them on his nose.

'What for...?'

'Wait a minute and I'll tell you...' Anthony thumbed through the pages then looked up triumphantly. 'I knew I was right.'

'Right about what...?' said Jasper, his tone rife with irritation.

Anthony pressed his index finger on a line on one of the pages. 'We bought the house...'

'*You* bought the house,' corrected Jasper, pernickety as ever.

'*I* bought the house from a Mr and Mrs Toplin who in turn bought it from a Miss Thelma Stokes.'

'What are you saying?'

'I'm saying that if what the old lady says is true, she supposedly murdered her mother in this very house.'

'Ooh!' Jasper flung the newspaper at Anthony and leapt to his feet. Clasping his hands to his cheeks, he cried, 'Does it say where the crime was committed? I mean, was it in the front bedroom...' his voice rose, '...the room where *we* sleep?'

'It doesn't say.'

Jasper paced the floor, gesticulating wildly. 'We can't stay here. It's a crime scene,' he shrieked.

Anthony burst out laughing. 'Don't be so melodramatic, Jasper, this Stokes woman is probably round the bend.' He scrutinised the rest of the article. 'It says she's been sailing around the world for the past couple of decades with a male companion. Apparently he died recently.' He quoted: *overwhelmed with grief at losing her beloved Leslie, Thelma Stokes decided to return to her roots and confess to the crime which had been weighing on her conscience over the years.* Anthony folded up the newspaper and let it drop to the floor. 'There didn't I tell you, the woman's clearly beside herself with grief?' He gave a chuckle. 'But it would make a lovely talking point at a dinner party.'

'How can you treat this so lightly, Ant? What if the police take her seriously and decide to come and investigate?'

'I don't think it will come to that.'

'What if it does?'

Anthony got impatient. 'It's just a silly story the newspaper has latched onto, Jasper.'

'I hope you're right,' Jasper slumped back into the chair he had vacated and wrinkled his nose. 'Just the same, I think I'll sleep in the spare room tonight.'

The production of *La Cage aux Folles* went very well. It was originally scheduled for a three-month run but due to its success this was extended for another two months. Although proud of his young partner and pleased by his success, Anthony couldn't help wishing the show would end. But worse was to come. After a short break it was announced that *La Cage aux Folles* would be moving on to the Mayflower in Southampton, which of course meant that Jasper would be away from home for even longer. Jasper was lucky because some of the cast had been *let go*, including his counterpart, Renato, whose replacement hadn't yet been decided.

'Let's make the most of your three-week break,' said Anthony, 'we could to go on holiday, maybe take a trip to Italy or the South of France.'

Jasper yawned. 'I don't know about that,' he said, 'all I can think about now is having a lovely lie-in each morning after a relaxing evening in front of the TV with you.'

Anthony knew he should be glad that all Jasper wanted was a quiet break at home but he couldn't help wishing he could whisk him away to a place where nobody knew them, to a place where they could be themselves for despite the easing of attitudes during the eighties, he had noticed the aloofness of some of their neighbours and he knew by the behaviour of one or two of his regular customers the word had got around that he was gay. Much as he loved his partner's flaunting conduct, he sometimes felt the urge to rein him in.

In the end, they stayed at home in Number Seven with the occasional day out when weather permitted. They took a trip to London to visit an Andy Warhol Exhibition at the Tate Modern. This wasn't to Anthony's taste but he was anxious to please Jasper. However, it seemed that pleasing his partner was well nigh impossible because the young man soon lost interest in the exhibition.

'This is getting boring,' moaned Jasper slumping down on one of the couches in the centre of the exhibition hall.

'You're the one who wanted to come here.'

'I know, but if you've seen one you've seen the lot. Let's go and have a drink; I know a nice place not far from here.'

Anthony felt uncomfortable when Jasper led the way to a gay bar. Never having been overtly gay, he was sensitive to remarks made by so-called *straight* people, especially men. He was inherently gentle both in speech and manner. As a twenty-year-old he had been unwilling to acknowledge his sexual proclivity and had played the macho man. At six foot two and with a heavy build this had been relatively easy. He would not admit, even to himself, that being called a *queen* or a *fag* could cause him as much pain as a physical blow.

He looked at his companion who took pride in being gay, envying his ability to cast aside prejudice with a flick of the wrist. Anthony had not officially *come out* and he wasn't sure whether even his cousin James, with whom he had spent much of his childhood, knew he was gay.

Jasper noticed his discomfort and said with a laugh, 'Cheer up, Ant, they serve good coffee here if you don't want a beer.' When Anthony didn't reply, he added, 'What's the matter? Oh, I see, it's not upmarket enough for you.'

'It's not that.'

Jasper wrinkled his brow in comprehension. Rolling his eyes, he said, '*I'm* not ashamed of what I am even if you are.'

'I'm *not* ashamed,' protested Anthony, 'I prefer to be discreet that's all.'

The door to the bar was pushed open and a couple of men emerged, walking away arm-in-arm. Jasper disappeared inside but Anthony hesitated on the threshold, unable to stop himself from glancing back over his shoulder to see if anybody was looking at them. He caught the eye of a delivery man who was carrying a bulky parcel into a nearby shop. When the man winked at him, he felt his cheeks redden and hurriedly followed Jasper into the bar.

'Not all of us want to be stuck in a time warp,' sniffed Jasper continuing the conversation they had started outside. Luckily, the loud music precluded further argument.

The day didn't turn out the way Anthony would have liked. After only a few moments inside he noticed that many eyes were turned on Jasper, who cut an attractive figure with his slim physique and classical bone structure. His piercing violet blue eyes were his best feature and had he been born a woman he would undoubtedly have been proclaimed beautiful. Anthony knew that Jasper was beginning to get concerned that his sandy hair was thinning and he took great pains to comb it across his head and to add a little gel to keep it in place. To make matters worse, Anthony himself had a head of thick dark hair. Jasper didn't cope easily with envy and frequently moaned that it wasn't fair that his much older partner should be so blessed.

Against his natural inclination, Anthony put his arm possessively around Jasper's waist. Generally, he kept demonstrations of affection strictly private but he felt the need to lay claim to the young man by his side. After leaving the bar, Anthony couldn't keep a lid on his jealousy.

'You didn't have to flirt with that good-looking black guy by the counter,' he said.

Jasper took delight in deliberately misunderstanding him. 'Why, because he's black? I didn't know you were racist, Ant.'

'Don't be a fool! You know what I mean. We're a couple and you shouldn't play around like that.'

'Ooh, do I see traces of the little green god?'

'You're behaving like a child,' grumbled Anthony, ignoring the fact that it was he, not Jasper, who was unwilling to acknowledge his sexuality.

They travelled home in silence, sitting as far apart on the train seat as possible.

TWENTY-FOUR

Jasper felt peeved about the incident in the coffee bar. All he'd done was flirt with a good-looking guy. Anthony didn't *own* him. It wasn't as if they had gone through a civil ceremony tying them together. Anthony had hinted at it once, saying that if they were legally bound, he would arrange for Number Seven to be held in joint ownership. Jasper was aware that Anthony had a nice little nest egg stowed away in a building society. If their relationship were legalised, he would have claim to that too. But for the moment, he couldn't rid his mind of his irritation when Anthony behaved so covertly. Why was he ashamed of his sexual predilection? He, Jasper, was proud of it.

The atmosphere during the remaining days of the three weeks was strained. Anthony wanted to put things right but didn't know how to and Jasper seemed to take delight in winding him up with caustic comments about his old-fashioned attitude. They slept in the same bed but their relationship had changed and their *goodbyes* on the day Jasper departed for Southampton seemed to Anthony almost like a final farewell. For the rest of that day, he moped about the house, leaving the care of the shop to his part-time assistants.

As promised, Jasper phoned him on his arrival, assuring him that his digs were fine and that he would begin rehearsals the next day.

'It's going to be great here. It's a pity you won't be able to see the show with its new cast.'

Anthony had never suggested that he wouldn't travel to Southampton to see the show and felt slighted that Jasper assumed he wouldn't make the journey. As the weeks went by, he sank into depression, feeling ill both mentally and physically. He had always suffered from indigestion but now the pain he suffered in the evening was getting worse. Unwilling to admit that he might be ill he put off visiting the doctor.

The heart attack hit him during the night. He struggled from his bed and was able to phone for an ambulance but in an attempt to get downstairs to open the door, he fell headlong in the hallway. His last thoughts were uncharacteristically dramatic: *so close to help but yet so far.*

When the paramedics couldn't gain entry to Number Seven they knocked at Number Five but Anthony had never entrusted anyone except Jasper with a house key. The woman next door hastened to explain that Anthony's partner was away - she had seen him depart with a suitcase - but she didn't know where he was.

The police broke the front door down but had difficulty pushing it open as Anthony's body was in the way. Eventually, a slim WPC managed to squeeze her way in and ascertain that he was dead.

'What's his partner's name?' the Police Sergeant asked the neighbour but all she knew was that he was called Jasper.

'No surname?'

'I'm afraid not but I think he's an actor.'

'Is he in a show now?'

'Possibly; maybe he was going to a rehearsal when I saw him with a suitcase.'

This new clue soon brought to light Jasper's whereabouts. He took time off from rehearsals and rushed home, arriving later the same day.

'Oh my God, oh my God!' he kept repeating while the patient Police Sergeant tried to question him.

'Do you know if Mr Sanders had any relatives, Mr Cole?'

'How would I know?'

The Police Sergeant exchanged an exasperated glance with the WPC who speaking very quietly, said, 'We do need to know whether Anthony has any family.'

Jasper started to calm down at last but he wasn't able to furnish them with much information. 'I believe there's a cousin somewhere in East Sussex,' he said, 'but I don't know whether his surname is Sanders. He could be a cousin on Ant's mother's side.'

'Please try and remember the cousin's name,' insisted the WPC.

'I can't, I can't,' howled Jasper, 'why can't you leave me alone, I'm so upset.'

The Police Sergeant lost patience. 'Get him out of here,' he grunted.

Jasper scurried out of the room accompanied by the WPC. In the corridor she spoke to him again. 'Don't take offence, Mr Cole, it's just that we need a lead to help us contact Mr Sanders' next of kin.'

Her kindness sobered Jasper. 'I know,' he muttered, 'and if I think of anything I'll let you know.'

That night, Jasper slept in the spare room. The very idea of sleeping in the bed they had shared appalled him. *I'll never be able to set foot in that bedroom again,* he told himself. He tossed and turned all night as the repercussions of Anthony's demise sank in. *La Cage aux Folles* was expected to run for at least six weeks at the Mayflower but there were rumours that when it came off the director intended to put on a different play and he had no idea as to whether he would be included in the cast.

While acting he earned a reasonable salary but he was quick to spend it, never bothering to put any money aside for a rainy day. Why should he? There was always Anthony to fall back on. Now the future looked uncertain.

He remembered Toby and his thoughts flew back to pre-Anthony when he had almost become a down-and-out himself. On one occasion he had even sunk to prostituting himself because he was skint. He had meant it when he'd told Anthony that Number Seven was his first *real* home; the likelihood of losing it was too awful to bear. Then he brightened. Ant had once mentioned adding a codicil to his will. Was it possible that his name had been added? He ran a hand over his balding head reminded that he'd been going to ask Anthony for the £500 needed for a hair transplant. Perhaps it was still possible. Reassured by this hope, he at last fell asleep. Never once did he reflect on Anthony's suffering.

The police questioned him again the next day, at the Police Station this time. Although they offered him a cup of tea and a cigarette, he felt like a criminal. Nothing would convince them that he had no knowledge of Anthony's cousin. However, to his relief, during the interview the WPC came in to say they had located James Sanders.

'You may go now, Mr Cole,' said the Police Sergeant, 'but please leave your address and telephone number in Southampton at the desk when you go out.'

Jasper made his escape, sloping off down the steps of the Police Station as if he had something to hide. He departed for Southampton the following day, anxious to make the acquaintance of the new Renato.

He was pleasantly surprised when he met Robin Ballantyne-Smith who turned out to be a distinguished-looking man in his early forties. He spoke with an educated accent, letting the company know soon after he was introduced, that he was a Cambridge graduate. He had studied law but had discovered, after practising the profession for a couple of years that he was more suited to entertaining a theatre audience than convincing a courtroom jury.

Jasper and Robin hit it off right away. The director was delighted that they worked well together, feeding off one another's cues so that there was never the slightest moment of hesitation in their performance.

After a week of rehearsals Jasper received notification of Anthony's funeral. It came in the form of a letter from James Sanders' solicitor and it also demanded the return of the house keys to Number Seven. The director agreed to Jasper taking a couple of days off and since this made rehearsing the Renato part difficult, Robin was also granted free time.

'How about I come with you,' he suggested to Jasper, who although taken by surprise, readily agreed.

Wistfully he explained that Anthony's demise made him virtually homeless.

'You can come and stay at my pile any time you like,' said Robin. 'There's plenty of room…' He laughed, '…I've got twelve bedrooms.'

'Twelve?'

'Well, there are only six available given that the west wing has been closed up for years.'

The following day when they arrived at Number Seven, Jasper was horrified to discover that repairing the broken front door had necessitated a new lock being installed so that his key didn't fit.

'This is embarrassing,' he moaned, before remembering that he also had a key to the back door.

Fortunately this hadn't been changed, so they were able to let themselves in.

'Oh my word, what a dinky little house!' gushed Robin going from room to room, opening cupboards and peering into drawers.

'Will you mind staying here tonight?' asked Jasper, feeling anxious that Number Seven wasn't up to Robin's standard; maybe he would opt to book a room in a hotel.

'Duckie, I love it.'

'There's a choice of bedrooms,' explained Jasper, 'you can take one of the spares or...' He looked coyly at Robin, '...we could share.'

'Sharing would be much cosier,' replied Robin.

When they went to inspect the damage to the inside of the front door, Jasper discovered a pile of newspapers. Robin picked up the top one. 'This must be the local rag...' he said, 'maybe there's an obituary about your former lover.'

Jasper snatched the paper from him thumbing through the pages until he came to the right one. Here it is...' He stabbed a finger at the heading. 'What a load of waffle? You would think James and Ant had been best buddies over the years...' He shook his head in disbelief, 'when in fact they hardly ever saw one another.' He went to fling the newspaper aside but another heading stopped him. 'Wait a minute...what's this?' Beneath the name of Anthony Sanders was that of Thelma Stokes. It announced that Thelma had died in a mental institution still asserting that she had murdered her mother. So Anthony had been right! Thelma Stokes was nothing more than a nutcase.

Robin turned out to be as much a chatterbox as Jasper so they spent half the night exchanging anecdotes. Jasper talked in depth about his childhood experiences, revealing things he had never revealed to Anthony, who had always drawn the line at discussing emotional angst. When Robin's turn came to describe his growing-up years it seemed at first that they were worlds apart but Jasper began to realise that Robin's misery during his public school years had been parallel to his own suffering at the children's home.

'I shall never forgive my father for the torment he forced me to undergo,' said Robin. 'He used to tell me to stick up for myself. Your brothers came out unscathed, he'd say, so why can't you? Then he would draw comparisons...'

'Comparisons...' repeated Jasper.

'Yes, comparisons with my brothers; Douglas is a successful lawyer and Henry, the eldest, is a colonel in the Guards.'

'So he doesn't approve of your pursuing a stage career?'

Robin threw back his head and gave a caustic laugh. 'The old boy nearly had an apoplectic fit when I said I wanted to be an actor. Acting is for nancy boys, he said. He was going to disinherit me. I've got Douglas to thank for stepping in and talking sense into him.' He heaved a sigh. 'Yes, Douglas is a good sort.'

Jasper wanted to question him further: *was his mother still alive, did he have any sisters?* But a twinge of envy held him back. It seemed that everybody had family, even Anthony. *His* death had brought a cousin out of the woodwork. A feeling of abject self-pity swept over him. If *he* died, who would care? Who would bother to come to *his* funeral?

Anthony's funeral took place at the local Crematorium. Jasper and Robin took a taxi there, arranging for the driver to pick them up an hour later. Jasper was surprised to see a big crowd standing outside the chapel but soon realised they were attending another funeral. Anthony's funeral was sparsely attended. He recognised James Sanders quite easily because of his resemblance to Anthony. He was with his wife and two sons and an older woman, presumably Anthony's Aunt Florrie.

James left his family and approached Jasper and Robin. Shaking hands with obvious reluctance, he gave Robin a questioning look.

'This is a friend of mine, Robin Ballantyne-Smith,' said Jasper, hoping Robin's double-barrelled name would impress him.

James wasted no time in making it clear that neither of them was welcome, especially Robin and once the undertaker gave the signal for the mourners to go into the Chapel of Rest, he went back to his waiting family.

Jasper and Robin sat in the row behind them, joined by Anthony's two assistants from The Sanders Menswear Shop as well as Mavis Shuttleby from the jewellers and old Geoff Norton from the newsagent, both of whom had worked on the parade of shops for over twenty years and knew everybody. There was a reading from what, according to the vicar, had been one of Anthony's favourite scriptures and a eulogy from James, who described exploits he and Anthony had got up to in their youth. Jasper felt irritated when James insisted on referring to his erstwhile lover as Tony. During the time he'd known him everybody had called him Anthony. He of course had called him Ant.

The service took twenty minutes. Afterwards, the mourners gathered outside to inspect the wreaths which were laid out along the wall. Jasper's was predominant. Even in this sad moment he couldn't refrain from flamboyance. His was larger and more colourful than all the others. Jasper and Robin were obliged to wait a further fifteen minutes for their taxi. James came over to see them again.

'Don't wait around for us,' he said pointedly. Clearly the family intended to go on somewhere to drink a toast to their departed relation. 'Can I have the keys please?'

Jasper raised his eyebrows. 'Later, I've got to collect my things from the house.'

'I would appreciate it if you would do that as soon as possible as I want to put the house on the market.'

'Hadn't you better wait until after the reading of Ant's will?' Jasper sneered.

'That won't be necessary, I'm the legal heir.'
'Are you sure?'
'James!' Anthony's cousin turned when his wife called him.
'Coming, darling.'
Turning back to face Jasper, he scowled and said, 'Just make sure you're out of the house by tomorrow. Leave the keys on the kitchen table.'

The taxi took them back to Number Seven and after ordering a take-away, Jasper and Robin settled down to watch television. They smoked weed and drank several cans of lager before going to bed.

'I suppose I'd better sort out my things,' said Jasper the next morning. He gave a yawn. 'I've got a thumping headache. Now, where did Ant put that packet of paracetamol?'

He found it and took two capsules, feeling slightly annoyed that Robin seemed not to suffer any ill effects from their evening of indulgence.

'I'll help you sort things out,' said Robin. 'There's no point in leaving anything of value for James to confiscate. I wonder whether the will is going to change things.

Jasper shook his head, causing a rush of nausea to join his headache symptoms. 'I don't think so.'

'Well...' The other man gave a sly grin. 'What's stopping you from helping yourself to whatever you want? Some of this furniture is antique.'

'We can't remove furniture,' protested Jasper. In any case, he had no use for furniture antique or otherwise. The only item he coveted was Anthony's Bang and Olufsen stereo system, and that was too large to steal.

Robin pinched the bridge of his nose with his thumb and forefinger. 'Well, there are plenty of smaller items we can help ourselves to, things that bigoted cousin won't miss. After all, as Ant's partner, you're entitled to them.'

They spent the rest of the day searching through Anthony's personal belongings and, to Jasper's surprise, finding two pair of expensive gold cuff-links, a Rolex watch, and a state of the art camera. There was also a copy of his will, which clearly stated that everything was going to James Sanders.

Jasper flew into a rage, bellowing, 'You can't do this to me, Ant you fucking bastard, not after all I've done for you. I've given you the best eight years of my life, caring for you, filling your pathetic empty life with love. Before we met you were a sorry soul, lonely, miserable...'

'Calm down, Jasper.' Robin put a restraining hand on Jasper's arm but he shook it off.

With the copy of the will screwed up in one hand, he paced the floor, the clenched fist of the other hand pounding his forehead, reawakening the earlier headache and causing his left eye to twitch.

Robin tried manfully to pacify him until gradually outrage was replaced by a determination to take what he could from Anthony. Together the pair set about filling several large suitcases with anything of value and, by four o'clock, satisfied with their trophies, they ordered a taxi to take them to the station.

'You've got a lot of luggage,' grumbled the taxi driver, 'I should charge extra for that. I don't know how I'm going to fit it all into the boot.'

But they managed it and Robin climbed into the cab, holding the door open for Jasper.

'Just a minute...' Jasper remembered that he had agreed to leave the keys in the house when he left. Going back inside, he stood for a few moments looking around and as he felt his anger seep away, a tear rolled down his cheek. There had been so many happy moments: the evening he'd clowned around making Anthony laugh until he'd cried; the occasion when Ant had eased his disappointment with kind words after he'd been by-passed for a role he passionately wanted; the sunny day on which they'd strolled, arm-in-arm, to the end of the pier to watch the wind-surfers skull across the water.

He put his hand in his pocket and drew out the gold St Christopher his partner always wore round his neck. Ant had died during the night; he must have removed the necklace and put it on the dressing table when changing into his pyjamas, never doubting that he would fasten it round his neck again the next morning. Fingering it lovingly, Jasper fastened it round his own neck and with a lump in his throat he went out to join Robin in the taxi.

*****

THE DIGITAL AGE

James Sanders inherited Number Seven in 1990. He was a busy man and it took him a while to take stock of what his cousin's partner had purloined. He didn't bother tracing Jasper as the Southampton show had closed by now and he had no idea where Jasper had gone.

The early 1990s saw Nelson Mandela released from prison, the onset of the Gulf War and outrage at genocide in Bosnia. The cloning of Dolly the Sheep in 1996 caused controversy and in 1997 there was an outpouring of grief throughout the nation on the news of Princess Diana's tragic death.

James decided to let Number Seven rather than sell it. By doing so, he didn't have the bother of disposing of furniture although he put a classified in Friday-Ad advertising Anthony's collection of suits - all too large for him since James was a much slimmer version of his cousin. When he found a box of Jasper's theatrical costumes and masks - presumably left behind by mistake - he locked it away in the attic box room intending to get rid of it later. The Sanders Menswear Shop was put on the market as a going concern but failed to find a buyer. This was largely due to its old-fashioned sartorial stock and the fact that business had dropped off, the majority of its regular clientele having dwindled due to the passing of the years.

At the start of the school term, four students from the local college moved in. Simon and Max arrived first, claiming a bedroom each. Holly and Mel came two days later, agreeing to share the largest room. The girls already knew one another as they were second year students but for the boys this was their first time away from home.

'I hope you realise you've got to muck in with the chores,' announced Mel.

'Of course...' Simon winked at Max.

'We're not going to let you off because it's your first year. Your mothers may have done everything for you at home but me and Holly aren't going to step into their shoes.'

Holly looked a bit uncomfortable as she listened to Mel laying down the law although, having three brothers herself, she knew how easy it would be for the boys to get away with not pulling their weight.

Thus with four young residents Number Seven took on a new lease of life.

TWENTY-FIVE

As friends go, Mel and Holly were miss-matched. Mel was the only child of divorced parents and it hadn't taken her long to learn how to manipulate them. She only had to ask for something and one or other would provide it. Holly, on the other hand, had been brought up in a large family and was used to mucking in and doing her bit.

'Look Mel, the garden's lovely!' Holly exclaimed after they had unpacked and found time to go and inspect outside. 'The landlord must have got a gardener in to tidy it up before we arrived.'

'It says in the contract that we can help ourselves to all the fruit and vegetables but we've got to mow the lawn and do a bit of weeding. The boys can do that.'

'I don't mind doing it,' said Holly. 'I like gardening. We're lucky, the house has been spring-cleaned; it's much better than the place I rented last year.'

'Mine too,' agreed Mel, 'and we've got to keep it like this; we've got to start off on the right foot with the boys.'

However, her good intentions came to nothing. Both Simon and Max left unwashed plates and dishes on the worktops and forgot to clean the hob after they had used it. They hogged the television and left coffee stained mugs on every available surface. It became clear that neither of them had ever used a Hoover and Max had to ask Holly how to work the washing machine. Tempers erupted when Mel came home one day to find Simon's bike in pieces on the dining room floor.

'What the hell's going on?' she demanded.

Simon looked up from his kneeling position. 'I'm mending a puncture.'

'Well this isn't the place to do it.

'Don't fuss, I'll be finished soon.'

'I'm not fussing. You should mend your bike outside in the garden.'

'I couldn't, it started to rain.'

'That's your problem. I dread to think what the landlord would say if he could see you. Don't splash that water and make sure you don't get grease on the carpet. We don't want to forego our deposit.'

Simon lost his cool. 'I've spread newspaper over the precious carpet so it won't get damaged. What more do you want?'

'I would just like to know where we're supposed to eat this evening?'

'Off our laps?'

'You can but me and Holly are civilized and we want to eat at the table.'

'Stop going on, Mel, you're worse than my mum.'

'Well, I'm not your mum and as we all have to share this house, you've got no right to bring your bike indoors. Trouble is with you Si, you've been mollycoddled.'

Simon stood up and waved his spanner at her. 'Shut your face!'

'Don't threaten me!'

Simon took a step forwards, obliging Mel to back away.

'What's going on?' Holly stood in the doorway. Looking from one to the other, she repeated her question.

'Simon and I were having a little altercation,' said Mel, her tone rife with sarcasm. She gave a sniff of disdain as Simon sank to his knees again.

Holly dropped her rucksack and pointed at the dismantled bike. 'What's that doing in here?' As she spoke, she realised her words were the echo of her mother's on the day she had come home from shopping to find one of Holly's brothers cleaning the engine of his motorbike on the kitchen worktop.

'You may well ask,' replied Mel.

Simon opened his mouth to explain when Max turned up. Looking over Holly's shoulder he raised an enquiring eyebrow.

Mel lost patience. 'Get that fucking thing out of here a.s.a.p. and don't bring it in again.' She stamped her foot, reminding Holly of a naughty toddler. 'Never again, got it?'

'I could hear you shouting halfway down the road,' said Max.

Simon stood up and pointing at Mel, said, 'That bossy bitch is laying down the law again.'

'Well, if she's objecting to bike parts being spread out in here, she does have a point.'

'Okay, okay,' said Simon realising that he wasn't going to get support from Max. Sinking down onto his haunches, he spread out his hands, palms upwards. 'I'll clear it up and finish off outside.'

For the time being, the squabble was over but as the weeks passed tension between Simon and Mel developed into outright warfare. The other two kept their distance although occasionally they found themselves drawn into the arguments. Quite often Holly or Max would go the extra mile and tidy up after Simon in a bid to avoid yet another confrontation.

By Christmas the atmosphere was so tense that they were all relieved to go home to their families for the festivities.

After the Christmas break, Holly returned to Number Seven with mixed feelings. During the vacation she described the situation to her mother, who advised her to take a softly-softly approach.

'I expect it will blow over,' said her mother, 'but of course if you're not happy staying there then find other digs.'

'I don't want to move out,' explained Holly, 'I like the house and I like the other students most of the time. Actually, I like Max all of the time and I'm prepared to put up with Simon's couldn't care less attitude so long as the arguments stop. Maybe I ought to have a word with Mel.'

'Well dear,' said her mother, 'just don't get too involved.'

But Holly was determined to sort things out and the opportunity arose that evening when Mel arrived home ahead of Simon and Max.

'Can you go easy on the boys, Mel, especially Simon...' she said after they had exchanged their news.

'He's a bloody troublemaker, that one,' sniffed Mel.

'He's all right as long as you don't rub him up the wrong way.'

'He rubs me up the wrong way, you mean.'

'Whatever. But we've all got to live together and it doesn't help if you and Simon are at loggerheads.'

'I can't bear the way he takes advantage, he's lazy, he's rude...'

'He's been better lately.'

'I'm simply sticking up for our rights as sharing tenants; there's nothing wrong with that. Sorry, Holly, I won't let him get away with it.'

Holly gave a shrug, knowing there was no way she could change Mel's attitude. She decided to have a word with Max but it was tricky trying to catch him on his own. As luck would have it, she bumped into him in the corridor at college the next day.

'Hi, Max, have you got a moment?'

He grinned at her and she warmed to his friendly smile.

'What's up?'

She briefly explained her worries about Mel's obdurate standpoint.

'Yeah, I know what you mean but what can we do about it?'

'Erm, I was wondering whether you could talk to Simon, get him to ease off a bit; you know, fall in with Mel's rules whenever possible. Actually, her rota system is pretty fair.'

Max nodded. 'I'll have a word.'

Over the Spring Term things improved and Holly could only imagine that Max had worked his magic on Simon. She never got around to asking him because the explanation was unexpectedly revealed. One night she woke up feeling thirsty and decided to go downstairs to get a glass of water. Without switching on the light, she crept past Mel's bed so as not to wake her. On her way back, on hearing voices as she passed Simon's door, Holly paused to listen. They had all agreed that there would be no overnight visits from girl or boyfriends. She heard giggles followed by a high-pitched 'shhh' then the unmistakable sound of noisy bedsprings. With a gasp, she hurried along the landing to her own room. It seemed that once again Simon was breaking the rules.

In her haste, she accidentally knocked her leg on the end of Mel's bed. 'Sorry,' she whispered, hoping she hadn't woken her room-mate. There was no response.

Climbing into bed, she drew the duvet up to her chin and glanced towards the other bed squinting as her eyes became accustomed to the darkness. The bed was empty. Suspicions arose: had Mel and Simon become more than flatmates?

For the next few days, Holly kept her suspicions to herself. She didn't want to admit it but she felt jealous of Mel, who seemed to have everything: long blond hair, large grey eyes, a figure to die for added to which she seemed to sail through her course work without any trouble. Now she had gained the attention of Simon who oozed charm despite his argumentative nature. He was tall and athletic with fair wavy hair and had the good looking square-jawed features of a Hollywood star. It didn't seem fair.

Holly studied herself in the wardrobe mirror and grimaced at her sleek black hair and well-defined eyebrows. Her skin colouring was quite dark, a throwback to her Sri Lankan grandfather. Her mother, who was light-skinned, assured her that she was lucky because she didn't get sunburnt but Holly didn't see this as a great consolation.

She kept her suspicions about Simon and Mel's relationship to herself, surprised that their friends hadn't spotted it. One day after college, a group of students decided to meet for a BBQ on the beach. It was a pleasant evening and the tide was out. As the light began to fade, Holly noticed that Simon and Mel were no longer in the midst of the gathering. This was unusual since Simon was nearly always the life and soul of any party. All at once, she saw them running towards the pier, hand-in-hand. Unable to contain her curiosity, she slipped away unnoticed and followed them. On reaching the pier instead of heading for the entrance, they sneaked underneath it and, although by then the sun had set and it was quite dark, Holly couldn't miss seeing Mel leaning against one of the stanchions with Simon pressed close to her. His hands pushed up her skirt and then he lifted Mel off the ground so that she could wrap her legs around him. Holly gave a little gasp: she had seen enough. Turning on her heel, she raced back along the beach to rejoin the others.

Holly continued to behave normally towards Simon and Mel. It was easy with Simon because he seemed so besotted by Mel that he didn't seem to notice her anyway. As for Mel, Holly deliberately avoided girlie chats with her, claiming that she needed to study. At college they went their separate ways since Mel was doing geography and biology and Holly, English literature. Then one day Mel cornered her.

'Do you fancy changing rooms, Holly?'

'What d'you mean?'

'Well, you must have gathered that Simon and I are an item.'

'So?'

'We thought...'

'We...?' Holly wasn't going to make it easy for her.

'Me and Simon thought you would like to have a room to yourself. I mean to say, you'd have more privacy and you wouldn't have to worry about me chattering on all the time.' She gave a laugh. 'You know how you like to get your nose into those books of yours.'

Holly took time to reply. Obviously it would be more convenient to have a room to herself. 'I'll have to think about it,' she said. She was taken by surprise when Mel rushed over and gave her a hug. 'I haven't said yes,' she muttered, pulling away.

'No but you said you'd think about it, and that's great.'

Of course, in the end Holly agreed to change rooms and the swap went without a hitch except that Max looked a bit surprised when he came home and found everything different.

'I didn't know they were together,' he said to Holly. 'Why didn't you tell me?'

'It's up to you to notice things for yourself,' she retorted, then felt guilty when she saw the hurt look on his face.

Everything continued smoothly until the middle of the Summer Term when Mel came home from college with a furious look on her face.

'What's up with you?' asked Holly, backing away as Mel strode though the dining room into the kitchen.

'You'd better ask that bastard Si,' she stormed.

'Why, what's he done?'

'The two-timing moron is chasing after that ginger-haired Scotch bitch...'

'Scottish,' corrected Holly automatically.

'...whatever, that airhead in Biology.'

'Who? Tamsin Kennedy? She seems nice to me.'

Mel grimaced. 'She's sugary sweet, behaves as if butter wouldn't melt in her mouth but underneath she's a bitch.'

'Are you sure they're seeing one another?'

'Of course I'm sure.'

'What are you going to do?'

'I'm going to have it out with him. He's in deep shit I can tell you.'

Mel flounced out of the room and stomped upstairs.

Holly got on with cooking her omelette but she couldn't help flinching when Simon came in.

'What's up?' he asked, seeing the expression on her face.

'You'd better ask Mel?'

'Oh shit, she's seen me and Tamsin. What mood is she in?'

'A not very good one,' replied Holly, adding grated cheese to her omelette.

They both jumped when they heard a thump from upstairs.

'What was that?' said Simon.

Holly checked her oven chips. 'I think you'd better go and find out,' she said, switching the oven off.

Simon dashed through the dining-room bumping into Max on the way. 'What's going on?' he demanded.

Holly rolled her eyes. 'Mel's having a tantrum.'

'It sounds more like a revolution.'

'That too!'

By now they could hear the fighting pair's shouts and more thumps on the landing.

'I think she's chucking him out of her bedroom,' said Max, 'it looks like you might have to move back in with her so that Si can have his room back.'

Shovelling her omelette and chips onto a plate, Holly snapped, 'She can't do that.'

'She will.'

'No way, I'll not stand for it.' She tossed her head. 'I like being on my own, why should I jump to Mel's command?'

'I agree with you,' Max said with a grin. 'Look, if it comes to that, I mean if they don't patch things up, I'll back you all the way, Holly.'

'Thanks Max,' she said impulsively planting a kiss on his cheek.

For a moment he looked surprised. Then he grinned and took off his glasses to give them a wipe and, as he walked away, Holly couldn't help thinking that without them, Max was a good looking boy.

TWENTY-SIX

The next morning things turned out differently to the way Holly expected.

'You'd better hurry up, Mel or you'll be late for college,' she said when Mel trundled downstairs still wearing her pyjamas.

'I'm not going in,' she said.

'Why not, don't you feel well?'

Mel shrugged. 'What's the point I'm not interested in either geography or biology. I only stuck it out because of Simon. Honestly, I never wanted to do further education, my dad made me.'

This surprised Holly. Perhaps when his daughter reached the age of eighteen, Mel's indulgent parents had decided to put their foot down and force her to take her studies more seriously.

Holly tried to cheer her up. 'You're just feeling low. Why don't you come to college with me and later on today, maybe you and Si will make it up.'

Mel glowered. 'Not likely, yesterday he made it perfectly clear that we're finished. And do you know what...' She jutted her chin. 'I'm glad because now I can leave college with no regrets.'

'But surely he was only flirting with Tamsin. You're far prettier and more fun than she is, Mel. He won't last long with her.'

This wasn't quite true because Tamsin Kennedy was a very attractive red-head with green eyes and pale freckles across her nose. She was quietly spoken with an Edinburgh accent.

Mel shrugged. 'I'm not interested in Si any more. He's history...' She paused, '...but out of curiosity, where did he sleep last night?'

Holly wasn't sure about Simon being history. Mel's interest in where he slept last night didn't seem like idle curiosity, but she kept her opinion to herself. 'He kipped down on the floor of Max's room. Anyway, get dressed and come to college with me. You'll feel better later on.'

But Mel couldn't be persuaded, so Holly went off on her own.

At four o'clock she went home hoping Mel would have changed her mind but once inside Number Seven, the house seemed unusually quiet.

'Hello Mel,' she called up the stairs but there was no answering greeting.

She went out to the garden but although there was an open Danielle Steel novel on the grass beside a garden chair, Mel was not there. Going back indoors she went upstairs and knocked on the bedroom door. No reply. Tentatively, Holly opened the door and peered inside. The room was empty and it didn't take her long to realise that all Mel's possessions had gone. Rushing back downstairs, she found a note on the dining room table, which said: *Dear Holly, can't hack it, gone home, now you can have your old room back, love Mel.*

Holly sat down at the table with the note in her hand. She hadn't taken Mel seriously enough. She had been confident that Simon and Mel would soon be back together again. They were an ill-assorted couple but they had seemed genuinely fond of one another. She wondered how Simon would react when he heard the news.

In the event, both Simon and Max were shocked to learn that Mel had left.

'Why on earth does she want to give up now when she's nearly finished her course?' said Max.

'She told me she doesn't want to do either geography or biology,' said Holly.

'She wanted to do a beauty and hairdressing course but her father wouldn't let her. She dreamt of opening a beauty salon one day,' mumbled Simon. 'She told me she hated what she was doing and the people on the course.'

'But why wait until now to leave?' asked Max.

Simon lowered his head into his hands. 'This is all my fault.'

Holly cast him a searching look. 'Don't be dramatic, Si, how is it your fault?'

'I let her down. The Tamsin incident didn't mean anything. I told her that but she wouldn't believe me. She might have stuck it out if I hadn't messed around.'

Holly shook her head. 'No, Si, it would have come to a head eventually. She's never been happy here. Look how she bossed us around when we first moved in; it was because she didn't want to be here. It's got nothing to do with your relationship.'

But Simon wouldn't be convinced. Shaking his head, he said, 'No, I'm responsible.' He went to the door then stopped and said, 'If you want to move back into the big room, Holly, it's all right with me.'

There was a strained atmosphere in Number Seven during the last few weeks of term. To cheer them up, Max suggested throwing a party before they left to go their separate ways and it was arranged for the following Saturday.

Thirty students descended on Number Seven, filling the rooms and overflowing into the garden. The music which started at a reasonable level soon reached untenable decibels and it wasn't long before the neighbours started to complain. Holly did her best to pacify them. But worse was to come. Vodka and lager flowed like water and when one or two of the students were seen sprawled on the lawn out of their heads she got really worried.

'It's time you left,' she shouted above the din but nobody heard her.

Max joined her. 'This wasn't a very good idea was it?' he said. 'I didn't count on so many gatecrashers.'

'Yeah, head bangers too! Where's Simon?'

Max looked at her with soul-full eyes. 'He's upstairs with Tamsin.'

'Oh God, thank goodness Mel isn't here.'

She spoke too soon.

'Hi...hi every...everybody.' Mel stood in the kitchen doorway with a bottle of Vodka in one hand; the other was planted on the wall to steady herself. 'I heard you were having an end-of-term shindig so I thought I'd come along.'

'She's well tanked up,' Max whispered to Holly, who hurried over to the latecomer.

'It's lovely to see you, Mel,' said Holly. Taking her arm, she led her to the patio and sat her down on one of the garden chairs.

'Where's Simon?'

'I don't know.' Holly looked pleadingly at Max, hoping he would take the hint and warn Simon.

It was too late. At that moment, Simon and Tamsin came into the garden. His arm was draped around her neck and she was giggling, her head leant on his shoulder. They were clearly drunk.

Mel stood up. 'You bitch,' she shouted at Tamsin, who looked back at her with a vacant expression on her face. But Simon was not so far gone and he quickly ushered

Tamsin back into the house. Mel picked up her bottle of Vodka and stumbled after them.

'Stop her, Max!' cried Holly.

Max reacted quickly and ran after her but he was stopped when she slammed the kitchen door in his face. He wrestled with the door handle but Mel's back was pressed against it and through the window, Holly saw Mel smash the Vodka bottle against the worktop. What followed was like a slow motion scene from a movie. Simon stationed himself in front of Tamsin to protect her and because of this he took the full force of the broken bottle as Mel brandished it in the air and brought it down on the side of his head.

He fell to the floor, blood pouring from a wound on his forehead while Tamsin screamed hysterically. Shocked by what she had done, Mel dropped to her knees beside Simon, whimpering, 'I'm sorry, I'm sorry…'

Max pushed the door open and he and Holly rushed inside. Taking out his mobile, he called for an ambulance while Holly ran upstairs to fetch a supply of towels in order to staunch the blood. All the while, the music gained momentum and the other students continued to drink, smoke and chatter, oblivious to the drama unfolding in their midst.

While waiting for the ambulance, Max took charge. Switching off the stereo he told the party-goers to leave. Some of them were so far gone that it was up to the more sober amongst them to organise their departure.

By the time the ambulance arrived there were only half a dozen people left. The paramedics carried Simon out. The police came too, wanting to question Mel but she seemed unable to comprehend that she wasn't allowed to go in the ambulance with Simon and it took a long time for a WPC to calm her down. They took her away in a police car leaving another policeman to talk to Holly and Max.

'Do you know what motivated the young lady to do this?'

'It was an accident,' said Holly, casting a sideways glance at Max.

He backed her up. 'Yes, the bottle got broken and Mel, being a bit the worse for wear, picked it up and dropped it accidentally hitting Simon on the head.'

'I doubt that she actually dropped it,' said the policeman.

Yes, thought Holly, *Simon's six foot two and Mel is only five foot six so she could hardly have dropped it on his head.*

Max tried to explain. 'Well, she kind of flourished it but she didn't mean to hurt him.'

The questions went on and on but at last the policeman left.

'Do you think they believed us?' asked Holly. 'I mean, that it was an accident.'

'Time will tell,' replied Max.

'We'll be off now,' said one of the lingering partygoers and the others followed him out.

'Let's ring the hospital,' said Holly. 'God, I hope Simon's all right.'

Their enquiry revealed that Simon had a slight concussion and needed stitches to the wound on his forehead

'Phone again tomorrow and we'll know more,' the nurse advised.

'Have his parents been told?' asked Holly.

'Yes, they're by his bedside. I expect they'll want to have a word with you tomorrow.'

Holly's heart sank. Suppose Simon's parents blamed them for what had happened! She looked around at the chaos left since the departure of the students and then gasped, 'What happened to Tamsin?'

'I haven't seen her,' said Max.

'You look in the garden, I'll look upstairs,' said Holly.

She found her curled up asleep on one of the beds in the front bedroom and even though she shook her several times, it was clear that Tamsin would have to stay there until she woke up the next morning.

Neither Holly nor Max was able to sleep that night. At two o'clock Holly went downstairs to find Max nursing a cup of tea.

'So you couldn't sleep either,' he said, 'the kettle has only just boiled if you want one.'

'Thanks.'

'I would never have believed Mel could do something like that,' said Max.

'I know; it was an awful shock.'

'You've known her a while, was she always hot-tempered?'

Holly shook her head. 'To tell you the truth I hardly knew her at all. We were casual friends at college last year but we weren't in shared digs. I suppose you only really get to know someone when you live under the same roof as them.'

'I suppose so.'

'Well,' said Holly, finishing her tea, 'we'd better go back to bed. I hope Tamsin doesn't wake up too early tomorrow morning.'

'So do I.'

'I keep wondering what the repercussions are going to be,' said Holly.

They found out the next day when Simon's parents came to call on them. Graham Bellingham was a daunting figure. He was a mature version of his son but several stones heavier, his hair which must once have been fair was grey where it existed for it encircled his pate like Friar Tuck's. His wife, Marjorie, was a small mouse-like woman who remained mute throughout most of the encounter, content to let her husband do the talking.

'Simon tells me it was your idea to have a party, young man,' Graham Bellingham said, addressing Max.

'Everybody agreed to it,' replied Max defensively.

Mr Bellingham looked around the room, taking note of the chaos from the night before. 'It looks more like a pub brawl than an end-of-term party,'

'It's still early and we haven't had time to clear up,' protested Holly.

'I don't think your landlord is going to like the mess you've made of his premises.'

This thought had occurred to Holly too but she didn't want to face that problem yet.

'How is Simon?' she asked.

Graham Bellingham's frown deepened. 'He's recovering but he'll have a permanent scar on his left temple.'

Holly clapped a hand to her mouth. 'Oh dear, I'm so sorry; poor Simon!' She rushed on, 'Please give him our love…'

Max nodded in agreement but Mr Bellingham cut them short. 'I hope you realise this situation could bring your studies to a short, sharp end. The Head won't like students causing mayhem; it brings the College into disrepute. I'd like to know what possessed you to ask so many louts to your party.'

'We didn't,' said Max, 'they were gatecrashers.'

'You should have been more careful about the people you let in,' thundered Mr Bellingham.

Holly shivered as his voice reverberated around the room.

'Can I get you a cup of tea?' she asked in an endeavour to calm the situation.

'Yes please.' Marjorie Bellingham spoke for the first time. When Holly started towards the kitchen she found her close on her heels.

'Can I give you a hand?'

She was about to refuse the offer of help then realised that Simon's mother wanted to speak to her on her own. From the other room, her husband was still grilling Max, who surprised Holly by patiently standing his ground. She felt sorry for him and nervous too and she had to make a conscious effort to stop her hand from shaking as she filled the kettle.

'His bark is worse than his bite,' said Marjorie in a soft voice. 'You see, Simon is our only child and he's the apple of his father's eye.'

Holly lit the gas then said, 'You know, Mrs Bellingham, we had no idea that Mel was delusional and we didn't expect her to turn up at the party.'

'Yes, I've heard the police are referring her for psychiatric treatment. Poor girl, I'm sure she didn't mean to injure Simon. Did she show any signs of her condition when she was living here with you?'

'None at all,' replied Holly although several scenarios where Mel had seemed somewhat unbalanced flitted through her mind. 'But she was a bit possessive of Simon.'

When the kettle boiled, Holly made the tea and went back into the dining-room, followed by Mrs Bellingham. Both Mr Bellingham and Max were sitting down now and although the former still looked annoyed, the atmosphere seemed to have cooled. Over a cup of tea, things improved even more and by the time the couple left, Graham Bellingham's expression was less disgruntled. He strode off without a backward glance but Marjorie Bellingham hesitated. Taking Holly's hand she addressed them both, saying, 'Despite what my husband told you, I don't think Simon's scar will be permanent.'

After they had gone, Holly and Max looked at one another with relief.

'We'd better start clearing up,' said Holly, 'and I think Mr Bellingham is right, our landlord is not going to take kindly to the damage…' She glanced around at the stains on the walls and the scratches on the table. 'We'll lose our deposit.'

Several days later, the landlord, James Sanders, came to inspect the damage.

'Of course, you'll lose your deposit,' he said, 'but I realise what happened wasn't your fault. The police have kept me informed and from what they've told me, you two tried to keep order. I gather that the young lady who made the attack was of unsound mind. It's lucky she didn't cause more harm to your friend.'

'She didn't know what she was doing,' said Holly. 'We're really sorry about the mess. We've cleaned up as best we could.'

'I can see that,' said James. He smiled. 'As a matter of fact, I have teenage children of my own so…'

'Thank you for being so understanding, sir,' said Max.

'Just the same, young man,' replied James, resuming a more serious expression, 'you will have to forego your deposit.' His gaze went to the suitcases standing in the corner of the room. 'Are you leaving today?'

'I am,' said Max, 'but Holly's dad is picking her up tomorrow.'

'Well, you're welcome to stay until Monday; that's when your lease runs out.'

'Thank you,' said Holly and Max together.

After James Sanders had left, the pair looked at one another and burst out laughing. 'Well, that wasn't too bad, considering…' said Max.

'I thought he was very reasonable,' said Holly. 'What time is your train?'

Max hesitated before replying. 'It's at six o'clock but I don't have to leave today. I could stay and we could spend our last weekend together.'

'God, Max, you make it sound like a final farewell, who knows we might bump into one another again some time.'

Max looked doleful. 'I doubt it, after all, you've graduated and you'll soon be busy job-hunting.'

'You're coming back next year, aren't you?'

'Yes, my final year.'

'I don't live all that far from here, Max and my dad's promised to buy me a car now that I've passed all my exams; I could drive down to see you sometimes.'

'I'd like that.'

'Will you rent a room here in Number Seven again?'

'Oh, I don't think I'd want to, Holly, it wouldn't be the same without you and Simon.'

'I know.' Holly did a mini-pirouette, swinging her arms. 'I've loved living here despite the ups and downs.'

'So have I.'

Max went to pick up his suitcase but Holly stopped him. 'Please stay. You're right, we could have a lovely weekend together just to wind up the college year. I'll ring my dad and tell him not to come until Monday.'

*****

THE NEW MILLENNIUM

At nearly one hundred years old, I had seen many changes. The early years of the new century brought disasters including Nine Eleven; the Iraq War and the Indonesian tsunami; Wikipedia was launched and the Apple I-phone heralded the demise of the landline; Prince Charles married Camilla Parker-Bowles and in 2009 Barack Obama became America's first black president.

All along the South Coast the New Millennium was celebrated with parties and fireworks, and beacons were lit on the seafront as part of a string across the country.

In 2003 James Sanders took early retirement and decided to sell Number Seven. He sold to a couple of teachers from the local secondary school. Katherine's recent divorce settlement from her accountant husband and Olivia's legacy from her grandmother prompted them to pool their resources and purchase a property together.

Olivia, who was single, had so far been living in rented accommodation so she was excited at becoming a first-time buyer.

'It's just what we've been looking for, Kathy,' she enthused when they viewed Number Seven.

Katherine wasn't so sure. 'It needs some t.l.c. and I'm wondering whether we ought to look for something overlooking the sea.'

'It's only a five-minute drive to the pier and ten minutes from school,' pointed out Olivia, who was quite taken with Number Seven.

The quick sale of Katherine's marital home forced a decision and six weeks later these upwardly mobile ladies moved in.

Katherine and Olivia planned to take up their paintbrushes and start decorating Number Seven during the school holidays and they poured over copies of 'House and Garden' in search of ideas.

'We'll get rid of most of the carpets and put down wooden floors,' said Katherine.

'Yes, and we'll transform the garden. Decking close to the house and a gazebo at the end...' Olivia gathered pace, '...and of course we'll have to get some garden furniture.'

'We'll need a new shower,' said Katherine, ever practical...'that one's as old as the ark.'

Clearly things were looking up for me

TWENTY-SEVEN

'Well,' said Katherine as she and Olivia stood in the middle of the room surrounded by furniture and boxes, 'we're going to be a bit cramped until we sought this lot out.'

'Most of it's yours,' Olivia pointed out with a giggle.

Katherine grinned. 'I know...I should have let Pete take more of this stuff but he put my back up with his unreasonable demands over the divorce. After all, why should he take all this furniture when my money paid for it? We'll just have to sell some of it...or give it to a charity shop, more like.'

'Let's start unpacking some of these boxes and at least get the beds made up so that we'll have somewhere to sleep tonight. Which bedroom do you want, Kathy?'

'Why don't we toss for it?' suggested Katherine taking a pound coin out of her purse.

'Tails!' said Olivia.

Katherine wrinkled her nose. 'Sorry, it's heads, I win.'

'Well then?'

'I'll take the bigger room in the front.'

With the important decision of the room resolved, the pair set about unpacking essential items. Katherine, a natural organiser, directed operations with Olivia obligingly jumping to her command. By the end of the day they had stored away most of the crockery and glassware into the kitchen cupboards and the food in the fridge; beds had been made up in the allocated rooms and the furniture arranged around the remaining packing cases. They stopped for a Chinese take-away at seven thirty then carried on until midnight.

'Let's call it a day,' said Olivia, sinking into a chair and wiping a hand across her forehead. 'I'm knackered.'

'So am I, but it's been a good day, hasn't it?'

The next day the girls were due back at school so the rest of the unpacking was going to have to wait until the evening.

Olivia pulled a face. 'I'm sorry, Kathy, but I've got an after-school rehearsal for the end-of-term play,' she confessed, 'so I won't be home until about six o'clock'

'The rest of the unpacking will have to wait,' replied Katherine with a smile, 'there's really no hurry; we've moved in, that's the main thing.'

'But I want to get started on the decorating.'

Katherine shrugged. 'What's the hurry, we've got the summer holiday ahead of us so there's plenty of time.'

The girls usually cycled to school during the summer months and later in the week, as they wheeled their bikes to the cycle shed, Olivia said, 'Kathy, have you seen the key to the attic room?'

'No, I didn't realise it was locked.'

'Yes, isn't that strange?'

'The key will turn up sooner or later.'

'Did you look in that room when we viewed the house?'

'I don't think I did.'

'Neither did I. That's a bit odd, isn't it?'

'I think the agent said something about a missing key. It doesn't matter. If necessary, we'll have to get a locksmith in.'

Olivia finished padlocking her bike and slung her hold-all over her shoulder. 'I wonder what secrets that room holds.'

Katherine laughed. 'It will be empty; don't let your imagination run away with you, the previous owner wouldn't have left anything behind.'

'I think we should force the lock and find out,' said Olivia, clearly keen to do a bit of investigating.

They went their separate ways: Katherine to the Science Room and Olivia to the Main Hall where she was due to give a drama lesson.

As soon as Olivia got home she started searching for the missing key. It was nowhere to be found. Impatient as ever, she said, 'We'll have to force the lock.'

'It can wait, it's not *that* important, ' Katherine disagreed.

'I think it is,' insisted Olivia.

For several days Olivia let the matter drop. She had entered into the purchase of the house with Katherine without giving much thought as to how well they would get on. At school, during breaks, they had always sought one another out. This was partly because the other members of staff were either of a different generation or unwilling to spend time with their fellow teachers. Olivia and Katherine often made fun of the ungainly maths teacher, Vera Wiley with her old-fashioned tweed skirt and her grey hair cut like a member of the armed forces; they sympathised with poor little Angela Thompson who couldn't control her pupils during history lessons; they sniggered at Phil Matheson who took his gymnastic class too seriously, sometimes resulting in one or two of the girls bursting into tears. Of course, these teachers never knew how much amusement they provided. Certainly, neither Olivia nor Katherine considered that their secret ridiculing was unkind.

One afternoon Olivia arrived home earlier than Katherine and curiosity about the locked attic room got the better of her. They had both looked for the key but it had never come to light. *The time has come to find out*, thought

Olivia, running up the two flights of stairs to arrive on the top landing slightly out of breath. She had brought a screwdriver with her and, armed with this, she set about forcing the lock.

Half an hour later, impeded by the need to stay alert in case Katherine caught her red-handed, she managed to release the obstinate lock and the door swung inwards. There were scratches and gashes on the doorframe but Olivia didn't care: too bad if Katherine was annoyed!

The room smelled musty as she tentatively stepped inside. Venetian blinds were drawn over the window and when she pulled them up a cloud of dust rose into the air. She turned away from the window coughing and sneezing and then let out a shriek of alarm when she caught sight of a ventriloquist's dummy balanced on a wooden kitchen chair against the wall. Its eyes seemed to bore right into her and its bright red mouth gaped revealing a set of startling white teeth. Recovering, she inspected the rest of the room. There was an old iron bedstead covered by a stained ticking mattress, a large free-standing mirror and several theatrical posters on the wall. One showed an actor in drag with a date on the bottom: Eastbourne 1985.

Then she spied a large wooden trunk. It too was covered with dust. Olivia brushed her hand across it, screwing up her nose at the dirt on her palm. But it needed more than a brush of her hand so she raced downstairs to fetch a damp cloth and a duster. A good clean revealed a barrel-topped chest with pine and brass fittings. It was unlocked.

Olivia held her breath as she lifted the lid. The contents astounded her. The trunk was crammed full of theatrical costumes; some were silk, some velvet, some brocade. She pulled one out and held it up. It was the one depicted in the poster on the wall above the bed. So an actor had resided in Number Seven. She was puzzled. While negotiating the price of the house she and Katherine had, on one occasion, met with the owner and he certainly didn't fit the image of an actor.

'Hi, Livvy, where are you?'

Katherine had arrived home. Forgetting all about her dread of annoying her housemate by forcing entry into the attic room, Olivia called back, 'Up here. Come and see what I've discovered.'

Katherine was as surprised as Olivia. 'Fancy someone abandoning all these expensive costumes! They must be worth a fortune,' she exclaimed. 'Let's clean the place up and have a good look at them all. It seems a shame to bring them out with all this dust around.'

'Good idea. We'll have dinner and then get to work.'

Over dinner they couldn't stop discussing it.

'I think we had better get in touch with the previous owner,' said Katherine, 'after all he may have forgotten all about them.'

Olivia looked indignant. 'No way, it was up to him to clear the room before the sale.' She couldn't bear the thought of relinquishing her find.

'He certainly didn't look like an actor. Maybe it was left by one of his tenants. He did say he'd let the house for a couple of years.'

'He let it to students. They wouldn't have been able to afford costumes like those. I think they were left by the people before what's-his-name…'

'James Sanders,' supplied Katherine. 'Perhaps we ought to find out.'

'No!'

Katherine's eyebrows rose in surprise. Olivia wasn't usually so adamant.

Dinner over and the washing-up done, they trudged upstairs to do the cleaning. It was beginning to get dark and the only light was a single bulb hanging from the ceiling. Olivia rushed to get a table lamp to plug in so that they could see better. With two pairs of hands it didn't take long to clean the place up.

'Wait a minute...' said Katherine, 'I think we should spread a sheet over that dodgy-looking mattress before we start sorting things out.'

She dashed off and returned with a sheet from the airing cupboard, which they spread over the bed. Their inspection revealed a mixture of items: pantomime dame dresses, Halloween outfits, pirate gear. There were also a few stage props.

Olivia sat back on her haunches and shaking her head in puzzlement said, 'How could anyone forget to take these?'

'It's a mystery,' agreed Katherine.

They were both exhausted by the time they went to bed. Olivia found it difficult to fall asleep. All she could think about was the possibility of utilising some of the costumes in the up-coming end of school year play which was set in the late 1700s.

Olivia went to school next day having decided that her lead heroine would wear the dark green velvet number. It would need a tuck or two here and there but she was sure Chloe Kennington would look quite fetching in it even though she was a bit thin. Certainly, it would make the performance of Jane Austen's *Pride and Prejudice* look more authentic.

Back at home she noticed that Katherine seemed a little subdued.

'Is something wrong?' she asked.

Katherine shook her head. 'No. I'm tired, that's all.' She went silent for a while then said, 'By the way, I've been in touch with James Sanders about those costumes.'

'What!' The book Olivia was holding landed with a thump on the table. 'Why on earth did you do that?'

'They are rightfully his.'

'No they're not, they came with the house that *we* bought.'

'Technically, they could be construed as stolen property.'

'What are you talking about? And more to the point, what did he say?'

'I didn't actually speak to him. I left a message on his answerphone.'

Olivia relaxed a little. 'Thank goodness for that,' she said, 'with a bit of luck he won't pick up.'

But he did pick up the message and luckily, it was Olivia who took the call.

He sounded impatient. 'Those old things, they're no use to me. Get rid of them, they belonged to the partner of the previous owner...' He paused, 'he's an actor and if my memory serves me right his name is Jasper King...what's the name of that singer...Cole. Yes, it's Jasper Cole. You can probably trace him through Equity.'

'Thank you very much.'

Olivia put the phone down, her heart pounding. She had no intention of contacting Jasper King, Cole, or whatever his name was.

When Katherine came in she broke the news to her, omitting the actor's name and the possibility of being able to trace him.

'Well, there you are,' gloated Katherine, 'now you can make use of those costumes with a clear conscience or of course, we could make some money selling them on ebay.'

But Olivia wouldn't hear of that and the incident was soon forgotten. The school year was drawing to a close with all the usual extra activities: sports day, the concert, the school play. Olivia enjoyed the buzz, especially this year. Her lead, Chloe, was delighted to wear the green velvet dress and the performance looked to be the best yet.

TWENTY-EIGHT

Olivia walked out of the school gates with all the paraphernalia from the play. She had ordered a taxi to take her home because it would have been impossible to manage everything on her bike. After a successful school year - *Pride and Prejudice* had proved to be the best performance yet - she was looking forward to the long summer holiday. Work was to commence the next day on the alterations they had decided upon. The downstairs floors would be pulled up and replaced with real oak floorboards, a new shower would be installed and while the builder and the plumber were busy with that, she and Katherine would start painting the upstairs rooms.

When she got home she found Katherine seething with anger.

'What's the matter?'

'You may well ask,' stormed her housemate. 'That bloody ex-husband of mine was supposed to pick up all this stuff this morning but he didn't turn up.'

The stuff she was referring to was the excess furniture she had brought with her. She seemed to have completely forgotten that she not Pete had insisted on claiming it.

'He'll turn up later.'

'He'd better, otherwise all this rubbish goes out into the garden.' She frowned angrily. 'And I hope it rains and ruins it all.'

Katherine in a fury was a sight to behold. Olivia held her breath as she continued to rant about her errant ex-husband. Olivia had never met Pete and was now consumed with curiosity. The picture Katherine painted of him was far from complimentary.

He rang the doorbell just as his ex-wife was giving her a colourful description of his bad eating habits, his untidiness and his lack of consideration.

Katherine stomped down the hall to answer the door, stomping back again followed by a tall good-looking man in his mid-thirties. His frown changed to a broad smile when he saw Olivia.

'This is Pete,' said Katherine, 'Pete, meet Livvy.'

Olivia shook his hand and found herself staring into a pair of twinkling grey-blue eyes. Was this the monster Kathy had described?

'I've hired a van,' he said, 'I hope it's not blocking you in.'

Olivia laughed. 'No, that's Kathy's new car, I've got a moped but we go to work by bike when the weather's good.'

'For the exercise, I suppose,' he laughed. 'Look, my mate's outside; he's going to give me a hand.' He promptly went out into the hall to call his friend.

It didn't take long for the two of them to remove the unwanted furniture, leaving the room looking more spacious. After the pair had lifted everything into the van, Pete came back inside.

He took Olivia's hand again, 'Nice to meet you, Livvy.' Turning to Katherine he said, 'By the way, Kath, I didn't see my antique wine rack amongst that lot. Where is it?'

'*Your* wine rack...?' Katherine looked apoplectic and Olivia guessed this was because he addressed her as 'Kath' which she hated. 'I got rid of it.'

'You've done what? But Kath, it wasn't yours to get rid of. It was a present from my dad.'

'Well, that's too bad. If you'd been around when the removal men picked up the furniture you could have claimed it.'

Pete's expression hardened. 'It was *mine*, Kath.'

'Not any more.'

Olivia cringed as they glared at one another. She didn't want to be privy to the argument and tried to sneak out of the room but to her dismay she found herself pulled back when Katherine said, 'Livvy will back me up.'

She held up a restraining hand. 'Don't drag me into this.' Swivelling around, she went into the kitchen, closing the door behind her.

Olivia put the kettle on and tipped a spoonful of Nescafé into a mug seeking any distraction from the row taking place in the next room. Katherine's voice rose stridently whilst Pete's was more like an angry mutter. Then the front door slammed. Hastily Olivia took another mug out of the cupboard and made a second cup of coffee.

After a couple of minutes, the kitchen door opened and Katherine faced her. 'Why did you walk out on us?' she demanded.

Olivia tried to keep her voice neutral. 'Because it was none of my business.' She pointed at the mugs of coffee. 'Here, drink this and calm down.'

The incident upset Olivia. This was a side of Katherine she had not seen before. She recalled that sometimes at school whilst walking past the Science Lab, she would hear Katherine shouting equations at her reluctant pupils but so far, outside of school, her housemate had been good company. There had been one or two disagreements, like Katherine's call to James Sanders over the costumes episode but since then things had run smoothly.

Half an hour later it was as if nothing had happened. With Katherine again directing operations, they set about preparing the downstairs for the workmen's arrival the next day. Later, they went to B&Q to buy the necessary paint and brushes ready to start work in the morning. Agreement over the colour scheme had been reached quite easily: a neutral ice blue throughout.

'That will be nice and cool in the summer,' said Katherine and Olivia agreed. 'We'll open a bottle of that Gran Reserva Rioja tonight,' she went on. 'Do you remember? I got it from Waitrose on special offer.'

It was a pleasant evening so they ate a ham salad with crusty rolls outside on the tiny patio. Olivia was never sure whether it was the relief that school was finished for a few weeks or the balminess of the air, but they had soon consumed the bottle of red wine.

'Don't worry,' said Katherine, getting to her feet, 'I bought two at the same time.'

She promptly disappeared inside the house to return with the second bottle. Opening it, she poured a generous amount into each glass.

'I shall sleep well tonight,' said Olivia, sinking back into her chair, the glass in her hand.

'Me too; by the way what did you think of Pete?'

Olivia straightened up, spilling some of her wine over her wrist. 'What d'you mean?'

Katherine laughed. 'What did you think of Pete?'

Had Olivia felt inclined to tell the truth she would have said *I think you were mad to divorce him.* Instead she said, 'He seemed quite nice.'

'Huh, you don't know him like I do.' Stating the obvious was Katherine's suit.

Olivia tensed. 'Of course I don't.' She hoped the matter would end there.

This wasn't to be. 'We were so much in love when we got married,' said Katherine, her eyes glazing over at the memory, 'they called us the *perfect couple.*'

Olivia grunted, knowing that more was to come. It came in the form of a soliloquy.

'I thought we were made for each other. For me, there was no one else but Pete thought otherwise. It didn't take him long to stray off the path of marital bliss into the arms of some hussy with big tits and a slim waist.' She patted her hips. 'I've always been a bit chubby but he didn't seem to mind that when we got married. He used to tease me, saying I was lovely and soft and cuddly.'

Olivia kept silent, knowing intuitively that Katherine was about to confide more. It was true that Katherine was a little on the plump side but she didn't look overweight because she was taller than average. Her best features were her naturally blond hair and large blue eyes. For the first time, Olivia noticed the light sprinkling of freckles on her nose and cheeks, no doubt brought out by the sunny weather.

Katherine went on, 'He wanted babies you know, but I'm not the motherly type. To tell the truth, I hate children especially little ones. They're so messy and demanding. And if I'd got pregnant I would have ended up getting really fat and he would have played away from home even more.' Looking directly at Olivia, she asked, 'Do you want children?'

Lulled by Katherine's meanderings, Olivia's eyes had started to close. She blinked them open. 'Yes, I suppose I do,' she giggled, 'but I've got to find a man first.'

Katherine flicked a nonchalant wrist. 'You will. Why, you're only twenty-five but look at me, pushing thirty and already divorced.'

As Katherine rambled on, Olivia's thoughts turned to her own situation. She had been in a long-term relationship but it had not been serious enough for her to consider getting married. Splitting up had been a relief rather than a disaster.

Katherine poured herself another glass of Rioja and took a gulp from her glass. 'Of course, Pete's a wonderful lover,' she murmured dreamily. 'I knew he was experienced the first time we had sex. Gosh, when I think back on it...' Her words faded into a deep sigh.

Olivia tried unsuccessfully to suppress a yawn. Katherine was getting carried away with her reminiscences and she didn't want to hear any more about Pete's accomplishments between the sheets.

The light faded, leaving only a flickering candle in the middle of the table to cast shadows on the fence. A gentle breeze stirred the trees, somewhere an owl hooted and a pleasing scent wafted over from the Choisya. Olivia was finding it more and more difficult to keep her eyes open. She wanted to put a stop to Katherine's confidences but hadn't the energy to get up from the chair and plead that it was bed-time.

'Maybe that's the reason he got fed-up with me,' continued Katherine in a low monotone, 'but he could have said...'

'Said what?'

Katherine's head jerked round. 'Livvy, aren't you listening?'

'Yes...no...I'm tired.' She dragged herself up straight. 'Let's go to bed.'

'Okay...okay...' Katherine tried to stand up but slumped back onto her chair. She hiccupped and muttered with a giggle, 'I'm...I'm very...very drunk.'

This sobered Olivia. She stood up and placed a guiding hand under her friend's elbow. Somehow, she managed to lead her indoors where they both stumbled over the doormat and burst into peals of laugher.

'Look at us,' said Olivia, 'two lonely school mistresses pissed out of our heads.'

With more peals of laughter they made their way upstairs to their bedrooms.

TWENTY-NINE

Work on the house went according to plan although Olivia had to pacify the plumber when Katherine found fault with the grouting in the shower.

'What's she complaining about?' he asked her in a quiet moment when Katherine wasn't around.

Olivia could see nothing wrong with it and she accepted that the man was justifiably indignant. She said awkwardly, 'I'm afraid my friend is a terrible nitpicker. Actually, I think you've done a good job on the tiling.'

Frowning grumpily, he said, 'She shouldn't interfere; why doesn't she let me get on with the job? I know what I'm doing.'

'She means well,' said Olivia, 'and in future, I'll try and keep her out of your way.'

It was even worse with the carpenter. First of all, Katherine didn't like the colour of the oak; it wasn't dark enough and there were too many knots in the wood.

'That's one of the characteristics of oak,' explained the carpenter patiently, but it was difficult to convince her.

She got annoyed when on one occasion he didn't turn up until half way through the morning.

'Sorry,' he said, 'but my wife's ill and I had to take the children to the Play Centre.'

'We're not paying you to take a half day off,' protested Katherine.

Afterwards, Olivia reminded her that they were not paying him by the hour. 'He quoted us for the entire job so an hour or two here or there doesn't make much difference,' she pointed out.

By the middle of August the dining-room floor had been fitted, they had an efficient power shower and the upstairs decorating was almost finished.

'It's time to buy new curtains and a couple of rugs. This is the exciting bit, Kathy,' said Olivia enthusiastically. 'Let's go to IKEA.'

They drove to Croydon in Katherine's car and spent a couple of hours deliberating over furnishings.

'I can't wait to put these curtains up,' said Olivia on the way home. 'I hope we can do it by ourselves. Apart from painting I'm not very good at DIY.'

'I'll get Pete to come and give us a hand.'

Olivia looked at her friend in astonishment. Only a week ago she had been rowing with her ex-husband about the wine rack his father had given him.'

'He won't want to after the way you parted the other day.'

'Oh that...' Kathy took her hand off the steering wheel and flicked her wrist. She gave Olivia a sideways grin. 'If he's a good boy he can have his wine rack back.'

'I thought you said you'd got rid of it.'

'That's what I told him but, actually, it's hidden in the shed.'

And so Pete came to help with the curtain hanging. Olivia was out when he arrived but she came back to find the pair laughing over the number of times Pete dropped the curtain hooks.

'What's the matter with you, you butterfingers?' said Katherine. 'Stop making me bend down to pick the stupid things up.'

Then he said the wrong thing. 'It's good exercise, Kath, you could do with losing some of that spare tyre.'

Olivia hesitated in the doorway, knowing that there would be a reaction.

Katherine threw down the curtain she was holding. 'Get out!' she shouted.

'Don't you want me to finish the job?'

'I said *get out!*'

Still balanced on the ladder, Pete said, 'Let me finish, I didn't mean to upset you.'

'We can manage on our own.'

'Then why did you ask for my help in the first place?'

'I didn't, it was Livvy's idea.'

Olivia burst into the room and faced Katherine. 'It was *not* my idea,' she snapped.

Katherine shrugged and muttered, 'Whatever.' Then turning on her heel, she stalked out of the room.

Pete looked down at Olivia with a perplexed expression on his face. Clearly, he was of two minds as to whether he should he finish the job or down tools and leave.

'Please stay,' whispered Olivia. 'I'll hand you the curtain hooks.'

'How do they look?' he asked as he fixed the final hook.

'They look really nice,' said Olivia, reaching out a hand to steady him as he climbed down from the ladder.

He stood back to admire his work. 'Yes, I've made a good job of that. I only hope madam is satisfied.'

'Oh, she will be. Don't take any notice of her she can be a bit moody sometimes.'

'Tell me about,' grinned Pete, 'I was married to her for five years.'

Olivia clapped a hand to her mouth. 'Of course, I'm sorry, you must know Kathy better than anybody.'

He shrugged. 'I hope you two get on better than we did. I'll get off now. See you around…'

With that, he headed towards the door but she called him back. 'Won't you stay for a cup of tea, or a can of lager; I think we've got one in the fridge.'

He grinned again. 'Better not. I think I should make my escape before…you know…' He edged further along the hallway.

Olivia smiled back. 'Ciao and thanks for all your help.' It was only after he had left that she remembered Katherine's pledge to return Pete's wine rack to him, but it was too late.

She decided to make a cup of tea for herself and Katherine. Going to the bottom of the stairs, she called up, 'There's a cuppa ready for you down here.'

Katherine came downstairs looking sheepish. 'Sorry about that,' she said, 'but Pete really knows how to rub me up the wrong way.'

'Well,' said Olivia pointing at the window, 'what d'you think of the new curtains?'

'They look lovely.'

The start of the new school year was drawing near. Olivia decided to go into Brighton to buy a few things for her autumn agenda. It was a beautiful sunny day and she spent time walking along the promenade before doing her shopping. The sea was a deep blue, almost navy in places and the beach was crowded with tourists. She felt tempted to take a walk along the pier but knew that would take up too much time so she made herself a promise that at half term she would have a sight-seeing day in Brighton and visit the Pavilion and the Aquarium.

She was turning the corner into New Street to go and pick up some leaflets from the Theatre Royal for her sixformers when she bumped into Pete. They both stopped in surprise.

'What are you doing here?' he said.

'Fancy meeting you!' she gasped. 'I…I…'

'Let me buy you a drink, Livvy.' Before she could refuse, he took her arm and led her to a nearby café. 'What about a glass of wine?'

Olivia looked at her watch. It was almost five o'clock. 'Wine would be lovely,' she said, thinking guiltily about the list of stationery items she still had to buy from W H Smith before going home.

'Did you come on your moped?' he asked.

She shook her head. 'Brighton's traffic is too hectic for that. I came on the train.'

'Have you finished your decorating?'

'Almost.'

He gave a chuckle. 'I can't honestly see my ex-wife wielding a paint brush.'

'She did her bit,' replied Olivia defensively, although she had noticed that Katherine always seemed to have something important to do on the days they set aside for decorating.

They remained in the café until six o'clock discussing a variety of topics. It seemed they liked the same films, shared the same taste in music and enjoyed an outdoor life. When Olivia took another glance at her watch and decided it was time to leave, Pete said, 'Can I see you again, Livvy?'

She stiffened. She had enjoyed herself but somehow it didn't seem right to arrange another meeting - effectively a date - with her friend's ex-husband. She wrinkled her nose. 'I don't think that's a very good idea.'

'Why not?'

'Well...'

He grinned. 'You mean, because of Kath. She doesn't have to know.' He frowned. 'At least give me your mobile number.'

She shook her head. 'Don't get me wrong, Pete, it's been lovely talking to you but I think we'd better leave it at that. I've no doubt we'll bump into one another again through Kathy.'

Then she got up from the table and left, making her way to the train station. But she didn't notice anything or anybody on her way there because in her mind she kept re-running the unexpected meeting. On reflection, she knew that she *did* want to see Pete again and wished she had given him her number but commonsense told her that the decision she had made was the right one.

Katherine greeted her cheerfully when she got home. 'Hi, did you have a nice day in Brighton?'

'Yes it was great.'

'Did you manage to buy everything you needed?'

'Nearly everything...'

Something held Olivia back from mentioning her encounter with Pete. She tried to second guess Kathy's reaction. Would she be angry, upset or just plain uninterested? It was better not to put it to the test.

A week later, Olivia was surprised to get an email from Pete. It was just a friendly message saying how much he had enjoyed seeing her and would she consider meeting up with him? She couldn't imagine how he had obtained her email address and decided not to reply for the time being. But curiosity got the better of her and she asked Katherine casually, 'Have you seen Pete lately?'

'No, why do you ask?'

'No reason. Did you happen to give him our phone numbers and email addresses?'

'Why would I do that? I want to be rid of him, don't I? The only number he's got is our landline.' Katherine gave Olivia her full attention. 'What brought that up? Did he call?'

'Not as far as I know.'

'Good, I'm glad he's taken the hint.'

She went back to her task of marking homework. Olivia was puzzled and for several days she was plagued with indecision: should she reply to Pete or simply wipe his email off her computer? Unable to get his image out of her head, she couldn't help thinking that Katherine and Pete were an unlikely partnership. She fleetingly wondered whether *she* was Pete's type and *he* hers. Leaning her elbows on the dressing table, she stared at her own reflection. A pair of hazel eyes in a heart-shaped face stared back. She flicked a strand of dark hair away from her forehead and smoothed her slim fingers across high cheekbones. Then, jerking away from the mirror, she gathered her hair into a ponytail and fastened it with an elastic band. *Enough of that*, she told herself, Pete was Katherine's ex and as such, was out of bounds.

For the next few days she determinedly put Pete's image to bed but one day Katherine began to rant about his wine rack. 'It's still in the shed, why didn't you give it to him when he put the curtains up, Livvy?'

Olivia couldn't believe what she was hearing. 'It wasn't up to me to hand it back to him,' she protested, 'and anyway he never asked for it.'

'Well, it's going to the tip this week when I get rid of the garden refuse.'

'You can't do that.'

'Why not, if he loves it so much, he should come and collect it.'

'But Kathy, he still thinks you got rid of it.'

Katherine gave a shrug. 'Hard cheese.'

That settled Olivia's dilemma. Without hesitation, she sent a reply to Pete's email, telling him about Katherine's intention to dispose of the antique wine rack.

He replied immediately: *So she kept hold of it, did she? Will it be convenient if I pop round and collect it this afternoon?'*

As luck would have it, Katherine was giving one of her pupil's an extra-curricular lesson after school so Olivia emailed back, inviting him to come before six o'clock.

He arrived at five and when Olivia opened the door, he grinned and said, in a theatrical whisper, 'Is the coast clear?'

Olivia grinned back. 'Yes, she'll be out until six. You're quite safe.'

'*We're* quite safe,' he corrected her.

'Come in, and by the way, how did you get hold of my email address?'

He laughed. 'Oh that! I rang up the school and spoke to the secretary, said I was a parent of one of the pupils and I needed to contact you during the holidays.'

Olivia was aghast. 'She had no right to give it to you.'

'I was very convincing.'

'I bet you were! That was an awful thing to do Pete; it could get her in trouble.'

'Hmm, only if you let the cat out of the bag.'

Olivia couldn't help smiling. 'You're incorrigible. Wait here, I'll go and get the wine rack.'

Pete didn't wait. He followed her out of the back door and down the garden path to the shed. 'I hope it's not got damp and warped in there.'

'The shed's waterproof,' said Olivia.

The shed was clean and tidy, Katherine's doing. Olivia would never have had the urge to spring clean a shed but her housemate did.

'My, oh my, this place shrieks of Kath,' said Pete as Olivia handed him the wine rack, 'and to give her due credit, she has wrapped this up rather well.'

He pulled aside the bubble wrap covering it.

'Yes, Katherine is meticulous,' Olivia agreed.

To her surprise, he put the wine rack down and took her hand, pulling her towards him. 'Come out with me, Livvy, please. Kath and me, we're history. We've both moved on. Honestly, there's nothing to stop us seeing one another.'

Still Olivia hesitated. She wanted to believe him; she wanted to get to know him better but something held her back. Pete might have moved on but she wasn't convinced that Kathy had. Her hostility could disguise her true feelings.

He squeezed her hand. 'Please, Livvy.'

His eyes crinkled at the corners and she found it hard to refuse, especially when he drew her close and kissed her on the lips. Her resolve melted away and the friendly hug became something more sensual as his tongue explored her mouth. She couldn't resist, she didn't want to resist.

The shed door flapped open in the wind and that's when they heard the sound of Katherine's car drawing up. Olivia drew away from him. 'Quick,' she said, 'go out the back way so she won't see you...oh God, she'll see your car.'

'No she won't because I parked round the corner.' He took her hand again. 'Tell me I can see you again, Livvy. What's your mobile number?'

Hurriedly, she reeled it off. 'You won't remember it.'

He gave that captivating grin of his. 'Yes, I will, I've got a good memory for numbers.'

With that, he picked up the wine rack and slid out of the shed door to make his escape along the back alley.

THIRTY

Katherine appeared at the back door just as Olivia walked down the garden path.

'You look a bit flustered,' she said, 'what's up?'

'Nothing, I was just thinking the garden needs weeding,' said Olivia, aware that her cheeks were burning. She hated lying to Katherine and she was angry for allowing herself to be coerced into Peter's conspiracy.

'Yes, we'll have to make that trip to the tip. I can get rid of that stupid wine rack.'

'Let's have a cup of tea,' Olivia suggested in an endeavour to stop Katherine from going in search of the wine rack straightaway. Maybe by the time they went to the tip she would have forgotten all about it.

Olivia spent the rest of the day mulling over the events of the half hour with Pete and, although she felt guilty about the kiss and its implications, she very much wanted to see him again. It worried her knowing that Katherine wouldn't be happy to learn that her housemate and her ex-husband were going out together.

A few days of rain put paid to a visit to the tip and then the Autumn Term began and the occupants of Number Seven settled into a routine. Pete didn't contact Olivia until a week later.

'Sorry I haven't been in touch,' he said, 'but it's been a bit hectic at work. Are you free tomorrow evening? I thought we could go and see a film. They're showing "The Da Vinci Code" at a cinema at the Brighton Marina.'

'Yes, but what am I going to tell Kathy?'

'Tell her the truth; after all, we're doing nothing wrong.'

'I don't think I'm brave enough,' replied Olivia.

'Livvy,' Pete sounded exasperated, 'you're not beholden to Kath.'

'I know that. I just don't want to hurt her feelings.'

The only excuse she could think of was that she was meeting an old friend. This sounded tame and she realised that had she not been feeling guilty, she would not necessarily have bothered telling Katherine who she was meeting. She began to wonder whether it would be easier to ring Pete back and cancel the date.

He was waiting for her at Brighton Station and as soon as she saw him she was pleased she had agreed to come.

'You look very nice,' he said, appraising her up and down, 'that shade of blue suits you.'

He led her to the car park and they drove along the seafront to the Marina. It was a balmy evening with the sun beginning to set; the sea was calm and the mild air had encouraged people to stroll along the promenade.

'We've got time for a drink before the film,' said Pete as he drove into the Marina car park.

A glass of wine relaxed her. Pete was easy to talk to and he had a good sense of humour, something her previous boyfriend had lacked. She reflected that after a couple of celibate years it would be good to be in a relationship again. Then she scolded herself: this was a first date not the start of a long-term liaison.

On the way home they discussed the film and agreed about its good parts as well as its shortcomings.

'It was a bit unrealistic in parts,' said Olivia, 'but on the whole I enjoyed it.'

'Me too...' He turned to look at her. 'Can we do this again, Livvy?'

'Watch the road!' she cried as they narrowly missed scraping a stationary vehicle.

At her request, he parked a short distance away from Number Seven. Killing the engine, he leant over and kissed her and she wished they were anywhere other than in the car. She caught a waft of his aftershave and touched his chin.

He closed his hand over hers and said, 'I'm sorry, I came straight from work, didn't have time to shave.'

She laughed. 'I like a stubble.'

Until now, she had not realised how much she missed a man's company. When she and Katherine had pooled their resources she had not taken into account that living with another woman could become tedious. She and Katherine were very different: Katherine was meticulous, not only in matters concerning the house but she was also irritatingly knowledgeable about most things. Olivia was more easy-going but she sometimes found it difficult to relax in Katherine's company.

She released her seat belt and opened the car door. Pete grabbed her hand, 'Don't go yet.'

'I must.' Leaning over she kissed his cheek and withdrew her hand. 'It's late and I've got an early class tomorrow. Thank you for a lovely evening.'

He drove slowly along behind her until she reached the house, then after watching her make her way to the front door, he drove off.

Katherine was still up. 'Did you have a nice time?' she asked.

'Yes thanks.'

'Where did you go?'

'To the cinema...'

'What did you see?'

Olivia gave her a brief description of the film and then pleaded tiredness. 'I've got a busy day tomorrow. Good night, Kathy.'

'Night Livvy.'

In her room Olivia kicked off her shoes and sank down onto the bed fully dressed. She wanted to run through the events of the evening. She liked Pete but she could see that he was a bit strong-willed. Perhaps that was why he had split up with Kathy. Two dominant characters together would certainly spell trouble. But who had been the most dominant: Katherine or Pete? All at once she felt a frisson of alarm. What was she getting herself into? If she continued with the relationship it was bound to force a wedge between her and Kathy and since they were financially tied to one another mortgage-wise, this could prove to be a problem. She drew in a deep breath. On the other hand, she really liked Pete and she knew that had he asked her to spend the night with him she would have found it difficult to say *no*.

Half an hour later, having decided that it would be best to let things run their course, she roused herself to undress and clean her teeth. Why worry about it? She was making too much of it. Their relationship would probably fizzle out.

But the next morning, during her first drama class of the day, she found it difficult to concentrate. Pete's image had a way of sneaking its way into her thoughts. By lunchtime she had decided that it would be sensible to end it. As soon as the lesson was over she would send him a carefully worded text saying she didn't want to see him again. This didn't happen because before she could find a suitable slot in her busy schedule, he sent her a text inviting her out to dinner the following night. She stared at the message, her heart pounding then made up her mind to accept the invitation and tell him face to face.

Things changed when she got home that afternoon. She walked into the house to find Katherine in a rage.

'Livvy, do you know what that moron has done? He's had the nerve to come in round the back and take the wine rack away.'

Olivia thought quickly. 'Well, it is technically his,' she said.

'No it isn't and, besides he's got no right to break into our shed and help himself.'

Olivia felt the colour rise to her cheeks. 'He...he didn't,' she said.

'What d'you mean?'

'I gave it to him.'

'When? Oh, I know, it was the day I caught you coming down from the shed looking all flustered.'

Olivia nodded. 'I'm sorry, I should have told you.'

'That would have been nice,' retorted Katherine.

'It's just that you put such a lot of store on that wine rack I couldn't bring myself to...'

Katherine's eyes narrowed. 'What's going on between you two? Are you ganging up on me?'

'Certainly not...'

Katherine's frown was intimidating and, not for the first time, Olivia wondered whether the children she taught were being bullied into submission. There had been rumours going around the staff room that she was unnecessarily hard on them. 'Don't let him charm you, Livvy, he's always on the lookout for an easy lay.' Staring pointedly at Olivia's chest, she added, 'and he likes bit tits.'

'How dare you!'

Olivia's indignation was lost on Katherine, who turned around and headed upstairs. Olivia waited until she heard the bedroom door slam before going to her own room. What was her housemate insinuating? She went to stand in front of the full-length mirror, angry tears pricking at her eyes. She couldn't help noticing the male teachers at school eyeing Katherine's cleavage; a blond bombshell one of them had called her and Olivia sometimes felt small and insignificant beside her. How she wished she was tall and voluptuous!

Balling her fists, she stared angrily at her own image, regretting that she had gone into partnership with Katherine. What if things became unbearable? How on earth was she going to get out of it? It would be easier to curtail her friendship with Pete and solve the problem that way. After all, their romance had hardly got off the ground. She shook a clenched fist at herself mouthing that tomorrow over dinner she would put an end to it. That way, this silly disagreement with Kathy would blow over and things would get back to normal.

The incident had brought on a splitting headache so she went downstairs for some paracetamol. While she was searching the medicine cabinet Katherine came to stand behind her. 'I'm sorry, Livvy, I shouldn't have said all those things. You weren't to know what a moron Pete is. There's nothing else of his here so he won't be coming back.'

Katherine was especially friendly with her for the rest of the day and Olivia began to wonder whether she was right about her ex-husband. Perhaps he was showing her his charismatic side; maybe this charisma masked a different Pete.

She glided through the next day as if in a dream. She was impatient with the children and even upset one little girl by speaking to her sharply. By the time she got home, she was in a state of nerves.

'I won't be in for dinner tonight,' she said to Katherine, hoping she wouldn't be curious enough to ask her where she was going.

'Okay, then I'll order in a pizza.'

Olivia's gloomy mood wouldn't allow her to wear anything colourful. This was going to be a serious evening so something sombre would suit the occasion. She chose a short black skirt, teaming it with a black and white silk shirt. A tailored black linen jacket completed the outfit. High heels were essential so she chose her stilettos; she needed height to boost her confidence.

She managed to leave the house without bumping into Katherine. On the way to Brighton, she felt so nervous that when she stood up to get off the train her legs started to tremble.

Pete was waiting for her at the station entrance. He took her hand and kissed her cheek saying, 'I hope you'll like the restaurant I've chosen. I've only been there once before.'

'I'm sure it will be good.'

They walked towards North Street avoiding late commuters on the way up to the train station. She felt tongue-tied: *how can you make polite conversation with someone you are about to ditch?*

'You seem pre-occupied this evening, Livvy,' he said.

'I've had a busy day,' she replied.

The waiter showed them to a place near the window.

'I hope you like Thai food,' said Pete, reaching for her hand across the table.

'I love it.'

'Shall we go for the set menu or do you want to choose individual dishes?'

'The set menu will be fine.'

The wine waiter arrived and Pete withdrew his hand and scoured the list, pointing to a white sauvignon. 'I hope white wine is all right with you.'

'Yes, of course.'

After the waiter had left them, he said, 'What's the matter, Livvy?'

'Nothing...nothing at all.' She pretended great interest in the ornate table decoration. 'I wonder how they fashion these artificial flowers; Thai people are so artistic.'

Another waiter came to take their order, placing a dish of sweet chilli crisps on the table between them.

Throughout the meal their conversation was strained. Olivia knew she owed Pete an explanation for her detachment but couldn't bring herself to broach the subject of Katherine. Of course, she told herself for the umpteenth time, the whole incident of the wine rack was trivial. Nonetheless, the food stuck in her gullet. Normally, she truly loved Thai food but tonight she had no appetite. The waiter hovered, frequently replenishing their wine glasses and Olivia knew she was drinking far too much too rapidly.

THIRTY-ONE

Olivia toyed with the food on her plate, picking at it with her chopsticks although usually she was a dab hand with chopsticks. Pete managed efficiently but, sensing her unease and in the mistaken belief this was the cause, he said, 'If you find them difficult we can ask for some ordinary cutlery.'

'Oh no...I mean, it's all right. I'm afraid I'm just not very hungry this evening.'

'Aren't you feeling well?'

'I'm a bit off colour, that's all.'

'I expect you've been working too hard.'

She nodded and took another gulp of wine. The waiter replenished her glass.

Although the menu they had chosen contained many of her favourites - crispy aromatic duck, chicken satay, prawn tempura and spicy squid - there was a lot of food left over.

Pete said, 'They always give you too much.'

Again she nodded, knowing that he was trying to make her feel less uncomfortable.

'Coffee or tea?' he asked when they had finished their meal, 'I don't mind foregoing coffee is you don't want it.'

She picked up her wine glass again, drinking from it despite the cotton wool effect it was having in her head. A strong black coffee would be a good idea but she refused it.

'I'll get the bill,' he said, calling for the waiter.

She excused herself and went to the ladies powder room, tottering on her high heels. The mirror over the wash-hand basin revealed a slightly intoxicated female with narrowed eyes trying to focus. She attempted to re-apply lipstick but gave up. Why had she allowed Pete to order that second bottle of wine? He had only drunk a couple of glasses himself. Throughout the evening she had been trying to find a way to tell him they were finished, bolstering her confidence by drinking too much. Straightening her shoulders, she returned to the table determined to broach the subject.

'Are you all right?' Pete asked as he tucked the receipt and his credit card back into his wallet after paying the bill.

'Yes, of course I am.'

'Let's go,' he said, ushering her ahead of him to the door of the restaurant. Outside, the fresh air took her breath away and the traffic seemed to rumble like thunder. For a moment she felt overwhelmed and stumbled as they crossed the road. He steadied her.

'I'll see you home,' he said, 'but I'll have to pick my car up first. It's parked outside my flat in Hove.'

'There's no need for that,' she murmured, 'I can take the train and pick up a taxi when I get off. By...by the way, I've...I've been meaning to talk to you about...'

'I knew there was something up; have I done something wrong?'

'Oh no...!' Her denial burst out spontaneously. How was she going to tell him she didn't want to see him again, when in reality, nothing was further from the truth?

'What is it?'

'I...I...'

Somebody pushed past her and she almost lost her balance. Damn these high heels. She stopped to slip one of her shoes back on.

Pete hailed a taxi. 'Forget the train,' he said, 'we'll take a cab to my place and I'll drive you home.'

In the back of the taxi, she couldn't stop herself from resting her head on his shoulder, almost nodding off. On arrival, he somehow manoeuvred her out of the taxi.

'I'm taking you back to my place,' he said. She didn't resist.

Next morning, Olivia blinked open her eyes and tried to focus but she didn't recognise where she was. She was lying on top of a maroon and navy striped duvet. Pete's bedroom! The next minute a rush of nausea forced her off the bed.

'Where's the bathroom?' she shrieked.

Peter appeared in the doorway and pointed along the hallway.

With a gulp, she stumbled in the direction he had indicated, getting there in the nick of time. After washing her face, she peered into the wall-mounted shaving mirror. God, what a sight she looked! She ran her fingers through her tangled hair but it needed a good brush.

Pete was waiting for her in the bedroom. 'Are you feeling a bit better now?' She shook her head and immediately regretted it. 'No worries,' he said, 'you'll feel more like your old self after a strong coffee and a piece of toast.'

'What?' she cried.

He grinned. 'I can do eggs and bacon if you'd prefer it.'

She grimaced then realised he was joking and tried to see the funny side. 'I'll settle for a cup of coffee, thanks.'

'Your clothes are hanging over the chair in the bedroom,' he said, 'as you can see, I didn't remove your bra and panties, although I was tempted.'

'So nothing...nothing happened?'

'Of course not,' he said, disappearing along the corridor in the opposite direction to the bathroom. Hurriedly, she got dressed and, running her tongue across her teeth, wished she had a toothbrush. Pete was waiting for her in his tiny kitchen. A typical man's abode it was far from tidy with unwashed dishes piled on the draining board. She perched on a stool by the worktop, mechanically brushing crumbs from its surface and emptying them into the pedal bin.

'How's the head?' he asked.

'Thumping.'

'Never mind, it's Saturday so you haven't got school.'

'I've got a pile of homework to mark,' she moaned.

The freshly-made coffee and a piece of toast and marmalade did help, but she wondered how she was going to balance on the high heels when it was time leave.

Starting to replenish her cup, he pre-empted her. 'I'll run you home when you're ready, Say when?'

She laughed. 'The coffee or the lift home…?'

'Both.'

They grinned at one another and in that moment, Olivia knew she was not going to be able to break up with him.

'We could spend the day together,' he suggested.

She frowned and stopped making little circles on the table-top where sugar had been spilt. 'What about Kathy? She'll be worried about me; I've never stayed out all night without telling her.'

Pete placed a hand on her shoulder. 'You're a big girl Livvy; Kath's not your mother.'

'Just the same…' She looked down at her feet and wiggled her toes. 'If I stay I can't walk around in those high heels all day long.'

'Who says we'll be walking around?'

'You mean…?'

'Only if you want to.'

Olivia's mind whirled. Since finishing with her last boyfriend she had stopped taking the pill. 'I'm not prepared,' she said, adding with a frown, 'and I'm not sure I'm ready for that kind of relationship.'

He moved away. 'Have I annoyed you?'

'No...yes...it's just too soon.'

He reached for her hand. 'In that case, run yourself a shower while I pop out and get the newspaper and we'll spend the morning sunning ourselves on the balcony, reading all the latest gossip.'

She nodded. 'That sounds good, but I'll give Kathy a ring to let her know I'm all right.'

'Will you tell her where you are?'

With an impish smile, she replied, 'Of course not.'

Olivia decided on a long hot soak rather than a quick shower and by the time she emerged from the bathroom wrapped in Pete's navy blue bathrobe, he was sitting on the balcony with his feet up on the table and the broadsheet spread out in front of him.

'At last,' he said, putting the newspaper down. 'I was beginning to think you'd drowned.' He pointed at the *Hello Magazine* on the table. 'I bought you that.'

'Thanks,' she said, 'I only ever get to read it at the hairdressers.'

'When we were married Kath used to buy it every week.'

For some reason this irritated Olivia. Until now Pete had only ever referred to his marriage to Kathy in a derogatory way. In this instance he sounded quite wistful. But she soon forgot the incident and began to enjoy the morning.

'Has your headache gone?'

'Almost.'

'Would you be able to stomach a pizza if I sent out for one?'

She wrinkled her brow. 'I think I might.'

After a late lunch, they went indoors to watch football on TV. Olivia was happy to sit quietly while Pete shouted each time a goal was scored. When the match ended, he switched off the television and went to his CD player.

'What kind of music do you like, Livvy: rock bands, ballads?'

'Have you got Michael Bublé's *Lost?*'

'*Voila!*'

He flourished it in front of her before inserting it into the machine.

As Michael Bublé's dulcet tones filled the room, Pete took hold of her hand. 'Let's dance.'

She slid into his arms and they swayed to the music. Dusk spread its mantle across the room throwing their elongated silhouettes onto the wall, shortening and lengthening as they moved over the floor. Olivia rested her head on Pete's shoulder. How was she going to break up with him when she was on the brink of falling in love? When the number drew to a close he pulled her down onto the sofa and started kissing her and she knew she would end up spending the night in his bed.

Peter woke up first. Olivia was still asleep, her dark hair spread like a halo on the pillow. Gently kissing her cheek, he swung his legs off the bed and shuffled into the bathroom. He paused in front of the shaving mirror, razor in hand, thinking about the wonderful day they had spent together. He had fancied her from their first meeting but if truth be told, asking her out was more of an emotional jibe at his ex-wife than the wish to date her. After all, the long-legged Linda from Chelsea he had been seeing recently was far more sophisticated. He stroked the razor down his cheek and shook off the excess shaving cream; but there was something endearing about Olivia's naivety. She had told him she had been in a long-term relationship, which had ended a couple of years back. He suspected this was the extent of her sexual experience. He finished shaving and patted aftershave on his cheeks. He had achieved what he wanted: he had got her into his bed. Why: to spite Katherine of course? He frowned at himself in the mirror filled with a sense of disgust. Olivia didn't deserve to be exploited like that. He would cut loose before it was too late.

Olivia was awake by the time he got back to the bedroom. She was sitting up with two pillows propped up behind her. She smiled at him. 'Good morning.'

'Good morning,' he replied, 'did you sleep well?'

'Like a baby.' Her smile broadened and he noticed what perfectly even, white teeth she had.

'I'll go and make coffee.'

'Come here first,' she said, patting the duvet cover and when he approached the bed she encircled his neck with her arms and kissed him lingeringly. 'You smell nice, darling.'

Peter felt the familiar stirring in his loins and he pulled off the towel wrapped round his waist. This time their lovemaking was even more urgent than the night before. *Naive or not,* he thought fleetingly, *this woman knows instinctively how to please me* and, for the first time in his entire life, Peter Faulkner felt the overwhelming desire to fully satisfy his partner. It was, he reflected afterwards, probably the only unselfish feeling he had ever had.

THIRTY-TWO

Despite Pete's offer to run her home by car, Olivia insisted on catching the train. She knew she would have to face a deluge of questions from Katherine even though she had sent her a text explaining that she would be staying overnight with a friend. She was surprised at how quiet it was when she entered the house. She sniffed as a sweet-smelling aroma reached her: weed! Both she and Katherine had smoked Cannabis occasionally but it was always in the company of others.

'Kathy! she called out but there was no reply.

Kicking off her high heels, she ran upstairs to the front bedroom and knocked on the door.

'Who is it?'

'Who do you think it is?' replied Olivia.

'Oh you, Livvy, come in...come in...'

Katherine was sitting up in bed with a box of Kleenex next to her. 'I've got a cold in the nose,' she mumbled almost incoherently.

'Have you got a temperature?' asked Olivia.

'How should I know?' She blew her nose on one of the tissues then aimed the crumpled up missile at the waste paper basket, missing it by a foot. 'If you must know, I've been stuck indoors all weekend with no one to help me out by going to the chemist for some flu poison.'

'Some what?'

'You know...that latest remedy they keep showing on TV.'

Olivia approached the bed but immediately took a step back. 'You smell awful. Why haven't you opened the window? You've been smoking weed and that's not a flu remedy.'

'It's the only thing left in the house, what else was I to do?'

Olivia gave a snort of disdain and turned to leave but Katherine called her back. 'Don't be angry with me, Liv.' Her bottom lip drooped and she put on a little girl voice. 'Why did you have to stay away on the very weekend I needed you?'

Olivia started guiltily. 'I sent you a text telling you I wouldn't be home.'

Katherine's eyes narrowed. 'You weren't staying with a girlfriend were you?' She wagged a finger. 'I know you've got a secret boyfriend; why don't you tell me about him?'

'You're wrong,' retorted Olivia hotly, 'utterly and completely wrong.' She felt the colour rise to her cheeks and hoped Katherine wouldn't notice.

'Oh well, suit yourself...' Katherine patted the side of her rather red nose with her index finger, 'but it's written all over you. I can always tell when someone's just had sex.'

'Huh!' Olivia turned on her heel and hurried out of the room.

'Make me a cup of tea, Livvy, pleeeeese,' Katherine called after her.

'Later, I've got to take a shower first.'

She went to her room and wriggled out of the tight skirt and bra and panties then went to run a shower. It was refreshing to let the warm water run over her body. She wrapped her arms around herself and closed her eyes. Two could share a shower. She allowed her imagination to conjure up Pete's strong arms around, the soft hairs on his chest against her breasts, his knee forcing her thighs apart. Unwillingly, her thoughts flew back to the early days of her co-habitation with Andy. At first they had often showered together but over time Andy had begun to shower alone. It hadn't taken her long to realise why: he was carrying on with a new member of staff at his office. Olivia had seen her once: a shapely red-head with a cleavage to die for.

A rush of panic engulfed her. Would it end up the same with Pete? She knew she was playing a dangerous game. Her friendship with Katherine was at stake; if they fell out how could the two of them go on living under the same roof? She bit her lower lip. One would have to leave and she knew who it would be. Splitting up with Andy and moving out of their rented flat had been traumatic enough: the curtailing of the contract on the lease, the division of their possessions, settling the final household bills. Moving out of Number Seven would be even more complicated. There was her share of the mortgage for starters. She had invested the entire amount of her grandmother's legacy into buying the house whereas she knew that Katherine still had a nice little nest egg stowed away. She let the water run for a long time as she pondered on the 'ifs' and 'buts' of the situation. Agreeing to go out with Pete had been a mistake; she should break it off before it was too late.

She went back to her bedroom to find a message on her mobile. Pete's image appeared on the screen. *'Did you get home safely, Livvy?'* Just seeing the tiny image of his face sent her heart racing. She texted back *'Yes'* and tossed the phone onto the bed. Going to the wardrobe she pulled out a pair of leggings and a loose top, slipped on a pair of flip-flops and went downstairs to make the tea. By the time she went upstairs again, Katherine was fast asleep.

The next day, Katherine was back to her old self and, thankfully, she didn't bring up the subject of the date. After a good night's sleep, Olivia told herself she shouldn't make a mountain out of a molehill and it would be best to allow events to take their course. Pete sent her several texts during the day but she was too busy at school to reply straightaway. As soon as she got home, she phoned him.

'What have you been doing; why didn't you reply to my texts?' he demanded.

'Some people have to work for a living,' she replied with a laugh.

'Are you suggesting that I don't work?'

'Well, I'm sure you're not tied to a strict timetable like me.'

'You've got me there,' he said, 'it's true, I am more or less my own boss.' He paused. 'When can I see you?'

'I'm free tomorrow evening.'

'Hi Livvy.' Katherine burst through the door laden with her briefcase and a carrier bag of groceries. 'There's more in the car so I could do with a hand...oh sorry, I didn't realise you were on the phone.'

Pete must have recognised his ex-wife's voice in the background because he lowered his own voice as he said, 'Tomorrow, seven thirty by the pier.'

'Yes,' agreed Olivia, 'I'll be there.'

Katherine dropped the carrier bag onto the floor and said with a grin, '...so I suppose this is another friend from your all girls school.'

Olivia snapped shut her mobile and told a half truth. 'It is a date, but these are early days so I don't know where it's going.'

'Tell me more, what's his name?'

'Kevin,' she said, borrowing the name from one of her cousins.

'Kevin? And where does Kevin live?'

'Brighton.' That seemed a safe enough answer. Eager to conclude the conversation, Olivia pushed past Katherine and went out to the car to bring in the remaining shopping.

Katherine seemed satisfied once it was established that the boyfriend was called Kevin and that he lived in Brighton, and for a week or two she refrained from asking more probing questions.

Both girls were busy during the Autumn Term, especially Olivia who had a concert to organise and the production of the Christmas show. This was traditionally a light-hearted production and this year they were doing *Mary Poppins*. Olivia was excited because she would be able to use some of the costumes stowed in Jasper Cole's dressing-up box.

'These will make the play much more realistic,' she said to Katherine as she rummaged through the costumes. 'And the kids will love them, especially the girls.'

'Are you sure you should be using them, Livvy, only technically they belong to someone else.'

'Don't pour cold water on my production,' snapped Olivia.

'I was only saying…'

'Well don't!'

'Perhaps you should double check before you use them.'

'I'm only borrowing them. When we found them way back in June you were all for selling them on ebay.'

'I didn't say that.'

'Yes you did. Borrowing them isn't like selling them for profit.'

It was clear that Katherine didn't agree with her but she gave a shrug and muttered, 'Suit yourself.'

There were two days left until the final rehearsal of *Mary Poppins*. Olivia had grabbed some time off to do some Christmas shopping and on her way back to the bus stop, she chanced to glance at the placard advertising *Cinderella* on the wall of the local theatre. She stopped in her tracks as a name jumped out at her. Jasper Cole was playing one of the ugly sisters.

With a gulp of dismay she stood rooted to the spot. The bus she was intending to catch drove past but she didn't bother to run for it. Gripped by indecision, she was oblivious to shoppers hurrying past her but all at once she knew what she would do. Crossing the road she headed for the theatre box office and bought a ticket for the evening performance.

'I'm going out tonight, Kathy, so don't put the chain across the front door.'

'Seeing the boyfriend again?'

'Not this time.'

Before Katherine could question her further, Olivia disappeared upstairs to get ready. The show started at seven fifteen and Olivia arrived to find the theatre foyer packed with children. It was a long time since she had seen a pantomime and she was happy to share their excitement.

The rustle of sweet papers and the crunch of popcorn accompanied her to her seat. While waiting for the curtain to go up she studied the programme. There was a photo of Jasper in costume and another of Jasper in mufti. She scrutinised his face and decided he looked amiable.

The Safety Curtain was raised, the orchestra tuned up and the lights dimmed. Then as the overture began, an expectant hush fell on the auditorium. Buttons appeared in front of the heavy red velvet curtains with ER embroidered in gold and asked the audience to remember to switch off their mobile phones. Then the pantomime began for real.

Five minutes in and Olivia felt as if she had been transported back twenty years to when her Auntie Jean had taken her to see her very first pantomime. The music was loud, the singers mediocre, the jokes corny but none of this mattered to Olivia. She soon picked out which of the two ugly sisters was played by Jasper. He was wearing a blue crinoline with pink sleeves and pink pantaloons. His blond wig looked incongruous against his tanned skin. However, she came to the conclusion that he wasn't a bad comic actor.

During the interval she joined the queue for ice creams with the children, listening with interest to their chatter and, not for the first time, she wondered whether she herself would one day be a mother. All at once, the yearning to settle down and be part of a family enveloped her. Would it ever happen and who would become the father of her children, Pete? She thrust the idea from her mind. Her affair with Pete was exciting and spiced with an element of danger. If Katherine found out that Kevin was really Peter, there would be hell to pay.

'Vanilla, strawberry or chocolate?' asked the usherette.

'Vanilla, please.'

She returned to her seat just as the musicians made their way back to the orchestra pit. Act Two began and the children, even livelier now, responded eagerly to Buttons' encouragement to join in the fun. Several little ones were invited up onto the stage, each returning to their parents carrying a Goodie Bag. Then Buttons tossed lollypops into the audience. Olivia caught one and handed it to the little girl seated next to her. Prompted by her mother, she smiled shyly and murmured, 'Thank you'.

At the end of the performance, amid loud clapping and shouting for an encore, the curtain eventually came down. Olivia took her time following the crowd from of the auditorium. She had figured out where the Stage Door was and she intended to wait there for Jasper Cole. But there was plenty of time because she knew he would have to change and remove his makeup first.

It was raining when she got outside and, putting up her umbrella she stood shivering in a cold wind at the side of the theatre. The performers came out one by one. She studied all the men carefully afraid she might not recognise Jasper without his theatrical makeup. He emerged arm-in-arm with another man, the other ugly sister she surmised.

'Excuse me, Mr Cole.'

He started in surprise, clearly unused to being accosted at the Stage Door. 'Yes?'

Olivia cleared her throat, not quite sure how to broach the subject of the costumes. 'I very much enjoyed your performance this evening,' she managed to say.

'Thank you.' He smiled and went to walk off with his companion.

Olivia touched his arm. 'Can you spare a few minutes?'

He looked even more surprised. 'You'd better make it quick.'

'Look,' she said, 'there's a pub just round the corner, could I buy you and your companion a drink?'

'Well...'

'Certainly,' said Jasper's friend, deciding to take charge. 'Let's not hang around here getting wet.'

They found a quiet table and Olivia asked them what they wanted to drink. She was rather taken aback when they both ordered a rather expensive cocktail. Returning with the drinks, she found they had removed their coats and were sitting holding hands, their heads almost touching. They drew apart as she placed the drinks on the table.

'My name's Olivia Manning,' she said. 'I recognised you, Mr Cole but erm...can I ask your name?' This was directed at Jasper's companion.

'Robin Ballantyne-Smith,' he said and she couldn't help noticing that despite his grey hair and sideburns he was a handsome man, possibly in his early sixties.

'Well...' Olivia took a deep breath and started to explain how, after moving into Number Seven, she had found the costumes. 'When I discovered who they belonged to I wanted to meet you, Jasper. You see, I'm a drama teacher and I was hoping to borrow some of the costumes for my school play. In fact, I was relying on using them but since they belong to you and you're actually here in town I felt I had better get your permission first. Of course, if you don't want me to use them I'll just have to think of something else, but the kids will be so disappointed. They would love those costumes.'

Looking surprised, the pair listened to her story until Jasper burst out laughing. 'To tell you the truth, I'd forgotten all about them.' He wrinkled his brow. 'Fancy you living at Number Seven. Robin, do you remember our narrow escape from Anthony's cousin James?'

They both rocked with laughter while Olivia looked on not knowing what to think.

'When is the performance?' asked Jasper when at last their mirth had subsided.

'Next Thursday afternoon.'

Jasper looked at Robin, who nodded his head. 'There isn't a matinee that day...' he turned to Olivia, 'so if you can get us tickets?'

Olivia's hand flew to her mouth and her eyes widened. 'Of course I can. Does...does that mean we can use your costumes?'

'It would be a pleasure to see them being used on stage,' he said. 'Can you give us the details?'

Hastily, Olivia searched for a piece of paper and scribbled the address of the school and the time of the performance. Handing it to Jasper, she said, 'Thank you so much, your being there will inspire my pupils. I am so grateful to you.' She rose to her feet and picked up her bag. 'I hope I haven't delayed you too much.'

They both stood up and Robin took her hand and gave it a theatrical kiss, while Jasper smiled broadly. She felt their gaze upon her as she walked to the door of the pub.

'*Toute a l'heure*, dear lady,' Robin called out.

After Olivia had left, Robin and Jasper looked at one another and grinned.

'What a sweet girl!' said Robin.

'Yes,' agreed Jasper, 'she's really excited about those costumes. I'd forgotten all about them, you know.'

'What are you going to do?'

Jasper flicked a wrist. 'Let her keep them. They're of no use to me...' He winked at his partner, 'unless you want them, duckie.'

'What would I want with them? I've already got a cupboard-full of party outfits; let the school teacher have them. But what are we going to do about her school play?'

'Let's go, it will be a bit of a lark. I mean, watching all those school kids strutting around the stage in professional costumes!'

Robin ordered another round of drinks and they chatted on for a while. Half an hour later, they left the bar. As they walked hand-in-hand to the car park Jasper could easily pick out Robin's beige Jaguar, its sleek surface glistening in the rain. Robin was paranoid about maintaining its appearance, both inside and out. Jasper couldn't resist smiling as he ruminated on how lucky he was. The costumes he was giving away were worth a lot of money but what did he care? Meeting Robin had been the turning point in his life; he now had a wealthy partner who doted on him and furthermore, unlike Anthony, Robin paraded his homosexuality quite openly. He did a miniature time-step and patted his head of implanted hair - courtesy of Robin - then puckering his lips he planted a wet kiss on his partner's cheek.

'What was that for?' laughed Robin.

'I just felt like it,' was Jasper's response.

THIRTY-THREE

'Real actors!' gasped the fifteen-year-old who was playing the lead, 'real actors in the audience? I shall be soooo nervous.'

'There's nothing to worry about, Debbie,' said Olivia, 'they're just ordinary people like you and I; they just happen to be actors, that's all.'

'But...but I won't *know* them.'

'You won't know half the audience so you won't be able to pick them out. I bet you've never met the parents of most of your classmates, so what's the difference?'

Olivia left Debbie giggling excitedly with the rest of the members of the cast. She had to admit that she too was apprehensive. Jasper and Robin had seemed really eager to see the production but she wondered whether they would, in fact, turn up on Thursday. Worse, they might show their disapproval or worse than that, get up and leave during the interval.

She needn't have worried. They arrived at the school entrance where Miss Trencher, the teacher on box office duty, had their complimentary tickets ready. There was no mistaking them: Robin wore a dark overcoat with a Russian-style astrakhan collar; he took it off and handed it to the gobsmacked teacher, who called over one of the prefects detailed to usher people to their seats. The boy gave an amused smirk but dutifully took it to stow away on a hanger in the Staff Room. Beneath the overcoat, Robin sported a slim-fitting wine-coloured velvet smoking jacket. Jasper was equally dapper in a gold brocade dinner jacket with black satin lapels and a bow tie. They nodded graciously to the teacher, clearly pleased to be the centre of attention as the families of the performing pupils crowded into the entrance.

Olivia was too busy back stage to witness their arrival but afterwards Katherine gave her a minute-by-minute report on the spectacle. 'You should have seen them,' she chortled, 'they paraded like peacocks; any one would think they'd come to collect their Oscars. And the parents...well some of them tittered and the kids, of course, couldn't stop giggling.'

'I hope Jasper and Robin weren't embarrassed, Kathy, because honestly, they're awfully nice.'

'Don't worry about that. They were too self-absorbed to notice anybody else. But tell me, when you saw them afterwards did they say what they thought of the performance?'

Olivia chuckled. 'They were quite impressed and they didn't even comment about the boy playing George Banks forgetting his lines, which I thought was pretty decent of them. Of course, Jasper made a lot of the fact that we had used his costumes, brushing off my thanks with a lot of hand waggling and pseudo modesty.'

'What's happening about the costumes now? Does Jasper want them back?'

'I'm not sure. He didn't say so I'll have to ask him.' She heaved a sigh. 'I must say they really helped the production.'

On the day of the final performance of *Cinderella* she sent Jasper a message via the theatre inviting him and Robin to tea the next day, but he sent her a letter in flowery handwriting explaining that they were too busy rehearsing for a new musical they were hoping to take part in. He told her to keep the costumes, and said how much they had enjoyed the performance of *Mary Poppins*, adding as a postscript: *If you ever decide to leave teaching and take up employment in the theatre, just let me know.* He forgot to include a forwarding address.

On Christmas Eve, Katherine went to stay with her sister in Norfolk and Olivia divided her time between her divorced parents, which involved travelling between Somerset and Leeds. They both returned to Number Seven in time for the New Year celebrations. Olivia had been too busy before Christmas to see much of Pete but they had texted one another every day and she was eager to see him again.

'What are you going to wear for Jake's party?' Katherine asked.

'Oh, didn't I tell you, I'm not going.'

'Why not...?' Katherine stopped unpacking the jars of homemade jam and pickle her sister had insisted on giving her and looked at Olivia.

'I'm seeing Kevin...' She only just remembered to call Pete by his alias. 'I sent Jake an email a few days ago.'

'Why don't you bring the new boyfriend with you?' Katherine started stacking the jars in the cupboard above the microwave.

Olivia gave a shrug. 'He wants to spend New Year in Brighton.'

Katherine looked exasperated. 'Isn't it about time you introduced him to me; after all you two have been seeing one another for over three months.'

Olivia forced a laugh. 'Oh, you'll meet him sooner or later.'

'I'm beginning to think you've made him up or worse...' she shuffled the jars around so that they were in date order, '...you think I won't like him.'

'Don't be ridiculous, Kathy, it's just that I want to wait and see how things go.'

With that she turned round and sped upstairs to her room.

Olivia went to Brighton on New Year's Eve. Pete met her at the station.

'Come here, you gorgeous girl, I've missed you so much.'

'Me too,' she whispered as he pulled her into his arms.

'Do you realise it's been three weeks, two days and ten hours since we were last together?' he said as they walked arm-in-arm to the car park.

'That long?'

'I'm not letting you out of my sight for the next two days and I almost wish we weren't going to that disco tonight?'

'Which disco?'

'Mike, that friend I told you about. Didn't I mention that he's invited us to go clubbing with his gang this evening? I hope you've brought your best party dress.'

Olivia laughed. 'What I've brought will have to do.' She giggled. 'Kathy wanted me to go to a party with her tonight.'

'What did you tell her?'

'I said I was meeting you.'

Peter looked surprise. 'So she knows about us? What did she say?'

'Well...'

Pete took his keys out of his pocket and unlocked the car. She deliberately took her time making her way round the back of the car to get into the front passenger seat, hoping that he wouldn't press her on the subject. He started the engine but was forced to brake abruptly when a vehicle shot out in front of him.

'Moron!' he shouted and went into a rant about white-haired drivers. 'They're past it and they shouldn't be allowed on the road after they reach sixty.'

The diversion gave Olivia time to gather her thoughts and she hoped that by the time he had manoeuvred his way out of the car park he would forget to repeat his question. This wasn't to be and, as they swung into the traffic, he said, 'What did Kath say?'

It all spilled out then.

'You said I was Kevin?'

Much to Olivia's surprise, Pete seemed to think this amusing but his smile didn't last for long and she knew that inside he was angry. He parked the car outside his apartment block and they made their way upstairs to his flat in silence.

'Are you annoyed with me?' she asked.

'Should I be?'

'About calling you Kevin…'

He turned to face her. 'I don't know what your problem is, Livvy, we're both adults, free to go out with whom we please and yet you refuse to acknowledge me.'

'I don't,' Olivia protested, 'it's just living in the same house as your ex-wife is awkward to say the least…'

'Well it shouldn't be, like I told you Kath and I are over and done with.'

'I know that but Kathy and I see one another at home and at school and I don't know how she would react if I let the cat out of the bag.'

He took hold of her shoulders and gave her a gentle shake. 'Grow up, Livvy, stop being such a baby.'

Olivia pulled away from him, her temper flaring. 'How dare you call me a baby. I haven't noticed you offering to confront Kathy with the truth.'

He flared back. 'If that's what you want, I'll do it'

'No…no…'

Before Pete could reply, his mobile rang and he reached into his pocket for it. After a few mumbled words, he turned back to her and said, 'It's Mike, he was checking to make sure we're going tonight. He says if we are we'd better get a move on.'

Olivia tossed back her long hair. 'In that case let's hurry up. I'll go and change.' With that, she slung her hold-all over her shoulder and disappeared into Pete's bedroom.

Fifteen minutes later when she rejoined him the atmosphere had improved although they walked down the stairs to the street keeping distance between them. By the time they arrived at the agreed meeting place, Olivia had decided it would be better to call a truce before meeting Pete's friends, so she slipped her arm through his as he introduced her.

The evening went well and after midnight when the DJ played a romantic number, she found Pete's arms tighten around her as he nuzzled his face into her hair.

'I can't wait to get you home,' he whispered, 'let's leave now.'

Taking her hand, he led her out of the hall and they ran through a chilly drizzle to his car.

'I hope you're not over the limit,' Olivia said.

'I didn't need booze tonight,' Pete replied, 'dancing with you was intoxicating enough.'

She gave a giggle. Clearly, the question of his alias had been forgotten, at least for the time being.

Olivia was in a happy mood when she let herself into Number Seven the next day. Over a late breakfast she and Pete had talked rationally about the problem of breaking the news to Katherine and she had promised to bring the subject up at the first opportunity. Katherine arrived home a couple of hours later, banging on the door and calling Olivia's name in a loud, slightly strange, voice.

'Coming,' Olivia called out as she hurried to open the door.

Katherine pushed past her swinging her high-heeled sling-backs in her hand.

'Hey, you nearly hit me in the face,' grumbled Olivia.

Then she saw that her friend was coatless and was wearing a flimsy off-the-shoulder dress. Katherine skipped through the house into the kitchen, apparently unaware of the cold tiles under her bare feet. Momentarily she slumped against the worktop and then sprang away from it to resume her agitated movements.

'Hadn't you better sit down, Kathy, you look a bit unsteady?'

But Katherine ignored Olivia and skipped back through the kitchen to begin an ungainly waltz with an imaginary partner, her shoes still clutched in her hand. She accompanied her own cavorting with a trilling *la...la...la.* Again Olivia tried to calm her but Katherine was in a world of her own. She touched her arm several times but Katherine swept her away and continued her extemporised dance routine.

Olivia gave up, and going into the kitchen she took a tumbler out of the cupboard. A glass of cold water might help. It was clear that Katherine had taken drugs and she guessed it was something stronger than cannabis. They had both smoked weed occasionally and she knew the effect was not like this. It crossed her mind that someone must have brought her home because clearly Katherine could not have made it on her own.

All at once she noticed that the trilling had stopped and she found Katherine slumped on the sofa. She tried to turn her and to her horror saw that Katherine was laying face-down in her own vomit. Running to the kitchen, she fetched a damp face flannel and gently cleaned her friend's mouth and cheeks. The fine blond hair was sticky with vomit too and Olivia did her best to wipe it away. It was obvious from the smell on her breath that Katherine had been consuming a lot of alcohol. She felt her forehead and noticed how hot it was.

She needed to wake her up and tried shaking her but although she could hear faint breathing, Katherine didn't stir into life. Alarmed, Olivia looked around for Katherine's mobile but it was nowhere to be seen so she raced up to her room and found her address book, thankful that her housemate was meticulous in keeping it up-to-date. Thumbing through the pages, she found Jake's number and rang him. It took several rings before he answered.

'Jake, what did you give her?' she burst out when he answered.

'What...what...who is this?' Clearly, she had woken him up.

'Jake, it's Livvy, Kathy's arrived home stoned up to the eyeballs; do you know what she's taken?'

'What are you talking about?'

Quickly Olivia described her friend's condition.

'It must have been that fucking Stuart,' he said angrily, 'I'll find out and get back to you.'

Olivia ran downstairs to find that Katherine had rolled off the sofa and had vomited again. One glance told her that the situation was serious. She dialled for an ambulance.

THIRTY-FOUR

It was touch and go for a few hours while they stabilised Katherine. Olivia stayed at the hospital while they tried to work out what drugs she had taken.

'Did your friend give you any indication as to what substance she took or who gave it to her?' asked the doctor.

Olivia shook her head. 'She was in no state to tell me anything.'

The hospital must have called the police because a PC turned up and started asking more questions. 'Did you and your friend come home together Miss…?'

'Olivia Manning. No, we were at different parties.'

'Who got home first?'

'I did, but only by a few minutes.'

'Do you have any idea what your friend took?'

'No.'

'Would her boyfriend have fed her anything?'

'She hasn't got a boyfriend, not a regular one anyway.'

'Whose party did she go to?'

Olivia took a few seconds before answering. Should she divulge that Jake had been the host? Would this get him into trouble? He had sounded genuinely shocked when she'd spoken to him on the phone. Besides, he taught maths and geometry at her school and, although their paths rarely crossed, he had always seemed a responsible sort of person.

'I…I don't know,' she said at last, 'I'm sorry I'm not much help.'

Then the doctor came back. 'Well,' he said, 'your friend is lucky to be alive. She was fed a strong concoction of Ecstacy laced with cocaine.'

Olivia was horrified. What had induced Katherine to take such a risk? Surely she knew the consequences of accepting drugs at a party! She chided herself for not having realised that Ecstacy was involved when Katherine arrived home: the high temperature, the elation, the dilated pupils, the dancing. She should have guessed but she had been on a high herself, not from drugs or alcohol but because she was falling in love.

Olivia didn't leave the hospital until ten o'clock that evening. Looking at her mobile for the first time since going there she found a text message from Jake: *Olivia, it must have been a gatecrasher. None of my friends knew Kathy was stoned.*

She texted him back: *Did anyone see who took her home?*

His reply wasn't encouraging: *I didn't nor did anyone else. That's all I know.*

Olivia bit her lower lip. Maybe Katherine wasn't brought straight home, maybe she was taken somewhere else first. God knows what could have happened to her. Instead of texting, this time she dialled Jake's number and he answered at once, sounding guarded. 'What is it now?'

'Where's her coat? She didn't have it when she got home.'

'How would I know? The last I saw of her she looked all right. In fact, she was more than all right; she was doing an energetic jive and enjoying herself.'

Olivia was getting angry. Although it was now almost midnight, she needed to share her misgivings with someone. She opened *contacts* on her mobile and was on the point of dialling her mother when she remembered she had gone to Scotland with friends for Hogmanay. She didn't want to ring her father because she knew this would annoy his new wife Carol. In the end, she rang Pete but as soon as he answered she regretted making the call.

He listened while she told him about Katherine then said, 'What do you expect me to do about it?'

Olivia couldn't believe her ears. 'Don't you care; after all you were married to her once?'

'There's no need to point that out. Livvy, how many times do I have to tell you it's over between Kath and me? She's no longer my responsibility. Are you always going to let her shadow loom over our relationship?'

Without replying, Olivia snapped shut her mobile. How could he be so cold hearted? Surely at one time he must have felt something for Kathy. All at once, she was aware that tears were streaming down her cheeks; hot angry tears she couldn't control. When at last they began to abate, she made herself a cup of cocoa and took it upstairs to her room and got ready for bed. But it was hours before she was able to fall asleep.

The Spring Term started without Katherine. The headmistress called in a supply teacher to help out and Olivia resumed her own duties, noticing a new respect from the drama pupils after the surprise appearance of Jasper and Robin at the performance of *Mary Poppins*. She didn't seek out Jake, only nodding a greeting to him when they happened to meet in the corridor.

After being discharged from hospital, Katherine went to stay with her sister in Norfolk and Olivia learned that she had fallen into deep depression. With the house to herself she realised that she and Pete could have continued their relationship quite openly, but her feelings towards him had changed. She couldn't come to terms with his lack of concern for his ex-wife's wellbeing. He rang her several times over the next couple of weeks but gave up when she made excuses for not meeting him. Sometimes she regretted their break-up. He had been a wonderful lover and an interesting person to talk to. They had got along well on all levels. Would she ever find anybody else to fill his shoes?

After three weeks, Katherine's sister, Nicola telephoned to tell her that Katherine would not be coming back for the foreseeable future.

'I'm afraid she's had a breakdown, Livvy. I'm awfully sorry to leave you with the responsibility of the house and everything but rest assured, you won't be out of pocket because me and Malcolm will sort out any money owing to you for gas and electricity etc.'

Olivia liked the sound of Nicola although she had never met her. 'That's very kind of you but I don't want to put you to any trouble.'

'It's the least we can do,' Nicola assured her.

'Please give Kathy my love.'

'I will when I next go and visit her.'

'Visit her? I thought she was staying with you.'

Nicola heaved a sigh. 'I'm afraid, for psychiatric reasons, she's had to be admitted to a special unit in the local hospital.'

Olivia was shocked. She hadn't imagined that her housemate was mentally ill. All at once, she experienced a rush of panic. Katherine had always been the one to take care of the household bills and when she herself had lived with Andy, he had been the one to organise their finances. Now it seemed she would have to take charge.

This realisation sent her scurrying upstairs to Katherine's bedroom. Her desk was under the window. It was clear of clutter; the household files and Katherine's personal folders were stacked on a shelf underneath the desk. Each drawer of the desk was arranged in an orderly fashion with pens and pencils lying in neat rows, scissors, stapler, hole-punch and paperclips likewise. There was a letter rack with several letters in it: a telephone account, a bank statement and another letter. Olivia took it out of its envelope. Clearly Katherine had read it because the envelope had been slit open and a date in the body of the letter was highlighted in yellow.

Olivia took a step backwards and sank down onto the bed. Her hands shook as she read the words. It was from the Borough Council and it stated that a compulsory purchase order was being placed on the entire terrace from Number One to Number Eight. She dropped the sheet of paper to her lap, squinting into the evening sun as it set over to the west. How could this happen? Why hadn't Kathy mentioned it?

She looked at the top of the page. The letter was dated 20th December. She reached for the envelope and saw that it was addressed to both of them. Trying to calm herself, she re-read the letter. The meaning was clear. The whole terrace was going to be pulled down and sold to a construction company. The shock was so great, she couldn't even cry.

At school the next day, Olivia could barely function. Her mind kept winging back to the contents of the letter. By the weekend she still hadn't taken it in. Staring out of the back bedroom window at the leafless trees she thought about how pretty the back gardens would look in two or three months' time. There would be primroses and daffodils brightening the borders and then cherry and apple blossom would appear, the lilac tree would spring to life and bright red peonies would show their heads. Was the construction company going to build a high-rise block? If so, what would they do about the trees and plants? Would this private oasis become a communal lawn for the flat owners or would it become a tarmacadamed car park?

The letter had stated that the occupants would be given further information by March and Olivia decided to give her friend the benefit of the doubt. Perhaps she had thought it wise to delay sharing the dreadful news until nearer that date.

March came and went and there was no further news and even when Olivia made enquiries at the Council Offices, their official prevarication failed to cast light on the situation. In the end, she was so worried she telephoned Nicola and asked her if Katherine had told her about it.

'Good lord no!' gasped Nicola. 'I had no idea. Kathy could surely not have forgotten about something as important as that. I suppose she just couldn't face it, especially under the circumstances; I mean it must be the last thing on her mind.'

Olivia felt puzzled. 'What do you mean?' she asked.

She heard Nicola give an intake of breath. 'Of course, you don't know, do you?'

'Know what?'

'Kathy's pregnant.'

'What?'

It took a while for the news to sink in. Kathy the child-hater was to become a mother!

'Who...is she happy about it?' Olivia said, her voice rising to a squeak. 'No of course she isn't. How silly of me! But what is she going to do about it?'

'To tell you the truth, Livvy, she's all over the place at the moment. As you probably know, she's always been adamant about not wanting kids. That was always a bone of contention between her and Pete.'

'How far gone is she?' Olivia knew this was a silly question because clearly conception must have taken place during the New Year incident.

There was silence for a while then Nicola said, 'You're one of her closest friends so I may as well tell you, she was date-raped at New Year. I suppose you had already guessed that.'

Olivia's breath came out in a hiss. It was what she had not dared to contemplate. 'That's terrible, Nicola. Poor

Kathy!' She tried to marshal her thoughts. 'Has she told the police? You know, they questioned me when I took Kathy to the hospital. She ought to take it up with them; after all date rape is a criminal offence.'

Nicola's reply was subdued. 'That wouldn't be a good idea, Livvy. Kathy's in no state to face a barrage of questions and possibly a court appearance.'

'Look, can I come up to Norfolk to see her during the Easter break?'

'Ye..es.' The reply was hesitant.

'I won't come if you don't want me to, it's just that…'

'I know you want to see Kathy and I understand that but can I test the waters first, see how she feels and then I'll give you a ring? You would be welcome to stay with us overnight.'

'That's kind of you, Nicola, but I don't want to put you to any trouble.'

'You'd be welcome. Leave it with me and I'll get back to you.'

After the call ended, Olivia sat thinking about their conversation. She had suspected that something more than the taking of drugs had been involved way back on New Year's Eve. Now she knew the worst had happened. She wondered how Pete would react if she were to tell him but pushed the idea out of her head. It was stupid idea.

THIRTY-FIVE

Olivia travelled up to Norfolk during the Easter break. Nicola and her husband, Malcolm greeted her warmly and their two little girls were delighted to meet their Auntie Kathy's friend. They wanted to hear all about the famous actors who had watched the Christmas play. This amused Olivia; it seemed that Jasper Cole and Robin Ballantyne-Smith had been elevated to stardom when, in fact, they were barely known nationally.

Nicola took her along to the Psychiatric Unit to visit Katherine. Olivia gave a little shiver at its clinical white walls and furniture as she entered the building. But she guessed - correctly as it turned out - that her friend would approve of its orderliness.

The sun was shining and the temperature was pleasant as they were taken to a large balcony with tables and chairs. Katherine was sitting there alone. She jumped up when she saw Olivia and rushed over to give her a hug. This seemed a bit strange to Olivia since her housemate was not in the habit of showing her feelings.

'How are you, Livvy? Come and sit down I want to hear all the gossip.'

Olivia allowed herself to be dragged by the hand to a pair of wicker chairs by a small glass-topped table.

'I'll leave you two to have a chat,' said Nicola.

Olivia felt as if she might need a third person there. 'Why not join us?' she said.

'I'll go for a stroll around the garden and come back later when they bring some coffee.'

Olivia guessed that Nicola was going in search of the Charge Nurse to make enquiries about Katherine's progress.

'You must have lots to tell me, Livvy,' said Kathy, 'what's been happening at school? What's the supply teacher like?'

The questions poured out endlessly until Olivia broke in with a laugh. 'Give me a chance, Kathy, and I'll give you the low-down on everything.'

She proceeded to describe the succession of supply teachers who had taken Katherine's place, the occasion when one of her drama students complained of stomach ache and had to be rushed to hospital to have her appendix out. She gave her the news that the headmistress would be retiring at the end of the school year.

Kathy gave a short laugh. 'You know, I quite liked old Maudie Bridges. Do you know who's going to take her place?'

'They haven't told us yet.'

'What about Jake?' Katherine's frowned. 'I hold him responsible for getting me high that night.'

Olivia's brows raised in a perplexed frown. 'Did *he* give you the Ecstacy?'

'Of course he didn't.'

'Who did?'

Katherine's lower lip began to quiver. 'I don't know. Don't let's talk about it.'

'It was you who brought up Jake's name,' Olivia reminded her.

'Well, I want to forget it ever happened and get on with my life.'

Olivia couldn't stop her gaze from fixing on Katherine's stomach. She was nearly four months into her pregnancy and it was beginning to show yet so far her friend hadn't mentioned it.

'What are you going to do?'

'What do you mean?'

'About the baby?'

'Oh that! Nothing...'

She stood up and went over to the balcony, leaning her elbows on the railing and tapping her foot to the sound of distant music being played inside the building.

'I take it you are keeping the baby then?'

Katherine stopped tapping and stamped her foot like a naughty child. 'I don't want to talk about it. You can leave if you've got nothing interesting to tell me.'

Olivia got up and went over to her friend, putting an arm around her shoulders. 'You'll have to face up to it sooner or later.'

Katherine's face was red with anger as she turned and pushed Olivia away. 'Just go, damn you, you're just like all the others, trying to force me into making a decision.'

'But...' Olivia began, but her words were cut short when Nicola and the Nurse arrived.

Nicola hurried over and took Olivia's arm. 'She's having a bad day, ' she whispered, 'I think we had better go.'

Glancing back over her shoulder, Olivia saw the Nurse lead Katherine back to her chair. With a flick of her hand, she waved them away.

'How did you get on?' Nicola asked as they drove home.

'Not very well,' Olivia admitted, 'I didn't even get a chance to mention the compulsory purchase order.'

Nicola cast a quick glance in her direction. 'I'm afraid you'll have to deal with that by yourself, although of course Malcolm and I are always on hand to back you up.'

'Kathy doesn't seem to acknowledge that she's pregnant.'

'I know. We keep hoping that by the time the baby starts kicking, the truth will have sunk in.'

'Is it too late for an abortion?'

'I think so.'

The two women fell silent for a few minutes then Olivia said, 'This must be terribly worrying for you. I mean, what's going to happen to the child, will Kathy be well enough to care for it or are you going to advise her to go for adoption?'

'I don't honestly know.'

It was good to get back to Nicola's house where the two lively little girls took their minds off their worries. But in the evening once the children were in bed, Olivia, Nicola and Malcolm had a serious discussion about the situation although by the time they all went to bed, no real conclusion had been reached.

Olivia departed for the South Coast the next morning. She was relieved that she didn't have to return to school for a few more days. She needed a period of respite, time to think. Easter Monday was a beautiful day, crisp and sunny and she decided to go for a walk on the Downs. Walking in the countryside always helped to clear her head and by the time she got home, she had convinced herself that apart from the sale of the house, Kathy's problems were nothing to do with her.

She was unable to visit Kathy again until the middle of the summer holidays. By this time the baby was almost due and Kathy was staying at Nicola's. The day before she was due to go to Norfolk, Nicola rang her.

'Livvy, Kathy's had the baby; it was a bit early but they're both fine.'

'What is it?'

'A boy, he's a good size and he's a handsome little chap.'

'Is it too early for me to come up? I could delay my visit for a week.'

'Please don't do that. Kathy wants to see you.'

'I want to see her too so I'll be there around lunch-time tomorrow.'

So Kathy was now a mother. A year ago, this was the last thing Olivia would have expected and, in a way, she felt slightly envious of her friend. She pushed the mean thought aside telling herself that one day, she too would become a mother.

Nicola picked her up at the station. 'You'll be amazed,' she said, 'I would never have believed my big sister would take to motherhood.' She shook her head wistfully. 'How wrong you can be!'

'I can't wait to see them both. Has Kathy chosen a name yet?'

'She's toying with several names.'

Kathy was in the conservatory nursing the baby when they arrived. She looked up and laughingly said, 'As you can see, Livvy, I can't get up to greet you at the moment.'

Olivia dropped her overnight bag to the floor and went to kneel down beside Katherine. The baby was sucking happily at her breast and the mother's face was wreathed in smiles. Nicola's children were hovering nearby, excited at having a new baby in the house.

'Isn't he sweet?' one of them cried while the younger one gently patted the top of the baby's bald head.

'I never knew how marvellous motherhood could be,' said Kathy, 'you must try it one day, Livvy.' They talked about the birth and the baby for quite some time. Kathy pointed to the new baby paraphernalia she had been given. 'There are lots of toys too. See that one...' She pointed to a cuddly giraffe. 'Pete gave it to me...'

'Pete?'

'Yes, it's a pity you missed him, he was here only yesterday.' When Olivia didn't respond, she went on, 'I know you don't approve of him after all the horrible things I told you, but really he's not so bad.'

'I never said I didn't approve of him,' protested Olivia. She felt her cheeks burning and hoped Kathy hadn't noticed. She thought it best to change the subject. 'What are you going to call him?'

'I haven't decided yet. Pete likes Ethan but I prefer George.'

Olivia could hardly believe her ears. She found it difficult to concentrate as Katherine waffled on about nappies and Babygros and formula. At last, she said, 'I've brought you something. It's in my holdall.'

This gave her the opportunity to escape into the hall and forage through her bag. She told herself to breathe deeply and keep calm. After all, Pete meant nothing to her. Their fling was over and done with. She went back into the conservatory to give Kathy the present.

It was after Nicola had served dinner and the girls had gone to bed that Katherine dropped her bombshell. 'Pete and I are thinking of getting back together,' she said casually.

Olivia did her best not to look alarmed but the news shocked her. 'That's good,' she said.

Katherine went on, 'Yes, so when the house has been sold, we'll be out of your hair...' She bit her lip, 'I mean to say, it never really worked: you and me living together, did it?'

'It wasn't too bad,' protested Olivia, 'although we did have our ups and downs. To tell you the truth, I'm really sorry the house is going to be torn down.'

'Do you know what's going up in its place?

Olivia shook her head. 'They haven't told us yet but I think they'll build flats.'

The evening dragged on with Katherine extolling the joys of motherhood until Olivia felt like hitting her. When at last they said goodnight, she escaped to her bed and cried herself to sleep.

The following week brought a sense of reality to the termination of Olivia's occupancy of Number Seven. An official letter arrived giving the timescale for the compulsory purchase. She read through the pages of officialdom with growing panic, trying her best to concentrate on the small print. The letter stated that an assessor would be inspecting each house in turn in order to make a fair offer. Occupants were advised to instruct a solicitor to handle the documentation.

Katherine had dealt with the negotiations when they had moved in, declaring that prior to taking up teaching she had done a year of law at university. Olivia had been only too pleased to let her get on with it; she couldn't be done with crossing the 't's and dotting the 'i's. Now it seemed she would have to handle all the documentation herself.

She stabbed a pin into the *Yellow Pages*' list of solicitors, came up with a local company and made an appointment. She felt nervous when she crossed the threshold into a well-appointed suite of offices but the receptionist gave her a friendly smile as she directed her to take a seat in the Waiting Area.

After ten minutes, the girl answered the intercom then called over, 'Mr Jessop will see you now, Miss Manning.'

As she spoke a tall good-looking black man appeared from a corridor. He shook her hand and beamed at her, making Olivia feel less anxious.

'Come along, Miss Manning, my office is this way.' He ushered her into a large, airy room with a view over a garden where a gentle breeze stirred lingering leaves from the trees. 'Please take a seat.' He went to sit down at his leather-topped desk and studied a sheet of paper in front of him. 'I see you are the subject of a compulsory purchase order. I'm sorry to hear that. I gather you're not in favour of it.'

'That's right,' said Olivia, 'it came as a terrible shock and they still haven't given us, the occupants that is, a clear reason for the purchase.'

'Well,' he said, 'I can clear that up. They intend to widen the road because they consider the narrow bend is hazardous.'

Olivia raised her eyebrows in surprise. 'It was rumoured they're going to build an apartment block.'

'It's likely they'll sell off the gardens behind the houses to builders but the actual site of your house will become part of the road.'

'I see.' Olivia didn't see because as far as she knew there had never been any road traffic accidents at the bend in the road.

'Do you want to file an official protest?'

'What good would that do? The Council always do what they want in the end.'

'Hmm, that's true although in a few cases the residents have been successful in turning things around.'

'Have any of the other residents of the terrace approached you?' Olivia asked.

'I can't tell you that.'

'I suppose it's confidential.'

'Yes. Have *you* spoken to other residents? A joint protest would be far more effective.'

Olivia shook her head. 'I'm afraid I've been too busy with other things,' she said, 'you see the girl who part owns the property has been ill lately and now she's moved out.'

'But does she still own her share?'

'Yes.'

'Why don't you contact her and find out her views on this?'

Olivia sighed deeply. Why indeed? But she knew that Katherine was too involved in her new maternal role to bother about the problem of the house. Katherine had made it clear that she didn't want to move back and, as far as she was concerned, compulsory purchase would solve the problem of having to put the house on the market themselves.

When she replied, Olivia's voice was choked. 'She doesn't mind.'

'You mean, she's happy for the Council to go ahead with the purchase?'

'Yes.'

'I see. That changes things somewhat. Without her backing it would be difficult for you to protest.'

Tears welled in Olivia's eyes. 'What do you advise?' she whispered.

'I can see you're upset,' said the Solicitor, 'and to tell you the truth, under the circumstances, I think you'd be better off not joining any protest. However, once they make you a firm offer I will do my utmost to increase it because the initial offer is invariably low.'

'Thank you,' she said, wiping a fist across her eyes and wishing she was as tough as Katherine, who would never have been reduced to tears.

Gregory Jessop saw her to the door, shaking her hand again as they said goodbye. She looked up into his brown eyes, pleased that by sticking a pin into a telephone directory she had managed to come up with such a kind man.

THIRTY-SIX

Things moved swiftly after that. Gregory Jessop was as good as his word and, after weeks of negotiation, he was able to achieve a good price for Number Seven. During this period, Olivia visited his office on many occasions, sometimes quite unnecessarily although she wouldn't admit this even to herself.

She emailed Katherine to let her know how the negotiations were going but all she got back was a short message of acknowledgement and a photo of the newborn. She couldn't help wondering what had got into Kathy. How could anyone change so radically? Since there was no mention of Pete in the message she assumed they hadn't got back together after all. Maybe the possibility of reconciliation had been wishful thinking on Katherine's part.

She often thought about Pete, sometimes waking in the night after dreaming that he was making love to her. This was disturbing because since discovering about his renewed friendship with Katherine, she had made up her mind their relationship was over forever.

By late autumn, she realised it was time to look for somewhere else to live. Even with the price the Solicitor had negotiated, she knew it would be impossible to buy another property on her own. She decided to treat herself to a skiing holiday during the Christmas break and to put the rest of the money into a savings account with the intention of building on it until she had a sizeable deposit for a flat.

The next time she visited the Solicitor was for Exchange of Contracts. To her dismay, as she laid down the pen after signing the Agreement, tears began to spill down her cheeks. Covered with embarrassment, she reached for a tissue but Gregory Jessop handed her a handkerchief.

'I'm so sorry,' she murmured, 'it's just that I really like living in Number Seven. There have been lots of ups and downs but despite everything that's happened I've been happy there.'

'I understand,' he said, just as if seeing his clients burst into tears over the sale of a house was an everyday occurrence.

She wiped her eyes and blew her nose, feeling foolish.

'Don't worry about sorting out the finances,' he said, 'the co-owner's solicitor has been in touch and everything has been taken care of.' Then all at once, he took her by surprise. 'Miss Manning, eh Olivia, after Completion would you let me take you out to dinner?'

She clapped a hand to her mouth, looking at him in surprise. 'I...I...'

It was his turn to look embarrassed. With a flick of his wrist, he leant back in his swivel chair. 'Of course, I quite understand. I was out of order.'

She felt sure he was blushing but of course it didn't show. 'Oh no,' she gasped. 'I would love to go out to dinner with you.'

He leant forward over his desk. 'Are you free on Saturday week? Oh I forgot, you will be moving into your new place.'

'No...yes...' She paused to think. 'I'm sure Saturday week will be fine.'

Her heart gave a lurch as he smiled at her. 'My name's Gregory but everybody calls me Greg,' he said.

They both stood up and when he came round from behind his desk, she noticed he was taller than she had at first thought, six three at least. He held out his hand to shake and when she took it, the link between them seemed to linger. He let go of her hand and everything was formal again.

Several days later, Olivia began to prepare for the move into a rented flat. Katherine had emailed saying that, apart from a few items, she didn't want much of the furniture. 'I'll get the things I want picked up,' she wrote. 'Malcolm is going to borrow a friend's van and drive over on Sunday.'

This suited Olivia and she spent Saturday collecting Katherine's belongings together. They took up most of the dining room. She felt uncomfortable going through her bedroom drawers and wardrobe but, since Katherine had stated that she had no intention of sorting things out, it fell to Olivia to do it for her. She felt angry as she packed clothes, make-up and other paraphernalia into a large suitcase before having to drag the smaller items of furniture into the middle of the room.

Malcolm arrived, cheerful as ever. Olivia didn't know him very well but she had always found him amiable. Luckily he had a friend with him to help move the heavier pieces of furniture. They had trouble getting Katherine's king size bed down the stairs and by the time it had been loaded into the van, Malcolm was red in the face and gasping for breath.

'Are you all right?' she asked, handing him a glass of water.

He grinned. 'I'm not used to lifting stuff these days.' He patted his belly. 'I ought to go to the gym; Nicola's always nagging me about taking more exercise.'

When everything had been loaded up, she offered the men a lager and the three of them sat amongst the remaining debris for a short respite.

'Cheers!' said Malcolm, looking around. 'At least you won't have to clean up in readiness for the new people when you leave.'

'No, the bulldozers are moving in in a few days time. How's Kathy?' she asked.

'She's fine, moving out soon.'

'Oh, has she found somewhere to live?'

He raised an eyebrow. 'Didn't Nicola tell you? Kathy and Pete are back together. They're going to live in Horsham.'

'Horsham...?'

'Yes, Pete's bought a house there; quite a big place I believe, four bedrooms at least.'

Olivia couldn't hide her astonishment. 'Do you mean to say Pete has accepted the child as his own?'

Malcolm shrugged his shoulders. 'There's none so weird as folks. I'm blowed if I would accept another man's child like that.'

His friend butted in. 'Come on Malc, we ought to get going if we're to make good time.'

They made their departure and after they had driven away, Olivia went back into the house. Her feelings were mixed. After all that had happened: the acrimonious divorce, the bitter words, the mud-slinging, the ill-assorted couple were back together again. For some reason she felt culpable, as if the short-lived fling she had had with Peter had been adulterous and she was the guilty party.

She was too busy during the following week to fret over this turn of events. The man-with-a-van she had hired to move her belongings was due on Monday and she was wondering whether, even with Katherine's things gone, there would still be too much furniture to fit into the new flat. By Saturday morning she felt exhausted. How could she go out on a date and leave this muddle behind?

She decided to ring Greg up and put him off. At first, she couldn't measure his reaction. His tone was flat and she wondered whether he had had second thoughts about dating her. Then he came up with a solution. 'I'll come round and help you,' he said.

'What?'

'I'll give you a hand; that is if you'll let me.'

All at once, she knew that this was exactly what she wanted. 'Yes, I really could do with some help. Thank you, Greg.'

He arrived dressed in jeans and a sweatshirt, looking quite different. Until now she had only seen him in a formal suit and a white shirt, although she had noticed he went in for jazzy ties.

'Thank you for coming,' she said, 'I'd never be able to sort this lot out on my own.'

He rubbed his hands together and grinned, "Two pairs of hands are always better than one. Right, where shall we start?'

A couple of hours later they sat down on the sofa with a mug of tea each and surveyed their handy-work.

'My new flat will need a lick of paint,' she said.

'I'll help you; I enjoy a bit of DIY.'

Olivia bit her lip. 'You don't need to.'

'Why? Don't you trust me to do a good job?'

She threw back her head and laughed. 'I'm sure you can, it's just…'

'You've got a streak of dirt on the tip of your nose.'

'Have I?'

He reached over to rub it off then abruptly moved away, saying, 'Let's eat? Where do you want to go?'

'I can't go out like this; I look a sight.' She gestured to her dusty leggings and t-shirt.

'What about a pizza delivery then?'

'That sounds like a good idea.'

'What topping do you want?'

She told him and he took his mobile out of his pocket and dialled a number, placing their order.

'They said fifteen minutes. Can you last that long?'

'Just about and as luck would have it there are a couple of cans of lager in the kitchen. They won't be very cold though as the fridge has been disconnected. Oh dear, I've just remembered, I've packed all the tumblers.'

'Never mind,' he said, 'we can manage without.'

It was while they were slurping from the cans that Olivia was reminded of Jasper's costumes. Then she relaxed, the school would be only too pleased to store them.

Her new romance took Olivia's mind off the impending bulldozing. Greg had entered her life so unexpectedly that she sometimes couldn't believe what was happening. He was the most caring man she had ever met. She had never been out with a black man before, not from choice but simply because the occasion had never arisen. He told her how his parents had come over from Trinidad in the late fifties and settled in Notting Hill.

'It wasn't a very salubrious area in those days but, of course, things have changed over the years and property prices have gone sky high.'

'Do your parents still live there?

'Yes, they came out of it rather well. They started with a clothes stall in the Portobello Road and graduated to a shop selling all the sixties favourites. My father's retired now but my mother still insists on helping out in the shop even though they've got reliable staff running it. My eldest sister is married with a couple of kids and the youngest one is at uni studying to be a pharmacist.'

She told him about her parents, feeling instinctively that they would one day have to meet Greg. She knew her mother would welcome him but she wasn't quite sure how her father would react. Churning it over in her mind, she decided that although he would have reservations at first, Greg would win him round. When her thoughts wandered along these lines she told herself not to be foolish; after all, they had only just met.

Demolition took place during Half Term and she felt drawn to take a look. She stood on the other side of the road to watch two enormous bulldozers plough into the house. Of course a barrier had been erected to keep the public safe, but she watched the dust rise as bricks and mortar crashed to the ground.

She felt a wave of sadness sweep over her as the top floor of the houses disappeared and an enormous cloud of dust rose above the lilac tree in the back garden which was now visible from the street.

All at once, she sensed rather than saw someone standing beside her. Greg reached for her hand. 'This is not the end,' he said as he pulled her close, 'for us it's the beginning. We will never forget that Number Seven brought us together.'

*****

HOLLY HAS THE LAST WORD

'Darling, look at this!' cried Holly, pointing a finger at an article in the local newspaper. 'It says here that a row of terraced houses has been demolished in the road we used to live in when we were students.'

'They're going to build another block of high-rise flats, I expect,' said Max, stuffing a piece of toast into his mouth and snatching his jacket off the back of his chair. 'I must fly if I'm to catch my usual train.'

After giving his wife a peck on the cheek, he hurried from the house, leaving her still studying the report. The baby gave a gurgle, spewing mash all over the tray of his highchair and forcing Holly to give him her full attention.

While the baby was having his afternoon nap, Holly took another look at the article. It said the Council had been obliged to sacrifice the entire terrace for the sake of widening the road. She lowered the newspaper to her lap and, closing her eyes, leant back on the settee, her thoughts *winging back to her student days. Number Seven held a gamut of memories for her: the ups and downs of student life, the fun, the quarrels and above all the awful incident of Mel's unprovoked attack on Simon. She wondered what had happened to Mel and Simon. Had Mel recovered from her breakdown and gone on to open her beauty salon? Had Simon continued his studies and become a micro-biologist?*

The most nostalgic reminiscence of all, of course, was her last-minute decision to stay on in the house and spend her final weekend with Max. Would they have gone on to get married if she hadn't postponed her departure for a couple of days? She re-read the article, feeling sad that the house which held such mixed memories was no longer there and, much to her surprise, she felt the prick of tears at her eyes.

The baby's cries reached her and discarding the newspaper, she hurried upstairs to check on him. He was bouncing up and down in his cot, his cries changing to gurgles of delight when he saw her. Lifting him out of his cot, she hugged him close, silently thanking the good fortune that had made her choose Number Seven for a house share.

If you have enjoyed this book, why not read some of Elaine Hankin's other novels?

FROST ON BARBED WIRE

For readers who enjoy an exciting story set against a factual background.

West Berlin 1953: twenty-two-year-old rookie reporter, Erich Laube, thrives on adventure, nosing out stories from behind the Iron Curtain. But Erich is still haunted by memories of his escape from Poland during the final months of WWII when he led his ten-year-old sister to safety.

The question is, can he shed his terrifying past and find happiness in a free world?

LAWS ARE SILENT

Courage and sacrifice in war-torn Italy.

When tragedy strikes his family, Count Vincenzo Di Tomasi sends his English-born wife, Alice and his son, Beppe to England.

Appalled by the atrocities being meted out by the fascist blackshirts, Vincenzo joins the Resistance where he meets, Livia Carduccio. But their affair is doomed and the price Vincenzo pays for his lover's sake has a far-reaching effect on Beppe.

TWO SIDES OF A COIN

A young woman searches for her brother in the chaos of civil war.

1937: when her twin brother goes missing while fighting with the International Brigade during the Spanish Civil War, Maggie Morán makes a brave decision. Leaving England's tranquil suburbia she heads for battle-scarred Madrid to search for him.

But before long, her daring adventure turns into a nightmare as she finds herself drawn into Spain's conflict. Will she find her brother or will she be sidetracked by the horrors she encounters?

SWANS SING BEFORE THEY DIE

A woman haunted by her past.

Born into poverty during the 1920s, Jessica Brown has one thing in her favour: a beautiful singing voice. The outbreak of WWII gives her the opportunity to leave her Islington home and join ENSA, travelling to the Middle East and Italy entertaining the troops.

But in the post-war years, Jessie finds it difficult to make her way in show business. Her route to stardom is hampered by a terrible secret, a secret which corrodes her relationships and undermines her confidence. Will she have the strength to overcome her demons?

PORTRAIT OF ROSANNA

Romance in Rome.

The portrait, a parting gift from her Italian lover, dominates Rosanna's existence. Trapped in a loveless marriage, she cossets the bittersweet memories it evokes. When the portrait disappears, she tracks down its new owner, only to find herself faced by further decisions and heartbreak.

Should she reclaim her portrait or should she let it go? If happiness means confronting the past, only Rosanna can decide whether she possesses the strength or the inclination to do that.

HOUSE OF SECRETS

Suspense-packed thriller.

An unexplained death, a bundle of old letters, a wall of silence - incentive enough for Chantal Lawrence to launch into some private investigating. How did her mother, Madeleine, come to fall to her death seventeen years ago? And why is the incident still wrapped in secrecy?

Chantal embarks on a quest which takes her from a farmhouse in the Dordogne to a garret in Montmartre to a chamber d'hôte in Pierrefonds. How can she know that the trail she is following will precipitate her into a terrifying flight for her life?

Lightning Source UK Ltd.
Milton Keynes UK
UKOW01f0210100218
317664UK00001B/5/P